Henry T. Williams, C. S. Jones

Beautiful Homes

Hints in House Furnishing

Henry T. Williams, C. S. Jones

Beautiful Homes
Hints in House Furnishing

ISBN/EAN: 9783337416485

Printed in Europe, USA, Canada, Australia, Japan

Cover: Foto ©Andreas Hilbeck / pixelio.de

More available books at **www.hansebooks.com**

BEAUTIFUL HOMES.

OR,

HINTS

House Furnishing

BY

HENRY T. WILLIAMS

AND

MRS. C. S. JONES.

Vol. 4. Williams' Household Serie

NEW YORK:
HENRY T. WILLIAMS, Publisher.
1878.

PREFACE.

"One fair asylum from the world he knew,
One chosen seat, that charms the varied view,
Who boasts of more (believe the serious strain),
Sighs for a home, and sighs in vain."

ROGERS.

THE house in which we live does not constitute the entire home, yet inasmuch, as a well-appointed, tastefully furnished and comfortably arranged house, enters largely into the well-being, and happiness of the family residing in it, it becomes a matter of grave importance to select a dwelling, at once healthful and pleasant. The aspect should be so entirely agreeable, so bright and cheery, and the appointments within, should present such a combination of beauty and genial comfort that all who enter the doors will be impressed with the subtle power of the Beautiful pervading the entire household arrangement.

"* * if eyes are made for seeing
Then Beauty is its own excuse for being."

Household taste is but a synonym for household culture; and she is a wise woman who surrounds those she loves with objects of beauty ; for she may safely rely on the influences (so intangible) which the beautiful (both in nature and art) ever exerts in a moral, intellectual, spiritual and social point of view. The beautiful picture or softly tinted wall, the peaceful drapery or chiselled statuette may perhaps be the means of opening some fount of wisdom, else closely sealed, or touching some sensitive nerve of thought, otherwise dormant. As a late writer, (Mr. Conway,) suggests, "what germ in the child's mind may that picture on the wall be the appointed sunbeam to quicken ? What graceful touch to unfolding character may be added by the modest tint of a room. Who can say how much falsehood and unreality has been shed through the life and influence of individuals by tinsel in the drawing-room and "rags up-stairs ?"

The cherished aim of our life is to improve the aspect and surroundings of our American homes, to carry out (though in a most simple manner), the views of the lamented Owen Jones of whom it is said, "that the aim of his life was to bring the beautiful in form and color home to the household, to mingle its subtle influences with the whole frame-work of social and family life." The majority of American homes belong to the great and highly respectable middle class, who by industry and economy have amassed moderate wealth, or are making sufficient money to provide their families with comfortable, and in many cases elegant homes. But nowhere more than in these very homes is there such need of care in beautifying. Our taste needs education and culture, and in this day of cheap decoration and vulgar display, it requires both judgment and discrimination to carry out the entire scheme of household arrangement and embellishments in a manner so chaste and delicate that it cannot offend the critical eye of the truly artistic.

A house is not to be a mere show-room, or museum ; but a home! and each home is to possess an individuality of its own which is to make it as entirely distinct as any human character.

In his chapter on " Domestic Life," Emerson, that wise and sagacious writer of the day, says, " Let us understand that a house should bear witness in all its economy that *human culture* is the end to which it is built and garnished. It stands there under the sun and moon to ends analogous—and not less noble than theirs. It is not for festivity, it is not for sleep; but the pine and the oak shall gladly descend from the mountain to uphold the roof of men as faithful and necessary as themselves, to be the shelter—open always to good and true persons,—a hall which shines with sincerity, brows ever tranquil and a demeanor impossible to disconcert, whose inmates know what they want; who do not ask *your* house how *their's* shall be kept."

It is by the thousand little felicities in shape of a pretty bracket here, an artistic gem of picture, statuette, or bust; a gauzy curtain veiling some little recess ; a pretty hanging draping, but not excluding the warm glow of color from yonder brilliant window ; a graceful stand of flowers ; a tiny cabinet of choice treasures ; a cozy chair or comfortable divan; these and many another object, trifling in itself and of easy manufacture, are the " traps to catch the sunbeams," which shimmer and lighten up and glow through the dwelling where taste dwells in unity with utilities and love. Sunbeams of both a physical and moral character, for where such surroundings as we have described fill and environ a dwelling it is sure to be a home in which dwell the " graces of which the Spirit, love, joy, peace, gentleness, goodness, faith, meekness, temperance," spread their sweet influence and affect each member of the household.

TASTE

—in—

Furnishing and Embellishing the House.

CHAPTER I.

FURNITURE.

THE first point to understand as regards the furnishing of the house, is that use and beauty must stand united.

The desire is felt to make for one's self *a home*, a place of beauty, yet embracing all the requirements of a habitation, in which people are to live, to eat, sleep and pass their hours of relaxation and pleasure; and with many of the family, of busy care as well; therefore, though beauty may ever be the queen, utility must reign as the lord and master, the two forming a perfect pair, (and united,) a perfect whole.

Nowhere more than in the dwellings of the American people is felt this need for the exercise of the beautiful; here the *useful* governs without any aid, but the great tendency to conventionality, often lapsing into mere vulgar display, is demanding some set rules by which the mind, anxious for improvement, and the deft fingers tingling for a guiding hand, may be led into right paths.

The time has come when beautiful homes can be made, at a cost, within the means and desires of our most humble, but tasteful people.

Each person is to first understand what they desire and what is truly beautiful and appropriate; the decoration and furnishing of the house will then expand into beauty as the foliage of a tree, commencing inward with the germinating leaf, and opening outward until, leaf by leaf and branch by branch, the perfect verdure is formed into a symmetrical and beautiful object. As a *home*, what does a man need in the dwelling he has provided? What is the actual requirement of this house-holder, who day after day goes forth from his door to make, "by the sweat of his brow," or the activity of his brain, a livelihood for the dwellers in his house?

Is it all sufficient that the bread he has earned should be made and placed before him ? That the bed he has purchased should be daily re-arranged, or further still, do these simple acts suffice the wife and mother and daughter? Are they willing to give him no more? The daily toil on the farm, or in office, store or shop is perhaps cheerfully endured by this father of the house ; the work carefully, even willingly performed, but it necessarily brings weariness, and the daily life in the busy world, though in a sense one of enjoyment, is among *men*, perhaps strangers, and a man of business is "everybody's man"; but when the long shadows tell that even-tide has come, and turning from plow, or desk, or counter, this man shuts the door behind him and carefully locks back all the day's perplexities and cares; what is he to find when he opens the *other* door, and his own bit of life is reached; when the one fragment of day he may call his own dawns down upon him? House-wife, "house-mother" you are to answer. You are to make the home. A home which has been aptly defined as

> "A centre amidst a busy and weary world, for
> Friendship, love and repose."

In the able work on decorative art, Scott's "History and Practice of the Fine and Ornamental Arts," we find taste defined as "that faculty by which we distinguish whatever is graceful, noble, just and loveable in the infinitely varied appearances about us, and in the works of the decorative and imitative arts. The immediate impulse in the presence of beauty is to feel and admire; when the emotion and sentiment are strong, we are compelled to *imitate*."

On the correctness of the taste displayed in furnishing the apartments of a house depends entirely the air of comfort or elegance they will wear and the sensations of pleasure or unrest to be felt by those inhabiting them. Many rooms, expensively furnished, will have something dragged into them that will not only detract from the beauty of really elegant surroundings, but produce as well, a sense of irritability to a critical eye, for, as Mr. Conway says, "it is a large part of the art of decorating to know what *not* to have in a house." Studied elaboration in a small or unpretentious dwelling, and without means to support elegance is not a mark of good taste; this holds good as regards massive or highly decorated furniture, as also confusion of color; masses of vivid shades offending the eye of correct taste. Let us suppose that our walls are covered with paper of tasteful design and quiet shades, (unless paint or wash of some lovely tint has been preferred) ; that carpets, oil-cloth, or rugs, unobtrusive in design, deep and rich in tone cover the floors, and also we assume that these are adapted to the particular uses and positions they are to occupy ; we are now ready to introduce our furniture. In doing this we must constantly bear in mind the color and character of our back-ground and ground-work. As a picture with warm Italian sky would appear absurd with houses capped and covered with snow, so would richly tinted hangings and furniture trimmed with heavy materials, illy compare with light bamboo furniture, or rustic decorations. This nice discrimination must be carried out in all apartments, and each must be adapted to the special use for which it is designed. Furniture, hangings, and indeed all the appointments of a house may be simple in the extreme, and yet strike the critical eye as being perfectly harmonious, just so long as each part is kept constantly in view, as the furnishing is carried along. The cry constantly made that a tasteful house is "too expensive a luxury," is an excuse that will no longer stand, for this is the day when invention has given us too much cheap luxury in furniture of every kind; for is there not luxury in the highly polished crystal upon your neatly furnished side-board, in the burnished silver plate that graces the snow-white tray-cover upon your table; in the beautifully embroidered linen of your bed; in the thousand little et ceteras entering into your daily household furnishing, which may be purchased at so trifling a cost, and in many cases is mere imitation. This is so far correct that it is doubtful whether there is not a far greater lack of taste in the houses where the cut-glass remains unpolished and frequently unwashed; the "solid silver" tarnished, bruised and worn; while the linen of both bed and board, and the entire list of household articles bear the marks of the "hard wear and tear" of the careless hireling.

Cheap luxury *is* easily obtained in this day by any woman who possesses the use of hands and head.

What a woman *has* done, a woman *can* do; and we hold that any woman of ordinary strength, and enjoying an average of usual health, may by management of details, and judicious expenditure of time, make for herself and those she loves a home, beautiful in embellishment, and furnished with comparative luxury.

The truth is, the chief beauty of decoration does not consist so much in the costliness of the materials which compose it, as in the taste displayed in its design, and the appropriateness of its position. The beauty of the picture you so admire is not enhanced by its being portrayed upon a certain kind of canvas, but in the arrangement of the landscape and figures; true, the finest pictures are upon canvas and not cabinet-board, but only a close critic with educated eye can detect the difference; so an elegant and lofty apartment best displays the elaborate, the costly hangings and the exquisite frescoes; still the more humble room may have its walls so carefully and tastefully painted that even the eye of the *connoisseur* is caught and held by the exquisite coloring.

The rules to govern the furnishing and embellishment of a house are these:

1st, beauty of form; 2d, the harmonious combination of color; 3d, the fitness of each article of furniture for its special office, and the adaptation and appropriateness of each ornament for the particular purpose to which it is applied.

This chaste and delicate taste would lead to the following results in furnishing: if the paper was of an olive green with gold lines and spots, the carpet deeper shades of green, brightened in spots with touches of primary green, and careful arrangement of some deep-toned colors; then the covers of tables, curtains and upholstery would harmonize best if they were tinted with shades of dull red or crimson; but it is best to bear constantly in mind that as a rule, the primaries are best confined (in their pure shades) to the objects and ornamental details to which the general masses serve as back-grounds. For instance in the case supposed, the reds should not be too positive, but of a subdued tone, say inclining to purple, while the green should be of an opposite character and contain a yellowish tinge, while any bright spots or masses of decided color being introduced in borders of table covers, bands of chair and sofa seats, edgings to Anti-macassars, borders of rugs, curtains, etc., would "stand out," as it were, and produce their proper effect.

As regards styles of furniture for various apartments, in this day, it would appear almost fruitless to attempt the descriptions of varieties, and the application of styles to positions, there being such a vast number that a person about to furnish their house, may choose *ad infinitum ad libitum.* Perhaps, though, we may be able to give a few hints that will aid our young housekeepers, at least, to make such selections as will allow them no grounds for after regret or self-reproach, which we will do, before entering upon the principal object of our work, which is to give directions for furnishing and embellishing THE HOUSE of which they are to make A HOME by their own hands.

CHAPTER II.

SELECTING AND ARRANGING HOUSE FURNITURE.

As a means of aiding you, our ambitious and tasteful housekeeper, in selecting and imitating beautiful models and artistic arrangements, let us walk through the various establishments, whose furniture, carpets and upholstering are spread before us in all the rich profusion which is so enchanting to the eye of those women, whose taste hungers to be fed with beautiful objects.

Here we find exquisite furniture of every description, and for each apartment in the house. For the dining-rooms, bed-chambers, sitting-rooms and halls, the quaintly simple English Gothic styles, after designs by Eastlake, are appropriate, and possess the recommendation of being easily copied, as we show in a following chapter. Many do not admire this style, but among the lovers of ancient and mediæval art, those rather simple forms present peculiar attractions. It consists of low, square and straight form, in wood of various colors and kinds, embellished with illuminated designs in blue, scarlet and dead gold, arranged after mediæval patterns. The curious oxidized rings, screws, hinges and locks give a massive appearance to some of the "pieces," and are suggestive of utility as well as age.

Butternut wood of light yellowish-brown, maple both curled and bird's-eye, white poplar, and other light wood is suitable for dining-room, chambers and living-room ; walnut for library, hall and parlors in the majority of houses, and in many is preferred through all. The ebonized and highly ornamental furniture in imitation of the exquisite Japanese lacquered and inlaid work, Chinese papier-mache, omolu, gilded and painted fancy suites are highly esteemed for parlors and drawing-rooms, and can be so perfectly imitated that the great fear is, persons will be apt to overdo the matter and run into extremes that will tend rather to vulgar and pretentious display than to chaste and elegant adornment.

Many persons of moderate means will prefer suites of black walnut, and we would mention to those not aware of the fact that exceedingly tasteful chamber suites with marble top to bureau, wash-stand, *commode* and candle-stand may be obtained for $75 to $100, while simple suites of walnut without marble, cost from $30 to $50, and these can be so exquisitely embellished that, after coming from the brush $500 would scarcely purchase them.

Suites of parlor, dining-room or chamber furniture, made neatly and strongly, may be gotten up for about $15 to $25 (or purchased directly from the factory).

Of well-seasoned pine wood, which can be rubbed down and polished, we can make furniture *en suite* for each separate room ; and though it will require time, industry, and a modicum of artistic skill, we need not fear but we can adorn every apartment in our house, not merely with taste but with elegance of no mean order. As we proceed with this work full directions will be given for enriching these plain sets, but for those with means at their disposal for purchasing elegant furniture directly from the establishments, we have butternut suites with blue and red illuminations costing from $600 to $2,000. Dark old walnut mediæval suites relieved by scarlet, gold and ebony figures, at $1,200.

For dining-rooms there are side-boards from Eastlake's designs, that bring to mind the comfortable old affair of our grandmothers, filled to repletion on Thanksgiving or Christmas ; a set of deep shelves above, with the cupboards below closed in by heavy doors furnished with hinges, rings and key-shields of dull oxidized silver or brass. In some cases these are made of the bright cheerful-looking butternut wood with designs in marquetry, either of stained or self-colored woods.

Chairs of square form, upholstered with leather, or the leather cloth. The wooden mantel may be made to correspond with the furniture ; indeed may almost be said to make a portion of the suite ; above it a shelf and tiers of brackets, with picture of fruit, game or suitable figures.

For chambers, the same square style appears to be preferred to the high-pointed forms of years back. Solid walnut suites, well made, and simply embellished with mouldings, consisting of seven pieces, viz. : bedstead, bureau, wash-stand, candle-stand (or small table), rocking and two side chairs (cane-seated.) may be bought for $50. A dressing-table, with mirror from four to six feet long, with drawers on the sides furnished with drop-handles, costs $25 to $40, and is a great comfort in a ladies' dressing-room.

The "cottage suites" of enamelled wood are exceedingly pretty, particularly for country houses or children's chambers. The sage gray tints are specially lovely with scenes in oval frames of ornamental gilding ; or charming floral designs of moss roses and buds, or clusters of violets, or creamy white lilies. These are easily and beautifully imitated (as we shall hereafter show) and can be made to form exquisite combinations, with colors of carpet, walls, etc. The low head-boards of these fancy suites are extremely quaint looking and the pretty tints above the snowy linen present a charming appearance, and the drop-handles of nickel or wood added to these light suites, appear peculiarly effective. French-gray grounds with scarlet and gilt illuminated designs ; black enamelled with blue, scarlet, and mingled tints of gorgeous color, blended with gilding ; oak with bands of blue and gold enclosing exquisite landscapes, form some of the combinations which appear naturally to suit this style of furniture.

The fancy for mediæval furniture, which is now the caprice of wealthy people, can be brought to impart a special beauty to the homesteads of the more humble housekeeper inasmuch as it is a style peculiarly adapted to the quaint rooms belonging to many of our country dwellings.

For the pretty cottage suites, just described, this form is exceedingly appropriate, and a set of such furniture with carpet and walls corresponding in tone, mantels stained, enamelled and painted, (or imitated with Decalcomania work) will be found to produce a most pleasing result, and is an inexpensive one with all.

For parlors, drawing-rooms, or saloons, ebony, (which may be so beautifully imitated), is the wood in special favor. It is used for entire suites and appears peculiarly adapted to the many pieces of furniture now brought into requisition, to add to this the treasure-house of the ambitious housewife. So she may have her entire parlor suite, made of well-seasoned pine, after certain patterns which correspond with her peculiar taste, and proceed to ebonize and embellish after the true mediæval style.

The long straight sofas, and chairs with square arms and backs, cabinet with shelves and case for the *bric a brac*, the massive table, frames of mirror and pictures, case for the (otherwise simple) clock, easels for choice pictures, pedestals for busts or statuettes, and brackets for the tasteful vase or other pretty adornments.

The enrichments for this sombre ground-work are gilt traceries, marquetry of tinted wood, inlaid ivory, tiles of antique color and design and Oriental painting with vivid transparent tints.

For some rooms, light woods may be preferred, indeed, where the aspect is a north or north-easterly one, or the apartment somewhat shaded and gloomy, we would recommend this style.

In this case the walls are painted in imitation of fresco, or with dado and frieze of deeper shade and the intermediate walls a light tint of a similar color, or the walls may be white or some very pale tint, with gilt mouldings or a dado of cloth-paper with gold figures.

The carpets here should be of white or very light lavender, pearl or dove color, with designs in primary colors, or a square of Aubusson tapestry, with floor tastefully painted to represent tiles—or again the entire floor may be stained and carefully colored to represent inlaid woods, with only rugs placed about in true Eastern style.

Renaissance chairs of various kinds — some with low oval backs, covered with rich embroidery;—light fancy reception chairs, stools, ottomans, *brioches*, etc., are scattered carelessly about; and draperies with white ground and gay figures, give the whole a light, bright appearance that will at once change the gloomy apartment to one of brightness and cheery light.

The invaluable "bracket" saws, carving and ornamenting tools, which are now to be procured for so small a sum, place household decoration, indeed the complete furnishing, within the means of every one, and where any member of the family with sufficient strength can use one of the finer foot power scroll saws, we should say that it were money well invested to secure one of these never failing sources of satisfaction and pleasure. With such a saw, and tools (such as are shown on in a later chapter), a person may furnish their entire house. Taking a set of furniture, piece by piece, it is not after all an impossible thing (for a man at least), to make every article desired ; and with the small saws and carving tools, a lady will find it a most pleasurable occupation to fashion all the lighter articles of household decoration and light fret-work panels for even heavy furniture. This application of dark fret-work upon light wood or *vice versa*, will be found one of the most elegant methods of embellishing panels of doors, wainscoting, window-frames, broad, flat spaces on furniture, etc.

Low book-cases of walnut or light wood may be beautifully enriched (in imitation of the costly specimens we see) by using the Egyptian, Roman and Grecian heads which come in such perfection among the artificial wood carvings. The highest part in the center of these cases is five feet, fitted with shelves set in graduated distances for volumes of different sizes, while on the sides are low wings three or four feet high, inclosed with doors, furnished with locks and rings, which adds greatly to their quaint look. Ladies' Davenport desks, corner cabinets, with shelves and spaces inclosed for curiosities, low easels and upright portfolios for engravings and pictures of other kinds, brackets in Gothic style, and quaint, massive table, constitute the library furniture ; while for halls are chairs of heavy carved wood, with wooden or cane seats ; hat-rack, inclosing mirror, and drawer below for brushes, bracket with broad shelf for shawls ; wall pockets of wood with embellishments to correspond with furniture for gloves etc., chandeliers with wine-colored shade, and the usual mats and rugs upon the floor. All these things we are to reproduce by imitation.

As regards the upholstering we may not fabricate the rich damasks, cretonnes and Indian silks which, accompanying the furniture we have described, make the dwellings of the rich so luxurious ; but, thanks be to innate taste and the ingenuity and enterprise of American manufacturers, we *can* cover our sofas and chairs, can make our cushioned couches and tufted ottomans, can drape our windows with materials so beautiful in design and soft in texture, and withal at such prices, that we are enabled to make up fully by extra lining and quantity for the heaviness of the imported article.

For parlors, drawing-rooms and *salons*, rich Oriental damasks, raw silks of rare Indienne designs, Persian silk, cashmeres and tapestry are used.

The silks are soft and fine in quality, in delicate shades ; while the rich Indienne fabrics called lampas, a kind of figured satin, and Persian silks, cashmeres, in pale tints or white grounds, strewn with dark figures ; some satin damasks have black grounds with heavy brocaded or embroidered designs covering them ; these and tapestries are of light fade hues, with curious, quaint arabesque figures ; a Louis Quinze rose color, with lovely blue, pale-drab, pearl or gray, blue-green with embossed velvet figures, and a clear amber-brown with self-hued brocaded figures, or the many charming shades of brown, blue, drab and dull red wrought in golden yellow.

Bed-chambers are upholstered with fabrics equally rich, or with the beautiful Cretonnes, satteens, cashmeres and chintzes in various styles. Striking contrasts are avoided, and in rooms appropriated for family use serviceable colors are preferred; blue furnishes more tastefully perhaps than any other, but no color fades so quickly.

Country houses, during Summer, appear best with light or white-grounded chintzes or Cretonnes, quaint blue or buff backgrounds, with arabesque designs thickly covered over the plain surface ;—drab, gray, black or brown, with bright colored flowers or figures ; so perfect in shading as to appear as if painted in delicate water colors. Rich plain fabrics have bands of velvet stitched on the edges, or plaited bands with ruchings on the edges completely cover the woodwork of chairs and lounges.

Curtains, mantel hangings and covers of tables and stands are of like materials as the upholstering ; or in summer linen damask, or Swiss embellished with applique work. Bedsteads are again furnished with curtains and valances (physicians to the contrary notwithstanding), and with the Arabian bedsteads, form a most charming arrangement. We confess to having a strong predilection for the quaint, comfortable, and even elegant bed-hangings of the olden times. These of course correspond with the remaining drapery and may be of any of the new quaint stuffs now used ; the curtains attached to rings which slide readily upon poles of wood or metal.

For plain houses the new gray linen damasks are as beautiful as appropriate. This may be bordered with embroidery, figures cut from scarlet cloth, or blue, green, or other desirable color, or from cretonne-chintz, and fastened with applique stitch ; chain-stitching, a braided design, or even wide bands of color stitched on each edge with sewing machine work, finishes them equally well. A pretty fancy of the times is to make Summer covers, anti-macassars, etc., of Swiss, with fluted ruffles as a finish, curtains and hangings to correspond, as also a bed-spread and pillow covers, which must be lined with color to match or contrast with furniture, &c.

Libraries and dining-rooms are upholstered largely with embossed leather ; leather-paper on walls, plain, or stamped in bright or somber colors—brown, stone, dark green, crimson or dull red. The enrichment of furniture here consists in bands of dark velvet thickly studded with gilt-headed nails, heavy woollen fringe. Curtains of damask or furniture crash, bordered with velvet to match upholstery, and lambrequins of leather-cloth decorated with designs to match the tiles of the furniture, fire-place, &c. In libraries where more warmth of tone is desirable, richer fabrics are used for the hangings ; plain rooms having the cheaper worsted stuffs, such as Tycoon and striped reps, in rich Indian tints, lined and bordered with velveteen.

Of the principal feature of the dining-room, the sideboard, we have already spoken, but would add that the former taste for marble slabs is entirely superseded by the plain, highly enamelled tiles, with heavy ornaments of nickel or brass—in ring-handles, hinges, keys, etc.

For sitting (or living) rooms there are lovely chintzes, cretonnes, and heavier woolen fabrics; a host of rich tints of blue, drab, gray and pale rose, that catch the tints of rosy morning or golden evening, and diffuse brightness and a glowing warmth through the room, in which various light furniture eminently for ladies' use is scattered about, though the deep "Sleepy Hollow" chair, with tufted foot-rest of carved wood, upholstered cushion, and carved newspaper portfolio, indicate that the gentlemen too are expected to enjoy this general room. Quaint sets of cottage or Japanese furniture in colored wood or bamboo, upholstered in bright colors; cabinet to correspond, and rich, folding screen, with "couches that invite repose," and every variety of "knick-knackery," are shown for this apartment devoted to the family circle; and, perhaps despite the housewife's laudable ambition to ornament the parlor, the dearest, most carefully embellished spot of all her house.

The illustrations we give will afford some idea of the embellishment and decoration of these various kinds of furniture, and will aid in their being imitated.

CHAPTER III.

THE HALL.

THE VESTIBULE.

MANY halls, instead of having a vestibule at the entrance, open directly upon the portico or steps, and as the staircase and doors to various apartments generally stand in this passage, screens will not only be found a comfort as regards privacy, but also in breaking those draughts of air which rush through the building upon opening the outer doors in cold or stormy weather. In many cases an *impromptu* partition reaching from floor to ceiling, with a door, will be found to answer admirably as a screen.

Such a partition may be made simply of canvas neatly papered, with the door of light frame-work covered in the same manner, and present a really tasteful appearance. Or where elegance of a more artistic character is desired, nothing can yield such an air of comfort and taste as warm, bright colored curtains separating hall and vestibule.

Where the ceiling is high, a deep lambrequin may extend for a distance below it with the curtains fastened beneath; but where the space will admit, a more simple method will be to fasten brackets upon the side walls, into which a pole is set, with the curtain falling in long, heavy folds and readily drawn aside by means of large rings, fastened to it and on the pole.

In arranging such curtains both sides must be neatly finished, as either will be equally conspicuous, the one from the entrance, the other from the hall.

When possible, the entrance door should be made with glass transom and side lights, as upon these depend the brightness of an otherwise gloomy apartment.

We have frequently heard it asserted and believe it to be a prevalent idea, that the entrance to a house should be made as bright and dazzling as possible; that the hall should, from floor to ceiling, be covered with brilliant colors in carpet and paper, and furnished in the most sumptuous manner, presenting the person entering with an immediate sense of the ability of the house (whether it be great or small), the millionaire setting the example, the more humble neighbors following on as closely as possible.

Whereas both are wrong, for whatever may be the state of finances, and whether the hall may be wide or narrow, the same rule should govern; which is, that here the light must be soft and the colors subdued; the furniture a shade *more simple*, and the aspect slightly *less sumptuous*, than in the surround-

Fig. 1. Home-made Hall Curtain.

ing apartments; to carry out, in fact, the old idea of a vestibule, that it is to be "a sheltered cortile," into which our beloved home-comer and stranger guest may turn as to a haven of rest, and find that he has not entered into a scene of dazzling and oppressive light, but to a soft, subdued shade, as restful as it is refreshing when compared to the garish light just shut out with the closing door.

Mr. M. D. Conway, in *Harper's Monthly*, in speaking upon this subject, tells us that "in the majority of beautiful houses, the first effect at the entrance is that of shade," and he adds, very aptly: "The visitor who has come from the blaze of daylight is at once invited to a kindly seclusion. Beyond the vestibule the light is again reached, but now blended with tints and forms of artistic beauty. He is no longer in the hands of brute Nature, but is being ministered to by humane thought and feeling, and gently won into that mood

> 'In which the heavy and the weary weight
> Of all this unintelligible world
> Is lightened.' "

To produce this sense of refreshment, whether from the bleak cold winds of winter, or the hot sultry heat of summer, becomes a subject worthy of careful consideration.

To the wealthy it will be easy to produce the results so ably held up to us as examples by Mr. Conway; but to our more humble housekeeper and that large class who "desire but have not the means to gratify," to these it becomes a matter of real unrest, that with earnest desire to make home as inviting as possible, they lack the ability. Though "on hospitable care intent," to just as great a degree as her more wealthy neighbor, our less wealthy woman feels unable to so furnish her hall and apartments that they will yield the dreamy satisfaction, the luxurious refreshment just described. What then? Must she succumb to her stringent circumstances, and with bare floors and dazzling panes of transparent window glass, endure the mortification and sorrow perhaps of knowing that her friends and even her own household are uncomfortable?

No! Thanks to those who with laudable anxiety to aid that large class who have no means to purchase costly luxuries, have given us means of imitating beautiful and even artistic objects, we may, by exerting ourselves, obtain descriptions of them, or perhaps secure the use of some costly specimen for a time, be able to make such perfect imitations of the same that all who see them will enjoy the copy as much or more perhaps than the original. Let us see therefore, first, what we can do to produce that mellow glow, so beautiful when diffused through a vestibule; this in handsome dwellings is the effect of the light through stained glass in the side and transom lights of the front door. But in this day when men of taste and culture resort to the recent imitations of Diaphanie, Vitromania, etc., for the embellishment of churches and other *public*

2

buildings, surely the finger of scorn cannot be pointed at those who apply these really exquisite kinds of work to the embellishment of their own homes.

There are such a number of charming methods for changing plain panes of glass into transparencies of no mean order, that it becomes a matter of wonder that so many (even tasteful persons), are willing to submit to the glare of the unornamented glass, or even worse, to the obscurity and *ugliness* of the thick green paper which has been used so long for covering the hall door lights.

Diaphanie and Vitromania are such perfect imitations of stained glass that the plates are being largely used in Europe for the windows of handsome public buildings, dwellings and churches, and have become wonderfully popular with decorators. The art of transferring these plates is fully given in "Household Elegancies;" and among the designs, borders, grounds, corners, etc., of which there are between three and five hundred different plates (in manufacturers' catalogues), a large number will be found peculiarly adapted to our present purpose.

Pieces of a sacred character are only appropriate for churches, chapels or the *Sanctum Sanctorum* of the clergyman; but for those who admire mediæval and ancient scenes and decorations are offered an extensive assortment, consisting of knights, musicians, medallions, heads of various characters, groups of flowers and fruit, Rosaces, etc., in many styles of the thirteenth, fifteenth and sixteenth centuries and Renaissance period; while to those who prefer more modern styles are presented charming views in Switzerland and other countries.

Besides this method of enriching plain glass, there are numerous other ways of subduing the garish light which are even more simple.

By applying the Decalcomania designs in the usual manner and covering with bobbinet, then varnishing with Demar (which will fasten the lace to the glass), a beautiful effect is given, almost equal to Diaphanie. Or varnishing with Demar and applying figured lace and finishing with two after coats of varnish, the glass will appear like the figured ground glass and will bear washing.

Where an extremely subdued light is desired, a charming effect is produced by cutting thin card board of size of the panes, sketching pretty designs on them, then cutting slashes in the high lights; which work bears the imposing name of Epiphanie, but is really quite simple, though beautiful beyond description, looking like sculpture. To produce a different effect, line the design with colored gelatine or even tissue paper, and if crimson is used a rich glow like stained glass will be cast; or, better still, line the various parts behind the slashes, with the color required; for instance, if leaves, green; flowers, rose, blue, yellow, purple, etc., to suit the different varieties.

Photophanie too affords an exquisite means of embellishment; using a plain wall paper with a border of vine leaves, or ivy, maple or oak, and a group in the center of each pane; or extending from the center to each end, (diminishing from the center,) of larger leaves, with grapes, flowers, or whatever is desired, carefully pricked with needles of several sizes.

Where the family can boast of an artist, none of these imitations will be required, but they may resort to a still more artistic embellishment and paint directly upon the glass in transparent colors, which is certainly a most charming method of adorning the hall and other windows.

FLOOR OF VESTIBULE.

The floor of the vestibule should if possible be covered with oil-cloth, or some substitute for it, either matting—Canton or Cocoa-fibre—or the imitation of oil-cloth made with wall paper, or chintz.

This substitute or "imitation" we can highly recommend, having tested it for many years, upon a hall in constant use by a large family; and we would remark here, that those who have failed in making this cloth durable, have either not varnished sufficiently, or have neglected to give the "necessary" coat of shellac each spring, which if attended to, will insure long wear. The method of making this "home-made oil-cloth," is this: having the floor perfectly smooth, by puttying the cracks and rubbing down any rough places, give it a thorough cleansing with brush and soap-suds. Allow to dry, and having sufficient coarse muslin to cover the space, proceed to tack one end firmly and closely to the floor, stretch as tightly as possible, and fasten at the opposite side; proceed in like manner with the sides. Next paint the whole with smooth, thin paste, until the muslin is thoroughly wet, allow this to dry, and having selected wall paper with check, or mosaic design, cut into lengths, of size of room, matching each one carefully. Having a quantity of smooth, boiled paste, to which a half pint of thin liquid glue has been added to every gallon, with a small whitewash or paint brush, paint the under or "wrong" side of each strip, always keeping one covered ahead, in order to allow time for the paper to become thoroughly damp. The strips should be laid evenly, and carefully matched; then patted with a clean, soft towel, until they adhere to the muslin in every part. When dry, paint with two coats of shellac varnish, allowing the first to dry before applying the second. Lastly give two coats of Copal, and you have a handsome and durable oil-cloth.

When those parts in constant use, show worn and defaced spots, immediate application of shellac varnish, followed by a coat of Copal, will at once renovate them, and by this care, such a floor-covering, will constantly appear fresh and solid as when first made, and will withstand the "wear and tear" of many years.

Where Canton Matting is used, the bright crimson or deep brown and white checkered kinds appear to best advantage. Where the white matting is preferred, weekly washing (or rather sponging) with salt-water, will tend to retain the greenish-white color, noticeable in the new and genuine article.

White metal tacks should always be used for matting, as the rust of the ordinary iron tack soon discolors the edge, besides presenting an unsightly appearance.

STAINED AND INLAID FLOORS.

An elegant floor is made as follows :—

Take a quantity of fine whitening and mix with linseed oil, until sufficiently plastic to be worked readily, then with a glazier's knife, carefully fill each crack, hole and crevice in the boards, working the putty firmly in with the knife. Allow this to dry, and endeavour to make the entire surface as uniform as possible.

Next obtain a decoction of burnt-umber by mixing the powder, in scalding vinegar, and while it is preparing, proceed to sketch and cut out a border and center-piece of style, corresponding with the surroundings.

If the glass of your windows has been embellished with floral designs, (whether in Diaphanie or Photophanie work, is unimportant,) then a suitable design for the floor will be a conventional group of flowers, with a border of Oak leaves and Acorns, or Vine and Grapes. These must be large, and arranged carefully with the vines, starting from the center of sides and ends, and running out toward the corners, where ornamental squares may finish and connect them.

Cut these designs from stiff paper—and if care is used not to tear them while wet, the same strip, or succession of leaves, will answer for the remaining sides, and a quarter section of the center for the other three.

Fasten these patterns in position on the floor, by pressing pins through the paper and into the wood; then with a medium sized painters-brush, and the decoction of Umber, stain the uncovered parts of the floor around them, proceed thus with each section, and give successive coats until a rich brown color is obtained; when each part thus painted is dry, raise the patterns, and the design will appear in the color of the wood. Brush the surface of the stained parts with a soft brush, and rub thoroughly with a flannel cloth until perfectly smooth, then with a little of the stain, (made very light with vinegar) proceed to vein and mark the leaves, stamens of flowers and any fine parts, when dry oil or varnish the whole surface, and the effect will be that of a floor inlaid with butternut or other white wood on walnut.

Another effect is produced by staining the various figures with colors, such as are described in chapter on wood staining, etc., using yellow, purple, green, red, etc., in imitation of the marquetry art, but using only two colors, or two shades of one color in one design. Mosaic designs will be extremely effective for this work, producing most imposing results—and being besides, easy of execution, as they can be laid on with line and rule, with geometric figures—such as are shown in Fig. 2.

The idea is to imitate tiles, which are so various in character that all tastes may be suited, though we would suggest that two tints—or at the most three, is in better taste than a heterogeneous mass of colors, as this kind of polychromy is out of place on the floor of a private house. It is a pretty idea too, to imitate the old Roman fashion, and introduce some motto or legend upon the pavement thus made; thus following the lead of Minton, and others who copy the designs of the tiles of Herculaneum and Pompeii, and other ancient cities. Some of the designs and legends are peculiarly appropriate, as for instance that of the chained dog, with the motto "Cave canem," and that cheery word of welcome "Salve," "which," says Mr. Perkins, "the visitor to a Roman house, in the

Fig. 2.

palmy days of the empire, often found written beneath his feet, and heard re-echoed by the 'pica salutatrix' (the talking Magpie), from his gilded cage which overhung the door-way!"

DOOR TEXTS OR MOTTOES.

These cheery and beautiful door embellishments have become so common and deservedly popular that a tasteful apartment is scarcely considered finished without one or more of them.

We think the fashion (as is too frequently the case with these things), is in some instances carried to excess, but, as an ornament over the front door, the hospitable "WELCOME" or the cheery old "SALVE" amounts almost to a genial handshake; while over the entrance to the sitting-room, "SWEET HOME;" for a bed-room, "THOU ONLY MAKEST ME DWELL IN SAFETY," etc., are not only suggestive but highly ornamental.

At present we have only to do with the motto or text for the front door.

Fig. 3. Motto.

Of course the sentiment to be embodied in the word or words must be
entirely at the discretion and preference of the mistress of the house, but let it
be what it will, it should be (whether painted, illuminated or embroidered,)

Fig. 4. Motto.

carefully framed and glazed, and so placed over the frame of the door that it is "tipped" slightly forward in order to present a clear view, from below, of each word and letter.

Some persons paint the words in transparent colors upon the glass over the door, as a part of the illuminated transom, but this is open to the objection that from one side the letters must be transposed.

We believe the most popular kind of door texts are those worked on the beautiful stamped perforated card-board of which there are such an innumera-

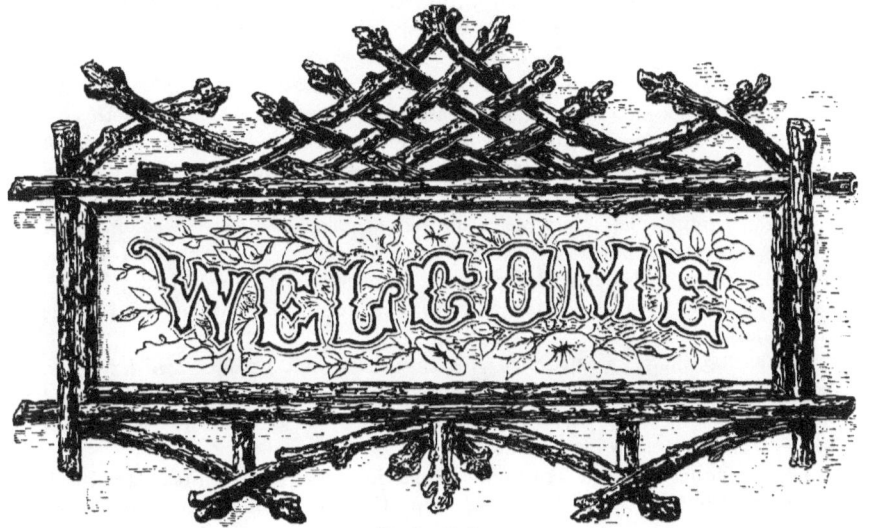

Fig. 5. Motto.

ble variety, embroidered with silk, chenille, gold and silver thread, cord or bullion, beads, or even zephyrs. These letters, especially when of highly ornamental character, are very beautiful.

An unexceptional mode of making these letters is by means of illuminated painting, and where the grounding is richly colored, with a large admixture of gold in the lettering the effect is wonderfully artistic.

ON GLASS.

Charming letters for this purpose may be made on glass by proceeding thus: have your glass cut of proper size, and having washed it perfectly clean, first, with soap and water, and afterwards with alcohol, cut a strip of tin-foil of the size desired for the letters, and make it quite smooth by rolling with a polished surface, such as an ivory paper-knife, and wetting the place on the glass (which the letters are to occupy) with a little *very thin* gum arabic mucilage, or the white of an egg dissolved in half a pint of cold water, lay on the foil, rubbing it down flat with a pad of cloth, and after it adheres, with a burnisher of some kind; the more it is polished the finer will be the effect. On this foil mark the pattern letters, which may be as ornamental as desired, and should be cut out from card board, or other material which will lay down flatly and admit of being cut around, (bearing in mind that as you are working on the back the word must be backward). With a sharp knife cut off and remove all superfluous foil from around and within each letter, pressing down carefully the edges, over which apply a little varnish to prevent the ground color from entering beneath the foil, which would ruin the work.

Next arrange any scroll-work, borders, corner-pieces, or other graceful ornamentation in the same manner, and finally apply over the whole a smooth coat —or several of them—of the desired ground color, which may be brown, of "Asphaltum varnish," or any colored paint, prepared with varnish as directed hereafter.

If transparent colored letters are desired, or gold alone or with colors, paint them with tube-paints mixed with Demar varnish. Thus: green, 1-5 blue, 4-5 yellow; purple, 1-6 blue, 5-6 crimson; wine-color, 1-12 blue, 11-12 crimson; pink, add crimson to white zinc; brown, dark purple with yellow until of the shade desired.

For back-grounds: white, zinc with turpentine and Demar varnish; black, lampblack with asphaltum varnish, turpentine and boiled linseed oil in equal quantities; light flesh-pink, white zinc with a little crimson and a touch of yellow; blue, Prussian blue, white zinc and Demar varnish.

For sketching out the figures or letters in colors, use a little lampblack rubbed in asphaltum varnish, adding turpentine until it flows easily under the brush.

The colors used are of the transparent class, Prussian blue, crimson and yellow lakes, No. 40 carmine, Roseau and white zinc, sold by druggists in tubes.

An exquisite shade of green for various kinds of fancy work is made by putting green coffee into white of egg and keeping for two or three days, until of shade required.

CARPETS FOR THE HALL.

Having finished the vestibule, our next duty is to furnish the hall proper, and as the most important feature will speak of the floor.

In one of the pleasant notes, appended by the American editor to Eastlake's "Hints on Household Taste," he says, in answer to Mr. Eastlake's assertion, that "the best mode of treating a hall-floor, whether in town or country, is to pave it with encaustic tiles." If Mr. Eastlake were speaking of a vestibule, we should agree with him. That appears to be the true place for a mosaic pavement, or a pavement of encaustic tiles, but a parquet floor is better fitted for the hall, especially in a cold climate, etc.

For real comfort we believe that in winter a carpet on both floor and staircase is preferable to either, giving an air of warmth and comfort that is most delightful on coming in from the cold vestibule.

We would therefore suggest that a floor be first ornamented by any one of the methods described for the vestibule, and thus present a cool, pleasant aspect in summer, which at the time of the Autumn "cleaning," upon being covered, will not only produce the results described, but afford a pleasant change. The style of carpeting for the hall, should be rather bright and cheery, small figures, and with a warmth of tone, contrasting rather strongly with the coldness outside. An appropriate border adds greatly to the effect of this carpet, but better even than this to have the floor painted or stained with a border, and allow the carpet to extend only to the inner edge of this, is still more appropriate.

On the stairs, use a striped design, and finish the edges and face, not covered with paint, of shade contrasting or corresponding with the color of walls or wood-work.

In all these different parts, whether in coloring wood-work, floors, carpets or wall, let one thing be kept constantly in mind, that as a possible rule, too many colors must not be introduced. However imposing the effect of vivid and numerous colors may be in shop, hotel or restaurant, such polychromy is in bad taste when applied to a private dwelling.

Two colors or two shades of the same color, will give a chaste effect, and as regards walls or floor—never attempt to produce a raised appearance.

WALLS OF HALL.

As regards the mural embellishment of the hall, there can be but little doubt, that panels are the most appropriate, and produce the finest results. It is not difficult to procure wall-paper which imitates oak, walnut, etc., with the borders, corners and other "*trimmings*," that will simulate dado, frieze and panel, and with the directions we have already given for hanging to apply these to the walls with the most happy effects. A beautiful mode of beautifying such apartment, is to imitate an inlay of encaustic tiles to a height of three feet from the floor above that, to calcimine in some pleasing tint or paint with flat color, for where it is possible a hall should be painted rather than papered. Another and most artistic method is to paint the walls as directed in chapter on papering, etc.

There may be found some ambitious and truly artistic housekeeper, who would persevere in the effort to paint the walls of her house, one after another, but we fear these would be greatly in the minority, and that if one or two pet apartments meet with the indulgence of having their walls painted, it will be all that most dwellings can boast, still by one or two of the methods given in another chapter, any walls may be thus embellished without such vast expense of time, labor and patience, and we can assure our readers " it will pay." The color of the walls if painted or calcimined, or the tint of paper must necessarily depend upon circumstances, color of floor or carpet, amount of light, style of glass in transom (" fan-light " as some call it) or window. If rather dim as regards light, a warm pomegranate, delicate green, or soft gray will be well chosen, but where the light is vivid, as through " illuminated glass " dull reds, browns or darker grays will be found excellent as surface colors, but in any case divide the wall into three parts, dado, frieze and intermediate wall, and in forming panels, go closely by the rules given in section on Paper Hangings.

HALL FURNITURE.

The furniture of a hall, should be simple in form, and not over abundant in quantity, as nothing appears so offensive to a truly fine taste, than an apartment intended only as a place for a transient sojourn to be crowded with an indiscriminate mass of " odds and ends," placed or left there apparently because not being constantly occupied, things are not so carefully noticed. This is a mark of wretched housekeeping, and as first impressions leave a lasting trace upon the mind, which is never wholly obliterated, so does the effect produced upon the mind upon first entering a dwelling, continue to color all succeeding recollections of that house, and the mistress thereof will receive her full share of blame or praise according to the merits of the case.

But inasmuch as it appears natural for most persons, to do those things most easily and readily done, it is the result frequently of necessity, that, hat, cloak, gloves, umbrella, whip, etc., are thrown down, no appropriate place being furnished for their reception. Therefore every hall should have its hat-pegs, its wall-pockets for gloves, veils, hoods and scarfs, a table for the book, paper or parcel carried by visitor or member of the family, and to be taken at the end of a call, or when again going out; the card receiver, case for letters or papers for the post-office; chairs for those waiting, or weary, and perhaps a sofa or lounge, for in most houses, especially in the country, should be something more as Mr. Perkins truly observes, " than a mere *locum tenens* for the staircase."

We would pause here to make one remark regarding the style of furniture designed by Charles Eastlake, and which he so enthusiastically urges the public to adopt; concerning it we would say that inasmuch as it exhibits, all severe simplicity, solidity and (where desired) cheapness, of much of the odd old articles of our great-grandfathers, it would appear to be conveniently adapted to the requirements of many persons, especially those residing in quaint, old-fashioned dwellings, or to those who can utilize the hoards of old furniture, which, since their mother's childhood, perhaps, has been collecting dust and cobwebs, under the moss-covered roof of the garret. By this time, the old side-board, secretary, chairs and other ancient pieces of furniture have acquired the very shade of darkness, and mellowness of tint required, and can be made into the quaintest Gothic pieces that can be desired.

Nevertheless popular fancies are so changeable even these, by their very sameness of simplicity, will give place ere long to styles more ornamental.

A hundred years ago, the hall was a most important part of the dwelling. With its heavy cabinets, chairs, and quaint upright eight-day-clock, standing, sentinel-like in the corner; this apartment presented a most inviting appearance. We confess to a lingering love for "the old clock that ticked on the stairs," and would advise its introduction in every hall, though it might not be the veritable " old eight-day," which is fast becoming extinct, still let there be a substitute, which may be either suspended or placed on a bracket; if the latter it should correspond with the furniture of the hall.

With regard to brackets, we would suggest the use of plaster or clay colored, some dark brown or stone color, and sanded, or the brackets sold at the picture-frame stores, made of some composition, which has a beautiful gray tint, that is certainly artistic, and of which picture and mirror frames are moulded, prior to gilding.

French clocks are expensive, but the elegant imitations made by our

Fig. 6. Fig. 7.

American clock companies, are not only perfect " time-keepers," but have cases of exquisite workmanship in marble, bronze and other materials, and above all, have, as regards price, been brought within the means of our tasteful and moderately wealthy classes.

Many beautiful forms of these clocks may be purchased for ten to sixty dollars, and are adapted to the various apartments, from the parlor to the nursery, some of the forms being eminently adapted to give pleasure to the " little folks."

For a hall, such clocks as Figs. 6 and 7 are most appropriate, and would impart a truly artistic air to the apartment. In Fig. 8, in the bronze figure with arm uplifted, the clock is not given, but such style (of clock) as is shown in Fig. 7, is designed for it, to be held in the raised arm. These figures are surpassingly beautiful but though not expensive, if considered too much so by some possessing but limited means, we would suggest, that such figures may be obtained in plaster, and after being bronzed according to one of our methods,

Fig. 8.

will if placed on a bracket, correspondingly embellished, and a clock (of the marine class) also, ebonized or bronzed, fastened in position on it, be found to make a beautiful substitute for the one shown in this illustration. For a hall the marine clocks are eminently adapted, and as they are not remarkably ornamental in their unadorned form, the plan of obtaining really chaste and artistic plaster figures of proper size with a bracket, (if necessary) and bronzing them all skillfully, with some one of the fine bronze powders, elegant clocks are obtained at one-fourth the cost of the bronze ones.

If preferred the marble cases may be imitated in a similar manner, by having a wooden base made and staining it, then imitating some one of the rare kinds of marble.

It is by such wise discrimination in selecting fine models, that a house is made, not a mere show-room, or museum, filled with every variety of cheap and flimsy imitations, but an enchanting spot adorned with objects at once interesting, chaste and even elegant in appearance.

A charming arrangement—illustrative of our idea regarding the union of Use and Beauty—is made by utilizing the usually unoccupied corners behind the front door. These spaces may be changed from useless triangles—too frequently presenting the ever-ready spot for umbrellas, canes, and other articles (which are necessarily desired to be quickly rid of), into tasteful alcoves, which not only afford a far more convenient receptacle for the various articles named, but offer a beautiful position for the bracket, on which a statuette may stand, unless a statue of large size (from four to seven feet in height), is to be accommodated; where these triangular cases may be made only three feet or less in height, and thus form pedestals at once useful and ornamental.

To make these corner wardrobes and arched recesses for the umbrella, canes, etc., have a panel (fitting across the corner) more or less wide, according to the size of hall, from the center of which saw an arched opening, as shown in Fig. 9. In a large hall the space thus enclosed may be of considerable size, the hyphothenuse of the triangle be four or even five feet, thus affording ample space for cloaks and other "wraps." The lower part has a drawer or box (at pleasure) one foot in height, made by nailing cleats within the triangle, and on them fastening a light board, which if the case is desired in box form, must have hinges and a handle, wherewith to lift it; but should a drawer be preferred, this board is merely nailed on the cleats and the drawer fitted in the case in the usual manner, (which will require the aid of a carpenter).

These cases may be arranged so that one answers for a coat-rack and wardrobe, the other, with umbrella stand, and hat-pegs above. One of these recesses should be furnished with mirror and wall-pocket, containing clothes and hair-brush; the other a companion wall-pocket for gloves, etc., and other small articles. A shelf fitting beneath the hat-rack, will be found a great convenience for laying shawls upon. The wood-work within these cases must be nicely painted, or covered with paper, while the frame on the outside, may be cut out with the fret-saw, and finished with carving tools, or the artificial wood carvings may be used with fine effect, and the same scheme of embellishment be carried out in all the furniture, and adornment of the wood-work.

The effect of these little alcoves is extremely imposing where they are arranged in a handsome manner, but even where only a simple panel is used, embellished with lines of paint in contrasting color, the effect is at once neat and tasteful. Nothing of an ornamental character, appears more imposing in a hall than statuary.

We are well aware that elegant specimens of carved and richly sculptured marble, are costly luxuries, wherewith to satisfy the artistic taste; but by visiting one of those underground workshops,

Fig. 9.

where the Italian plaster-moulders hold dominion, and form their huge tubs of mushy plaster, producing such pure white, and marvellously lovely forms, some of the most exquisite copies of celebrated works of art that eyes ever beheld may be procured. True they are but copies, but they are nevertheless so exceedingly lovely, majestic, or graceful as the case may be, that we would urge upon our readers, the importance of securing them if possible, for to an artistic taste, no adornment or ornament can afford such an amount of satisfaction (after a beautiful picture) as a piece of statuary of marble or bronze if possible; otherwise of fine plaster purely white, or carefully bronzed.

Fig. 10.

In this connection we would speak of the more recent improvement in plaster casts, by which the material is made much harder, and presents a creamy-tint peculiarly beautiful; this plaster is also capable of being beautifully bronzed in any of the various shades of green or crimson.

We would suggest with regard to selecting plaster casts that great care and discrimination be used in making selections. Secure only copies of fine models, or pieces strikingly beautiful.

Take such forms as Fig. 10, supposing they may be found in statuette or statue size, (and these or equally beautiful forms are to be constantly obtained in plaster). Then making a neat pedestal by ornamenting a box, fitted in the corner (if the piece is of large size), or forming a tasteful bracket if it is merely a statuette or other small figure, bronze the figure, and arrange it either as a support for some object, such as a clock, vase for flowers, tasteful *Jardiniere* or card-receiver. For such purposes nothing forms so elegant and artistic a base, and these plaster casts are at once inexpensive and yet in perfect good taste.

One great reason why plaster casts are in bad repute with tasteful people is from the fact of so many ill-shapen, rough and ordinary looking specimens having been thrust upon the public, by the Italian venders who perambulate the streets of our cities, and even by means of the railroads, who carry their very worst specimens into the country towns and villages; thus the taste becomes vitiated, for it is not mere "imitations" which tend to mar the artistic beauty of our homes and deprave the public taste, but the making of imperfect and crude copies, and ungraceful, ordinary models. Thus in selecting a statuette for the hall, instead of taking a statue of Washington in his military suit and cocked hat, or Napoleon Bonaparte, booted and spurred and the inevitable folded arms, we should prefer the more graceful figure of the Lasquinet shown in Fig. 8, whose richly embroidered dress and beautiful trappings would present an imposing appearance if skillfully bronzed. The gracefully lifted arm may support any suitable article before named, and thus add utility to beauty; or if a different class of figure is preferred, the grace and loveliness of Fig. 10 will make itself apparent to any artistic mind.

In a hall of large or even moderate size pictures add great beauty; these should be arranged carefully however to produce a good effect, and great attention must be paid to this class of adornment.

Oil-painting will perhaps be selected as the most appropriate by the wealthy, but good chromos will be found to yield a vast deal of pleasure to many an artistic soul *whose purse cannot be extended over the oil-painting.*

Figures are especially attractive here, for a bright face beaming upon one as they pass the threshold of the entrance door, has almost as magical effect as the heartsome welcome, or the genial " Salve," speaking from the pretty frame over our head.

We would take this opportunity to introduce a variety of colored pictures, which coming within the ability of almost every one, will be found at once chaste and beautiful. We allude to the German Lithographs. These are not as expensive as the imported Chromos and cannot, we believe, fail to afford satisfaction to any but an æsthetic taste. We are speaking of *figures* entirely, a few of which we can recommend from the fact that we have used them in some cases ourselves; and though a severe critic may perhaps feel justified in censuring us for recommending this class of picture and consider us devoid of all taste, we venture to assert that " The Seasons," in these German Lithographs, are four as lovely faces as one who has not means to purchase costly pictures, need desire. The colors are soft and delicate, no single tint being either garish or positive. The complexion is soft and creamy, without any of the vivid tints on cheeks and lips which render cheap pictures so offensive to a truly artistic eye. Another called " Blonde and Brunette " is extremely lovely; the ivy leaves adorning the head of the dark-haired beauty, and the narrow fillet of blue the fair one, are the only touches of color that can be called bright in the least, and even these are so very delicate and there is so very little of them that they are not offensive in the slightest degree. For the rest, the silvery gray mantle and the glimpses of the silken dresses of some negative tints, are all the color seen, so that the entire effect is chaste and simple. The size of the piece within the oval, 19×22 inches; the entire square black mat, with gold margin around the oval, 22×25 inches.

The Transfers of various kinds are also particularly appropriate for this position and may be applied to the face of the staircase, on the panels of the doors, and even upon the walls; but in the latter case, of course this embellishment would supersede the use of framed pictures.

Such figures if desired for door panels may be obtained from mediæval paper-hangings, and small spaces from catalogues of various kinds, such as are used by dealers in gasaliers, lamps, clocks, and other establishments where metal articles are sold. Many of these are finely engraved, and make transfer or antique designs of the finest character. For hall embellishment we should merely touch these up with Indian ink and Sepia; with no color deeper.

CHAPTER IV.

WALL-PAPER.

BEFORE entering upon the details of furnishing and embellishing the particular apartments of the house, we think we may confer a favor on some of our readers (young housekeepers, particularly), by selecting a few special features of the interior decoration, with the view of illustrating the application of certain principles of correct taste and artistic arrangement ; and select as our first subject that of *wall-paper*.

In many houses, the paper-hangings constitute one of the largest features in the embellishment since they extend over a large surface, and though they should never be the most conspicuous, or important parts of the enrichment, they must either enchance or destroy the artistic effect of an apartment, by imparting brightness, or a soft glamour reflected from the light, or completely destroy the harmony of the general effect, by untasteful designs and ill-assorted colors.

The lack of taste or heedless negligence, in selecting appropriate and tasteful coverings for the walls, is one of the most noticeable, as well as unfortunate features in the furnishing of American homes.

So that a paper is of a " lovely shade," and covered with " splendid figures," it matters little, whether the colors be tertiary, secondary, or primary—or the design mosaic, or floral, representations of " still-life," or of " fish, flesh and fowl ;" and as to the importance of the position being upon a flat surface against the wall, why this is ignored entirely ! Herein lies a great mistake, and until we rectify these erroneous ideas of what is truly according to the rules of art, we shall continue to err in each separate detail of our household furnishing and adornment. The old Latin adage tells us there is no disputing concerning taste, and if persons insist upon preferring sprawling vines, monstrous bouquets, and groups of cats, dogs, or lions on their paper and carpets, to the conventional designs adopted invariably by artistic persons, and always used by Indian and Turkish weavers, they must be left to their own devices, but it must be obvious to a sensible person that a wall presenting as it does, a perpendicular, flat, solid surface, should be decorated in accordance with these facts.

In examining a painting, the background does not appear an important part, yet it frequently gives the artist more trouble than the entire remaining parts

3

of the picture, so the covering or embellishing of the walls, which bear the same relation to the room, requires to be so carefully chosen that it will act as a "foil," throwing out in relief the pictures, mirrors, and other wall-ornaments.

The first and most important question to be decided in selecting a wall covering is, whether it is to form a decoration in itself, or to become a background alone for pictures; for in certain cases where no pictures or mirrors are hung, (these occupying a room to themselves,) the superb Japanese hangings, with their wonderful combinations of brilliant hues, and grotesque patterns, make a room pictorial of themselves.

But as a general thing a wall-paper should never be obtrusive, and there are certain principles to be observed, which will insure a good selection. *First*, that the surface to be embellished is *flat*. *Secondly*, that the wall being *perpendicular*, the *designs* must be in accordance with this fact. *Thirdly*, that the paper on the walls being relatively a *background*, it is to serve the end of *exhibiting the furniture and wall ornaments*.

With regard to the perpendicular position of the surface, we will endeavor in few words to make this point clear. Supposing the design is a repeated succession of small single figures, such figures should be alike on each side, or in other words, if the design is a symmetrical unit, constantly repeated, such unit should be by-symmetrical, or if the figures are irregular, as in floral or other vegetable forms of design, the adaptation must still be arranged for an upright surface. Therefore in selecting hangings with such designs, use particular care as regards these points.

With respect to the second principle, relating to the embellishment of a flat surface, light shadow reflection, or indeed, any effect producing the idea of relief, or doing away in any degree with the flatness, is not admissible; and when animal or floral figures, or designs like baskets, vases, etc., are used, such representations should be treated with due regard to the flat surface. For instance, in a sample paper, a regular trellis is shown with foliage, vines and flowers, colored and arranged as in a painting, with light and shade carefully portrayed, (which cannot be clearly illustrated in an engraving). Now this literal imitation of foliage climbing up trellises, is in *bad taste*, let the workmanship be ever so perfect; for it is not a literal imitation of natural figures that are required for wall enrichment, but merely such an ornamental treatment of them *as is appropriate for a flat and upright surface*.

Thirdly, as regards the paper in its relation to the furniture, carpets etc.

Paper that is the most quiet and unobtrusive, will be found to produce the finest results, and in order to make it *subordinate* and *retiring*, all conspicuous contrasts, both of color and form must be carefully avoided, and here we can understand the popularity of those lovely grays, pearl, sage, stone, or that exquisite "Ashes of roses-tint," that has been copied from the imported paper-hangings of the celebrated Morris Company of London. But although these subdued shades produce such wonderful effects, and are so altogether charming to a refined taste, we seldom see them on the walls of the "million," for they do not readily adapt themselves to the ordinary houses of ordinary people. Yet we have happily seen them in the four rooms of a simple cottage near by, where they aid in imparting a rare, chaste beauty, to humble rooms, and go to illustrate our text, that fine taste does not dwell alone in "marble halls," but that the dweller in a cot may understand the philosophy of the poets lines

"The eye made quiet by the power of harmony."

In some papers where the colors are carefully and even tastefully applied, without any violent contrast to disturb this harmony, the eye is disturbed by a dazzling appearance as if the figures danced in a whirligig, with an almost painful effect. This is owing generally, to the figures being oft repeated in strong contrasts of light and shade, with an isolation of detail, by which a sort of prominent patched appearance is produced, which constantly striking the eye gives the persistent motion described.

Still another class of designs requires particular care, and as they are unusually popular should receive our special notice; this comprises the whole and immense variety of striped paper, which with an equally disagreeable effect upon the eye, adds the still more unfortunate result of marring the effect of pictures, mirrors and even curtains and hangings; inasmuch as, when the stripes extend perpendicularly, they not only give frames and hangings an unequal breadth but appear like posts around the room.

We might extend these strictures upon false taste ad infinitum. but it were better on account of space and fear of wearying you, to give some general rules whereby those about to select paper may be governed. One of the principles which it is safe to accept as a positive rule is, viz.: that a paper should be of secondary, tertiary and gray colors; and where the primary colors are introduced, let them appear only in small spaces or figures, for, by such a display of them sparingly applied the effect is enhanced, just as the background of a painting, by the shades being "broken" into irregular lines of brightness upon the gray body-color.

Paper-hangings in small figures of gold, rose, blue, red. etc.. so arranged as to produce a soft mottled appearance, a sort of "neutralized bloom," will have a fine effect when the furniture is upholstered, and the draperies are of deep, rich hues; while carpets and rugs have embodied in them the like mellow tints found in the paper. The only care required here is to be mindful of allowing one bright shade too great a preponderance.

Disagreeable effects are easily avoided by selecting only those papers in which the designs are so blended with the ground-color that no offensive contrasts disturb the quiet tone.

It matters not whether the design be of graceful floral character, or of rigid geometrical or mosaic pattern, so long as the delicate contrast of tone is preserved, which will insure an agreeable effect. ·

The lovely sage-grays, pearl and stone shades, and the corn tints which the Morris Co., have introduced to us from England, are unexceptionable as regards color—presenting delightful effects, both during summer and winter; in the one affording a refreshing sensation of coolness, as from the spicy air on first entering the shade of a wildwood on a hot July day; while in the other, no more beautiful background can be conceived for the glowing firelight, brilliant hangings and autumn leaf decorations of the frosty *Christmas* morning. Or quite as beautiful are the sea-greens, the frosty and delicate blues, and that indescribable blue-green, which gives us all the changes of tint from the robin's egg to the ocean wave just touched with the delicacy of sea-foam—these with the creamy buffs and that royal kingly color, lavender, in all its many shades, the rosy pomegranates and shell-like peach blossom tint afford every variety of color adapted to each special location. Many prefer the enamelled, plain "selfs," or solid colored papers, so figured, and they certainly present many recommendations, yet we would caution our readers concerning them, as they are easily soiled both by abrasion, finger-marks and fly-specks. In this connection we would remark that the commonest shilling or ten cent papers (if sufficiently heavy to hide the figure), make a neat solid ground of most pleasing color and surprisingly fine as a background for bright ornaments and hangings.

There is a certain class of persons who appear to think that to secure gold-figured papers is to furnish the room; yet a gilded pattern is generally the very worst possible one that can be selected, appearing in one light like a splash of dazzling spangles, while in another a dark blurred spot gives the effect of some dark wash having been struck against the delicate ground; the constant change from dazzle to gloom is exceedingly unpleasant, and the effect does not remain the same for two minutes together, and never shows the same aspect to any two persons. The imitations of stamped leather-hangings in mediæval patterns are exceedingly elegant for libraries, but cost from $10 to $50 per roll. The colors and designs of many low-priced papers are exceedingly soft and chaste, and although the lightness of texture may be urged as an objection, with ordinary care even thin paper may be hung and made to appear smooth and beautiful.

HANGING PAPER.

We trust many of our readers belong to that independent and helpful class of women who are willing to make exertion to render their homes tasteful, and surround themselves with elegancies which are perhaps beyond their means to obtain by ordering or purchasing; and to such a few plain and simple directions for hanging paper and embellishing their walls may perhaps be of value.

Paper-hanging, though by no means an impossible operation to the amateur, does not consist in merely fastening paper against the walls, but it is attended by some difficulties which if described may perhaps prevent disappointment and failure.

First. The walls must be put in a proper condition. If they have been whitewashed or calcimined so frequently that a rough coat has been formed, recourse must be had to scraping and washing until the whole is removed, using great care not to cut into or indent the wall beneath as the scraping is continued.

The angles, top and bottom require particular attention, and all holes or inequalities must be filled with plaster of Paris mixed to a paste with water (a very small portion at a time as it hardens rapidly). This done, give the whole a thorough painting with hot size, made of glue well dissolved, to which sufficient hot water is added to make a smooth paste about the consistency of thin syrup.

PREPARATION OF DAMP WALLS.

Where walls are affected by dampness, several methods may be resorted to as a preventive, the most common of which is to cover with canvas.

Battens of wood are driven into the walls, over windows and close to ceiling and wainscot, or long strips such as laths may be nailed along the upper and lower edges of the wall, to which strong muslin cut in proper lengths and sewed together to fit sides and ends, spaces over and under windows etc., are tacked with tinned tacks. This canvas must be tightly stretched and have a coat of strong size, before applying the paper.

Another method is to obtain the strong brown paper sold at the paper-mills, which should have the rough edges removed, be cut into lengths, saturated with water until thoroughly damp, then pasted on with heavy paste. When it is possible damp stone or brick dwellings should have ivy, ampelopsis or other vines planted and trained over the walls, which will be found an effectual preventive to damp walls.

PASTE.

There are several kinds of paste used for paper, and it is of great importance that particular kinds should be used for certain purposes. We therefore give the method of making, first,

COMMON PASTE.

Which will answer for all ordinary paper-hangings. Take 4 lbs. of clean, good wheat flour, sifted through an ordinary flour sieve; to which add gradually, sufficient *cold* water to make a stiff paste, entirely free from lump and perfectly smooth; then add cold water until a thick batter is formed, which beat and stir until light and creamy; add two ounces of powdered alum, and one-eighth of a pound of nice glue (the common kind).

Have a pot or boiler with five gallons of boiling water on the stove, into which stir the paste gently and rapidly until the entire quantity is added, when continue to stir until the mass swells and assumes a white cream-like color, when it is sufficiently cooked and may be removed from the fire.

This will afford nearly one bucket-full of paste, which when cold will become jellified, but this does not injure it, and each time it is used sufficient cold water must be added to make a smooth paste that can be easily worked under the brush.

If there is necessity for keeping the paste on hand for any length of time pour cold water over the top to prevent a skin from forming on the surface; and it will not ferment for a long time, though mould may form which, however, will do no harm if removed carefully.

PASTE NO. 2.—FOR HEAVY CLOTH OR VELVET PAPERS.

This paste is unusually adhesive and of great strength, and will seldom be used by ladies; still there are times when it is required, and it will be found useful for other purposes than paper-hanging.

In a pot of proper size have two gallons of boiling water; mix two pounds of fine flour to a paste with cold water, thinning until creamy, add one ounce of powdered alum and stir slowly into the boiling water, with one ounce of resin (carefully melted) to each gallon of paste; stir constantly until thoroughly cooked, and after removing from the fire until cool. To thin this paste add a thin mucilage of white glue or gum arabic.

Every house should contain a step-ladder, easy of ascent and safe withal, which article must be now *on hand*, with a table as long as possible and perfectly clean. We will suppose the walls have been measured, and the lengths of paper cut, matched and trimmed *close to the* pattern on the right edge, and within one-eighth of an inch on the other. Lay these one on another upon the center of the table, with the remnants cut, trimmed and arranged for the spaces over and under doors, windows, etc.

Now draw one strip of paper (the upper one) to the very edge of the table, have the paste-bucket at your *right* side and loading the brush, pass it from left to right until all resting on the table is covered, then taking the two corners in the hand, double the paper over, letting the pasted side adhere slightly, (this must be the bottom of the paper). Carefully slip the strip along, with the one edge directly within the touches of paste, (that will necessarily be on the next strip,) and the edge of table, and cover in like-manner. Then commence hanging; have the ladder in front of the left side of the mantel, or in some position where there is a straight facing, and the beading of a mantel is as good as any other, for you do not wish the place at which you stop to show; taking the upper end of the paper (the bottom folded up to keep from striking and sticking to the wall) ascend the ladder, and place the paper against the wall, and with the towel, which should hang over the arm, wipe quickly down the center and out upon each side, to remove all air bubbles, descend from the ladder, loosen the end and with the same movement fasten it in position, then take your plumb-line and ascertain whether the edge is perfectly perpendicular, for upon this first piece depends the symmetry of the whole. A paper in which each figure appears as if toppling over, is sufficient to disturb the equanimity of temper in a person with a correct eye.

Work always to the left, and you then have your piece constantly on your right, so as to be easily fitted into the corners. If possible make the lappings face the light, as this prevents their being so conspicuous. By passing a clean smooth castor down the seam, it may be made so flat as to be invisible.

Many paper designs require care in arranging as in stripes and uniform designs; here take conspicuous places as over the mantel or doors, and measuring the distance across, cut a strip of blank paper of needed size, which try across the wall-paper, until you ascertain which part of the pattern will come in similar position on both sides, then cut off each strip (or breadth) on each side, until you make the part measured come each side.

Use care not to touch the outside with paste, and keep the towels perfectly dry and clean. We have found a clean, new broom, an excellent article for using on high walls; with a little practice a person can work rapidly in this way.

Place the pasted paper over the end of the broom, with the upper edge hanging over about a quarter of a yard, raise the broom and placing the paper against the wall, pass the broom quickly up and out upon each side, then loosen the doubled-up end and sweep down the center to the bottom, then out upon the sides.

VARNISHED PAPER.

The walls for paper intended to be varnished, must be sized with fine white glue. By covering the glue with cold water for a few hours, it will readily dissolve upon adding boiling water.

Clear Copal varnish is generally used for paper varnish, as only such styles as imitations of wood, paneling, etc., admit of so glassy a surface; the object in most papers being to obtain as soft a surface as possible.

Where a very fine varnish is desired it may be made by melting four pounds gum Copal, in a very little boiling Linseed oil, and adding it to one and a quarter gallons Linseed oil, eighth of a pint Sulphate iron while boiling, when cool add two and a quarter gallons Turpentine, stirring until quite cold.

ARTICLES FOR PAPER HANGING.

Scissors, plumb-line, paper brush, paste brush, (like painters large round brush, or a small whitewash brush,) step-ladder, table, soft towels, a porcelain bed-castor, and vessels for size and paste.

Regular paper-hangers have a rapid way of throwing up the paper, passing the "roller" down one strip after another, that is "delightful to behold," but we *unprofessionals,* who are mere amateurs cannot work in this "*manner of the craft,*" and as we have hung many rolls of paper, and succeeded in a manner to receive the commendation of a *professional* paper-hanger of fifty years experience, we feel warranted in giving our own method, to those ladies who may desire to cover their walls as elegantly, or as tastefully as those of their wealthy neighbors.

PANELING.

In many apartments, as dining-room, hall, or perhaps an office, study or plain library, it becomes desirable to use panels and varnish finish. Indeed in old houses, this style imparts a certain quaintness that is in keeping with the ancient wood-work and other finishing. But aside from this, there are circumstances which render such hangings valuable, as where flies, dust or rough usage would mar the beauty of more delicate wall-covering.

To give opportunity for such finish, we therefore give directions for its accomplishment.

In this style of paper much depends upon the taste, some preferring one color and style, some another; but for ordinary use we would recommend oak with rosewood mouldings, or walnut and ebony, or walnut and rosewood.

On account of pictures, each space in the room should be in one panel, as the least deviation from uniformity will produce unpleasing results to a critical eye. By using care in cutting and fitting the mouldings most pleasing results may be obtained in applying paneled paper; for where the tinted grounds and shaded mouldings are desired, exquisite designs in Decalcomania may be applied, and produce charming groups : scenes, floral-arrangements and other styles of picture equal to beautiful paintings. In many cases, such wall-enrichment will be found wonderfully effective.

PAINTED AND ILLUMINATED WALLS.

Mr. Conway in his papers on Decorative Art in England, very ably elucidates this subject and describes the exquisite embellishments, enrichments and decorations of the dwellings belonging to certain millionaires, artists and virtuosi residing in England. These artists will no doubt go far towards raising the tastes of our people, and not only exciting in the minds of many an ambition to possess like beautiful surroundings, but also inciting them, we trust, to create for themselves homes of beauty; added to the joy of daily beholding our treasures. to say nothing of exhibiting them to husband and children, is that of the satisfied consciousness of having created them ourselves by our own efforts and skill and taste. One special feature noticed by Mr. Conway is the wall embellishment of the dwellings he mentions; this exquisite dado—the other imposing frieze; and in many cases the description of the entire walls and ceiling are given.

Now these wonderful creations are the work of famous artists, designers and decorators; many requiring years to complete them; and we know full well how inappropriate they would be for ordinary dwellings, even were we able to design and paint them, but we may imitate and apply so far as is consistent with our means and ability.

Supposing for instance you desire to embellish your walls, whether of parlor, living, dining or bed-room, with panels to be surrounded with garlands of flowers and foliage, scrolls, or other designs appropriate for the apartment; this may be accomplished by painting directly upon the prepared wall, or upon their tracing-paper, to be fastened directly on the walls, or in like manner with Decalcomania; or, if preferred, canvas of dimensions corresponding with the spaces may be prepared upon stretchers fitted to them and the painting done upon them. This, though apparently a Herculean task, bears the recommendation of being transferable in case of removal; and when we consider the mammoth undertakings and achievements of some artists, perhaps a large number of our American women and girls will be glad to thus apply a portion of their time and talent, especially those upon whom large sums have been expended in bills for instruction in oil and water-color painting, illuminating, etc.

For this kind of painting the finest English colors (Winsor and Newton's) must be used, not the oil tube-colors, for the grounding, as a large quantity is required, but the colors sold by the bulk, in ounce or pound packages, called " W. & N's. Prepared Levigated Oil-Colors."

The walls are divided into dado, frieze and cornice; the space between the dado and frieze may be divided into panels or otherwise left for any enrichment desired.

In many houses—especially old dwellings—the narrow wainscot of this day is extended upward for a height of four feet, with moulding more or less heavy along the upper edge; and we confess to admiring this finish, which imparts to the walls an appearance of solidity and comfort that no arrangement of paper or coloring can bestow. We find that the eye of decorators is acknowledging this fact, and there is even in elegant mansions an effort made by the decorative artists to return to this ancient finish, shown by using a dark ground with moulding along the top as a sort of substitute for it. But in painting or papering artistically at the present time, the wooden wainscot of a few inches in height is the only wood-work on the walls; above this for about three feet, a band of body or ground-color; next a foot for the dado; and below the cornice (separating the ceiling from the sides), the frieze one foot (more or less) deep.

A wall to be painted must be thoroughly cleansed from lime, paper and smoke; then well painted with best boiled linseed-oil. After this, three coats of best white paint, called "zinc-white", which is an oxide of zinc, and the most durable and whitest of all white paints, never becoming yellow, and producing a finer surface than any excepting pearl-white (a sub-muriate of bismuth), which is exceedingly delicate and used where any unusually high finish is desired.

Should grease or greasy smoke upon the walls prove difficult to remove, wash off with soda-water, weak lime, whitewash, spirits of nitre, or sulphuric ether; then rinse in clean soft water.

Prior to commencing the designs, apply a coat of zinc or pearl-white, mixed entirely with turpentine, in order to obtain a soft surface free from glossiness. This "flatting" produces what painters term a *dead surface*. Upon this and with the preparations here described, any style of ornamental painting may be executed.

CEILINGS.

It is a vexed question with professional decorators, whether colored and figured ceilings add to, or detract from the fine effect of walls and furniture. Now this depends upon the height of the walls.

But even though we do not advise rich painted or highly ornamented ceilings in apartments ranging in height from eight to fourteen feet, we certainly do insist upon the beauty of tinted and even simply enriched ceilings. Not the shade of the walls, by any means, but a color some three shades lighter, and here calcimining will be found invaluable, as it is a difficult task to apply paper-hangings to a ceiling.

As we have suggested the wisdom of further enrichment of ceilings after the mere tinting, we will mention one or more methods by which this may be effected without any extraordinary means.

The first of these is by means of ornaments in plaster of Paris. Ceilings thus ornamented are of the class constantly seen wherein appear cornices, center pieces, and corners more or less elaborate.

But a very beautiful and far less troublesome and expensive embellishment is found in the application of the beautiful artificial wood-carvings. Here we have a large number of designs, which fastened securely to ceiling or cornice, and painted with plaster of Paris give an enrichment, not excelled by the plaster mouldings.

A few dollars will furnish sufficient of these beautifully moulded *wooden* castings for an ordinary room, and we can recommend them as durable and elegant, and easily put on with plaster mixed with glue.

But as regards the painting of ceilings moderately low, we would suggest the use of straight bands of color, and as it is difficult to arrange these with due regard to distance and space, and especially so if shadow is to be depicted; it will be found quite satisfactory to obtain the shaded mouldings found in designs of wood-paneled paper. We have seen a room papered with a soft pearl-gray, with the ceilings tinted three shades lighter, (calcimined) and finished with these bands taken from a walnut-wood design paper, brown lines shaded with gray, and a thread of gold along the margin, fancy center and corner pieces of the same, made a lovely finish; and the paper was so beautifully applied that only a close observer could detect the *imitation*.

The effect is quiet and in perfectly good taste, despite the constant reminders that "all imitations are vulgar." Where greater outlay of time is warranted, the work may be made more artistic by measuring and drawing accurate designs, some in clusters of thread-like lines, with a broader band or two, to be painted carefully in with color, always remembering that, what is a mere thread seen from the floor, will be, or should be an eighth of an inch or more wide on the ceiling. If greater elaboration is desired, obtain the tracing-paper, (such as Artists and Architects use,) upon which sketch out any design suitable, whether scrolls, arabesques, floral or other figures, transfer these to the ceiling, and with a fine brush, trace them in desired colors.

We must certainly recommend one other, and perhaps the very best of all methods for ornamenting either walls of ceiling, in the most artistic manner and with the very least amount of labor; this is by the application of Decalcomania-pictures.

CALCIMINED WALLS.

The old fashion of "whitewashing walls," is almost entirely superseded by the popular process of Calcimining. Many imagine that this requires some secret knowledge known only to the initiated, but this is certainly not the case, or such a number of ladies could not do their own Calcimining, both in white and colors.

Very many artistic persons argue that pictures, mirrors, and indeed furniture appear to the best advantage, when surrounded by plain, tinted, or even white walls.

In the new house, the gleaming white "hard-finished" coat, (though exceedingly harsh to our taste) fully satisfies, even edifies the majority of people, but alas! time and smoke and dust soon discolor this polished immaculate surface, and with its brown and white rays, and yellow streaks, it looks altogether forlorn. Painting if even performed by one's own hand, and the materials purchased at wholesale rates, is (when applied to walls) a serious labor and heavy expense, no paper can be procured that will correspond with carpet and hangings, and "what is to be done?"

Here recourse to the Calcimining becomes a step of importance, and we will add one that may be made perfectly satisfactory.

Tints the most lovely and delicate, or deep and full-toned with a finish far softer and more beautiful than paint can be obtained with, but (comparatively) small outlay of money, and with less labor than either paper-hanging or painting.

For small rooms with low ceiling, no more beautiful, chaste and appropriate wall covering can be imagined, than one of the exquisite tints produced by adding a little color-powder, violet, lavender, blue, peach-blossom, straw-color or one of the lovely grays to the Calcimining mixture, finishing with a gilt moulding around the ceiling.

CALCIMINE WASH No. 1. Make a heavy glue by pouring cold water on the white clear sheets, called "bonnet makers glue," over night, and heating in the morning until dissolved, adding boiling water until of consistence of cream, while boiling stir in best Spanish whiting, until thick and smooth, when add any coloring desired.

This "stock" will become jellified when cool, but must be thinned with water, until of consistency of paint, and applied with a fine whitewash or paint brush, going over the space to be covered rapidly, and never repeating until the whole is dry.

No. 2. Dissolve one-half pound fine white glue as described above, and thicken with best "Paris White" while hot until a creamy liquid is formed, which may be colored to suit the taste and well stirred. This is a brilliant wash for ceilings or walls, and will give a finish as fine as the best plaster coat. A narrow gilt moulding around the edge of the ceiling makes a beautiful finish for such tinted walls.

Our professional artist will doubtless treat this idea with incredulity, perhaps with scorn, and as it is another of the "imitations" so obnoxious to many, we do not wonder, at the same time we can assure our readers that here they will find a means of enriching their walls and ceilings, which if carefully executed defies the closest inspection, as upon plaster it appears equal to fine painting.

The only objection to be urged against this work, is the difficulty of performing it, which can only be accomplished at the expense of considerable weariness; still proceeding slowly, and applying only a few designs each day, or at intervals during the day, the task is finally accomplished, and the reward is ample.

We shall have occasion hereafter to speak of this work as specially applied, and will then describe some exquisite designs for the purpose.

We would mention here however, that by applying to the proprietors of Art Emporiums, any number of one or more particular designs can be obtained, of whatever size, form or style is required.

A charming and rapid method of applying colored designs to walls or ceilings, is by means of stencil plates cut out of card or stiff paper, one of each figure answering for any number as they can be moved from place to place, and the colors applied in the open spaces in the cards, the edges of which may be dried to prevent the *dragging* of the color upon applying it to another position.

CHAPTER V.

CARPETS.

In a well furnished room we shall always upon investigation, find that the entire scheme of decoration possesses a character, a relation as it were one thing to the other. The background and groundwork of the whole represented by paper and carpet are subservient to the furniture and decorations.

So having enjoyed the luxury of a house perfectly furnished in all the details, one has a sensation of having received a blow in the face, when they enter a dwelling in which each separate piece of furniture or embellishment, appears as it were "to swear at its neighbor."

Yet leaving a house where from the entrance door through each apartment all things harmonize, one has that impression which is produced by viewing some lovely scene in nature at early dawn or sunset, a dreamy recollection of that subtle lulling of the faculties, as, under the soothing influence of an æsthetic, perfect bliss is mingled with the half consciousness of tangible things just passing away and being merged into the unknown; a dreamy impression of mellow tints and soft shades, mingled and fading one into the other of a room, the walls of which are tinted with the lighter shades, reflected from the deeper colors in frieze and dado, and carpets wherein are softly blended the same shades, brightened by some rare touches of the primary colors carefully bestowed, soft falls of curtain and hanging allow glimpses of other apartments, wherein the golden sunset and rosy morning light are broken into innumerable prismatic tints, as they strike through the colored window lights, and touching wall and floor are caught and held by the many pretty "traps to catch the sun-beams," which tasteful persons know so well how to form and arrange.

No "loud" and conspicuous colors to disturb the harmony; no garish lights to strike the delicate eye in the carpets of this house, but the whole is simple and unobtrusive without ostentation or vain show. In endeavoring to give some aid to those who appreciate the fact, that certain rules *do* govern taste; we feel we cannot confer a greater favor than to give, in preference to any observations of our own, the rules established by high authority, which affirm principles embraced by all artistic decorators, and illustrated in the dwellings of the true connoisseur.

First. The surface of a carpet serving as a ground to support all objects, should be quiet and negative, without strong contrasts of either forms or colors.

Second. The leading forms should be so disposed as to distribute the pattern over the whole floor, not pronounced either in the direction of length or breadth, all "*up and down*" treatments being erroneous.

Third. The decorative forms should be flat without shadow or relief, whether derived from ornament, or direct from flowers or foliage.

Fourth. In color the general ground should be negative, low in tone, and inclining to the tertiary hues, the leading forms of the pattern being expressed by the larger secondaries, and the primary colors, or white, if used at all, should be only in small quantity, to enchance the tertiary hues and to express the geometrical basis that rules the distribution of the forms.

As we have remarked, no part of the furniture of a room should be determined upon without reference to the whole scheme of decoration, to which it is to add to or impart a certain effect.

And as the color of the walls and style of the floor-covering are the key-notes to which the furniture, embellishments and decorations are to be attuned to produce that *harmony* we hold so essential, it will become apparent, how necessary it is to make a wise selection, of these noticeable features.

According to the first rule, we must adapt the carpet to the position which it is to occupy, and the purpose which it is to serve, "as a ground to support all objects," and should therefore be composed of quiet colors, and whether light or dark in shade, let them appear to lose themselves in each other when shaded, while if a primary color is introduced, be sure it is one that contrasts well, and as a guide we give the following table:

White, contrasts with black, and brown harmonizes.

Yellow, contrasts with purple and white, harmonizes orange and pale shades.

Orange, contrasts with blue, harmonizes rose pink.

Red, contrasts with green, harmonizes crimson.

Green, contrasts with red, harmonizes yellow.

Purple, contrasts with yellow and white, harmonizes crimson.

Black, contrasts with pale colors, harmonizes deep shades.

Brown, contrasts with white and blue, harmonizes yellow and black.

As ground colors —

White, produces good effects with shades of blue, purple, violet, reds, greens and browns.

Black, with drabs, pink, lemon, gold, light blues, greens, purples and salmon.

Blue, with yellows, pink, salmon, buff, light blues, yellows and drabs.

Green, with yellow, purple, pink, lemon, pearl, flesh, stone, dove, grays, lighter greens and maize.

Red, with yellows, pearl, pale blues and greens.

Many colors, such as light blues with dark greens, appear well if a line of white or such mutual contrast come between. Many colors, such as reds, blues and greens, if of the same depth of tone, produce a dirty "muddled" appearance when placed side by side without a neutralizing tint between.

Flowing arabesque designs in pale shades of blue and yellow on black grounds, have a beautiful effect, also brown grounds with mosaic designs, and shades of tawny yellow or dull reds on various grounds.

Japanese designs in quaint, minute figures and intricate tracery, appear in Brussels and Tapestry, and also in the three-ply imitations of Brussels.

On grounds of lovely grays, sage, olive, pearl, canary and various shades of brown, strewn with curious marks, odd little figures, leaves, flowers, etc., in red, yellow, blue, green and orange; these are appropriate for parlors, while brown-black, dark "invisible" green, and tan colors with scrolls and arabesque figures for libraries, and for dining rooms; the Indienne designs on deep-toned grounds in rich warm colors, blue with silver, crimson with yellow-brown, French-gray, and cherry, and those charming monotone carpets for country houses' bed-rooms or sitting-rooms, are deservedly popular.

The Tapestry or American Brussels come in the showy Moquette designs, but save for a nursery or sitting-room, where brightness is an object, we cannot fancy these vivid colors.

Wiltons will always hold their place as regards color and durability, and for halls, or any thoroughfare, they will more than atone for first cost, only $2.50 to $4.00 per yard. The soft thick piled Axminsters, costing from $3.00 to $5.00 per yard, are for a handsome, or even comfortable and tastefully furnished parlor or drawing-room, the most satisfactory perhaps of all carpets. The American Axminsters to be had for from $2.50 to $3.00 a yard, have designs of fine vine-tracery on pale tinted grounds in imitation of the imported ones which for beauty and durability they really exceed.

The newest French Moquettes come in monotone, or soft drabs and grays, tone upon tone that are lovely beyond description, as also the velvets in close imitation though the warmly blended crimson shades will be found charming for many apartments.

But to go into a Carpet store to-day is to wander over the lands of the Orient, not as in the days past to walk upon baskets and vases of flowers, and vegetation of every conceivable form; but upon imitations of ancient tiles, and floors of inlaid work of rare soft wood, porphyry and quiet somber stones upon designs of quaint and curious character, that lead the mind back to ancient days.

Before closing our suggestions regarding the color and tone of various styles of carpet, we must give a hint to those living in country houses; in the cottage orner in the suburbs of the city, or in the "flats" of the same, and to our young housekeeper as well. For this class of residence the charming colors and patterns of the Morris Company found in Ingrains, will be entirely appropriate.

The lovely pearl and gray grounds with scrolls, arabesques and fine tracery of vine and blossom in shades of deeper tone, finished by borders of scarlet or blue, or clear pearly white grounds bestrewn with vivid Persian or quaint Japanese patterns in either case, to match chintz covers to furniture and curtains. These from 75 cents to $1.25 per yard, afford even "the million," an opportunity to cover their floors tastefully. To our wealthy readers (if we have any) we would say, for your parlor or drawing-room use an Aubusson tapestry, as you would tread upon the fairy grounds of the Arabian Nights. These only cost from $7.00 to $15.00 per square yard! and come in solid squares to suit the size of room. It is needless to say that the colors are charming and the effect enchanting.

And by way of an excuse for even mentioning such extravagant floor-covers, we may say, that many persons would prefer to spend their " carpet-money " for a small square of Aubusson, to grace the center of that bijou-parlor or library floor, than to cover the whole with an Ingrain or tapestry Brussels.

Regarding the second, third and fourth rules, relative to the forms of design it must be borne constantly in mind that a carpet is to be viewed from above; the figures therefore should be quite suitable for being placed in a horizontal position for furniture and persons to stand upon, and to be viewed in various directions and not laterally as a wall-paper. These points are obvious, so much so that it appears strange that qualities so essential should in many cases be totally disregarded, by those who would appear under the necessity of understanding such plain facts, we mean designers and artists.

The bi-symmetrical designs which appear so well against a wall, are entirely unsuited to a floor which requires a pattern that will appear well from every point, or from all sides of the room.

Thus bouquets and baskets, are in bad taste no matter how carefully colored, inasmuch as from one side it will appear inverted. The arrangement best suited for floor decoration, is the radiating with forms springing from a common center.

Observe in Nature how this law is carried out. Plants which grow upon the ground or near it, will generally be found to have their parts radiating from one point, or arranged symmetrically upon the surface.

Being intended to walk or stand upon, all designs for floor decorations should invariably be perfectly flat, though to examine any collection of carpets, rugs or floor-cloths, one would suppose this idea was an entirely novel one, so large a number of the designs assume the very character we denounce as erroneous.

One obvious mistake is in designers imitating rather than inventing, and though baskets of flowers may be lovely in a picture, they are not suitable as covering for floors; though "music hath charms" it is not supposed to be a happy method of practising it, to walk, dance or stand upon the various instruments, or again to look down upon a fragment of landscape, or an entire view, although perhaps plainly illustrating the poets idea of "viewing the landscape *o'er,"* might give the unpleasant impression of looking into the antipodes transposed.

These flagrant instances of bad taste will be found in the designs of the handsomest carpets and rugs; we therefore call particular attention to this point, because so many persons about to purchase carpets, have these styles urged upon them.

A handsome carpet with border, or drugget or floor-cloth with floral figures properly arranged and distributed make appropriate patterns, but in an article like this, it is not possible to describe the various complications that would render each design a perfect one; but, with the rules and hints we have given, a person of ordinary taste may be able to decide upon what is proper and what the . verse in a floor-covering.

Borders are now so universally used, and add so greatly to the elegance of a carpet, that we advise their use whenever practicable.

Where border-finish is introduced to rest against the wainscot, the bi-symmetrical arrangement is not objectionable, inasmuch as it then assumes the same condition as wall-paper. Unusually elegant and tasteful designs are shown in the Kidderminster carpets, but the colors here which produce results wonderfully lovely, cannot be shown, but may be imagined, in varied shades of wood-color, with peculiar golden-green, melting into the golds of the wood-brown tints, and a mere brightening in the livelier tints of the light scattered blossoms, as delicate as if woven by the fingers of some fairy nymph, whose woodland haunts, were carpeted with just such soft feathery ferns, and tufted moss. Looking down upon such a floor-covering as this, one could almost fancy they inhaled the spicy, wild, "woodsy" odors of the Anemone and Arbutus, and feel ready to turn up the fern fronds in search of the blue-eyed Heptatica, or scarlet berries of the Partridge Vine. As the tread upon soft carpets is one of the luxuries even we, ordinary mortals, may enjoy; and as we must all admit it to be no trifling comfort, we should surely endeavor to secure it.

The sponge carpet linings, chemically prepared to prevent moths, produce a delightful elastic softness, and may be procured for 15 or 20 cents a yard; but, where unavailable, felting paper, or even several thicknesses of newspapers will answer the purpose. In the country, clean straw, smoothly spread, or even sweet well-dried and fine grass will be found a most pleasant strata, upon which to spread the carpet, and it is astonishing how very greatly these linings add to the apparent depth, heaviness and richness of the carpet. So, in any case, never lay a carpet, especially an Ingrain, directly upon the boards.

With stair carpets, always cover the edge of each step with several thicknesses of paper, felting, or other material that will prevent the friction upon the boards; and when measuring for these, allow a yard or less over the exact length, to afford an opportunity for changing the part trodden upon each time it is taken up, which will make it far more durable.

4

CHAPTER VI.

BLINDS,

CURTAINS AND LAMBREQUINS.

THE first thing to be attended to in house-furnishing is the windows; for it is as unpleasant to have the full glare of sunlight streaming through an apartment, as to be annoyed by prying eyes, or suffer the feeling of fear at imagining some outside spectator gazing into our apartments during the evening hours.

We will not enter upon the vexed question of the healthfulness of sun-baths, for we cannot imagine that any one of our readers will insist upon it that windows are to stand out, in all their bare, open-eyed boldness, without shade or curtain, at all hours, day and night, and so we will venture to give a chapter on this most important subject of window coverings, and "hangings" in general, hoping to aid some oft-perplexed friend to robe her windows and doors with beauty and grace.

The blinds of a house, it is a matter of elegance and comfort to arrange properly. They should be uniform in material and color throughout the front of the house, at least, for nothing so mars the beauty of a "front" than windows showing, even at a distance, all the colors of the rainbow, or even two or three of them.

Buff Holland produces a mellow, warm tone, when the light passes through it that is extremely pleasant; but white linen, and even muslin are so easily laundered, and harmonize so well with hangings and upholstering of all colors, that perhaps we cannot do better than to recommend the use of them to all persons about to furnish their windows.

Many persons have an admiration for transparent shades, and some of these are so lovely that one can scarcely wonder at this taste. To such we would say—you cannot do better than to obtain what is called architect's or artist's tracing cloth, which is a clear, transparent cloth, producing that mellow light seen through the white ground glass lamp-shades, and upon it to transfer some of the exquisite designs in Diaphanie and Vitromania work. These are of all varieties, from the Mediæval and Renaissance period, with its gorgeously robed knights lansquenets, musicians, saints and madonnas, to the lovely landscapes and Oriental groups, or domestic scenes of our own more modern times.

For many windows, shades of this description impart a wonderfully imposing effect, as, for instance, in the library, or bay window of sitting room or parlor, in the conservatory and hall,— for many prefer a shade that can be removed at pleasure, or rolled up and down when desired, to a window filled with ornamental glass, and whose frequent removals are necessary, it certainly possesses advantages of no light order. For dull, cheerless apartments, we should strongly recommend this variety of window covering, as it imparts a rich, bright glow to an otherwise gloomy room.

The patent rollers and fixtures for blinds are so readily adjusted that any lady may manage to fix all her windows without troubling any one.

Care should be used not to nail or tack the shade close to the ends of the roller; allow it to be one inch *wider* than the roller; cut off the selvage (measuring accurately with a tape-measure), and turn down each side a half inch, ironing or pressing them flat, and fastening by means of neat herring bone stitching, or else run through the sewing-machine.

For the lath at the bottom, turn down a hem and work an eyelet-hole in the center for the cord to pass through, which holds the tassel; turn down the upper raw edge and mark the centre of it with indelible or marking ink, also the window to which it belongs; mark the roller in the same manner, so that, in case change of blinds is necessary, it is known to which each belongs, without wasting time to measure each blind to the particular window.

In nailing on the blind, use small tin tacks, as iron rust will mar the material. Tack first the center, then the ends, and then try whether it will roll perfectly straight. If it will not, be certain it is not straight somewhere, and requires altering. It will pay to take time and do this work thoroughly, for there can be no more annoying thing than a blind that never rolls straight, and is always at "cross purposes" with the window sash.

Of the figured "oiled muslin," or transparent shades, none are as genteel and quiet in appearance as those with simple gold or silver bands around them, with perhaps a little ornamental scroll work in the corners. As for the gaudy, many-colored "horrors," that are offered in shops, they are better fitted for a saloon than a private dwelling, and should never be admitted into the tasteful homes. With regard to curtains—no dwelling should be without these graceful aids to comfort and elegance, for, let a drapery be ever so simple, it imparts a certain air of coziness and delicate taste that no other piece of furniture can afford. In connection with blinds and akin to them is the very simple machinery required for the curtain.

The ordinary window curtain is suspended by hooks to rings, which slide backwards and forwards on a pole or rod at the top of the window—behind the cornice or lambrequin, if there be any: or, if not, on a heavy pole with large ornamental rings, though some persons use small rings and a wire to hold the curtains, and arrange a heavy gilded pole and rich, ornamental rings in front.

but stationary. Heavy curtains are always appropriate for Winter, but for the warm season, should be carefully shut away from dust and sunlight and find a substitute in lace or muslin. In this day of Nottingham lace and Swiss both sheer and beautiful, at such low prices, where is the house that may not be furnished with this lovely addition? for, though lace so gossamer-like that it appears almost like a cloudy mist, is charming indeed to shroud the window of some palatial mansion, what can be more beautiful than the blue-white tints of the Swiss curtains, with their exquisite puffs and neatly fluted ruffles, or the soft, rich, yellowish-white Nottingham lace hangings, with lambrequins of feathery ferns and gorgeous Autumn leaves?

As regards these same Nottingham lace materials, the variety of patterns which are shown purchasers about to procure them, is confusing, but our advice would be to select only the more delicate designs, and small figures, such as a fine fern spray, the various conventional flowers of medium size, and the many imitations of old laces. Many really artistic patterns are to be found among the Nottingham curtain laces, and it is far better while purchasing an article of this kind to select an imitation of some really fine specimen, than a common pattern, that is a constant source of mortification to the critical eye.

As regards Swiss muslin, the coarser the texture the more sheer and light the appearance; besides this, the coarse is equally easy to "*do up*," and a set of these curtains will continue to present a neat appearance for several seasons. They may be trimmed either with a wide hem, or a narrow ruffle or ruffles, neatly fluted or crimped.

Point-lace making is now becoming as popular and ordinary an employment as the old tatting and crochet making, and, by using some of the coarser varieties of "point-lace braid" and thread very elegant curtain laces may be made, at comparatively small expense, and without any unusual labor, that is—a pair of curtains the materials for which would cost about ten to twenty dollars, would cost in the stores from five hundred to one thousand dollars. This may appear almost incredible, but it is a fact we can verify from actual experience. It is the *time* that it requires which makes point-lace so immensely expensive, for the knowledge of the stitches can be perfectly acquired in six lessons of one hour each.

There are many household expenditures in which it is wise to use economy, but there are few even of the elegancies which it were wiser to *so appear*, if not really to be, somewhat lavish; one of these is—curtains!

Curtains are well worth all they cost, and by some means procure them, or make them at odd minutes, or of some old material.

As regards heavy hangings nothing can be more elegant in appearance than some plain woolen material, green or brown, or any solid color, embellished with bands of the woolen strips used for saddle-girths. We learned this little secret years ago, and what was our delight on reading Mr. Eastlake's "Household Taste" to find the following:—

"Some very beautiful specimens of *portiere* curtains have recently been made from the designs of Mr. A. Blomfield architect, and Mr. P. Heaton, (of London); they are composed of velvet and other stuffs, embroidered by hand, and decorated with deep borders, consisting of alternate stripes of velvet and common horse-girths. It is a remarkable fact that horse-girths (as well as a certain kind of coach trimmings) traditionally preserve the spirit of some very excellent designs." All kinds of damask, moreen and rep will be found preferable for parlor, sitting-room or library, and we would speak here of that really valuable material for persons of limited means, the Tycoon reps. This material comes in rich colors and many really beautiful patterns, some of which possess a truly Oriental character in design, richness of color, and general soft warmth of appearance. It is now used extensively for hangings and upholstering, and when lined hangs in rich soft folds that rival many a more costly fabric.

Many really elegant curtains are purchased at the auction room, for wealthy people soon tire of their luxuries, and after a few months wear they are banished to the auction rooms to be knocked off to the highest bidder, hence many a costly piece of material, rich in texture, and elegantly made is sold for a mere tithe of its true value. With deep cornice and a heavy weight of fringe and tassels, such hangings would be most inappropriate in the pretty cozy home we have imagined our reader to be furnishing in very doubtful taste indeed. But to use rich material of quiet colors and sparsely trimmed, is always the perfection of fine taste, and that delicate refinement of mind which leads to the selection of the rich and substantial, in preference to that which is flimsy and tawdry.

Sometimes these costly fabrics are discarded, because they are really too begrimed and besmoked to be any longer endurable, still even then they may be renovated.

We have in mind an instance of this; a friend whose means were small and desires large, longed for a set of Winter curtains, so with contracted purse she hied to the auction-room, and among a quantity of curtains espied just what she so longed for, a set of double hangings, cigar color, with bands of Turkish embroidery and black velvet around the edges, rich, but quiet, and just suited to her carpet, but what a condition they were in! she almost feared to touch them, they were so grimy and smoked—so altogether disgusting with grease and dust; however they went off at a mere trifle, and knowing their full value she bid them in. The next day she spent in ripping them to pieces, then sent them to the scourers, paid two dollars for having them cleaned, and they came home as clean and handsome as new ones, she felt repaid a thousand fold, and was the happy possessor of a set of rich, though plain damask curtains worth several hundred dollars in the store. So much for visiting an auction room in time of need. Yes, it is rather disagreeable, but so are bare windows and ugly rooms.

We believe "it pays" in the end, especially if several friends go in a company. We have had quite a pleasant morning in an auction room.

To those who have never observed the fact, it will be a subject of astonishment to notice the remarkable effect of curtains judiciously applied, in apartments of inferior size.

When folding-doors divide two parlors, or parlor and library, or perhaps hall and parlor, or library, the very first step taken by the amateur decorator must be to remove the huge doors, and have them carried at once to the carpenter shop for the finishing of some dwelling whose mistress possesses less artistic taste; then take the money obtained for them, and invest it in hangings of some soft material, which though it may be inexpensive, will hang in heavy folds, rendered perhaps by an interlining of old dresses, sheets, counterpanes, or other worn-out and discarded articles.

Fig. 11.

"It is remarkable indeed," says Mr. Conway, (in speaking of this subject,) "how much may be accomplished with rooms inferior in size; * * * by the skillful use of curtains."

If a gentleman in London enters a house with the intention of decorating it in accordance with principles of Art, his first work probably will be to tear away the folding doors, or single doors which divide the drawing-room. For these he will substitute a draping, which having in itself an artistic effect, shall make what was a barrier into a beauty. Nothing is better understood than that no square angles should divide a room, and the curtain is more graceful than any arch or architraves for that purpose. The sketch we give of a curtained alcove in the drawing-room of Mr. Alma Tadema, the distinguished artist, will give some idea of these charming effects of hangings in place of doors.

Besides the graceful drapery between rooms and over windows, many felicitous impressions may be made by improvising little cabinets, and various Lilliputian "art shows," half hidden by a silken or gauze hanging, (which being of small size may be unusually elegant,) for instance, one unused window may be shelved and lined with velveteen, then filled with all the beautiful treasures that can be collected, and a silken curtain gaily embroidered in true Oriental style with vari-colored silks, be carelessly (and only partially) caught back by some tasteful band, a Parian hand or gilded ring, or as we saw a short time since a purple velvet band encrusted with "pearl" (otherwise the Roman wax) beads.

Or a corner may have a set of shelves fitted into it, one triangular shelf over another, each two, three or four feet apart, the topmost one, one or two feet from the ceiling, a beautiful bracket of some kind. Now these shelves are all tastefully painted and edged with some pretty border, or covered with tinted

Fig. 12.

Fig. 13.

paper, velvet or silk with a puff or little frill on the edges, here another *etagere* is formed, which may contain all the *bric-a-brac* of the family, and on the bracket above the stand some graceful figure.

It may be only plaster yet be very lovely, far up there against the deeply tinted wall, through the arm of "Euterpe" or crook of "the Little Shepherd" pass a long gauze or silken scarf, which allow to fall in graceful folds over the tasteful, richly laden shelves below. . It is by such felicitous ideas that plain rooms are rendered charming, and how easily they are accomplished after all.

In the parlors substitute curtains for doors where ever practicable; it may be a closet that presents an obnoxious feature, remove the door ornament, the shelves, and upon each side above the frame fasten brackets far up, three or four feet above in the center, (another perhaps a larger one,) on these place statuettes, busts, vases, or any pretty ornament that may be convenient; nothing however produces a more imposing effect than a few good pieces of statuary, and it is wonderful the remarkably perfect and fine copies from models of note that can be obtained from plaster casts. All the pieces we give in this volume may be obtained, we believe in this country in plaster.

Fig. 14.

On the side brackets of our closet just described, we would stand the statuettes such as are shown in Figs. 12 and 13, representing Music and Painting, while on the central one high above, an Urn similar to Fig. 14, would appear tasteful, and afford a beautiful position for collections of Ferns, grasses and other treasures during Winter and natural flowers in Summer. Pass long scarfs through the ring and arms of the vase in single widths two upon each side, then carelessly drape one on each side behind and partially over the figures, while the other two fall over the shelves of the closet and give them a loose tie perhaps below; these curtains may be merely of Swiss muslin or Tarlatan, lined or unlined, at pleasure, and will be a most lovely addition to the room.

It is thought, quickness of perception, innate love of the beautiful, and a certain amount of industry and perseverance rather than wealth, which creates the "Sweet home." These are some of the means for arranging hangings, but they may be multiplied *ad infinitum.*

The *regular* suite of parlor furniture consisting of chairs, table and sofa is generally accompanied by piano with its stool and stand for music, *etageer*, ottomans, and various knick-knacks, or *bric-a-brac* as these are now termed; also pictures, brackets, tasteful wall-pockets perhaps, and the mantel which is now almost a piece of furniture, while the windows are draped as has been suggested, those who can procure them will find a charming natural adornment for simple muslin or lace curtains, in Ferns, Ivy-sprays, and other woodland productions.

Autumn leaves sewed on bands of muslin, are arranged as borders along the edges of curtains and point of lambrequins. When carefully preserved, Autumn leaves afford a most charming embellishment for curtains of white Swiss, and will continue fresh and bright for a whole season. Instead of sewing them upon the material, it is a better way to fasten them with gum arabic as by this mode, the leaves are easily removed when done with, and the curtain itself is not so apt to become torn as when the bastings are drawn through it. By combining Ferns, Autumn leaves and a pressed Ivy leaf in tasteful clusters, or graceful garlands, designs appearing like beautiful embroidery may be made.

A tasteful cornice for such curtains is made of pieces of slender tree branches, ornamented with the delicate little spruce twigs, forming the most exquisite Gothic designs imaginable, and which from the floor appear like some old and curious workmanship of mediæval times, complicated in form, and rich in color as some wonderful mosaic.

The beauty of the spruce-pine twigs consist in their delicacy, and the richness and variety of the brown color.

All that is required to make these cornices is an abundance of small pins, by which the numerous little arches and points are fastened together. A coat of shellac varnish gives a fine finish to this work, and delicate fern-fronds with tiny sprays of pressed Autumn leaves, arranged as vines over them add to the artistic effect.

PORTIERE WITH LAMBREQUIN.

This *portiere* and the lambrequin are made of brown woolen reps, and are lined with muslin. The edges of the reps are trimmed with a border in applique and embroidery shown in Fig. 16.

For the foundation of this border use light brown cloth, and for the application a darker brown than the foundation and black velvet. The application is edged with yellow silk soutache. The design figures are worked with brown sadler's silk in two shades in satin stitch, and are edged with yellow cord fastened on with black silk. Work the knotted stitches with gold colored thread.

To make the lambrequin, measure one-third the length of the window for the length, and allow for the width—the width of the window frame, and one-half as much again, and shape it out as shown in the illustration, then measuring off equal spaces for each of the figures, mark out any design decided upon for the embroidery, which when finished must be lined with muslin. On the outer edge of the lambrequin apply black velvet, and cover the seam made by doing this with gold colored braid. Plate the lambrequin on the upper edge, and finish with tassels of brown woolen cord and black silk. The *portiere* is draped on the sides with brown cords and tassels.

This window may also be beautifully imitated by using the cheaper woolen materials, interlined with old soft material under paper cambric, (which gives a heavy rich appearance,) and using bands of black velveteen braided with yellow braid, with black braided designs for the embroidery on the lambrequins, and for the *portiere* use for trimming, light brown alpaca braided with black

Fig. 15.

and brown, with application figures cut from black velveteen. A few weeks of work of a most fascinating kind, will give in return a set of curtains that will afford rare enjoyment for several years, if carefully put away each Spring.

The cornice above these elegant curtains is extremely handsome, but a more simple and appropriate one for a plainer suite may be made by using figures, and scrolls of artificial wood carvings, and either ebonizing or bronzing them, or indeed they are sufficiently beautiful in their natural brown state.

Fig. 16.

WINDOW WITH DOUBLE CURTAINS.

The curtains and lambrequin shown in Fig. 17 are of figured damask—of cigar color—with a plain damask richly embroidered for the lambrequin, the lace curtains of costly point with under shade of fine muslin and embroidery. Any one desiring to furnish with such curtains, will not be apt to undertake the work themselves, but will probably order them from the upholsterer. But that larger, and perhaps happier class, who are eager to surround their windows with beautiful hangings, at as small expense as possible, will no doubt be glad to know that they may have them as effectively draped, without any vast expense. To do this, first procure of some one of the pretty woolen stuffs, now to be bought for a comparatively small sum, sufficient to make the curtains reaching from the top of the window to the floor, and should the window be small, better to measure far above it, which will give the impression of greater size. If the material is of double fold, one width on each side will be all-sufficient, and, if the material is not unusually heavy, it might better be lined throughout, purchasing a bolt or two of colored cambric, and thus obtaining it much cheaper. Procure also a few yards of plain material matching the ground of the color somewhat; this for the lambrequins and borders to the curtains. Get, also, an entire piece (or two, perhaps) of coarse Swiss muslin, or neat, small-figured Nottingham lace curtains. Now we have our materials, and will proceed to make up the curtains; but first, perhaps, we might better make the cornice, which is easily done by using the carvings before mentioned, first preparing a strip of wood five inches wide, on which the ornaments are fastened. If desired particularly elegant, the wood and carvings may be ebonized and gilded, or, if preferred, the entire work may be enameled and gilded.

Fig. 17.

The under-shade is made of Swiss and is pretty finished with a fluted ruffle and gathered into long puffs from top to bottom. The curtains trim with a band of the plain material, on which large figures of black velveteen are fastened with application embroidery, using gold-colored braid on the edges, or button-hole stitching of yellow silk. Instead of lace curtains, take a half width of Swiss muslin, trim the edge with fluted ruffles, and fasten on the inside of the heavy curtains. The effect is precisely the same as though the entire curtain were hung beneath, and, as will be seen, with far less expense. The lambrequin is "shaped" as shown in the illustration, from the plain goods, and a design cut from black or other colored velveteen, is embroidered in application work of chain or button-hole stitches, or edged with yellow braid. The lining is put in after this is done. Heavy woolen fringe finishes the lambrequin and curtains; cords and tassels drape back the curtains on each side.

Among the various designs given for embroidery, tassels, bands, and trimmings of different kinds, there will be found many that will well answer for these curtains, and thus obviate the necessity of purchasing the costly ones sold in the stores, though, we would add, that a fringe sufficiently heavy for curtains, lambrequins and other furnishings, may be bought for twenty-five cents per yard, and a neat tassel of wool and silk for 25 or 30 cents, and a larger size, six inches long, for 50 cents, cord by the piece for 25, 50, 75 cents and $1.00, the last sufficiently thick for the heaviest curtains. These are retail prices, and, by procuring such trimmings by the quantity, from a wholesale establishment, they may be had for very considerable less.

CURTAIN HOLDER.

A curtain holder for these curtains is made of pointed cotton braid and crochet, is 14 1-4 inches long, with a middle depth of 3 1-2 inches, and side 1 1-2. The run of the braid, crochet with medium-sized cotton to a border, widening towards the centre, can be easily followed. For the outer edges, going all around, coarser thread must be taken. The loops to drape up the curtains are of L Ch. crocheted over with SC. and can, of course, be made any desired length.

BED-ROOM WINDOW GARNITURE.

The accompanying illustration shows a most tasteful and quiet-looking window-hanging, which must recommend itself to all who have a taste for things both elegant and chaste, for though the whole appearance of this window garniture is so exceedingly luxurious, there is nothing about it at all gaudy or "loud." The simple curtain, screening the window behind the *curtain*, is of white dimity or brown with an edge of narrow scalloping, or Hamburg edging.

The cornice is merely a strip of wooden moulding neatly painted with enameled-paint of the tint used on the wood-work of the room, and a little gilding, or enrichment with lines of color if desired.

The curtains are made of plain dark crimson woolen reps lined with muslin

Fig. 19.

of the same or some contrasting color, and edged with a thick woolen cord of two colors, and held back by bands and tassels of the same kind. Within this curtain is an inner one of plain lace edged with a rich border of home-made point, but a neat Nottingham lace curtain would answer perhaps, and be far less expensive. Many ladies are, however, so interested in making point-lace, that they would prefer manufacturing their own lace, and certainly nothing can be more superbly elegant than a set of the home-made point-lace hangings, which now sell for a fabulous price, both in England and this country.

The lambrequin for our window is of a beautiful design, and can be easily cut by measuring the width across the window, and dividing it into the sections shown in the pattern, allowing the central point one-third wider than those on the sides. The material is reps or cloth a shade or two lighter than the curtain, or of a contrasting color, with a border of rich embroidery done in *petite-point*, with zephyrs of various shades of yellow and brown, using single design figures, instead of the coat-of-arms in the center as on the model—the monogram or initials of the mistress of the room is much more appropriate.

The lambrequin must be lined with heavy cotton, and finished with a cord on the edge. Any other colors may of course be substituted for those named, and should correspond with the surroundings, but the form of this hanging will be found unexceptionable, and it is also an economical pattern inasmuch as it has no plaitings on the lambrequin, and is so simple in its entire design.

CURTAIN TRIMMINGS.

Many persons, even after they have made their curtains and lambrequins, feel the after part of the work a matter of considerable trouble, especially if the purse has been almost drained by the purchase of certain of the materials. Some of this class of our readers may, perhaps, have leisure moments, and willingness to make such finishing parts as cord, tassels, fringe, etc., did they but know how to do it, and to such we offer a few suggestions and descrip-

tions as will enable them to do this work

In Figs. 20 and 21 are two styles of hand-made cord, which are so simple that any woman who can crochet will be able to make cord by the yard and with the greatest rapidity. These cords can be made of either wool or cotton for white or heavy curtains. Those with white cotton will wash well, and will be found useful for various purposes.

Fig. 20, No. 1, requires cotton No. 1 or 2, cast on 8 L. Ch., and close in a ring from the inside, with one row of SC. Continuing work-

Fig. 20.   Fig. 21.

ing in the round, only SC. are made, which, instead of being crocheted in the chain links are made between these, as shown in the illustration; the chain links themselves go entirely to the inside, and give the cord a proper firmness.

Fig. 21, No. 2, is crocheted with double thread or zephyr (if cotton, No. 4.) Cast on a ring of 11 L. Ch. Then working in the round, and from the inside the loop of every stitch is drawn across through two chain links lying together, For every new St., the hook is, however, put first backwards into the last St. (stitch). in order to be able to take on the hook the edge St. of the same with the following ones.

TASSELS.

Handsome tassels, bands, and other curtain trimmings may be made by a lady of taste and possessing some skill with the needle.

Some of the most elegant trimmings are made of portions of the material used in the hangings, united with other materials.

In Fig. 22, for instance, we show a tassel made of silk the color of the curtains it adorns. It is made thus: two large woolen balls are made in the usual way, by winding zephyr around circular pieces of card. The zephyr in this case is of two shades of brown, but may be made, of course, to harmonize with other colors. The upper ball is one-third less in size than the lower, and they may be of any size desired. Besides these, an elongated ball is made in a similar manner, on long-shaped pieces of card, cut down the center, filled in closely with zephyr, and cut around the outer edges. are stitched between

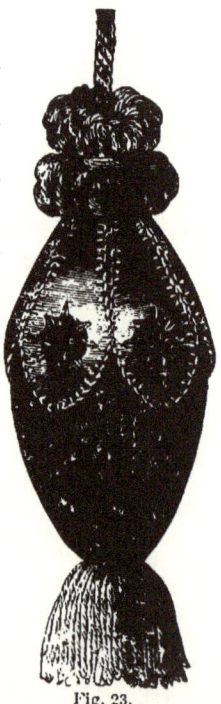

Fig. 22.

Fig. 23.

the two cards (instead of tying. as in case of the round balls). A large buttonmold covered with the material or zephyr. is placed on the large upper part of this ball, and six leaves of silk of a shade contrasting somewhat with the color of the zephyr, ornamented with buttonhole stitching on the edge, and herringbone down the center are arranged around it, as shown in the illustration, strands of coarse silk holding the points; similar leaves of one-third the size, cover the upper half of the lower round ball, and strands of silk ornament the upper one, a woolen tassel is fastened to the cord intended for suspending, which is then passed through the center of the three tassels with a large needle. or if this is a large tassel, a better way will be to put this cord through each of the balls, prior to cutting the zephyr and lying between the cards, the woolen tassel on the end may then be fastened to the cord by passing it through and tying.

The model from which our illustration is taken, was to adorn hangings of cigar-brown reps, the silk on the tassels was of golden-brown approaching yellow, embroidered with black, the tassel at the bottom three shades of brown.

Fig. 23 is of similar form, but made in a different manner, the lower part is made of four oblong pieces of card, slightly wider in the center than at the ends, which are covered with cloth sewed together and filled with cotton, this forms the egg-shaped pendant which is covered with a color harmonizing with the hangings, below this is attached a tassel of zephyr fastened to a cord passed through the pendant, leaves of silk several shades lighter, (six in number) are ornamented with buttons of black velvet, cut circular in form and held by stitches in point Russe embroidery, as shown full size in Figure 24; loops of double

Fig. 24.

zephyr several shades darker than the leaves, are arranged around the upper part in two circles, and make a pretty finish to this ornamental tassel, which is not only easily made but economical, for if preferred, scraps left from the hangings or lambrequins may be used to cover the pendant and for the leaves.

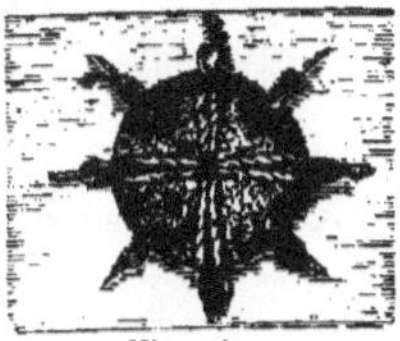

LAMBREQUIN AND CORNICE.

The accompanying cornice and lambrequin may be made entirely by a lady herself as they are quite simple.

The cornice consists of a piece of board six inches wide, and as long as the window is wide, sawed out upon the one side in rounded curves, (plainly shown in the

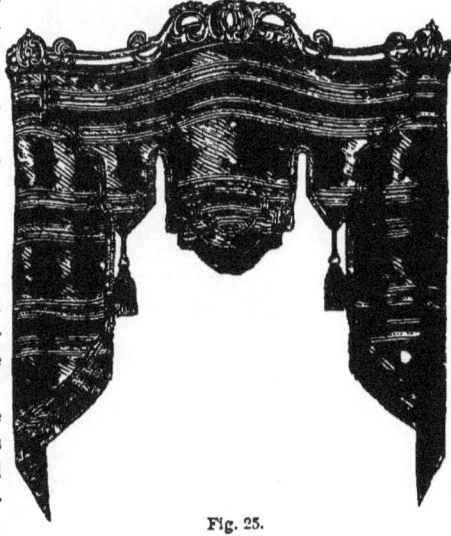

Fig. 25.

5

illustration, (on which is fastened a central and two side ornaments of the "Artificial wood-carvings" neatly bronzed.

The lambrequin is cut in the most economical manner, the two long ends

Fig. 26.

(eighteen inches in length from the point) are taken from the corners of a piece of striped rep, costing 75 cents per yard, which leaves a triangular piece extending from the opposite end, and running into a point between these two end pieces, as will be seen upon designing it, and it is then easily "shaped" as shown in the illustration. A double row of cord or braid fringe, and a pair of tassels finish the embellishments, and this tasteful lambrequin is highly recommended, not only for its beautiful form, but also from its utility, as it is readily kept free from dust owing to its simple arrangement.

In Fig. 26, we show a most elegant window arrangement, consisting of cornice, lambrequin, curtains and seat cushion, and drapery.

Many houses, especially the old residences scattered through our country, have windows which have become defaced, or are perhaps of unpleasing form, here, the drapery shown becomes invaluable.

The cornice is formed almost precisely like the one preceding it, but the lambrequin is merely a long strip of reps of solid color, costing $1.25 per yard, but only requiring 1 1-2 yards, as it is cut down the center longitudinally

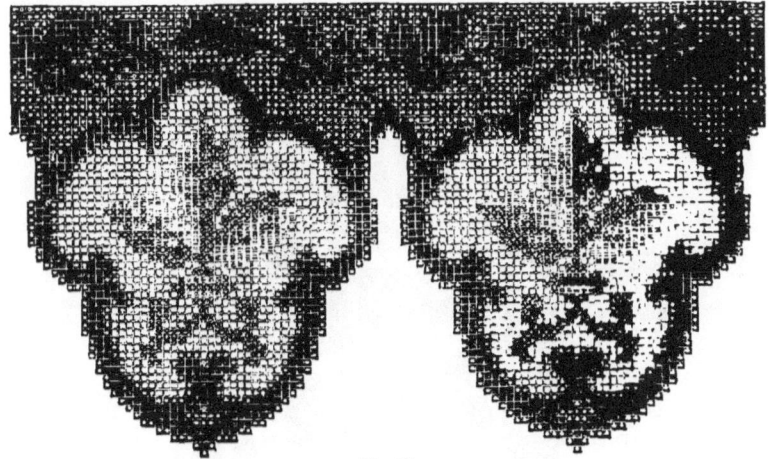

Fig. 27.

and pieced beneath the plaits, the form of which will be explained by the illustration. This lambrequin is trimmed on the edge with rows of worked braid, embroidered in herring-bone stitch with colored zephyr, which, by using several colors both of braid and zephyr, presents quite the appearance of Turkish work. Or a stripe of some kind, such as the bright saddle-girths, or an embroidered Berlin strip may be substituted, if you prefer. Swiss or Nottingham lace curtains constitute the hangings, and below these, the window seat is covered with a piece of the reps, from which depends a fall of rich embroidery in Berlin wool work, on extremely coarse canvas, of which Fig. 27 shows an elegant pattern.

In Fig. 28 is shown an entirely different style of *portiere*, and general door adornment. In this arrangement, three ornamental curtain rails hold cords and tassels festooned from one to the other, and also sustain a heavy rod, on which are hung the rings, fastened to the lambrequin. This rod and the rings may be of wood gilded, or black walnut and gold. The lambrequin here is cut from cloth with a contrasting color pinked out on the edge, and fastened on

Fig. 28.

with narrow braid, as shown in the design, Fig. 29, which is only one-fourth the size, but shows a beautiful pattern for such a point. An oval is cut out from the center, and an embroidered piece of light colored silk, richly embroidered with silk, in satin, half-polka and point Russe stitches, is inserted. A chain-stitching and running figures in satin and half-polka stitches fill the spaces on the corners, and hangings of striped rep fall below this lambrequin, or a lighter material interlined may be substituted, as shown in the illustration. A woolen

Fig. 29.

cord on the edge, and tassels and cords on various parts, make a rich finish to this elegant *portiere*.

DOOR WITH CORNICE AND LAMBREQUIN.

A richly adorned door-way is shown in Fig. 30, which exhibits a cornice covering the upper moulding. This may be by painting a "shaped" piece of wood in fancy colors imitating the rich illuminated designs in red, blue, gold, and other rich and brilliant tints. An artificial carving is painted white, and embellished with the same colors.

The lambrequin consists of a woolen damask, embroidered with application designs cut from cloth of contrasting colors, and finished with fringe. The form is simple and it does not require but the width of the door and one-fourth as much over. Lace curtains in Summer and heavy hangings in Winter hang below and sweep the floor, running on a wire extending beneath the lambrequin or cornice.

An elegant lambrequin is shown in Fig. 31. It is made by cutting a piece of yard-wide reps (of a rich brown shade) into three points with a straight piece between of one yard in length, which is plaited in two box-plaits, the points are each embroidered with an application design cut from large figured brocade silk or *Cretonne*, working the edges with button-hole stitching of the same color. The hangings below may be of Tycoon reps or richer and more costly materials

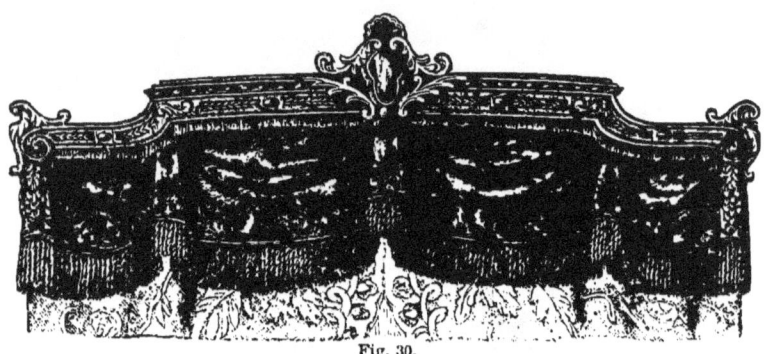

Fig. 30.

if preferred. Rosettes and cord on each plait of the lambrequin and ball fringe, with a pinked-out edge of cloth along the top forms the ornamentation of this tasteful door arrangement.

Fig. 31.

LAMBREQUIN FOR DOOR.

We have spoken of the fine effect given to rooms by the use of curtains instead of doors, and would urge upon our readers the importance of giving this class of adornment at least a trial, feeling sure they will at once adopt these *portieres*, and discard their doors to the "shady side" of the lumber-room, or as we suggested, dispose of them to some lover of doors. The illustration given in Fig. 32, shows an easy and yet beautiful lambrequin, which can be made of any material most convenient, the model here copied being Tycoon reps lined with some half-worn Turkey-red chintz curtains. A strip of scarlet cloth pinked

out on each edge, and fastened on with a buff braid in the center trims the
edge, while rosettes of the same scarlet cloth and home-made bands, with woolen
fringe at 28 cents per yard, finishes the ornamentation.

The bands are made of woolen cord of two colors of zephyr, with slides made
by cutting card-board in tasteful form, and covering with a piece of scarlet
cloth embroidered with wool-silk and beads.

Fig. 32.

Long curtains of the same material as the lambrequin or the contrasting color,
are fastened to small rings which slip on a wire extending beneath the lambrequin.

DOUBLE CURTAINS AND WINDOW-SEAT CUSHION, ETC.

The elegant simplicity (or simple elegance, perhaps), of the window furniture seen in Fig. 33, renders it very appropriate for chamber or living-rooms.
The cornice is quite simple; made by merely sawing a strip of wooden moulding, such as is used for doors, and adorning it with carvings, then ebonizing
and gilding certain parts, or bronzing the whole, as most admired, or it may be
stained in imitation of any one of the various kinds of wood.

The curtains are of plain material of any kind desired, simply trimmed with
cord of two colors, and finished with a fall of lace beneath, held back by bands
of gimp, while the colored curtains are looped with cords and tassels, tied in
graceful knots and loops. The seat of the window has a piece of the curtain

material braided in a neat pattern, and finished with a fall of embroidered cloth of some contrasting color, or several shades lighter, or a pattern may be worked on canvas according to Fig. 34, using coarse canvas, and, if necessary, repeating the upper part of the pattern. This design we have found

Fig. 33.

most appropriate for this purpose, the effect of the rich colors being extremely fine.

Our desire is to offer a variety of hangings, from which our readers may make a selection, and in Fig. 35 is shown a different style of window-hanging from any we have seen. The cornice is made by plaiting an oval piece of cloth in a frame, as the central ornament, and fastening it on a shaped piece of wood, ornamented with carvings and figures of gilded cherubs. The lambrequin is unusually rich and elegant, consisting of three festoons of the material, edged

Fig. 34.

with ornamental fringe and tassels, with long cords, festooned as shown in the illustration.

The hangings are of any heavy material convenient, trimmed simply with a bias band of contrasting color put on in scallops with light colored braid, harmonizing in color with the curtain. Instead of under-curtains of lace, a rich lace edge is fastened around the entire curtain, making a light and lovely finish to hangings otherwise heavy and rather somber. A rich lace shade, reaching to the floor, shades the window, behind the hangings. As may be imagined from the illustration, this window is one of unusually imposing effect, and would well adorn a room handsomely furnished and embellished.

Fig. 35.

WINDOW-SILL COVER AND BLINDS.

This cover is made of maroon plush and provided with a lambrequin of Java canvas, embroidered with maroon worsted, edged with like-colored cord, and decorated with rosettes and tassels of the same worsted. To make the cover, cut of the plush a piece wide enough to fit your window, and so long as to reach

Fig. 36.

the floor. For lining, cut a piece the same size of any kind, of woolen cloth. The cover is provided with three pockets—a large one in the center, and the small ones on either side—which are concealed by the lambrequin. For the small pockets, cut out of the stuff that serves for lining, two double pieces, each eight inches wide, and seven inches long. Round off at the bottom, sew together and insert into slits cut in the plush, at a distance of thirteen inches from the top, and four inches from either side. In like manner, make and insert the central large pocket, which is placed on a line with the others, and which is twelve inches wide and sixteen long. The seams where the pockets are inserted must be neatly finished off with woolen cord. Now attach the lining; trim at the bottom with wide maroon worsted fringe, and bind the sides and top with worsted braid, after affixing the lambrequin which covers the pockets.

Fig. 37.

This lambrequin is made of Java canvas, cut into three points at the bottom, a large one in the center, and a small one on each side. Embroider in any appropriate design with maroon worsted, having first drawn the shape of the points with lead pencil. When finished, cut away the canvas at about the distance of half an inch from the pencil marks, hem this over on the wrong side, finish off with cord, and decorate each point with rosette and tassel. The blinds are of Indian gauze ornamented with painted flowers, birds, etc., bound with silk ribbon, and fastened top and bottom by means of steel rods to hooks, as shown in the engraving.

DOOR CURTAINS, WITH EMBROIDERED BORDER AND DRAPED HEADING.

The illustration shows very plainly the handsome arrangement of curtains and heading. Their color should match the furniture, the border on the curtains being worked of two contrasting shades of cloth, on a light background. The fringe on the heading or lambrequin, the cord and tassels are chosen of a

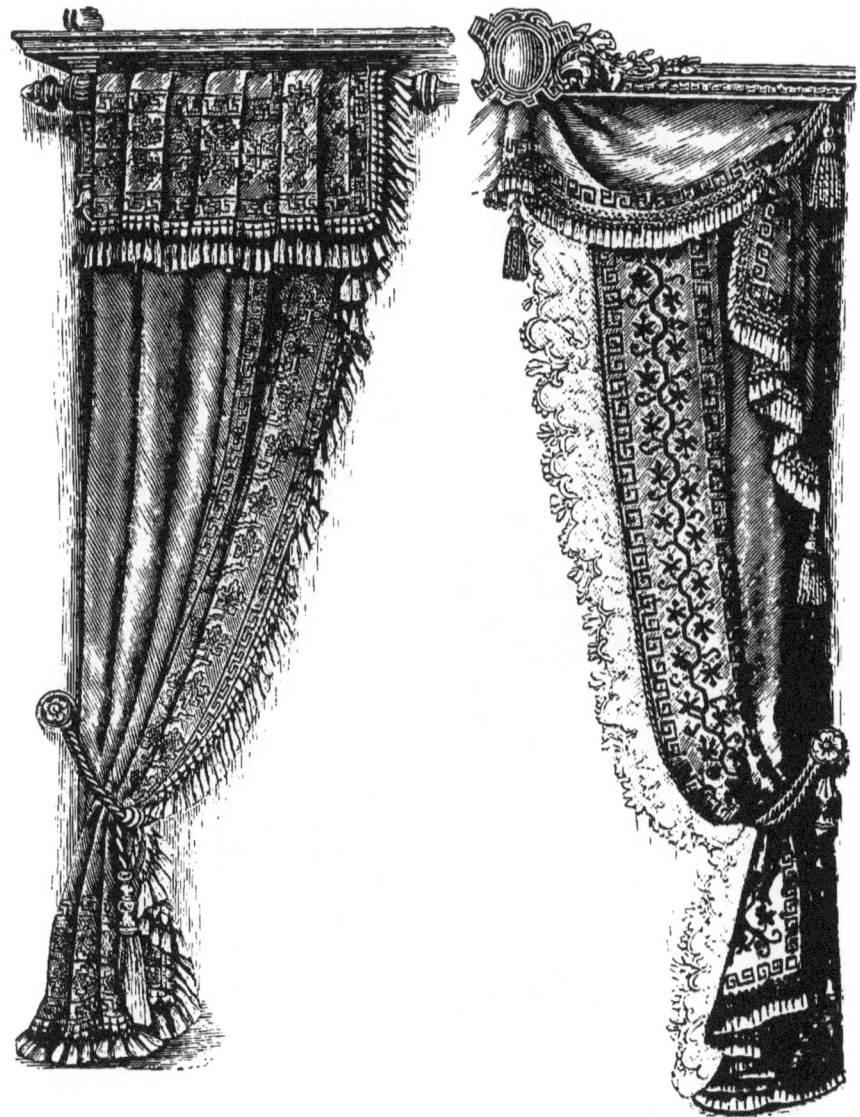

Designs for Lambrequins and Door Curtains.

color to match the border, which is finished off on each side by a neat little edging, worked of worsted somewhat darker than the color of the curtains.

Fig. 38.

WINDOW CURTAINS, WITH WHITE AND COLORED DRAPINGS.

The beautiful arrangement of this window is very plainly indicated by the illustration. Color and design may be chosen to suit individual taste. A deep ball fringe depends from the gilt cornice, and a like, though somewhat narrower fringe, finishes off the embroidered window-sill cover. The latter is made to match the border of the cloth curtain.

Fig. 39.

CHAPTER VII.

BED-ROOMS.

The furnishing of chambers affords wide scope for taste in selecting articles both expensive and plain, and for much ingenuity in fitting and adapting materials to the limits of small means, yet which shall not be devoid of beauty or elegance.

Black walnut has in a great measure superseded the mahogany of former years, but the many "fancy-woods" as they are called, such as the curled and birds-eye maple, birch, butternut, white walnut and silver fir, and the lovely enameled-pine have become so popular, and each one is so equally in favor that it is difficult to say what fancy-wood is most admired at present.

In the chapter on the present style of furniture, we described many of the new fancies and conceits for these various kinds, but after all the substantial black walnut which has stood the test of years, is the most generally used among those who having taste and only moderate means, desire to spend their money for the kind of furniture which will withstand constant usage, and present the best appearance for the least money.

Yet, even among this class, the charming "cottage-suites" will be found exceedingly satisfactory, inasmuch as by obtaining, or having made pieces, or entire sets indeed, of plain pine, and understanding the method of enameling in various delicate colors, and decorating or embellishing as may be preferred, these chamber-suites may be gotten up with but little expense.

From the furniture store, a bed-chamber may be furnished for from $15 to $100 in these cottage-suites, the heavy carved and painted furniture costing from $500 to several thousands, according to the elegance of the work.

The hangings and curtains for bed-chambers, may be of costly damask, reps, *Cretonne* or other expensive materials, but also of several low-priced fabrics, which cost but little and yet present quite rich and Oriental designs and colors, among which is the Tycoon reps, costing but 25 cents or less per yard, and with a coarse thread running through the chain, which gives it the appearance and durability of a more costly material.

The colors in a bed-chamber should be quiet and subdued, the forms the reverse of conspicuous and obtrusive, while a sense of warm, cozy comfort in Winter, and cool refreshing daintiness in Summer should pervade the whole from carpet to ceiling, and from wall to window.

Truly the life of an apartment depends upon the degree to which it subserves its end, and not as Madame De Guerdin facetiously defined it in "fires, mirrors and carpets."

In the parlor we may have all the brightness and glow of color, which will sympathize with the gayety of guests, or testify to the life of our hospitality; in the living-room we may gather all the various personalities which tend to the comfort or pleasure of each loved one of the family; while in the dining-room is collected all that can testify to a large hospitality, and give the apartment that charm belonging only to the spot where the "social board" is spread, but in the bed-chambers, where the tired limbs or aching head seeks repose and rest on bed or chair, the eye will require the refreshment of subdued colors, and that softly toned light which is at once grateful and suggestive of further comfort. A quiet room eminently restful and filled with real comfort, with no garish lights from brilliant windows, and no multiplicity of prominent embellishment to distract the weary senses, but pervaded by a refinement, simple as entire, and always remarkable for the impression given of its being the expression of peculiar and individual taste.

This should be particularly the case with the "mother's bed-room," but outside of this the guest-chamber, or "spare room" as it is called,—the rooms belonging to the children, and even the servants' chambers should each and all be furnished and arranged with a view to the characteristics of each individual.

The "mother's room" should be that most delightful retreat, which as the haven of rest for each afflicted or sorrowing member of the flock, is to be looked back upon and fondly remembered in the "after-time," when in recalling one by one the hallowed land-marks belonging to the old homestead, this spot stands out prominently above all the rest, as the sacred casket in which are enshrined the smiles and tears of childhood's hour, the joys and sorrows of youthful days, the confessions and confidences of maturer years, all poured into the fond mother's ear and hallowed by her admonitions and prayers.

In time of severe illness, no apartment is so well adapted to the trying necessities of the case as "mother's room," and the same plea goes forth, when trifling ills befall the flesh or imaginary woes afflict the spirit, from the *paterfamilias* down to the crowing baby; each one finds most comfort, and the heart's best solace within the enchanted precincts of "mother's room."

As regards the "spare room," we hold that instead of making it the stiff formal gloomy tomb, it too frequently is, no pains should be spared to give it an exactly opposite appearance, and make it a cheery inviting "homesy" place that the honored, or beloved guest will have cause to suppose is a harbinger of "good things to come," of the cordial large-hearted hospitality, the kindly word and good cheer awaiting them below.

Whether this guest-chamber is commodious and elegant with abundant means to embellish and adorn it, or its dimensions contracted, and its appointments of the humblest type matters little, so that "heartsome warmth" emanating from the truly hospitable soul is shown by the numerous little arrangements, which are really so trifling and yet speak so much. The sparkling fire, the cozy rocking-chair, the soft-foot cushion, the little bouquet and tray of fruit or refreshments; simple things taken individually yet testifying to such thoughtfulness as must be precious, to even a callous heart.

As the furniture, hangings and appointments of a "spare-room" are to prove congenial to various tastes, it is wisest to use only quiet colors, and no furniture that is ultra as regards form or arrangement.

Neatness and delicate cleanliness will atone for rich drapery or fine linen, therefore let everything about the room be *immaculate*, in the fullest definition of the word, "free from spot, stain or defect, spotless, pure, undefiled."— Nothing can compensate for this, and with this, plain furniture and coarse linen will appear well to the eye of the truly tasteful, for, after all, form and color are but arbitrary, and what pleases one will displease another; therefore, in an effort to suit all, the simplest forms and most subdued colors will best effect the object.

On this account, and also as a room more easily kept neat and clean than the remainder of the house, the furniture of the "spare-chamber," if to be purchased, might better be selected from the "cottage" styles, of which there are such a large number. Here the delicate ground of sage-gray, pearl-gray, or creamy-white, may be adorned with lines and narrow bands of color, black, brown or other contrasting tint, and perhaps some little designs on drawers and panels, such as we described in the chapter on the "Furniture of the Day."

Where it is inexpedient to purchase such furniture, entire rooms may be furnished *en suite* with impromptu furniture, and, as has been suggested, on account of the nature of this apartment, and its casual occupation, such furniture is peculiarly appropriate for it. Full directions for these dainty "*suites*" will enable any one to make them, and from the most simple materials. The walls of a "spare-room" may be treated in the most delicate manner, and made exceedingly beautiful both by the use of designs, the careful arrangement of three varieties of paper on dado, wall and frieze, or by the Oriental method of covering with hangings, and, when practicable, the latter is one of the most luxurious of arrangements for the Winter season, but, of course, requires abundance of material, and is (comparatively) an expensive wall covering.

BED-ROOM FURNITURE.

THE BEDSTEAD.

In examining Fig. 40 the impression of a costly and elegant bedstead is given, which, in its luxurious comfort and delicate beauty, presents an aspect so inviting that any one would desire to possess a fac-simile in their own house. This

Fig. 40.

might, perhaps, be considered an impossible thing, but is it really so? We will examine this beautiful arrangement and see.

First, as regards the bedstead itself, it is of the form called square Gothic, and of the simplest form, yet, because gracefully hung and tastefully ornamented and embellished, is the beautiful object shown in the illustration. Any ordinary workman may make such a frame, consisting only of two sides, a head and foot-board, the feet and slats for bottom. It is made of good one-inch plank-pine, which should be well seasoned, and of the best quality of lumber. The sides are seven feet in length, and two feet three inches in width, the head-board four feet eight inches wide and four feet ten inches high, the foot-board three feet six inches high. The square posts at the corners are eight inches on each side, and fastened securely to the head and foot-boards by mortising. The low feet are of turned wood, with castors, and must be secured carefully to the posts by long pins, entering holes in the posts several inches, or, better still, the feet may be a continuation of the solid wood of the post.

The ornamentation consists of corner pieces of artificial wood carvings, such as the right and left scrolls, Fig. 40. The entire ornament belonging to them, as illustrated by the whole figure, being the enrichment on head and foot-boards,—we would suggest, however, that the "Sleeping Cherub" as a central ornament is far more beautiful, and very appropriate; or, if the bedstead is designed for a boy's room, the Pointer's or Fox heads always give satisfaction; while for children's bedsteads, the "Flying Cherub," various arrangements of flowers, birds, etc., make characteristic ornamentation. This, however, will be at the option of the maker, of course, or, as directed by the mistress of the house, who will best understand the individual tastes she is laboring to satisfy.

The prices of a set of bedstead ornaments vary greatly, but it may be taken for granted that the richest ornamentation possible will not exceed $5.00, and those we have given cost, for central ornament and side scrolls for head and foot-boards, 50 cents each (entire); scrolls for four corners, 15 cents each ($1.60 cents, altogether); two figures for tops of posts, 50 cents each—and these last may be dispensed with, if desired, and a turned ornament substituted, such as we see on ordinary posts, ball, acorn, etc.

The bedstead is put together as described for table, book-case, and other articles given previously; then the whole is well polished and painted, either in colors, with zinc-white (enamel) paint, ebonized, or stained in imitation of any of the woods. By cutting out strips of paper and fastening them on the edges, also ovals in the centers, lines and panels may be simulated, as, upon staining the parts surrounding these pieces of paper, the designs beneath are left the color of the pine, which can afterwards be painted or stained with pure white and a light tint, such as gray, buff, or any light shade preferred. Where the artificial wood-carvings are used, it is not well to apply an over-abundance, which will at once give the impression of cheapness, whereas a few judiciously arranged, will produce a wonderfully rich appearance. We would suggest, as regards this bedstead, that it is ebonized on the darkest parts, stained with umber, in imitation of black walnut on the lighter panels, and finished with lines of white, in which a very little chrome is rubbed. The artificial carvings must be either black, or remain in the walnut-color natural to them, which, without either oil or varnish, presents a beautiful, soft, brown-color, that is extremely rich and chaste.

Since metal bedsteads—iron, brass, and imitation bronze—have become so popular, many may prefer to make light fretwork for the head and foot boards, setting such open panels in strong but light frames, and painting with bronze or lacquer, or perhaps gilding certain prominent parts. In such case the artificial carvings used may be bronzed or gilded and present a charming effect. For a "spare-room" this style of enrichment would answer well, as it will not require such constant wiping and cleaning as in rooms used more generally, though, as regards this, the bronzing, etc., may be renewed frequently with but little trouble or expense. The drapery of the bedstead in Fig. 40 is fastened to a projecting framework, which is arranged as follows: If the bedstead is to stand with one side against the wall, the frame is fastened as in the illustration; but if it is placed with head against the wall, or occupies an alcove or recess, the frame is held by hooks or staples driven through the plaster into the joist of the ceiling. For it, take a pair of iron or wooden brackets, which fasten securely against the wall, three feet apart (in the center of the space), and upon them nail a board four feet long and three wide, with the corners sawed off. This should be neatly covered with tinted paper or muslin, or a design may be substituted, if preferred, such as a wreath of colored flowers, painted or embroidered. Around the edge of the board fasten carvings to match those on the bedstead, painting them with bronze and a little gilding. Around this fasten hangings of Swiss, edged with embroidery or lace, or with a border in application of lace and bobbinet, or tucks appear neat and pretty, and spray-work will be found to make a charming finish. These hangings must be sufficiently full and long to cover the entire bedstead, and almost reach the floor. Around the ornaments on the top twine a scarf of material corresponding with the upholstery, and trimmed with fringe. The dainty furnishing of this beautiful bed will be given in an after chapter as also directions for making the quilt, linen cover and other tasteful equipments, of a well furnished bedstead.

If desired, an ornament of some kind may be placed upon the bracket, or shelf above the bed; a statuette of "The Graces," "Hebe," The "Sleeping Beauty," "Guardian Angel," Fig. 41, "Rebecca," *or the like being the most appropriate.* This bedstead belongs to a suite, the remainder of which will be described under the special chapters devoted to each one, and are designed to aid those who desire to make their own furniture, or, at least, have it made, and ornament it themselves. On account of the economy of this

course—for so very much more depends upon the after embellishment or adornment, that, as has been clearly shown, tasteful and substantial suites may be
thus made, which would cost from four to ten times the amount if selected from
the stores ; and, where bedsteads, or indeed any chamber furniture is concerned,
the auction-room, or second-hand articles from any place, are to be purchased

Fig. 41.

with great caution, lest in striving to economize, the house be filled with
vermin.

It is a disputed point whether drapery about a bed is detrimental to health,
or the reverse, many good and sound reasons being given on each side. We
would say where delicate persons, or the aged are occupying apartments exposed to cold winds, and there are drafts occasioned by badly-fitting doors and
windows, some protection is obviously necessary, and there is no doubt but
many a severe attack of neuralgia, catarrh or rheumatism have been occasioned
by the neglect of arranging some protection, such as curtains around the sides
and head of the bed, but where a room is perfectly close, and there can be no
drafts about the head especially, it is certainly more healthful to breathe the

pure air than that enclosed within the heavy folds of drapery used about many beds.

No doubt heavy draperies and bed curtains were well suited to the times in which they originated, and many persons still cling to the old "four-poster," and arrange tester and cornice year after year, as pertinaciously as did their great-grand-mothers a hundred years back. Our readers may have seen illustrations of the style of old fashioned bed-room furniture, or suites of a four-post bedstead, dressing table and chair of the time of Queen Anne. The whole is exceedingly elegant, but our present queens nor their subjects would be satisfied to arrange their dresses in front of such a diminutive mirror, as the three foot specimen of that day.

The Arabian bedsteads are now becoming more and more popular, and are so easily made that an ingenious boy could construct one. The advantages of these Arabians are that though whether for beauty or comfort, hangings are disposed about the head, they do not confine the air in the least, yet at the same time give a bed an air of cozy comfort during the Winter, when gay Oriental-looking stuffs hang about and protect the head of the bed; and when draped with soft fleecy-looking Swiss, lace or gauze in Summer they add such an air of breezy, dainty coolness to the pretty and inviting conch.

Any lady may add one of these Arabian canopies to her otherwise plain bedstead, and thus give it at once an air of elegance not obtainable by any other means. Supposing you have a bedstead, the tester-frame is made thus: Get two long wooden strips of one inch plank, about three inches in width, and seven feet long, and screw them firmly to the head of posts of the bed perpendicularly. (Judgment must be used as regards the height of these uprights, as this depends upon the height of the head-board or posts of the bedstead; the height from the frame of the bedstead should be eight or nine feet). These uprights should be screwed against the back part of posts or head-board, and stand perfectly upright, as nothing can be more objectionable than a crooked canopy, unless it is one that is constantly shaking.

Next to these perpendicular pieces screw two horizontal strips, which may be made of laths, as also the cross piece, if the bed is a single one, otherwise a strip of one-half inch plank, the width of the bedstead will be necessary; extending from this frame work may be an ornamental canopy of heavy wire, or two strips nailed across may suffice to form a square frame (which is made of solid wood and finished with a moulding). In the home-made canopy, however, this light frame is covered first with thin muslin, such as an old sheet drawn tightly over and tacked around the edges, thus covering the under part, which may be further and more tastefully finished by a cover of enameled paper, covered with moss roses and buds, if the color of the room is to be pink, or with morning-glories, if blue is the chosen tint, varying such embellishment to suit circumstances, or where a particularly handsome cover is desired, upon which to lie and gaze, a square of silk laid in large plaits along the sides, and taken to the center in close small ones, with a rosette finishes the connection.

This tester is now ready for the hangings which may of course be either costly and elegant, or simple and inexpensive. Supposing the latter, we may obtain (for Winter) some good pattern with rich colors of the Tycoon reps, our favorite of all low-priced goods; these we will make by cutting off three widths for each side of the bed, and sufficient Turkey-red chintz, or crimson paper-cambric to line them, also sufficient of the latter to cover between the two uprights at the head of the bed, stretching it perfectly tight, and tacking closely to the upright and also to the frame of the bedstead and top of tester frame; tack the curtains along the extended frame in the same way, and then finish with a shaped lambrequin, made according to any one of the various pretty designs given in chapter on curtains.

The bands for holding back these curtains may be made in various ways, beautiful ones are to be purchased for small sums, varying from fifteen cents to several dollars, but where the bedstead is embellished with imitation of marquetry, ivory-inlaying on ebony, or the artificial carvings; the curtain bands both for bed and windows, might better be made to correspond. Tasteful rosettes for such hangings as we have described may be made thus : take a piece of wood six inches square, and saw off the corners, bore a hole in the center then cover with cotton in form of a cushion raised on one side, and sew a piece of the curtain materials neatly over, next make a ruffle of a part (stripe if there is one) of the material or trimming, scalloping or pinking the edges, gather or plait this around the edge, and if it is to hold one end of the band, put a long screw through the hole in the center and fasten it in position, then cover the screw-head with a circular piece of the stuff sewed over a flat button-mold, and caught to the rosette with a few stitches ; to this fasten a band made of a strip of the material covered over card-board, with a flexible wire sewed in the edge, and ruffled with a tiny narrow strip of a stripe, or the trimming used for the curtains. Such rosettes may be put in various places where a finish is required, and add greatly to the appearance. Where striped goods are used, one of the stripes cut off lengthwise and trimmed on the edge, answers well as a border and for trimming.

At the approach of warm weather such heavy curtains and hangings are stored away, and dainty white ones, such as are described in the first part of the chapter, are substituted. These may be made of various materials—Dimity, Swiss, Victoria-lawn, Tarlatan, or Nottingham lace—either one of which presents a charming appearance.

The lambrequins for such light material should be of the same, either covered with puffings and ruffles, or lined with pink, blue, green or lavender paper-cambric, with bands of the same, and bows of ribbon, or the material lined and edged.

Many persons consider it worth while to renew these hangings each season, purchasing a bolt or two of the cheap Swiss or Tarlatan at wholesale prices, and discarding them at the end of the season. In this case, the best method of trimming them is to cut ruffles of the material, turn up only one edge, and pass it through the fluting iron, also to make puffs, and ruchings pinked on the edges. Such light trimmings present a delightfully cool, dainty appearance, and, with care, will remain in good condition during the entire season.

Another method of trimming these light hangings is by means of natural ornaments, such as fern-fronds, the climbing fern, Autumn and ivy leaves, etc., known under the name of "Artificial Vines."

There are many persons, however, who would prefer to enjoy the pleasure of preparing their own natural and, perhaps, artificial decorations as well, themselves, by making their collections of ferns, leaves and grasses during the Summer and Autumn, and finishing them while the long Winter evenings continue, and, for such, we append a few hints that may, perhaps, aid a few, at least, and those who already know as much and more than we can tell them, will patiently listen to an oft-told tale, if thereby even one may be made the wiser.

Gather your ferns as late as possible, and, whenever practicable, take them up "root and branch," for *a fern will not continue fresh for any length of time if severed from the root*, and, as some of the most lovely fronds are entirely too large to be at once pressed, many of the choicest are lost, for these are such delicate gossamer-like leaves that, unless each one is carefully straightened out, the greatest beauty is marred; if, however, the course we suggest be followed, the plume-like heads will be found as fresh the following day as when gathered, and then, rested after the labor of collecting, and with old newspapers for the large ones, and books for the small, the day may be pleasantly spent in arranging them between the leaves, and placing them under heavy weights. Each day the papers must be changed and those just removed laid in the sun or before the fire to dry out for replacement the following day. By this course, hundreds may be prepared with but little trouble, and with no disappointment and disheartening feeling of failure. We would remark here, though somewhat out of place, perhaps, that it will repay you to collect a quantity of the evergreen varieties, with the roots and a little soil about them, for the decoration of the table during the Winter, for, if placed in a box, in a cellar, or other shaded cool place, they will continue in perfection the entire Winter, and prove a vast comfort many a time when flowers fail for festive occasions.

Gather branches of gorgeously tinted leaves, and, after painting the right side of each one with nice linseed oil, to preserve the perfection of tint and render the leaves pliable, lay them, too, between newspapers or books, and laying them in a row upon the floor, place boards upon them, and all the heavy weights possible, such as stones, blocks or, indeed, anything that will add to the pressure.

(We are taking it for granted that large quantities will be required, you perceive). Quantities of single leaves, also, should be prepared, by wiping a warm (not hot) iron with wax, and passing it over the right side and placing them between folds of tissue-paper under weight. Late in October the bleached fronds of ferns may be procured and are specially lovely.

Bright scarlet berries and lichens, with moss-covered branches are also valuable, and should be prepared in abundance. and brakes, green, brown, white and yellow—the light green bracken is peculiarly lovely for this purpose.

During the Winter, make these treasures up into artistic forms of beauty; some in garlands, others in clusters, and a large number into "leaf-showers," as they call them, or "falling leaves of Valambrossa," still more poetical—whichever it may be, the effect is exceedingly fine. To make them, first arrange a cornice of Florida-gray moss around the very edge of the ceiling, sewing it on a strip of any material, and allowing it to droop gracefully here and there; then, at distances regularly marked off, place large circular figures of ferns of all shades, sewing them on card-board, and taking a spool of No. 40 cotton and tying bunches of bright leaves to one end, fasten it to one of the circles, and tie one, two, three, and so on irregularly at distances of all lengths from this to a height of seven feet from the floor. When these are arranged in the Spring, the effect from those standing or sitting below will be of a shower of leaves, and upon a white or delicately tinted wall, the effect is wonderfully beautiful. The white thread does not show at all, and, as may be imagined, the leaves will appear as though "floating in mid-air." A few ferns and sprays of delicate leaves carefully pressed may also be added, and will increase the beauty of the appearance still more. This same arrangement may also be placed upon the lambrequins and curtains, and present a truly charming effect upon Swiss or Tarlatan.

BED-CURTAINS, ETC.

There are many varieties of low-priced materials suitable for curtains and hangings in chambers, of which the striped chintzes, among cotton goods, are perhaps the most satisfactory, and as there may be some who feel at a loss, with regard to the quantity of material, etc., we will now give explicit direction that will enable any one to purchase and make up a set of hangings without trouble or loss.

Supposing the bedstead is of the kind we have described, the "Arabian" and full double-size, with a high canopy. Twenty yards of chintz, and twenty-eight of colored glazed lining, (both twenty-five inches wide,) will be required. This measurement allows of curtains three yards long, a foot valance of twelve breadths, and a head valance four and a half yards long before plaiting.

Every one intending to furnish a bed, must measure its size, and add to or deduct from these figures as required.

The three yard curtains will reach the floor, and though two and a half-yards will be sufficiently long for comfort, the appearance will not be nearly so handsome, though as regards material it will effect a saving of nearly two yards of outside material and lining.

To make the curtains, cut off three lengths of three yards each, fold one of these carefully and split it in half, this affords half a breadth for each curtain to be run to the whole breadth, that is, each curtain has one and a half breadths.

Cut three lengths of lining, each three yards long, split down one and join as before, pin the out and inside carefully together, and tack down the seams so that the whole is perfectly smooth and straight, as upon this depends the hanging. If the chintz and lining are not the same width, let the margin extend over which can be bound down afterwards. If trimming is to be put on, let it be basted on an inch from the edge, and bind neatly with curtain binding or tape of some of the fancy varieties. All this can be done beautifully on the sewing-machine. On the top of the curtain sew a dozen small curtain rings, which cost but about fifteen cents per dozen; these rings however vary according to size, as also the rods upon which they run, if they are desired to slip back and forth.

Nothing is handsomer than fringe around the canopy of a bedstead, and which may be obtained for 25 cents per yard, and as an edge to the curtains, narrower woolen fringe costing 15 cents per yard, will appear richer than the mere binding.

Around the frame-work of the canopy a scarf trimmed with fringe, and gracefully twined or looped is the handsomest adornment, but if this is considered too expensive, a row of fringe or a shaped lambrequin trimmed with the narrow fringe just named will appear extremely elegant. There are some persons however who would prefer the simple valance to any other finish around the top, and to make this take a piece of the chintz two yards long, split in half, and again in half these quarters, join on the selvage and if sufficient is not thus obtained to go once around the frame, and allow one-third more for fullness, add breadths until this length is obtained, cut a lining to suit and sew the two together, trim with the fringe and plait to fit the frame, binding the edge. A foot valance is made in the same way. If handsomer hangings are desired, two and a half widths should be allowed on each side for the curtains, and rich trimmings of cords and tassels be used, with gilt or ebony, and gilt cornice around the frame.

Having finished the hangings and valances, run together two widths of the lining with a half width on each side, or a half width between (according to size of bedstead) bind the top and bottom, and tack to the frame at the head of the bed, and to the head-board, (or frame of the bedstead,) then split two and a half yards of the chintz lengthwise and these again in two, make a box plait the entire length and fold over the edges, basting them down securely. Put these bands down the seams of the head lining just mentioned, and two others down the centers of the whole breadths, which makes a pretty finish to the inner part.

Fig. 42.

BEDSTEAD WITH CANOPY.

The charming effect given to the pretty bedstead given in **Fig. 42**, make one willing to take some little trouble to produce such a result. Yet this is not so difficult a matter that any one need fear to undertake it. The bedstead itself is really a most simple affair, and our model was made for the small sum of two dollars, though a home-made one consisting merely of a box of proper size with plain board, head and foot-boards are all that is necessary, as the entire wood-work is covered with a neat quilted rug edged with a border, embroidered by the hands of the fair mistress of the mansion, and finished with woolen fringe. This

Fig. 43.

cover may be of silk or any goods preferred, and is made to fit the frame, with a roll bolster fastened on the head-board. A frame of half-circular form placed on two brackets, is fastened against the wall ten feet from the floor, in the center of the side of the bedstead, and sustains the curtain and lambrequin of the canopy, the form of which is shown in the illustration. This frame should be sufficiently deep to extend across the bedstead for several feet. The curtains are held gracefully back by ornamental curtain bands.

BED HANGINGS.

Elegant bed curtains are made according to the design shown in Fig. 44, which displays only the upper part; but, as the lower portion of the curtains is merely a continuation of the two side pieces, their construction can be readily understood. The bedstead in this case (Fig. 42) is a handsome, carved frame, of the French style, placed with the head against the wall, the canopy extending towards the foot. The canopy is formed screwing a piece of one inch plank as long as the width of the bed, and four inches wide, against the wall, and to it fastening the tester, formed of three strips, two the length of the bedstead, the third the width across the bottom. On this, the cornice of walnut wood mouldings and artificial carvings are fastened, and, beneath this, the hangings. The tester is covered with a tightly stretched lining of white or colored muslin, which may be embellished with a lovely group of flowers in some beautiful "transfer" style, as Decalcomania or Antique painting, or, it may be covered with tinted paper.

The curtains of soft, rich woolen fabric, have a border of contrasting color, embroidered with a design such as has been shown in former illustrations. A

Fig. 44.

half-yard plaiting is fastened above these, with festoons of cords and knots, with tassels at various points. The form of the curtains and lambrequin is plainly shown in the illustration and will need no further description. The tasteful arrangement of the inviting looking bed, with its side rug and exquis- itely embroidered tidies, explains itself.

CHAPTER VIII.

TOILET-TABLES, WASH-STANDS, ETC.

A toilet-table is one of those tasteful additions to a lady's bed-chamber or dressing-room, which is, perhaps, more characteristic than any other portion of the furniture. The severely strict and eminently practical lady will show her proclivities in the arrangement and furnishing of her toilet-table, which may be seen at a glance; for here will be found the neat pin-cushion and box for the immaculate collar and cuffs placed within it conscientiously each night, while the prim bit of square mirror is suspended above it in rigid stiffness; but here will be found no frivolous or prominent displays, showing undue thought for the naughty "pomps and vanities of this wicked world;" no tasteful toilet-case with the "Satan's paint boxes," containing only two colors to be sure, but with which such wonderful faces can be made, to "play the mischief" with the world at large. This, and many another such pretty trifle is to be found on that other table, which shows a difference in many other points as well. It has rich lace hangings, interlined with the *couleur de rose*, which is to impart that exquisite glow to the complexion, and mirror so perfect that it reflects each image as clearly as though it were a mammoth diamond. This toilet belongs to the true "lady of the world," and, as she has procured it, with all its costly accessories, at an immense price, we will not debar her of it, but merely strive to cull from it any good points which we can make available. This table is seen in Fig. 43, and, as an accompaniment to the beautiful bedstead, also copied from the inlaid ebony and ivory, bronze and gold, of this same lady's chamber, is a fitting accompaniment for it.

Let us see, therefore, what are the peculiarities of this elegant table, the most conspicuous and prominent feature is (as it should be in a toilet table), the dressing-glass; but, for ourselves, we would suggest that, in this instance, beauty yield to utility and the mirror be of much greater dimensions, for a dressing-glass to be agreeable, should show, at least, one-half the person. We would, therefore, procure an oval or oblong glass, from two to four feet long, and, if an ornamental frame is desired, it can be readily made, by obtaining a strong box, one foot ten inches long, and one foot wide; to the sides of this screw two uprights two-thirds as high as the glass, two inches wide and one deep. This is the simple frame, to which adapt, first a lid on the top of the box, making it ornamental by adding a moulding around the edges and ornaments at the cor-

Fig. 45.—Toilet Table.

ners, with a large and rich center-piece of artificial carvings; the uprights ornament in the same way, unless it is preferred to procure circular turned posts. The cherubs on the scrolls, with the candelabras, may be imitated by using figures of Parian and a pair of tasteful candlesticks. These are to be bronzed or gilded, or the two combined, gilding the leaves and lily and bronzing the cherubs, also ornamenting the ebonized frame of the mirror with lines of gold.

The table is a semi-circular, pine top, supported on four strong legs. The top is first covered with a piece of heavy cloth, such as a section of old blanket or table-cover, over which is stretched a cover of dimity, embroidered with white or colored braid, in design adapted to the size and form of the table, which should be made to fit between two windows, if possible, as this affords the best light for dressing during the day. A dressing-table, or bureau, should never be so placed that the light is cast upon the mirror, but upon the person performing the toilet in front of it.

Around the lower part of the table, and covering the legs, is a drapery of *Cretonne*, or other material, headed by a Swiss ruffle, embroidered on the edge, designs for which are given in the accompanying illustrations. A narrow ruf-fle edges the top, and, at the bottom of the colored drapery is a plaited ruffle, half a yard deep, the upper edge of which is folded down, and a ruching made of a stripe contrasting in color is placed one inch below, thus making a beautiful heading to the lower ruffle.

To work this embroidery, transfer the design to the material, and run the figures and outlines with embroidery cotton; then work in satin, half-polka and back-stitches, as shown in the design. The scallops on the outer edge, and the shell-shaped ornaments above are worked in button-hole stitch. Bows of ribbon catch up the cover in four places.

There are many persons who have a prejudice against home-made furniture, and would prefer their rooms should present a bald empty inhospitable aspect, rather than resort to any of the numerous little contrivances which tend so greatly to give an air of coziness not otherwise imparted, even though it may be furnished with a regular suite fresh from the store.

We will not argue the question of "vulgarity," as connected with all home-made things, for it might be extended far into the complicated meshes of the household net-work, and countless questions as regards home-made dresses, home-made bread, etc., remain to be definitely settled.

If we can make pretty things that will give pleasure to ourselves and others, and that will save expense, (where need be to economize,) then it is wise to surround ourselves with them, and though it is just and right that the wealthy should enjoy all the luxury that money can procure, there is no reason why those less favored, and who perhaps enjoy beautiful objects just as fully, should not be allowed to make for themselves objects as nearly resembling the costly ones as may be, for as Mr. Conway justly observes, "take away all that has

7

been added to our homes by Art, and we all become naked savages, living in mud or log huts." These little adornments we describe, have a refining influence that will be felt by every member of the family, and a child brought up in

Fig. 46.

a family where attention is paid to the minute details of refined life, and who sees and is taught to admire even the simple beauties his parents strive to gather about the homestead, will if prospered and able to have a more luxurious

home for himself, be ready to appreciate the higher branches of Art, and cultivate to the fullest extent the taste fostered in him while a child, who was
taught to aid his tasteful mother to make simple elegancies for the home, he
loves to remember.

Each room therefore, is to be as beautiful as may be, not only the parlors or
parlor in which our visitors are ushered, but those other apartments which go to
make up the complete home, and above all, the rooms devoted to the loved
family circle, for it may not after all be a trifle that Charlie, upon coming in
on his twelfth birthday finds the tiny room over the hall, duly prepared for his
special occupation, furniture embellished with scenes of the Huntsmen in Decalcomania, and the carved heads of Pointer and Fox on door and drawer, or that
the industrious little Annie should be greeted on Christmas morning with the
tasteful little work-stand and chair made for her special benefit; such examples
might be increased multitudinously, but it is all sufficient to show that we cannot spend too much time and care on this house which is our home, and that it
is "worth while" to do our very best with the material within our reach,
simple though they be.

With this, then each piece of furniture we can make by means of our own
ingenuity and taste is of itself a treasure. In Fig. 47, we show another dressing-
table, which will be found quite as ornamental and more useful than the preceding one.

It consists merely of a plain dry-goods box for the foundation in size, three feet
in height, four in width, and two feet six inches in depth, (or about these dimensions,) this has four blocks of wood one inch thick and four inches square
nailed beneath each corner, to which castors are screwed. The box is placed
with open side out, and this fitted with a shelf or two of them for containing
various articles; the whole interior should be neatly painted or papered and
varnished.

On each side (at the back), of the top are fastened two long narrow boxes,
which may be obtained generally, from the drug or dry-good stores. These
should be about two feet long and one wide, and from eight to ten inches deep.
By sawing pieces of lath to fit the sides, and tacking them on in proper position,
shelves may be made that will be convenient for holding various articles. The
covers to the boxes fitted with small hinges will make doors, and the whole
must be neatly finished with mouldings put on with small brads, and an ornamental top and base made of square boards an inch or two deeper than the cases
themselves. To these are screwed a pair of the iron brackets, which we can
purchase for from 35 to 50 cents, or for 75 cents to $1.00 fitted with lamps
complete.

These cases are screwed or nailed very securely on the top of the table, as
they are to sustain the glass which as shown by the illustration is of " comfortable size "—perfectly plain but of good quality and neatly framed. Such a one

can be purchased new for three or four dollars, and at second-hand, frequently for the half of that sum.

Over the top of the glass is fastened a frame, similar to the one described for the bedstead, around which is draped a hanging made of Swiss (figured or plain)

Fig. 47.

lined with rose-color, (or other tint). First, a width reaching from the top to within a few inches of the floor, is fastened to the upper back-ends of the semi-circular tester, the ends finished with a deep ruffle of the same, then on the tester above this is arranged two pieces, made by tacking a width of the Swiss and lining two yards long, folding it diagonally from corner to corner, cutting and trimming the two cut edges with ruffles of the same, and arranging them as shown in the illustration, around the top tack another ruffle made with an edge above the cord, which runs along the center of all the ruffles.

The table-top is covered with a piece of the Swiss over a lining like the curtains, and a drapery arranged around the front, made with rings at the top, which slide on a wire beneath the narrow ruffle finishing the edge. This allows access to the shelves within. The wood-work of this beautiful table should be carefully polished and ornamented to correspond with the rest of the furniture, which may be ebonized, enameled in colors, embellished with marquetry, ivory-inlaying, Decalcomania, painting, bronzing and gilding or enriched with carvings at pleasure. Any one of these methods of beautifying will be found elegant, and may be made perfect of its kind.

BEAUTIFUL TOILET-TABLE.

The beautiful toilet-table, the model of which is shown in Fig. 48, may be adapted to the size of the room, and can be draped to suit the furniture. An ordinary dry-goods packing-box will answer for the lower part; to this is screwed two upright strips of wood, four inches wide, six feet long and one inch thick, placed one-fourth distant from each side of the back; small strips of lath are nailed from each end of the back, diagonally, across to these strips, and two end pieces, and a back of the inch plank, nailed on the box; then a hoop is securely screwed to the top of the two uprights, projecting over towards the front. Pieces of wood are nailed on the under four corners, and castors inserted in them. This forms the frame-work, which is covered with scarlet or other colored velveteen, as also the plain mirror hung between the upright standards. Two short posts, one foot in length, are nailed to the front corners, and also covered with the velvet.

The entire box is next covered with crimson (or color to suit other surroundings), glazed muslin, over which is stretched (in gathered folds) dotted lace or Swiss muslin, edged with lace, and a full puff of the thin material. Drapery of the same, with a lined and full-gathered lambrequin, cut with long points in front and edged with the lace, finishes the tester at the top. Around the table a long, straight piece of the Swiss is taken up in graceful loops, held by ruched bands and bows, made of ribbon of the lining pinked out on each edge, the same ornamenting the top. The inside of the box, shelved and lined, is convenient for holding towels, bed-linen, etc.

The dressing stool, or ottoman, placed in front of this tasteful table, is made of a section of a barrel. The lower and open part has two strips of wood (such as was used for the "uprights" of the stand) fastened across the open part of the barrel, to which castors are screwed. The upper part is stuffed and cov-

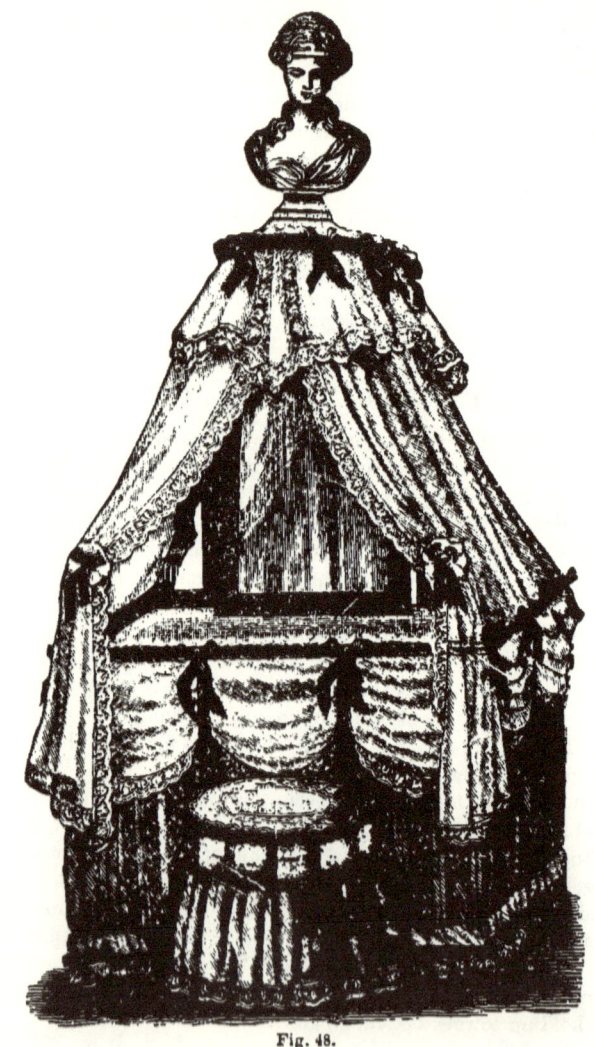

Fig. 48.

cred with an embroidered cushion, from which depends a curtain made of the Swiss, and lining like the table; a strip puffed around the edge with ruchings, as before described.

This table and stool are exceedingly elegant, and, in a small room, will be found very convenient, as even the ottoman, if turned the opposite way and fitted with a lid, may be made a convenient receptacle for shoes, etc.

WASH-STANDS.

The more simple and substantial articles of real service are made, the more consistent with wisdom, perhaps; yet one desires to see some little embellishment, even on these; and those not possessed with that æsthetic degree of taste, which can accept nothing that is not of the highest order, are willing, where they have not the means of procuring costly elegancies, to make a "virtue of necessity," and from "small beginnings" produce the "great endings," resulting in a handsome chamber suite, from a few dollars worth of plank, sundry empty boxes and barrels, upholstering materials, old or new, and the pretty embellishments now procured at so trifling a cost.

Thus, the pretty wash-stand belonging to the bedstead and dressing-table, we have described, will certainly excite the admiration of all who see it, and will, no doubt, create the desire to make a fac-simile, which, we are glad to say, may be easily done.

First, it will be perceived, that the table fits snugly in the corner, which is a great advantage where room is an object. A triangular box or case, made of a section of common packing-box will answer, and should be two feet on the sides, and two feet three inches in height, rounding out on the top and bottom in a gradual curve, two inches deeper at the center. Square blocks, two inches square, of inch stuff are nailed under the lower corners, in which castors are fastened. On the upper sides, are fastened two pieces of board, eight inches high at the front, and curved gracefully towards the back, where they unite in a point two feet high. This may be sawed out tastefully with the fret-saw, and carefully carved with tools, or merely sawed out in scrolls on the top, and embellished with painting, etc., according to the furniture, as before described. Against this back are fastened two narrow shelves, supported by brackets (the small ornamental iron ones answer well, and appear extremely tasteful, if of good design), or three single brackets of carved wood—a corner one high against the corner, one on each side, lower down, and placed flat against the sides.

These are to accommodate the various articles required on such a stand, the soap and tooth-brush vases, the mug and water-decanter, etc. The inside of the lower part is fitted with a shelf for the slop-pail, shoe-brushes, etc.

Six feet above the corner of the back a little corner bracket is arranged as a

Fig 49.

tester, and to hold a vase of flowers, statuette or other suitable ornament, and is fourteen inches deep on the sides, extending out about an inch and a half in a rounded form on the front. The wood-work of the stand is stained and embellished to suit the furniture of the room, and the top covered with a brown enameled oil-cloth, a lambrequin which is arranged to hang down one foot below the edge, and is cut out in a design figure, under which is laid oil-cloth of buff or other contrasting color, and the points bound with brown or buff worsted braid.

The hangings of Swiss muslin are to be lined and trimmed to suit the former pieces of furniture, though we give another style of hangings and lambrequins, in order to give our readers as great a variety from which to choose as possible.

This entire suite when tastefully gotten up, make as handsome an apartment as any one could desire, and when the beauty and substantial qualities of the work are considered, will amply repay for the expense of material.

Fig. 50, shows a more simple form of wash-stand still. An ordinary dry-goods box two feet six inches in length, and one foot ten inches in depth, two feet three inches high, has castors fastened on the four lower corners, and to the back is screwed very securely an upright piece about two feet high, (or the width of a board taken from the lid). To this are screwed two fancy brackets of iron or wood, for the support of a shelf fourteen inches wide.

On this is placed a looking-glass, which is screwed against the back-board and also further screwed, perhaps by a hook in the top passed through a nail in the wall.

This glass may have an exceedingly plain or shabby frame, as it is covered with a ruching of Swiss and lace over tinted muslin, and ornamented with full half-rosettes of the same.

The lower part of the box is divided into two parts, the one of which is shelved for the accommodation of towels, etc., the other covered on the bottom with oil-cloth for the slop-pail, etc. The entire case is enclosed and covered with Nottingham curtain lace in neat design over tinted muslin, and finished with a ruffle of lace and ruchings of the colored muslin worked on the edge or trimmed with imitation Valenciennes edging, which can be procured at wholesale for 25 cents per 11 yards. A full bow with a button and loop on the two sides of the curtains behind it finishes this beautiful cover. The top of the stand has a cover of white marbled oil-cloth, and the shelf and iron supports are painted with white zinc-enamel paint, and slightly marbled. For a small room this stand answers both for dressing-table and wash-stand, and for this reason is to be highly recommended.

A handsome and useful form of wash-stand is shown in Fig. 51, the foundation of which is a plain pine box, four feet long, two feet deep. This box is placed, with the open side out, and furnished with castors on the four corners.

The inside is divided into three compartments, each of the sides one and one-half feet wide, with shelves; the central one, one foot wide, for the accommodation of the slop-pail. On the back is arranged an uprihgt panel, three feet high, with side pieces, the center of which is sawed out to accommodate an oval mirror, which is screwed in through the outside. On the corners are fast-

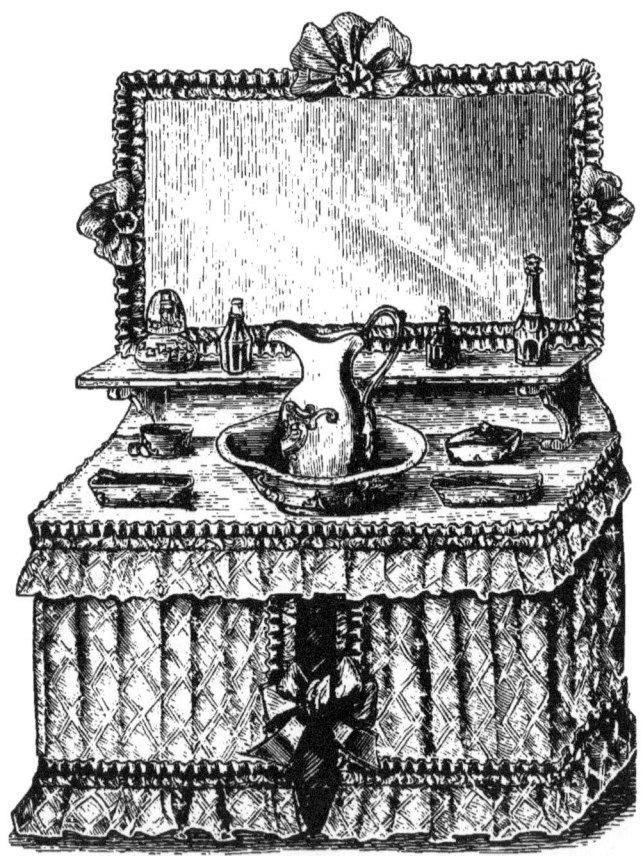

Fig. 50.

ened triangular caps, forming brackets, and, below these, are shelves, six inches long, supported by tasteful little brackets, which answer a useful purpose for holding various toilet articles. The manner of sawing out the back and side pieces, can be distinctly seen from the illustration. This back is made of nice, smooth wood, made smooth by rubbing with fine emery paper, and is painted with zinc-paint tinted a delicate pearl-gray, or lavender, and adorned with garlands of moss roses and lily of the valley, in Decalcomania. The front of the

Fig. 51.

stand has a curtain of material corresponding with the hangings of the room, finished with a ruffle and flat puff of the material, the same finishing the upper edge. An entire suite of furniture, made and finished to match this stand, would appear exceedingly handsome.

DRESSING–TABLE WITH HANGINGS.

Many families have plain wash-stands, such as are shown in the small illustration, Fig. 53, which may be made into charming dressing-tables in the following manner:

Take a piece of plank, four inches wide and eight feet long, which screw firmly against the back of the stand, as shown in Fig. 53; on this nail a circular piece of board, one foot six inches in diameter, around which fasten an umbrella frame, covered with muslin, and neatly lined, which will form a scalloped edge, which must be stiffened with wire. On this is arranged the canopy shown in the illustration, Fig. 52, made of figured Swiss, over pink or blue muslin.

Fig. 52.

Plait a circular piece over the top, and around the edge sew a strip twelve inches in width, around each edge of which are fluted and puffed ruffles; below this depends a curtain, one and one half yards long, also ruffled on the edge and drawn up into festoons. Beneath this, around the edge of the framing, is

Fig. 53.

fastened the long curtains, draped back and arranged on the arms or towel-racks of the stand (which must first be covered neatly with colored muslin and puffs of Swiss). The table is covered first with a colored cover and curtains of the lined Swiss; finished to correspond with the hangings. This curtain must open in front, in order to allow access to the drawer and shelf beneath, which is thus utilized as a receptacle for shoes, etc. A dressing-glass, cushion, and toilet-set ornament the stand, and bows of ribbon finish the different points where the curtains are fastened.

CHAPTER IX.

PARLORS AND MANTELS.

THE PARLORS.

In both England and America, the houses of the wealthy class, are generally arranged with a drawing-room, and parlors or *salons*. Where this is the case, the drawing-room is used as a reception-room, while the parlors are devoted to entertainment and the general use of the family, when guests are enjoying the hospitality of the house for an extended period.

Among the large middle classes however, the house is not usually so spacious as to admit of rooms being thus devoted to these separate interests, and we find in this country that the parlor or parlors, serve both as reception-room and that chosen apartment, which in the olden times was the " best room " of our grand-mothers.

As we are writing particularly for that large majority of Americans, " the million," who are walking in the enviable path, which is considered the happiest walk in life by the wise Apostle, who prays " give me neither poverty nor riches "—we shall devote no time to describing the " drawing-room," but confine ourselves to the embellishment and adornment of the parlors, making this apartment so complete and perfect in all its appointments, that it will be drawing-room and parlor combined.

Could we have the planning of each house in the land, whether large or small, we would say, if there can only be two rooms on one floor, let them open into each other with large double doors made to slide if possible, so that they may be rolled away out of sight, and allow graceful drapery to cover the opening. If there is a hall let it communicate in the same manner with the parlors.

This arrangement is not only far more conducive to health, but in case of company, it affords an opportunity of throwing the entire space into one, thus imparting an imposing appearance and an aspect of spaciousness, so pleasant when rooms are filled with company.

As the parlor in the majority of houses is the room devoted to the entertainment of guests, there is an apparent necessity for a liberal display of elegance, and those many attractions which tend to give pleasure to guests, and as it is a room sometimes (it may be supposed) opened for festivity, there may also be allowed a wider scope for embellishment and decoration, than in any other apartment. Here too are to be gathered whatever will amuse and entertain, and at the same time its arrangements are to be of such a character that they will afford comfort, and impart a sense of easy freedom to all gathered within its walls.

With these requirements, it is in the parlor therefore that we find the choicest treasures that the house can afford, that will tend to the hospitable entertainment of guests, just as in the sitting-room, or living-room are gathered the dearest tokens of love for the family circle. Here then we see walls softly but warmly tinted, and the pictures the handsomest and rarest the house affords; floors covered with the richest carpet that circumstances allow; the suite of furniture is covered with dark crimson or a rich glowing brown, covers, rugs, hangings, lambrequins and curtains correspond in color and tone with these surroundings; cabinet, *etagere*, brackets and shelves are laden with whatever will afford amusement or pleasure, while musical instruments, books, and the window with its tasteful floral arrangements, show the desire to make this pet-room the most attractive one to those outside, as well as to all within who enjoy its beauties. This is what the parlor of the beautiful and tasteful home should be, a room full of beauty and brightness, testifying at once to the large and generous hospitality, as well as to the taste and wise discrimination of the queen-mistress who reigns over the realm of which this is the state chamber.

Handsome or even tasteful furniture, rich hangings, gay covers, and beautiful carpets and paper are doubtless wonderful aids in making an imposing and attractive room, but far more necessary is judicious, artistic and wise arrangement.

Your carpet may be only a low-priced Ingrain, but let the colors be soft and warm, the design unobtrusive and the *making* perfect; and it will give only pleasure to the most fastidious, the walls may be rough and the ceilings low, but this will not be improved by a sprawling vine on the paper, nor a deep bright-colored border, cover such a wall first with a lining paper, and use a mere line for cornice, or better still, paper with dado and frieze, which will give apparent height.

Cover with some woolen stuff all the chairs and lounges, and let them all be noted for comfort rather than beauty, make the chairs low and improvise two or three lounging "Sleepy Hollows"; if you have none else, hang the windows with curtains even though they be but of coarse Swiss. Curtains are capable of giving such a deal of comfort to say nothing of *style*.

Scatter a few books and the latest papers on table and sofa, and let them look as if they had been so interesting that they had been read, yet never allow soiled books, or dirty crumpled papers to disgrace your neat room. Let dainty baskets of work occupy stand and window-seat, and never omit the daily bouquets, if only of bright Autumn leaves and grasses, but who cannot have a few sprays of blossoms during each day of Winter?

Keep every spot immaculately clean, but not distressingly so, that is do not among guests by dusting and wiping in their presence, nor show signs of terror if their rude children wipe their sticky hands on curtain or dainty tidy.

A pretty clock is admissible in a parlor, but it should be a tasteful one.

Place boxes of games, scrap-books and portfolios filled with pictures, photograph albums and objects of amusement, such as the stereoscope, kaleidoscope, and microscope, in appropriate places, and place chairs near them.

If possible, obtain one statuette, at least, supposing it be Canova's "Dancing Girl," in plaster. This is lovely, placed on a pedestal, near the piano, and stands, with the pedestal, five feet from the floor. Or, upon a pretty bracket, stand "The Fish Boy," no more graceful figure was ever made ; or, if not these, obtain that lovely group of "Aurora and her attendants." These may be obtained for from one to five dollars, and will add wonderful beauty to a room, especially if draped with fine white Tarlatan or soft Tulle.

Nothing imparts such an air of real artistic beauty to a room as pictures well framed, and a few pieces (one, if the room is small ; three, if large) of graceful statuettes, purely white, and copies of really noted works of Art.

It is by such tasteful arrangements that a room assumes that indescribable air of comfort and, perhaps, luxuriousness, which is so attractive to the eye of taste.

Many rooms, expensively furnished, are cold and barren, so far as real beauty is concerned, whereas, many a cottage house possesses that real attractiveness which makes all who enter it exclaim, "How lovely!" simply because the mistress, with an innate love for the beautiful, understands what to put in her house, and, better still, how to arrange it. It is the thousand little contrivances, the many little felicities that, emanating from a fertile imagination, always on the alert for "something *pretty* wherewith to beautify her home," inspires the tasteful woman and makes her work successful, and gives her the subtle power to make her home a little Eden.

MANTELS.

Within the past few years, there has been a change made in regard to the mantel, which is, in many respects, a decided improvement ; we allude to the use of lambrequins and covers of various kinds. A richly carved marble or wooden mantel is, in itself, an object of great beauty ; but so few can avail themselves of such an addition to their rooms, that resource has been had to miserable, bald-looking, stiff and most inelegant substitutes, in default of carving, ornaments (?) with most extraordinary achievements of the carpenter, in the shape of impossible figures, and astonishing mouldings, or those efforts the painter, with "splotchy" imitations of marble of all colors of the rainbow, or representations of wood that never had an equal in marvelous-

Fig. 51.

8

ness of "streaked and striped and spotted." To be allowed to cover all this with graceful hangings, or elegantly embroidered lambrequin, and find that even the indisputable Mrs. Grundy pronounces it "in style," is a satisfaction, indeed.

There is no portion of the room requiring greater care, and knowledge of internal embellishment, than the mantel, and, of late, it receives the attention due to such a prominent feature of the apartment.

Do not allow any apartment, unless it is a simple boudoir, to be destitute of this finish, for, even though the parlor, library, dining-room, or chamber, be ever so simply furnished, the addition of a tasteful mantel will, at once, change the whole aspect of the room, and give it a new dignity. Many will exclaim, "But there is not a mantel in my house, so I could not cover it, even if I had the material and was prepared to do so."

Once this was the case, perhaps, but, in this day, among other improvements and inventions, has appeared the beautiful "impromptu mantel."

MANTEL WITH LAMBREQUIN EMBELLISHED WITH AP-PLICATION OR DECALCOMANIA DESIGNS.

The superb mantel shown in Fig. 54 is made of richly carved marble, but a more simple one may be substituted, and we offer it, more to show a tasteful and artistic arrangement, than for the mere form of the mantel. An imposing effect is produced by applying heads found on *Cretonne*, or in the Decalcomania designs, or more artistic still by using photographs, to silk-merino or any smooth cloth; arranging one as a medallion, in the center of each lambrequin point, then surrounding with embroidery.

In the olden times, ladies wrought entire pieces, or "bolts," of rich material for hangings and "tapestries," many of them requiring years to finish; but, once accomplished, they were heir-looms, worth handing down to the "generations to come." Why should not our ladies employ their leisure in making hangings and other elegancies that need not require but a few weeks to complete?

The antique fire-screen in front of the grate, may be beautifully imitated by a painting, in Grecian style, directions for which are given in a later chapter on modes of embellishing, or it may be embroidered in silk or Berlin wool-work at pleasure.

The cover of this mantel is brown cloth, bordered with the lambrequins above described. On the center of each point, apply an oval medallion, four inches long, of black silk held with cord stitched on the edge, and on them place antique heads. Another way to make such heads, is this: Cut the heads from gray velvet, and coat them on the wrong side with a fine paste, made of starch and a little gum arabic. When dry, paint with Indian ink, executing the work with a fine camel's hair brush, moisten slightly, and apply these to the black medallion, and, when dry, outline with silk of same color in button-hole stitching. Embroider the remainder of the pattern with brown silk and gold cord or thread, with a little half-polka stitching of scarlet silk and satin, point Russe

Fig. 55.

and chain stitching of darker red. Work the flowers pink and the arabesques fawn-color, in satin stitch, using yellow or gold for the stamens. The application on the outer edge is of dark-brown cloth and fawn-colored silk, edged with gold cord. Fasten the dots of brown cloth with knots of gold thread.

Fig. 56.

The cloth application is bordered with ecru soutache, edged with light and dark-brown silk cord.

There may be some of our readers who would enjoy imitating the elegant mantel shown in the accompanying illustration, Fig. 59, which may be perfectly done by using a certain amount of care in finishing the various details. The form of the mantel is exceedingly graceful, and is made of a shelf, cut in projecting form, with a front made simply of matched flooring boards, fitted around its outer edge. This is placed upon strong brackets nailed against the wall, in order to give greater solidity to the framework. Upon each side of this central part, are placed large wooden brackets, sixteen inches from wall to outer edge, and twelve inches wide. As will be seen, these are sustained by panels reaching to the floor, and extending outward, resting on heavy pieces of wood fourteen inches long by twelve wide. This forms the frame-work, upon which the ornamental parts are arranged.

All the handsome scroll work of this mantel may be found in the rich "Artificial" wood-carvings previously mentioned, which after being completely finished may be ebonized or bronzed, either giving a rich and perfect finish.

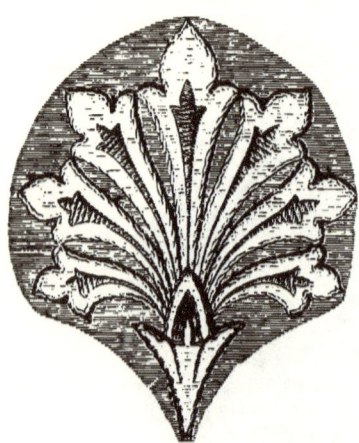

Fig. 57.

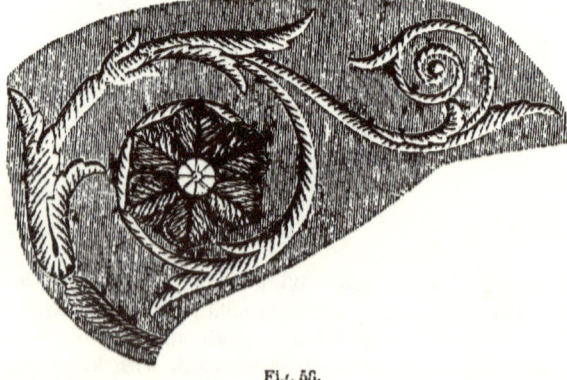

Fig. 58.

Fig. 59.

The ornamentation may of course be changed to suit the taste, as some may prefer Grecian or Roman heads, scrolls of certain form with other parts to correspond, but we would suggest the following, any of which may be obtained

Fig. 60.   Fig. 61.

from the establishments where these articles are kept. For the central ornament beneath the shelf, the Cherub, Fig. 60; for the panels on each side such a pair of scrolls as Fig. 61, which are arranged right and left for different sides; or the nearer imitation of leaves, and flowers of Fig. 62, at the bottom ornamental shells, and beneath the side brackets the exquisite Sleeping Cherubs, Fig. 63.

This would give sufficient embellishment to appear rich without being overdone, and when carefully finished appear what it really is, an elegant mantel, and a most perfect imitation of the original.

The front may be ornamented either with fret-work made of one-fourth inch wood, butternut or any light color, laid over a black, ebonized surface, or it may be em-

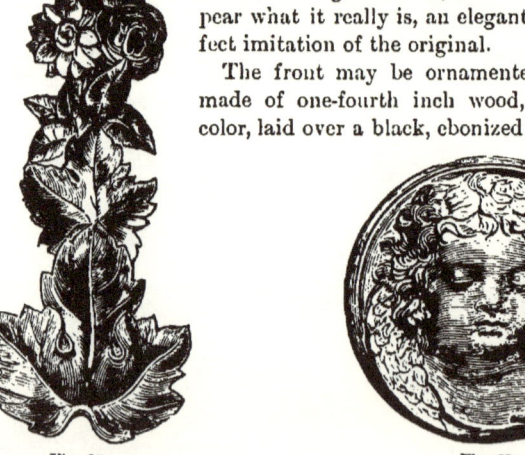

Fig. 62.   Fig. 63.

broidered with application to match the lambrequin which covers the front of the shelf. The chimney or grate is covered with a tasteful board ebonized and ornamented with a design.

This illustration is given merely to afford an opportunity for copying one of the richly carved mantels so highly esteemed.

There are many different modes of ornamenting this same mantel, and indeed of making the shelf itself, the simplest of which is to screw a plain wooden plank of desired length upon two iron or wooden brackets, and cover with material corresponding with the curtains and upholstering.

These iron brackets may be had in various forms, many of them exceedingly beautiful in design and finish, others of the most simple character.

Fig. 64.

Where these are impracticable, a wooden support may be substituted in two triangular pieces of wood, answering for the braces beneath the shelf, the drapery to be so arranged as to entirely conceal the rough frame-work.

We may cover such a shelf with paper or glazed muslin on the upper surface, (on account of the ease by which it may be dusted,) or if preferred this may receive a coat of paint and varnish, then a tasteful lambrequin cut like Fig. 64, which will be found an unusually elegant piece of work, and may be used just as described, unless any other style of embroidery or adornment is preferred.

This exquisite lambrequin is not difficult to make, and presents a charming appearance; it requires purple velvet, yellow silk, green merino or cloth of two or three shades, yellow and green embroidery silk.   The pattern for the pansies is shown in the large figure, and may be easily copied and arranged.

After cutting out the yellow petals, take black silk, and embroider the dots and long stitches, then touching the wrong side with a paste of starch and gum arabic, fasten them in clusters, as shown in the lambrequin, work the 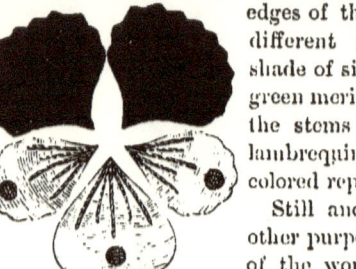 edges of the leaves, (cut from the green merino of different shades,) in button-hole stitching same shade of silk.   Make buds of the purple velvet and green merino, or embroider them if preferred.   Work the stems of green silk in half-polka stitch.   The lambrequin here shown, was made of dark amber-colored reps.

Fig. 65.

Still another beautiful lambrequin for this and other purposes, such as brackets, and baskets is made of the wonderful creations constructed of cork, of which we show a meagre sample in Fig 66, for it is utterly impossible in a mere engraving to show the surprising effects of which this material is capable.

In Germany, the designs are sold ready prepared for such fancy work, but here we are obliged to make them, and it is done by first cutting out medallions from some light colored silk, say gray, painting the sky with transparent colors, and lightly sketching a little landscape of some kind, such as an old ruin, a monastery building or a tiny castle, with moat and draw-bridge, then from the virgin-cork, shave thin pieces, which present all the beautiful shades of old stone and wood, cut these into shape with knife and scissors, make windows and doors, by building on small pieces and touching up with colored paint, glue these carefully on the medallion, and with pretty bark, dyed mosses, Autumn-leaves, etc., arrange trees, bushes and creeping vines climbing over ruined gateways, and hanging in long festoons from tower and battlement. When finished satisfactorily, edge the medallion with cord and long stitches and knots of colored silk.   In our model, the lambrequin is a dull red, almost a reddish brown, and the effect of the light medallion, with its lovely landscapes is wonderfully imposing, indeed the exquisite beauty of this work cannot be imagined from a mere description, but we assure our readers it is well worth a trial.

For bracket lambrequins, these cork-landscapes are exceedingly appropriate, and they are very durable if carefully glued together, only requiring a daily touching with the feather-duster, or bunch of feathers.   After the lambrequins are thus finished, fasten them on the mantel by means of ordinary tin tacks covered afterwards with cord or gimp, or use gilt headed nails, (the star-heads if they can be procured).   Place a tassel or woolen ball on each point.   Thus you have an elegant mantel at small expense, though it may be greatly elaborated if desired. Thus, in the center of each point may be embroidered a design either floral or other, in chenille and gold thread, or the material may be of the most costly description, and trimmed with rich gimp and fringe.

Imitation of marble with plaster, forms one of the most exquisite shelves imaginable. The shelf is supported by long flat wooden brackets, (as in the ordinary wooden mantel,) the whole is covered smoothly with muslin, and washed or painted with a mixture of fine plaster of Paris mixed in thin gum water; scrolls or flowers of muslin (or both) are then arranged, to form tasteful enrichment on the flat surface, care being observed not to be profuse in using too

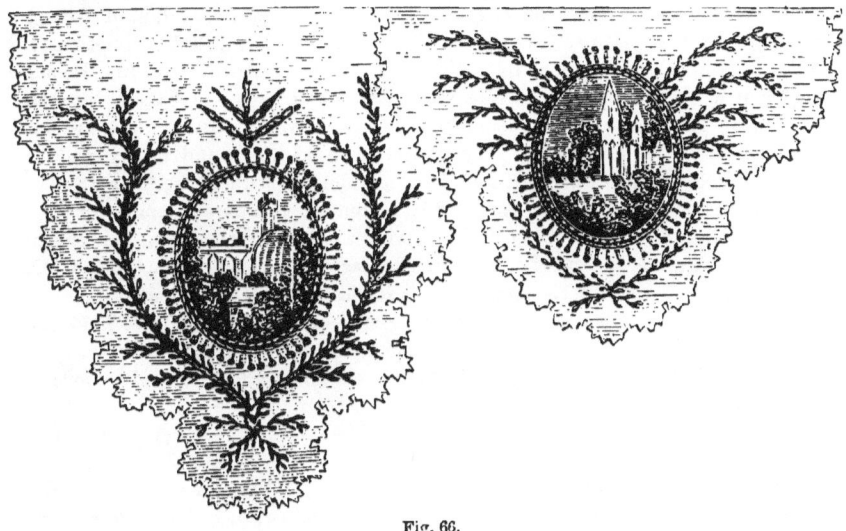

Fig. 66.

many, for this is the great fault with all imitations, they are applied with such a generous hand, that the critical observer is immediately led to imagine that the work is not genuine, and a close examination follows; whereas, were there no more ornament than one is apt to see on fine pieces of work, it would appear beautiful and perhaps genuine, at least it would not offend the eye of correct taste.

A neat braiding along the edge of the one inch (deep) shelf, is made by taking a long strip of muslin one and a quarter inches wide, and gathering it perpendicularly in spaces one inch apart, and tacking on with tiny thin tacks, a half wreath of lilies, roses, or other flowers with leaves on the board beneath the shelf, making it heavy in the center and gradually diminishing towards the ends ; a cluster of the same on each bracket, heavy at the top and lessening as it runs towards the base, with flutings of muslin on the various parts that appear too blank and bare ; this much ornamentation will appear quite perfect, whereas 'the entire wood-work covered with a heterogeneous mass of floral specimens would present a loose patchy appearance, not only devoid of good taste, but impossible to keep neat and free from dust.

The flowers, etc., for this work have been fully explained in "Household Elegancies," but lest any should not have this, we would merely say, cut the various parts from muslin as in wax-flower making, stiffen with nice flour starch with a little dissolved white glue added, (one quarter of a pound to a gallon of paste,) and put together with stems, copper wire, (or any material that will not rust). After finishing, dip into or paint with the plaster, then varnish with fine Demar sufficient to give the gloss of white marble. The flutings are passed through the fluting machine, and the various parts moulded while a little damp, and flat surfaces are ironed until dry. This mantel when carefully and neatly made is so exceedingly beautiful that it may be recommended without hesitation.

That it is constantly taken for marble, is but an indifferent point, for if an object pleases, and is perfect of its kind, what matter, whether it is *the* material or not, it is a material and the workmanship as fine of its kind as that of the sculptor, probably cost (comparatively) as much time and labor and skill.

We know this theory is considered treason, but as Americans we hold the right to have our-opinion, and though we enjoy works of real Art as heartily as "the others" do, we also enjoy just as fully the fine imitation, and believe it worth encouragement.

In elegant mansions, it is usual to have a sub-mantel above or below the major shelf, and a series of brackets or narrow shelves, extending above in some cases many feet. This is done to afford the connoisseur, and virtuosi, who enjoy collecting rare old pottery, and other *bric-a-brac*, an opportunity to arrange their treasures in conspicuous and appropriate position, and the effect is extremely imposing in the sketches of the drawing-room and library at Bellevue House, before mentioned a similar plan of making upper shelves to the mantel shows what fine effects may be produced by it, and to which Mr. Conway thus alludes in "Harper's Monthly ;"—" The artists (Mr. Scott's) collection of old majolica, china, and other objects of similar kind, serve to render his chimney pieces particularly beautiful, * * * in the drawing-room the jambs are paneled, the panels filled with mirrors, and divided half way down, two feet nine from the floor, by a shelf large enough to accommodate a lamp or candle, with a tea-cup or other object. The arrangement is admirable for utility and beauty. A supplementary chimney-shelf is added here also, a marble one ; and rising nearly to the ceiling is a surface of black-wood, with brackets for the exhibition of some very fine old Hispano-Moresque ware, the golden metallic lustre of which is favorably seen against the black. The center is filled with Mr. Scott's own most beautiful picture of " Eve," etc." We give this sketch that our readers may have a guide if they should desire to copy one of the celebrated mantels of England —and also that they may feel no hesitation in adopting this arrangement, which is common in houses where Art and Taste walk hand in hand, and " *dwell together in unity*."

Instead of filling such panels with mirror, imitation of tiles or glazed pictures might be substituted, and the little supplementary shelf is easily accomplished, as also the brackets running up each side, and the black " *surface of wood* " rising almost to the ceiling, while instead of the beautiful picture of " Eve," the lovely chromo of " Beatrice," or some fine engraving would appear quite as well to those who never saw the " Eve." On such shelves many articles valued for various reasons, could be conspicuously displayed, and yet be entirely out of the reach of "those busy and curious fingers," which make you tremble each time they handle your "heart's best treasures."

We cannot refrain from adding a brief description of the chimney-piece in the library from the same pen, and for a similar reason, for it will afford a still easier subject for copy. " The white marble jambs and architraves, are designs diapered with leaves —laurel and ivy of Indian red color, and above the chimney-shelf is a second chimney-piece and shelf, giving thus double accommodation for objects of ornament or use."

In this case, a beautiful chimney might be made by obtaining two largepanes of glass, and having them cut lengthwise, (or three long narrow strips to extend upon each side and across the top,) on these to paint or transfer Decalcomania pictures of the beautiful ivy and laurel leaves, (or other floral designs) and cover over with fine white paint, two or three coats, which gives *the effect* of fine tiles, upon being turned over and viewed from the polished surface of the glass ; these to be fastened against the sides and across the top with light mouldings of wood, and the mantel rising above the cross-piece or architrave, while three feet above is arranged another shelf, and on each side of this six inches above, neat brackets for lamps or vases. A chimney thus made would well imitate the elegant one described so ably by Mr. Conway, and perchance give as much satisfaction.

In the accompanying design will be seen one of Mr. Conway's sketches of a chimney-piece, which can be beautifully imitated, to occupy the position of the original, a dining-room where such ornamentation is more appropriate than hangings. In this case as before, either painting or Decalcomania will prove effective in imitation of tiles, or painted or transferred directly upon the wood, previously ebonized or enameled.

Such charming designs of animals, game and the other appropriate figures are found among the Decalcomania designs, that we feel inclined to urge our readers to procure these, explicitly stating when they order, that they require such and such figures. The scene in the circular frame in the center, with deer and stag, will be readily found, as also the various surroundings, and we would suggest the use of oval or circular frames, both for the deer and dog's heads, ebonizing them as also the surrounding wood-work, and putting them on the outside of the glass, the ground-work of which may be any color desired; white or buff will be found very beautiful for such panels.

Fig. 67.

The Minton designs exhibited at the Exposition in Vienna, were of the most exquisite character, and we feel glad to be able to show a few illustrations of these beautiful works of Art, hoping they may aid some of our readers who possess artistic skill, and can use the brush and colors effectively, to imitate them on plates of china or glass. The charming pair, shown in Figs. 68 & 69, would prove beautiful and most appropriate additions to the fire-place ; or, framed as *plaques*, they would add wonderful interest to a collection of pictures on the walls of any apartment.

Any blank space on the wall may be furnished as a chimney-place, where none really exists in the house, by arranging the shelves and space beneath as directed ; and if a still more decided imitation is desired, long, narrow pieces of board, beneath the shelf (against the wall), covered and dressed with plaitings of the Swiss or Tarlatan will still further give the impression. A tasteful picture of some kind, appears well in the space designed for the chimney-place, when viewed from a distance, but as the object is below the line of vision, it cannot be seen with good effect when close to it.

Where real utility is an object, covers of dimity, linen or muslin, will be found most satisfactory.

Upon plain surfaces, borders of braid stitched on with the machine, or narrow braid in figures ; gay *Cretonne* figures chain-stitched by hand or machine, or fastened with braid, or silhouettes cut

Fig. 68.

out from black muslin and put on in the same manner, will be found very appropriate. We have seen Decalcomania designs transferred to plain goods that presented a beautiful appearance as long as the ground remained clean, but of course couldn't be washed. Such a lambrequin is shown in Fig. 70, and is very elegant.

A beautiful hanging for a mantel or window-seat is shown in Fig. 71, consisting of black velveteen with medallions of application work, set in oval spaces cut out from the cloth ; or they may be stitched on it, and the stitches hid with narrow gimp or braid. These are on cloth of light ground, and surrounding them are groups of flowers and figures cut from dark *Cretonne*, with light tracery done with silk in chain-stitch. If desired, the lambrequin may have three instead of two points. The edge is finished with a narrow row of scarlet cloth pinked out and fastened on with machine stitching.

Any mantel-shelf is improved by a velvet hanging; if it is endurable in its plain state, the lambrequin will improve it; and if of bad form or shabby, it is rendered quite ornamental thereby. For this cover, measure the shelf, and get a board two feet longer than it, and half as wide again.

Fig. 69.

Velveteen answers well for this hanging, but cloth, reps, or damask will not collect the dust.

Tack this over the top and edges of the plank, straining it perfectly smooth; then add a lambrequin, either shaped out, or straight and laid in plaits; in the latter case edging with fringe. Tack a row of fringe along the upper edge with star-head-ed tacks.

Where a handsome form is desired, saw out the plank in form of Fig. 71, and after tacking on a straight valance of the velvet, edge with a heavy woolen fringe of the same shade, and over this arrange a tassel fringe of gold-color silk.

If the hearth is left bare (as some prefer), it should be washed or painted with fine plaster of Paris, put on hot. This will leave the stone or brick of dazzling whiteness.

It is so customary in this country to build houses with flues only and no chimney-places, that many do not possess this really beautiful finish to their rooms. To such, we would suggest that they make false chimney-places by putting up a mantel, and beneath it, arrange a panel with section sawed out in form of an arched or square chimney-place; into this they may fit one of the many beautiful fire-boards described in "Ladies' Fancy Work," or in Summer this may have one of the gauzy looking fire-papers tacked into the opening, the effect of which will be found charming. The panel of wood can be painted or covered to correspond with the mantel-shelf. These papers present a light airy appearance that is peculiarly cool and refreshing in Summer. The "gas-light green" and white Tarlatan with clusters of white Tarlatan moss-rose buds is specially lovely.

In conclusion, there is one point that should be particularly brought before our readers, which is, to fill the open fire-place, grate or even the hearth (behind the fender) with a large box, or several pots containing good soil with ferns, ivy and other climbing or green plants which will flourish in the shade. These will grow on during the hot Summer days, and give a bit of wild-wood greenness and a wild "woodsy" fragrance, to an otherwise black spot, looking only a little less grimy than "a blacksmith's forge on Sunday." A sprinkling of water each morning, a visit now and then to the glade and glen, and you may have the sweetest, the most refreshing of chimney-places, that neither English earl, nor French noble, may outvie with imported and costly tiles, or carved marbles, nor master-artist rival in fine form or rare color—for "behold the lilies of the field * * * Solomon in all his glory was not arrayed like one of these." For such a floral arrangement, a rustic fender is very appropriate, and may be readily constructed with gnarled and twisted branches and roots of trees, sprigs of spruce wood, and such ornaments as nuts, cones and acorns.

Fig. 70.

The frame or fender around the outside is made of plain plank, and will be found to be vastly improved by a padding and cover of black velveteen, secured by rows of gilt-headed tacks. Within this a cover of enameled oil-cloth will appear well, care being used to obtain suitable colors that will harmonize with the remainder of the mantel and wood-work of the apartment.

Many object to designs of game in a dining-room, and for such, there are fruit and flower groups of richest colors and most exquisitely arranged.

Where some member of the family has a taste for painting, time could be delightfully and profitably employed in painting, with transparent colors upon the glass, using foil to bring out the brilliant tints, and painting the groundwork.

The brilliant beauty of this style of work cannot be imagined, unless seen in all its gorgeous tints against the planished foil, and whether the design be some wonderful group of flowers tinted in Oriental splendor, or rich mosaics copied from Renaissance or mediæval designs, the work is sufficiently imposing to stand the test of close and critical observation, and comparison with the richest tiles.

If by any reason, persons are prevented from using such ornamentation as we have described for their dining-rooms; a simple lambrequin of brown, gray or dull buff-chintz, linen or woolen material may be embroidered in chain-stitch, or Berlin patterns of fruit, game, a hunting scene, or such characteristic arrangements will appear the next best mode of making a suitable mantel, the shelf or shelves of which can support various pretty knick-knacks, in the way of plates handsomely painted in colors or embellished with "smoke-painting,"

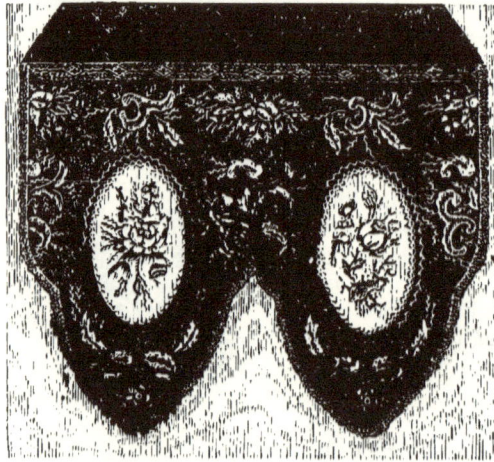

Fig. 71.

spray-work, etc., as also curiosities of appropriate character, and relics such as heir looms of china now so eagerly sought after.

It is a popular idea to have the various bed-rooms of a house called by the names of the color with which they are furnished, as "the Blue Room," the "Crimson Room," the "Yellow Room," and the idea is a good one, adopted by decorative artists generally, but care must be taken never to allow the predominating color to become "loud" and "obtrusive," with garish tints that strike with repugnant force the critical eye.

For the mantel-piece in the neat pretty chamber, nothing can be more appropriate than covers of colored muslin, blue, pink, green, or buff, (suited to the tint of the walls, carpet and upholstering.) over which dainty dresses of sheer Swiss muslin, or Tarlatan with fluffy puffs, and crisp ruffles, knots of ribbon and bands of the under material pinked out on each edge. Even should such covers require yearly renewing they are not costly, besides, this need not be the case, as we know by experience, having refreshed a set by careful washing, *clear* starching and ironing for three successive years.

Where there is no mantel, make one, by obtaining a board of proper length and width, and merely screw it firmly against two triangular pieces fixed like backets agaist the wall. Cover on top with oil-cloth or paper, (easily kept freer from dust,) and around it tack a cover sufficiently deep to hide the brackets; over this arrange a plaited ruffle, trimmed with narrow flutings and puffs, which if made on the straight thread of the material will be easily laundered. Two small bracket shelves above this main one covered in the same way, will give a pretty finish, while the space below, if not arranged as a fire-place, or filled with a grate, may have an ornamental paper according to directions in "Ladies' Fancy Work," or leather-work board.

9

CHAPTER X.

THE LIBRARY.

In every house where it is practicable there should be a room (even though a small one) specially devoted to quiet and retirement. There are always some members of a family who desire at some period during the twenty-four hours, to be alone for purposes of study, writing or reading; therefore, and also on account of having a proper place for the arrangement of the books, it is well to devote an apartment to the purposes of books and study, though in America this is not considered as essential to comfort as in Europe, where every house of ordinary size has its library.

In this room, the furniture should be of a simple and substantial character, oak or walnut wood being considered the most appropriate, though in houses where the back-parlor is used as the library, or living-room and library are merged into one, this stereotyped rule is in a measure overruled.

In small houses, it is a pleasant and most comfortable arrangement to furnish the sitting-room partially as a library; that is, with book-cases and the large table in the center of the floor; but of course this does away with any chance for quiet, and for this reason most persons prefer to devote even a small room to the sole purpose and legitimate objects of a library—that of a study, or the *Sanctum Sanctorum*. There are varieties of opinion regarding this subject of proper furniture for the library. Mr. Eastlake and his adherents advise old oak for material, with green as the best harmonizing color for upholstering and covers, and stern simplicity of style. His book-cases look like a portion of some old barn, with door in the roof and heavy iron hinges and bolts. With regard to this book-case, we quote from "Household Taste": "For material, oak is far the best wood to use both for appearance and durability. Unpolished mahogany (he might have added walnut also) acquires a good color with age. It also looks well, stained black and covered with a thin coat of varnish."

THE LIBRARY TABLE.

That important piece of furniture, the library table, should be of simple form and solid construction. The wood of which such a table is made is optional, but walnut, oak, or plain pine stained or ebonized, will be found the most appropriate.

As we have stated, it is our intention always to describe one or more pieces of each variety of furniture, which a person may make themselves, or have made at a merely nominal price; for during the leisure time always found in Winter, when carpenters are more or less unoccupied, such little jobs as ladies may require will be cheerfully—perhaps gladly—performed, and, as has been said, at low prices. We would take a moment to mention in this connection that it has been our custom for many years to embrace this opportunity, when workmen have really nothing scarcely to occupy them, to get trellises, pieces of furniture, and window-boxes or other floral "arrangements" attended to; and have always found (both in city and country), that the workmen are really glad to have

Fig. 72.

these demands made on them. Persons have frequently appeared surprised, when our yard, garden and porches were arranged in the Spring, to see many tasteful, and as has been (perhaps censoriously) remarked, extravagant embellishments added to our premises, for which upon attempting to copy, they were charged three times as much, simply because the workmen's hands were full. This will be found a new application for the trite proverb, "A stitch in *time* saves nine."

The style of furniture now so popular with many persons, that is the old Gothic, will be found exceedingly well adapted to ordinary use, and may be made to assume that quaint, ancient appearance so attractive to the artistic taste of certain persons who find the highest beauty in everything of a mediæval character; to such the furniture we describe as "home-made" would possess the greatest charms.

In making such furniture, the heavy iron hinges and locks, large screws, and indeed any such appliances as are seen on very old furniture or buildings, and which may still be procured at hardware stores, will be perfectly adapted to this purpose; and the real utility which will thus be attached to each article made, will enhance its value in the eyes of those who desire to furnish their homes with "beauty" that will in the true sense of the word prove "a joy *forever.*" The round-headed screws here mentioned are really objects of beauty when gilded, plated or bronzed; and a table, cabinet or other heavy piece of furniture fastened with them will appear massive and elegant, as we hope will be proved by all who make the library table about to be described. This is made of plain pine boards, the top of matched flooring, fitted up closely. The planks for frame are one inch thick, four inches in length, and the height from the floor two feet and five inches; the legs, which cross diagonally, are three feet long and four inches wide; in the center where they intersect, the width of the board is cut out from the inner side of the outer to form a neat joint; along the edges they are sawed out in any manner desired, to form an ornamental edge and render the weight lighter. They are screwed together at the center, and the cross-bar, is brought through by a mortise and secured by a peg of ornamental shape. The ledgers, which support the top are simply screwed to the outer side of the legs. The top itself is formed of half-inch board, nine inches each of which is secured to the ledgers by four round-headed screws; and after all are fixed in position, two supplementary ledgers are placed below to which they are all screwed.

Two triangular pieces are also screwed in to prevent any lateral weakness. The groove and tenon edges of the match-board admit of common match-boards, which may be used for the top, being strongly and easily put together. Next the cover is tacked on and held with strips of half-inch board an inch wide, which are screwed around the edges, and make a neat finish.

The longer pieces on the sides are first adjusted, then the corner ones overlapping the former are screwed down. The corner strips being fastened by two screws, will keep the others firmly in their places, and all the edges can then be trimmed, and after being rubbed off with sand-paper, must be stained and finally polished.

All screws used in this style of work are of the "round-headed" kind, which project above the wood-work, and assist in making it decorative.

THE CHAIRS.

The chairs of this style are of primitive simplicity as to form, but will be found most comfortable in form and handsome in appearance, which combined with their strength and utility, renders them all that could be desired for ordinary use.

The first is in height two feet nine inches, height of seat one foot two inches, its breadth one foot three inches. The six pieces of wood which form the sides of the seat, the back and legs are cut from one inch plank, the pieces across the back and seat are one-half inch plank. The form of the various parts must be sawed out according to taste, and this will not be difficult, as the form is clearly shown in the illustration. Care must be taken in screwing the legs together to saw the back ones so that the seat will be an inclined plane—and the back set back sufficiently to give a comfortable rest to the shoulders, which is done by making the back legs rather shorter than the front, and sawing off the front part of the bottom where they rest on the floor.

Cover the seat with canvas, stuff firmly and cover with cloth, oil-cloth or embroidery; for the library the leather cloth is much used, brass-headed nails, and a little lambrequin finish the seat, and the wood-work may be embellished in any mode desired.

The Arm Chair, is similar, but the seat should be one and one-half inches lower for a lady's use, and it is well to have a pair of these, the one high, the other as has been described. The dimensions too as to width and depth should be increased to twenty inches in breadth by eighteen in depth. Castors should be fastened beneath the cross-pieces below each leg, and the back and arms comfortably stuffed. Large round-headed screws and brass-nails give these chairs a most substantial and primitive appearance which, in this day, when mediæval furniture is bringing great prices, will be fully appreciated.

We confess to having a strong predilection for this sensible class of household furniture, which should certainly be popular in America during this time, when every pulse beats with the earnest desire to bring forth and possess old things.

All these articles will require a thorough and final polishing, and in case of the chairs, this might better be done prior to the upholstering.

Many kinds of light wood, pine, cedar, cherry and butternut, for instance, are made extremely handsome by simply oiling or varnishing, which darkens the color very slightly, and French polish will give a deeper tinge still.

The brackets accompanying this suite of furniture may appear severely simple in appearance, but will be found appropriate, and even elegant when made of richly grained wood, and

Fig. 73.

neatly adorned with fret-work and inlaying. As these require only small pieces of wood, the finer kinds may be used, and if the pine of which the furniture is made, is stained in imitation of walnut, oak or rosewood, the bracket may be made of the genuine article, the real wood, or better still elegant veneerings may be applied to the surface, and the finest effects result from the operation if well performed, for these veneerings of the finer kinds of wood contain the most elegant curls and markings from the heart of the tree, and are rich and beautiful beyond description.

When for economy's sake, deal (pine-wood) is employed, it is better to paint it in flatted color, because this can be renewed from time to time. Indian red and slate-gray are perhaps the best general tints when used for ordinary domestic fittings, but these may be effectively relieved by patterns and borders of white and yellow. Sometimes a mere line introduced here and there to define the construction, with an angle ornament (which may be stenciled) at the corners, will be sufficient. * * * * "It is usual for the lower shelves alone to be enclosed by doors, the upper being better left open for easy access to the books. The shelves themselves should never be less than an inch in thickness for a span of four feet. A little leather valance should be nailed against the outer edges. This not only protects the books from dust, but when the leather is scalloped (or we would add, pinked out) and stamped in gilt patterns, it adds considerably to the general effect. There is usually a kind of frieze running around the top, between the books and cornice above them. This space may well be decorated with painted ornament in the form of arabesques, armorial bearings, and appropriate texts. The pilasters which separate one compartment from another might be effectively treated in the same manner."

A quaint book-case of this style could be readily "gotten up" and ornamented to suit the taste, and prove really a most useful and surely (from high authority) *stylish* piece of furniture. On the top of such a set of book-cases, statuettes, busts and urns seem a fitting decoration, and, as Mr. Perkins says, is a custom of very ancient date, as proved from the lines:

"Indocti primum; quanquam plena omnia gypso
Chrysippi invenias. . . . .

and he continues, "the bust of a great author seems fitly placed on the top of a book-case."

Marble busts placed on pedestals and statuettes on brackets, with vases, bronzes and other articles of *vertu*, are most suitable ornaments for the library. To correspond with the old style book-case described on the preceding pages, a simple table, such as we gave for the sitting-room, and a chair of the kind called the "Cromwell."

The "Square English Gothic" style of furniture presents many advantages for the library, and when neatly and substantially constructed and embellished with taste is certainly the most sensible class of furniture that can be made.

Furthermore, as regards economy, a full set (or suite) of this furniture, from the stool to the book-cases,—including chairs, table, writing-desk, cabinets and wall-shelves,— may be made at home, or as has been suggested in regard to other pieces of furniture, by the neigh-boring carpenter, at a cost not exceeding twenty-five dollars; and when neatly stained (if the wood is pine) and em-bellished with marquetry, imitation of ivory-inlaying, or with a few simple carv-ings, forms a suite at once substantial and elegant. Some persons may object to the simplicity of form or, as they term it, "the old fashioned" appearance of this style, but the taste that has from association or education been taught to find the greatest beauty in simple forms and delicate colors, will at once accept these forms as portraying the highest style of Art.

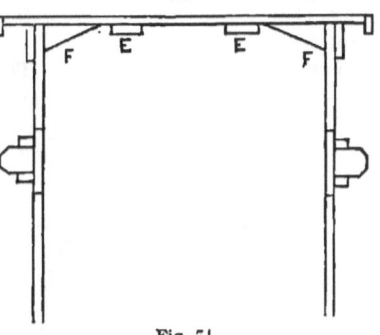

Fig. 74.

An apartment is furnished in good taste just so far as it subserves the end and occupation to which it is devoted. The library, therefore, as a place for study, or the quiet nook in which one is to lose one's self in a delightful book, or perhaps the apartment devoted to the most sacred hour of the day, the even-tide, when the family circle is drawn together, should be a domestic room, where the lamp should cast no garish light upon tinsel and tawdry finery of hangings and upholstery, but with quiet restfulness be caught by those subdued shades, that produce only a sense of every kind of warmth and comfort; that kindly seclusion and feeling of entire rest which shall not fail to distribute refining and happy influences on all who enjoy its care-fully appointed surroundings and be-longings, those artistic forms and beauty of tints which combine to form a perfect apartment.

Fig. 75.

The suite of Gothic furniture which consists of seven pieces, the table having been previously described in chapter on tables, the stool, there-fore, being the most simple article, will next occupy our attention. It will be found an exceedingly tasteful little piece of furniture.

To make it, take three pieces of one inch plank, one foot, ten inches long and two feet, six inches wide for the legs, which are arranged in an equilateral triangle, of which each side at the bottom measures fifteen inches, and at the top eight inches. They are screwed together by means of cross-pieces of one-half inch plank, as shown in Fig. 76. The top is sawed circular, one foot in diameter, of one inch plank, and is screwed to the cross-pieces. On this canvas is tacked (or a cushion), and tightly stuffed. The ornamental cover is then put over this and fastened with ornamental gilt nails. On each side (upon each

Fig. 76.

Fig. 77.

two feet,) is screwed the ornamental panel, below the top, while across the lower part, two-thirds from the top, are cross-pieces of the one-half inch plank, with an ornamental piece in the center sawed like Fig. 77.

All the ornamental open work on these pieces of furniture is sawed out with a small panel saw, and the whole surface is then rubbed smooth and stained either in imitation of oak, walnut or rosewood, or ebonized. No more appropriate embellishment can be added than simple lines of color, white or yellow, and a few figures added in imitation of inlaid-ivory work.

The library-table has been described; and almost similar in construction, as regards the lower part, is the writing-table, Fig. 78 ; the only difference being that the top is carried on a frame-work which passes all around and is dovetailed together at the corners, instead of being supported by cross ledgers merely. The materials used are of the same kind ; and also the ornamentation, which may be very much richer than that given in the illustration. After fastening oil-cloth or velveteen over the top, the back, sides, and strip on the front (which are dovetailed together at the corners), are screwed on with large round-headed screws.

The upright pieces which form the divisions between the pigeon-holes are next placed in position and screwed from the back ; then the board forming the shelf is fastened down on them ; and lastly the strips passing in front of them at the bottom and top (the last indented to form arches,) are screwed on. The whole of this upper part is formed of one-half inch board. The dimensions of this desk are : height, two feet four inches ; breadth, three feet three inches; depth, two feet three inches; cost of materials about one dollar.

If desired it may have the back made higher and be ornamented with brackets on the upper part. Or the lower part may form a closed case upon each

Fig 7b.

side, with an arched opening across the center which obviates the necessity of legs, and affords a convenient receptacle for paper, a few reference books, etc. The height of the case is two feet three inches; its breadth three feet six inches; the sides of the inclosed cases on the sides are of three-fourth inch plank placed vertically and screwed together by means of ledgers.

CHAPTER XI.

THE LIVING-ROOM.

The present living-room, but the dear old sitting-room of our grand-mothers' days, is perhaps after the "Mother's chamber," the dearest place in all the house. We say *after the* mother's chamber, yet in the Western states and indeed in many dwellings throughout our country, the sitting-room is the mother's chamber, two merged into that general sitting, lounging, and *dolce far niente* apartment, where all feel at home, and from which many previous memories are carried forth to the after days spent amid the busy, careless world.

It is taken for granted that every family has its sitting-room; it may be the elegantly furnished apartment of some lordly dwelling, or the one room of the poor mechanic, but if here the loved ones all gather, when the evening brings together the scattered band, whether it be from the banking-house of the wealthy householder or the workshop of the blacksmith, whether the children flock from the spacious nursery and fashionable academy, or from making mud-pies in the back-yard and from the close confines of the crowded public school, and whether they come to meet the beautiful mother clothed in "soft raiment," or the meek-faced woman, who in calico dress prepares the evening meal—it is all the same, she is mother; and it is her sweet and loved presence that cheers the dear old room, making, whether elegant or simple, the living-room the room where the real life of the family is felt, and wherein the sweetest associations are brought together to make this always and forever the most pleasant spot the world contains.

With these views then, we urge upon the "housewife" and "house-mother" the importance of rendering this spot in every way the most attractive one in the dwelling. Here gather together all that can most please and prove most conducive to the general satisfaction and comfort. Study the wants and pref-erences of each one and, as far as possible, gather them here to form one perfect whole; a room filled full of love, and made in every possible way attractive to old and young. For this reason select the brightest and most comfortable apart-ment in the house for the general room, for what are strangers and mere casual visitors compared with your own loved band? Therefore, if it be necessary, sacrifice even the parlor, if it proves to be the most popular apartment the house contains. We know of an instance where we believe a father and a grown-up son were saved from ruin by the mother and unselfish, loving sisters' sacrificing the cold, uninviting parlor to the requirements of the family, and using them daily to sit and eat in. Let this room, therefore, be the first to receive attention; and here bring the pretty home-made knick knacks which give such an air of cosy comfort; not bought articles, but things that you can say to father and brother, "I made this," and "mother made that," or such and such a one arranged the other. By such little devices, men are frequently brought to take an interest in home affairs, and this is not a feeling to quickly die out, but is rather one that luxuriates and grows by feeding.

The pretty sewing-chair and table shown in the illustration, Fig. 79, pre-

Fig. 79.

sent such a tasteful and inviting aspect, that any lady might desire to take a pattern by them (which may be easily done, as we will endeavor to show), for no prettier arrangement can be made for the sitting-room. Both chair and table, so far as the frame-work is concerned, are so exceedingly simple in form, that they may be made with but little trouble or expense by any person with a little mechanical skill, and with the directions given in a previous chapter. To make the chair more comfortable, it might better have a thick padded cushion placed beneath the worked strip.

The table-cover and strip for chair are made of gray pressed flannel, with a lining of soft colored stuff of any kind convenient; which tacked evenly together, is stitched in diamonds on the sewing-machine. In the center of the table-cover and down the center of the chair-pad are bouquets like Fig. 81, cut from gay woolen goods and embroidered with application work or, *petite-point*, zephyr, at pleasure. As a border, strips of scarlet and dark gray flannels are pinked out on each edge and fastened with half-polka and button-hole stitches, and a row of machine stitches on each edge. Heavy fringe finishes the edges of each.

Another handsome cover for the table and chair are made by quilting the lining and outside in diamonds, or other figures on the sewing-machine in various colors, and putting strips of contrasting color on for borders, finished with rows of alpaca braid stitched likewise on the machine. Gray and ecru-colored damask linens, embroidered in chain-stitch on the figures, make beautiful covers, and if done with scarlet and other fixed colors in embroidery thread, possess the valuable recommendation of being susceptible of cleansing; no light matter when they are in apartments constantly in use.

Fig. 80.

Fig. 81.

This class of table and chair-cover, we would particularly recommend to our readers, having found their value for week after week, to enjoy the luxury of fresh, glossy, carefully washed covers, is no small matter, especially during the hot weather, when everything that can add to the cool and refreshing aspect of the apartment becomes of momentous importance. And what imparts such a sense of heat and general aridness than covers of heavy bright colored woolen stuffs, which one fairly dislikes to handle. These may appear trifles to the busy housewife, but it is by just such little matters that the home is made delightful or uncomfortable.

SEWING-MACHINE AND RUG.

Our illustration in Fig. 82, shows a beautiful sewing-machine with its stool and rug, the latter being the article which we desire to describe to our readers, inasmuch as every sewing-machine should be furnished with this article, thus preventing oil from dripping on a handsome carpet perhaps, and also insuring it against the hard wear and tear, necessarily attending the constant use of an article of furniture in one position for an extended period.

The rug here, is made of a square of heavy cloth on the edge of which is a border of scarlet cloth, pinked out on the edge. as is also that of the upper part. The upper part of the rug is embroidered in application work, point Russe and

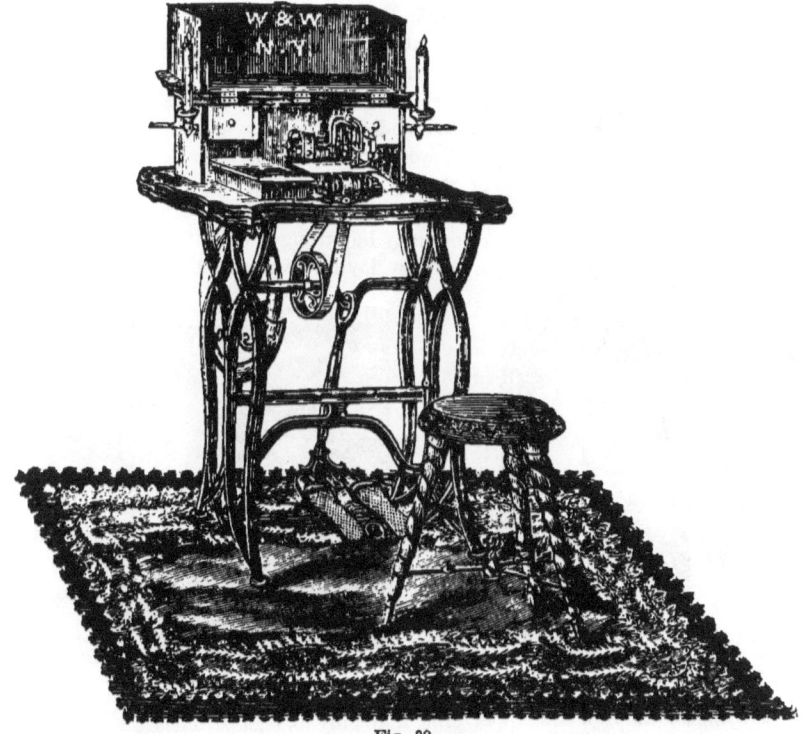

Fig. 82.

half-polka stitches, as shown in Fig. 83, which shows a section of one corner. The circular star-like pieces may be of scraps of various kinds of cloth held with stitches of contrasting color, while still smaller scraps are used for the dots, held by cross-stitches of bright colored zephyr. The coral work is in zephyr of bright colors, as scarlet, green, yellow, blue, etc., as may be convenient. Line the rug with a piece of oil-cloth, which will tend to hold it in proper position.

The sewing-machine or work-stand always needs some heavy or firm article, to which work may be fastened; some use for this purpose what is called a sewing-bird, others a pincushion screwed to the edge of the table, while many prefer a brick pincushion; the most convenient and at the same time handsome article, we have seen for this purpose, is a lead or stone cushion such as shown in Fig. 81. This is easily made at home, and requires for materials, medium sized canvas, shades of Berlin zephyr, merino, velvet, two yards satin ribbon one-half inch wide, card-board and corded silk braid, also two rings, ribbon wire, and a heavy stone or lead. Make a case by cutting the card-board into six pieces five inches high, four wide at top and three at bottom, covered with muslin, and a bottom cut to fit the narrow part of the sides making a hexagon,

all sewed neatly together. In this the stone is placed and covered to a depth of three inches with wool or bran; closely pack beneath a cover of strong muslin. Fig. 84, shows one complete square of the rug-work and size of canvas, and colors may be arranged to suit the taste in type style. In laying over the thick long stitches

Fig. 83.   Fig. 84.

which appear only on the upper side, and only as back-stitches on the under, the needle with the zephyr is always put through under every two threads of the canvas alternately on the one and other side edge, and so that between every stitch two threads of the canvas are left untouched.

The sides of the basket arranged in pockets requires a cross-piece of brown velvet twenty-four inches long and five inches wide, with stiff wire ribbon sewed into the upper edge, which is finished as also the lower edge with a corded silk braid, and the rug-work with either the same or a woolen one made of the zephyrs used on the work, straps of this also separate the divisions of the pockets. Two strong rings of covered wire or rubber, are securely fastened

Fig. 85.

to each end, and bows of ribbon finish the top.

The tasteful cluster of pocket shown in Fig. 85; is intended to be hung on the sewing-machine, and is useful for holding balls of cord, and the spools or other utensils required about sewing. They are made of five triangular pieces of canvas, (eighteen inches on the side,) embroidered in points with zephyr of four or five different shades of one color, (or one or two in contrast if preferred).

The upper edges are finished with woolen chenille to suit the color of the work, and if desired, tassels may depend from each point at the bottom. Each pocket is lined with bright colored muslin to suit the color of the zephyr on the embroidery, and ribbon loops at the top with a long one for suspension, finish the pockets.

VASE STAND.

The pretty stand, Fig. 86, is an artistic piece of work, and a specimen of the beautiful painting on wood, though if there be any one not possessing sufficient skill to perform this pretty work, there is another method by which it may be made. We will describe the wood painting first; a piece of hard close-grained wood is selected, or if pine is necessarily used, it must receive three coats of zinc white, in which sufficient lamp-black is rubbed to make stone color; when each of these coats has dried successively, another is given of Copal varnish, this must become perfectly hard and be rubbed off with pumice,

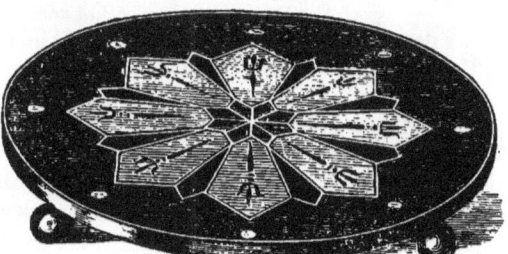

Fig. 86.

another coat of varnish applied, which when dry is to be highly polished with powdered pumice first, then with powdered Tripoli and oil until as smooth as glass, when rub off with finely pulverized starch; the design is marked off on this light ground by sketching it first on paper pricking the outlines, and then placing it in position and dusting with powder, the white lines are drawn with a fine camel's hair brush and white tube-paint; the lighter figures with bright colors and gold, and the black with black tube-color mixed with a little varnish. When done, a coat of outside varnish prevents injury. Four turned feet are placed under the lower edge, and a neat rim on the outside.

There should be no small article of furniture in which the housewife, imbued with delicate and refined taste, should take such interest as in her neat, and pretty work-basket. To carry light work to the parlor or other place she may

be called, a light, flat basket is, of course, necessary, but in the sitting-room or bed-chamber, beside the sewing-machine or window, a standing basket is by far the most appropriate. An improvised article of the kind is shown in Fig. 87. This stand may be made of any four light, round sticks; handles of worn out umbrellas or brooms answering well; when neatly painted, or covered with zephyr, and gilded or bronzed. These rods should be about twenty-seven inches in height, with two short cross-pieces screwed into them of nine inches in length, with ornamental rings, made of wire, covered with crochet-work. The rods and rings have scarlet braid twined around them, which give a beautiful effect. The tray-like basket, fifteen and three-fourth inches long, ten and one-fourth inches wide, and five

Fig. 87.

inches deep with handle one inch wide, eight and one-half inches high, and ten and one-half inches across; is made of stiff, heavy pasteboard edged with wire; and with a bottom of same, covered with muslin, and also stiffened with wire. This basket is covered on the outside with crimson or other bright colored glazed cambric, and lined with silk or the same colored cambric as outside, handsomely embroidered on the bottom, and fitted up with pockets and other conveniences. An edge like Fig. 88, of tatting, with a ring border above it is made, and stiffened with

Fig. 88.

thick glue; then varnished with Copal. The handle is finished like the rods, and ribbon is run through the rings. Woolen balls hang from the frame.

WALL-POCKETS.

As a general custom, wall-pockets are placed in the sitting-room, library, hall, or chamber, more frequently than against the walls of the parlor, but there are many articles even in the parlor which might better be kept in a handsome wall-pocket or basket, than littering tables, piano and even the sofas and chairs. Not that a little graceful confusion is unpleasant to the artistic taste, but that this license may be carried to that point which amounts to disorder, and is a sure sign of careless housekeeping; there-fore, though a few of the late papers and magazines, an interesting book, a basket of delicate work or even a game or two, may occupy appropriate positions on tables and stands—let the majority of such articles find an appropriate resting place in the beautiful wall-pocket or hanging-basket.

Fig. 89.

These articles, when used for the parlor, should be of the most elegant kinds, and may be enriched either with embroidery, painting, or other fancy work—of which we give a variety of patterns and designs in order that there may be different kinds from which a selection can be made, and which will serve as guides for making others, of differ-ent materials and modified forms better suited to the circumstances of various cases.

For Fig. 89, cut three oval pieces of stiff card-board; the middle one a third larger than the sides, and a back shaped like the three pieces when placed together, as shown in the engraving. The back and front pieces are lined with glazed muslin; the two lower front pieces, with blue merino, on which is em-broidered in satin stitch a pretty design, while the central piece (which it will be noticed is somewhat larger) is of a deeper shade of blue—or a contrasting color—likewise embroidered. By basting back and front pieces—both lining and outside on separate pieces of card, and overwhipping them together, a very strong case is formed; and the stitches may be covered with heavy cord. The back and front are connected by long, triangular pieces of morocco or merino, across the top of which is fastened an elastic band, holding them in plaits, and admitting of extension if necessary. Loops of cord at the top, and a full bow of ribbon at the bottom finishes this tasteful pocket—which may be used not

10

only for holding papers and other heavy articles, but forms a rack for cards between the edges of the oval pieces.

Fig. 90, is one of the richest wall-pockets that can be made, and though it requires some artistic skill, it will not be found a difficult task to make it, and no pattern we give will better repay the time spent on it. The form of the pocket must be accurately drawn off and enlarged, so as to give the correct outline of both back and front; the back ending in the scroll which shows below the pocket. The whole is cut from light-colored wood, and the appear-

ance of projecting frame and figures are produced by careful coloring with India ink and Sepia. The wood chosen should be hard and close-grained. The design is drawn in outline with a good pencil, the light spaces and white spots filled in with the best cake-white, rubbed fine, and the black portions in the same way with India ink — while the shaded lines are tinted with Sepia. The remaining portions may be left the natural color of the wood, or colored a warm gray. When thoroughly dry, go over with a fine pencil and India ink. It may be found necessary to go over the black portions several

Fig. 90.

times, which should be done before these final lines are drawn, as they give a certain prominent finish and decisiveness to the outlines not obtained by other means.

When perfectly dry, give a coat of fine Demar varnish, and when dry, polish with pumice-stone finely powdered and a wet flannel, taking care not to rub into the colors. Repeat this until a highly polished surface is obtained. Line the inside where the pocket commences with any material, such as crimson velveteen or green oil-cloth; and make a plaited strip of morocco of corresponding color, to unite the back and front; tacking it on with gilt tacks, and fastening an elastic band at the upper edges. Across the front of the pocket is fastened a polished or gilded rod, on which are suspended bunches of tassels; and two heavy cords, furnished with rings and screws, are arranged on each side of the back as suspension cords. The monogram of course may be changed to suit circumstances, or a small ornamental figure may take its place.

. This pocket is equally elegant made with pine-wood ebonized and ornamented with imitation of inlaying or gilding.

The form of Fig. 91 will be easily understood, and consists of a front about one-third wider than the back in order to make a projecting pocket where the two circular pieces at the bottom are sewed together. The materials required are two and a half sheets of stiff pasteboard, striped silk for lining the back, and a shade of velvet harmonizing with the most prominent shade, for the front, with sufficient satin or *gros-grain* silk of lighter shade to form the application design on the front, with coarse sewing-silk for the stitches inclosed in the scroll, and also the light tracery of point Russe embroidery on the outer parts of the arabesque design. Rich fringe with cords and tassels finish this

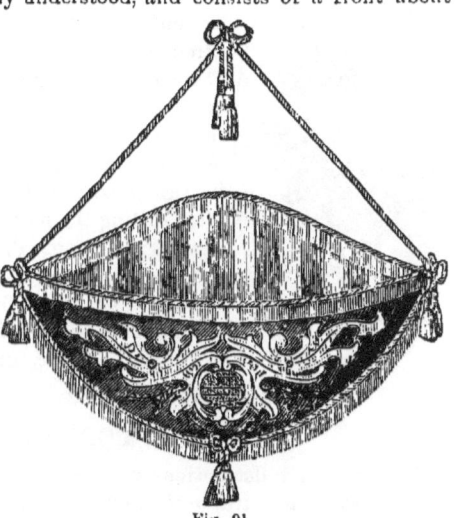

Fig. 91.

beautiful pocket, the beauty of which consists in the tasteful assortment of colors and richness of material.

The wall-pocket for magazines and journals, shown in Fig. 92, requires a half yard of scarlet or other colored cloth, and one-quarter of a yard of black velvet, two figures from *Cretonne*, various colors of silk and one sheet pasteboard. The form of the back is cut of pasteboard to suit the size of the journals to be accommodated, with the pocket corresponding with the lower part, and gracefully curved on the upper edge. The scarlet cloth covers the back above and an inch or two below the upper edge of the pocket, and the entire front of the pocket. On these is placed strips of the black velvet cut to fit the figure on the outer edge, and formed into

Fig. 92.

Fig. 93.

scrolls and arabesques on the inner part. This *applique* work is done with gold-colored silk in chain-stitching, and a cord finishes the edge around the outside. Two oval or round spaces are cut on each side of the pocket-front into which are fitted medallions of Chinese figures, or others cut from *Cretonne*. The lettering, flowers, etc, are done in various colored silks, in chain, point Russe, half-polka and satin stitches. A charming method of embellishing the ovals in such work is by means of photographs as shown in Fig. 93. Pretty faces or figure-pieces are selected and, after cutting the margin away carefully, paste the design against the material, and proceed to surround it with embroidery, as shown in Fig. 93. Or a pretty arrangement is a wreath of flowers in bright-colored silks, with a pretty face peeping from the center. Materials, heavy pasteboard, coarse, gray crotchet thread, cloth, velvet or silk in bright colors.

PORTFOLIO.

The frame and decorations of this portfolio, are of rods and rings of the thick heavy pasteboard, worked over with crochet as shown in Fig. 94 and 95. The sizes of the two card-board plates covered on both sides with the

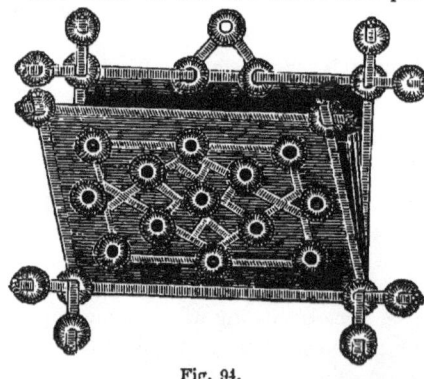

Fig. 94.

material used, and forming the pocket, are ten inches long, and eight inches deep for the back, the front being about one and one-half inches shorter. On the ends are folded pieces of strong muslin covered with the mantel, or better still of morocco. The size of the rings and rods may be judged by the pattern Fig's 94 and 95, and the arrangement from the illustration. These may be covered with colored zephyr, or the crochet-cotton, and if the latter, might better be varnished with Copal, which gives a beautiful effect. This kind of work possesses unusual beauty, and is not as widely known as it should be.

WALL-POCKET.

This wall-pocket is made of two panels of wood one-fourth inch thick, which can be easily shaped, as shown in the illustration, and must be carefully smoothed and ebonized as described in the proper chapter. The ornamentation is of Chinese character, consisting of paintings in gold, and where a person does not understand this class of fancy work, we would recommend them to use the gold figures in Decalcomania designs, which will be found well adapted to the work, and may be procured of any style desired.

The central oval panel on the front is ornamented with rich embroidery, such as the pattern in Fig. 95. An oval panel of binders-board is the foundation for the embroidery, which consists of an outer piece worked on scarlet merino with a piece removed from the center, into which a piece of black velveteen containing a monogram or other design is introduced,

Fig. 95.

and the edges finished with cord and stitches in half-polka or button-hole. The ends are connected by triangular pieces (*souffles*) of scarlet morocco, with bands of elastic let into the upper part, which is pinked out, and has slits five inches below for the elastic bands.

WALL–POCKET WITH EMBROIDERY.

The case of this elegant wall-pocket is carved from pine wood, and afterwards ebonized and gilded. On the front of the pocket is left an oval panel, in which

Fig. 96.

is fastened a piece of brown cloth with an application of ecru cloth on the center, fastened with gold braid in two rows one inch apart, with a herring-bone stitching between of coarse scarlet silk. Beyond this is a piece of embroidery with yellow silk in satin and half-polka stitch. The ecru cloth is embellished with a rich embroidery in application work, the details of which are clearly shown in the full-sized illustrations.

The cluster of circular flowers

are cut from scarlet and cherry-colored velvet, the stamens holding each petal are of gold-colored silk, with green heart in knotted stitches; the leaves are of green velvet, worked with two shades of darker and lighter green silk. The sprays of small leaves are of very light-green silk, with veins of yellow-green, while the larger ones are of brown cloth with vines of yellow. The berries are

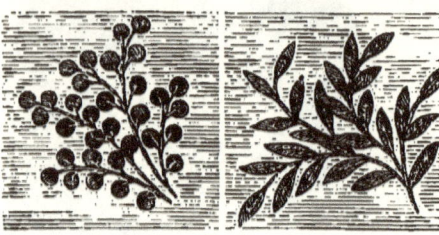

Fig. 97.

cut from purple velvet, held with a little fine gum arabic mucilage on the back, and stems of green silk. This panel is held in place by a frame of application work, consisting of lighter colored cloth, worked in chain-stitching half-polka point Russe, and satin stitch embroidery. This panel may be fastened in with gilt-headed nails,

which give a beautiful effect. Both sides of the pocket are lined with colored muslin or oil-cloth (of the enameled kind) while at the top are fastened screw-rings, with chains, which allow the front to fall open; thus forming a case or pocket.

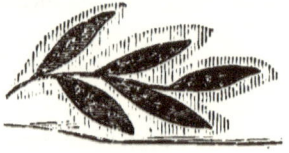

Fig. 98.

Fig. 99.

Fig. 100.

A similar pocket and sack may be made by ornamenting the front panel with a painted design, or by means of a "transfer;" then painting over with ground-color, and mounting with the painted side against the back; the glass on the front then presents all the fine effects of the rich, brilliant colors, thrown out by the ground painting. Or the panel may be of wood, highly polished and embellished with imitation of marquetry, ivory-inlaying or painting on the panel in transparent colors, in imitation of *papier mache*. Either one of these styles will be found exceedingly elegant, and where the entire hall furniture is ornamented and embellished to correspond, the effect will be found very beautiful, and, moreover, this result may be produced with very ordinary pieces of furniture.

CARD AND LETTER RACK WITH PINCUSHION.

All housekeepers know the importance of having the "convenient pin" always in readiness, yet frequently find it difficult to accomplish. For this reason it is always important to have a pincushion well supplied in some convenient position, and as there is no law which is against necessary things being likewise pretty, such a cushion should be made as tasteful as possible. We offer therefore a beautiful design combining the cushion aforementioned, and a rack for letters and cards, which also require some convenient receptacle.

Fig. 101.

To make this tasteful affair, saw out a panel of wood for the back, of one-half inch plank, making it fourteen inches long and ten inches wide, giving it the quaint form shown in the illlustration; next saw out the three pieces forming the racks, which is easily done with the fret saws and carving tools, or imitation carvings may be used.

Next, an oval cushion five inches long and seven wide is made of coarse cloth, and tightly stuffed with wool or bran. A cover of velvet, or other material is embroidered with silk or zephyr, and fastened over

Fig. 102.

the cushion with a heavy cord around the edge. Six tassels are fastened to the lower part and make a pretty finish. Fig. 102, the one chenille is worked thus: Transfer the design to the silk, and work the violets with fine violet chenille, and the leaves with green chenille. The veins and stems are worked partly in point Russe, and partly in herring-bone stitch with green silk and chenille.

We would suggest that the wood-work is handsomer when made of two contrasting colors, as walnut and whitewood; pine is good if oiled.

LAMP-SHADE.

This lamp-shade shows a new style of work, and is brilliantly beautiful. The materials required to make it, are white card-board, green, crimson, and white gelatine paper (or if this is not practicable, thin silk may be substituted, though not with equal effect), three yards of inch-wide ribbon, and a set of silhouettes three or four inches long, mucilage and six ornamental buttons.

The shade consists of six sections, each eight inches long and five wide, which

Fig 103.

are cut into a curved shape ending in a point at the bottom, and at the top gradually sloped to a width of four inches. These have traced upon them an arabesque design, such as shown in the illustration, the interior parts of which are carefully cut out with a very sharp pointed knife, placing the card on a solid cutting-board, and using care to leave a half-inch edge all around the outside and never dividing a figure so that it has no connection and will drop out; in the center cut out a space a trifle larger than the silhouettes, and interline with green gelatine paper or silk, leaving an equal margin entirely around the edge; the remaining open parts, line with the crimson and white gelatine paper. Catch the leaves together with strong thread or silk, and fasten one of the ornamental buttons on each connection, then at the top tie them together with the bows of ribbon, allowing a half yard to each. Lastly, having gummed the silhouettes, moisten them very slightly and fasten them carefully in place on the center of the green space. If these are made too damp, the gelatine paper will become drawn and present an extremely unpleasant appearance, looking wrinkled and sometimes cracking. If silk is used for these centers, line with tissue paper.

MOVABLE SCREEN FOR LAMP.

The stand for this screen is made of slender wooden rods, and four turned legs, all of which are finished with large agate beads. The upper part consists of two oblong four-cornered frames, which are joined in the middle by means of an upright pole fastened down into the bottom, and extending up to the top of the frames. Into each of these frames, which are ten inches long and five inches wide, is fastened a piece of card-board, either white or tinted, which has traced out upon it a design figure, and cut out with a sharp knife, placing the card on a piece of hard wood, and making clean incisions, so that each piece will come out clear. Behind this fasten marceline or colored gelatine paper, gluing it on the extreme edge with a narrow strip of fine muslin and lace, the panels into the frame with gold thread, making holes for the cord with a large darning needle or stiletto, and arranging the coils of cord evenly around the frame.

In cutting out the designs, prick all the stems, tendrils and other fine tracery with a No. 8 sewing needle. On the top of the frame, and on different parts of the base, arrange a few circles of wire, as shown in the illustration. The frame here described may be ornamented in several other ways—thus having cut out such a design as shown in the illustration, cover the back with two thicknesses of the vivid green Tarlatan, called gas-light green, which produces a beautiful effect; otherwise, cut from the card-board, a central and four corner sections, introduce into the central one a Diaphanie plate, representing some pretty scene or group of figures, and into the other medallions, Rosaces or bright groups of colors, found in some of the groundings and plates of borders. The effect of these plates is as imposing as the finest stained glass. Still another method is by means of Photaphemic and Epiphanie—which high sounding names are given to work as simple as beautiful. By Photaphemic is meant the pricking in of designs, with needles of different sizes, and in shades, or window transparencies, when placed against the light, the effect is exceedingly fine, as also is Epiphanie, which is, perhaps, still more effective, and consists in sketching a design very lightly upon a panel of thin card-board, and cutting slashes into the broad lights, cutting the points of leaves, petals, etc., and by bending the parts in slightly, admitting a ray of light to fall on this part, thus producing the effect of sculptured marble. On such panels as those shown in the present model, a group of vine-leaves, with a cluster of grapes, on one and an arrangement of flowers on the other, would give a beau-

Fig. 104.

tiful effect in either of these kinds of work. In some cases, this kind of work is lined with crimson, green, white or other color of gelatine paper, and the effect is surprisingly beautiful.

Another beautiful effect is given by cutting out a space in the center of each panel, and introducing photographs—then painting the panels around the medallions with black lacquer; or in this case it is better to use glass panels, gumming the photographs and painting around them carefully with a fine brush, then going over the remaining parts with smooth coats of black varnish until the whole is colored. The margin must be carefully cut from around the photograph, and the most appropriate characters are statuary pieces, or copies of Madonnas, saints, etc., from noted paintings.

LAMP-MAT AND SHADE.

The mat beneath the beautiful antique lamp shown in Fig. 105, is as simple and easily made as it is elegant, and our readers will not find a better pattern for this useful article.

To make it, cut of card-board one circular form, ten inches in diameter, which

Fig. 105.

cover with green satin or merino. Then apply at regular distances, three inches apart, around the edge, figures of green velvet edged with button-hole stitching of darker green silk, and embroidered with crosses of point Russe stitching; touch the back of the velvet with gum, and paste each figure closely to the foundation. Embroider, with herring-bone stitch, a piece of fine white silk or alpaca braid with green silk, and fasten it in loops around the edge of the mat so that one of the application figures shows between each loop, as shown in the illustration.

Then arrange a second row of velvet figures between those before put on, and within the divisions of the braid loops, as will be clearly understood by examining the illustration. Place a circular piece of velvet embroidered in button-hole stitch on the center of the mat, and line the whole underneath with a circular piece of green enameled oil-cloth, catching the edge to the cardboard of the mat, or fastening with a touch of glue on the center and edges.

The lamp-shade is one of the most *recherche* that can be imagined, consisting of green silk and crape or Tarlatan. The first thing to be done in making this shade is to cut out six pieces of green silk, six inches long and four wide; and after marking out a design, (such as shown in the illustration,) on each one, to button-hole stitch the outlines and then cut them out carefully, to be put on as application embroidery at a later stage of the work. These all embroidered, the most difficult part of the work is done; then cut a circular piece of card-board that will fit loosely around the lamp-chimney, and half an inch wide, allowing it sufficiently large to admit of a ring of tin within it to protect from the heat; cover this with green satin; next cut of card-board six strips, each one inch wide and six inches long; cover these also with satin, and trim with the white braid embroidered with green, (round the corners of the lower end of the card-board before covering,) then arrange these on the circular piece at regular distances. Next cut of the crape or Tarlatan twelve pieces, five inches wide and eight inches long, rounding one end gracefully to a point; place the sections two and two together, and button-hole stitch the lower part in scallops, as shown in the illustration; paste the application designs on, and after gathering each leaf, fasten them around the circular top-piece, with the edges under the bands previously fastened on. Catch the edges to the bands with a few stitches, and finish the top with alternate rows of embroidered braid and green satin folds half an inch wide.

LAMP-MAT IN CLOTH AND VELVET APPLIQUE.

Materials: gray leather, ends of cloth, in white, scarlet, orange-yellow, blue, and several shades of green and brown—pieces of purple and lilac velvet, shades of green, yellow, white, and red purse silk; also fine lilac sewing-silk, green zephyr, and three shades of ribbon (one inch.)

1.   Fig. 106.   2.

A circular piece of thin, gray leather, twelve inches in diameter, the edges cut out into six scallops of equal size. The six dahlias decorating these scallops, are made of cloth; a scarlet and white one alternately, made on small, circular pieces of card-board one and one-half inches wide; the outer edge having twenty petals, the next fourteen, the last eight. The largest of these folded like a cornet, is shown in Fig. 2, and spread out flat in 1; in 2 it is shown sewed together with a stitch or two. The calyx which holds the center is a knot made of two shades of green wool in loops, on a little circle of card. For the two acacia sprays, Fig. 106 gives the full spray with the pattern to be cut of yellow cloth, which is to be arranged as shown in Fig. 106. Yellow silk makes the center, and a calyx is made of light yellow-green zephyr. The bright green leaves of this blossom are cut out of green cloth, button-holed on the edge with silk of same color, and fastened on the mat with the veining. The beautiful convolvulus blossom is of blue cloth, with a white cloth calyx. The latter with red veins in stalk stitch (half-polka). The blue buds have capsules (or cups) of green silk, and a coil of red and white silk wound around, as shown in the illustration.

The veins of the full-blown flower are made of loose stitches in red, white and yellow silk, and resting on the blue worked calyx, (at the edge). The pansy is cut from purple and lilac velvet and yellow cloth. The petals are cut out and the edges touched with mucilage (to prevent raveling); they are then arranged on a small scrap of card or cloth; the lower single leaf one inch large and the two middle ones (on each side) are of yellow silk or cloth, the first join being hidden by those placed over it; requiring a piece of stuff folded a little in the middle and rounded at the ends one and one-half inches long and half an inch wide; these leaves having points of lilac velvet pasted on. The two upper rounded leaves each three-fourths of an inch high and half an inch wide, and the buds with green calyx are entirely of lilac velvet. Steel beads and loose lilac silk stitches make the blossom calyx of the pansies. Green silk ribbon gathered in the middle is put as a finish all around the mat.

Fig. 107.

RUG FOR DOG.

In the sitting-room we generally find these privileged members of the family, the dog, pussy, bird, and other pampered pets, belonging to the mistress of the household, and to make them comfortable is frequently as much a matter of grave consideration as to attend to the wants of any other of the home group.

In order to prevent the soil that of necessity comes from constant use of cushion, sofa-corner or even the rugs belonging to the room, dogs, especially, should be provided with quilted cushions, rugs, such as we show in Fig. 107, which is made of scarlet flannel thickly wadded and quilted on the sewing-machine, thus making not only a useful but quite an ornamental affair of " Fido's " bed. A fringe of woolen yarn finishes the edge, and a lining of oil-cloth, renders it durable and easily moved.

As a fitting accompaniment to the lace covers, anti-macassars and other furniture of this airy character, we gladly give a beautiful lamp-mat of the same

Fig. 108.

kind. This mat is equally suitable for vases, candlesticks, and on a tray beneath pitcher or glass. The materials required, are strong bobbinet, coarse crochet cotton, and if desired in colors, scarlet or other colored zephyrs. When done in white, it is easily washed, but the colors in zephyr retain their brightness for a long time. The star, Fig. 109, shows the manner of darning the lace, which is further explained in the full illustration which shows the mat in about one-fourth its size; the star being one-half the size if for a large mat, though for a small mat the star will be sufficiently large as it is shown here.

The fringe is crocheted of cotton rather finer than is used for the mat. The under part has a lining of bright colored glazed muslin sewed over a foundation of card-board. When washed this is cut from the outside, and replaced after

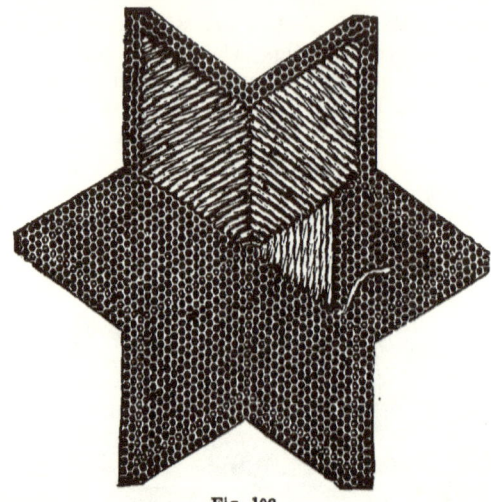

Fig. 109.

the mat has dried. These mats are not only tasteful but durable, and for the table or washstand answer admirably.

BRACKETS.

There is no ornament that can compare with the bracket in point of popularity, and it holds its position justly, for certainly as regards both use and beauty, it stands paramount in importance.

During the past few years, such wonderful improvements have been made in the form and workmanship of this piece of ornamental furniture, that one can scarcely recognize in the elegantly carved or painted specimen of to-day, the simple shelf of former times.

Whatever else, may from necessity be excluded from the house, brackets surely need not be one of them, for with the most ordinary materials and a hammer and tacks, the tastefully made lambrequin may be tacked around a simple shelf of pine nailed to two triangular braces, and an impromptu bracket, of no mean pretensions is at once formed. This, the very simplest form of bracket may be so greatly complicated, and richly embellished as to form one of the handsomest of the article.

Besides shelves draped with lambrequins, brackets are of various forms, as the corner bracket with its triangular shelf ornamented in front, the single and double shelf, and various arrangements as regards the braces, backs, and other variations of form. Next to the simple shelf described above, the plain corner bracket shown in Fig. 110, is the easiest made. The one here shown has a

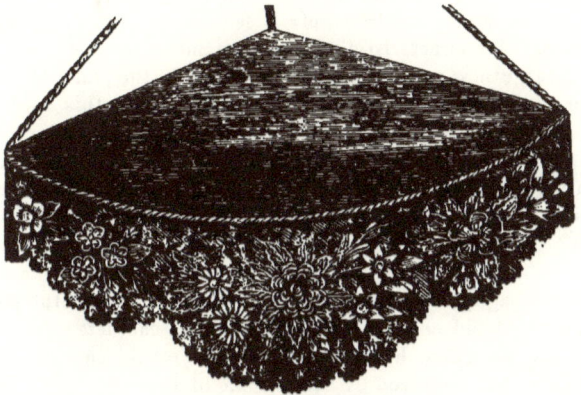

Fig. 110.

drapery of cloth embroidered with feather-work, which makes a most exquisite embellishment, the leaves and flowers are fastened on the cloth, which is pinked out on the edge, and stiffened with card-board tacked beneath it.

CHAPTER XII.

THE DINING-ROOM.

The dining-room requires less furniture than any other room in the house, but it must at the same time be carefully selected as regards appropriateness and usefulness. A characteristic of this apartment conspicuously noticeable should be its brightness; for this reason, if possible, the panes of glass should be colored or ornamented in some manner. Relating to this subject we have been pleased with a description of the window which lights the dining-room in the residence of Mr. George S. Boughton (the American artist), in Grove Lodge, Kensington, which is thus given by Mr. Conway: "Passing through the curtains, we enter a hall about two-thirds the depth of the house, to the dining-room. The hall is lined with fine, old engravings and cabinets, with here and there an old convex mirror. The general color of the walls of the dining-room are sage-green; thus setting off finely the beautiful pictures and the many pieces of old china. There are several cabinets which have been designed by Mr. Boughton himself, and a *bouffet* resembling one designed by Charles Eastlake, but improved by being made higher. * * * This dining-room is lighted by a large window set back in a deep recess, curtained off from the main room with hangings of red velvet, and exquisitely environed by original designs. The window is composed of the richest quarries, holding in their centers each its different decorative flower, or other natural form, and these being collectively the frame of large medallions of stained glass, representing Van Eyck, Van Orley and the Burgomaster's Wife, from Van Eyck's picture in the National gallery."

Now with the exquisite designs offered in Diaphanie and Vitromania, the hall, library and dining-room may be as artistically adorned as though done with the costliest stained glass. These designs must be adapted to suit the size of the panes; and no matter what these are, whether small or large, there are sheets particularly adapted to them. We are so partial to this class of work, that if it were possible we would insist upon every lady making a trial of it on some one window at least; for this done, we feel confident that others in appropriate places would quickly receive embellishment; and the change illuminated glass makes in a hall or dining-room can scarcely be conceived. Proper subjects for a dining-room window would be flowers, fruit and

Rosaces, or such figures as "Departure for the Chase," "The Seasons," "The Twelve Months," etc., with borders, corners, and groundings of rich brilliant colors. There is a lovely blue ground and another of crimson which are particular favorites.

A charming window is made from a Renaissance design, a medallion in

Fig. 111.

simple light and shade, with a lovely cherub in the center, and a clear blue back-ground. For small panes, from six to twelve in a window, there are figures representing Music, Painting, etc., of light and shade, or small Rosaces in Sepia and white, beautiful little landscapes, each a perfect gem pic-

11

ture in the most glowing colors, which, placed in the center of a pane and surrounded by a border and grounding, gives a lovely effect. Such windows light up a quiet-looking paper; and some graceful drapery will give an air of luxuriance to the room, even if the furniture be of simple form and unobtrusive in appearance; and for these nothing can compensate.

SIDEBOARD.

The old fashioned *buffet* of the French, which for so many years both in England and in this country was considered necessary in every dining-room,

Fig. 112.

has been superseded by the more modern sideboard. This piece of furniture is a necessity almost, inasmuch as it affords a place for various articles which are required in this room alone. Therefore, though it be ever so plain, every neat housekeeper should make an effort to have her sideboard, which may be improvised from very ordinary materials, and by the good housewife herself. It might appear almost absurd to state that the illustration, Fig. 112, which is a copy of a rich and costly piece of furniture, has been so beautifully imitated that it appears quite as handsome as the one here shown. The wood-work consisted of a lower case, three feet in height, three feet four inches in depth, and seven feet two inches long. On each end, closets were made as previously described, the center left open as a receptacle for the urn, wine cooler, or other high article. On this case was a second one, one foot less in length, five feet high and two feet deep, the ends of which are divided into little niches for lamp or they may be shelved, the center a cupboard, the door of which is one solid panel, ornamented with a picture upon the polished surface. If possible the wood-work of this sideboard might better be of black walnut, but pine neatly stained can be made to answer, and should be ebonized, in which case the artificial wood carvings with which it is enriched should be left in the natural color, but if the wood is walnut these should be ebonized.

Mouldings of walnut or pine can be procured, also neat beading, and these with a dozen or two of shell and scroll ornaments, four floral panels, three key

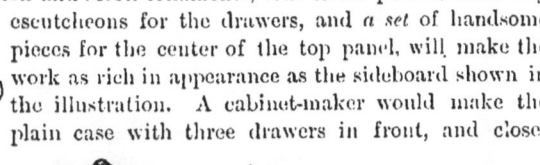

escutcheons for the drawers, and *a set* of handsome pieces for the center of the top panel, will make the work as rich in appearance as the sideboard shown in the illustration. A cabinet-maker would make the plain case with three drawers in front, and closet

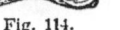

Fig. 113.   Fig. 114.   Fig. 115.

doors neatly paneled (of pine) for a moderate sum, probably from ten to twenty dollars, according to the price of work in the place, and the great beauty of the

Fig. 116.

piece of furniture consists in the finishing and embellishments, which when well done would make it worth ten times the amount. We give this as one of the best specimens of what the wood-carvings are capable of producing. The doors upon the sides are finished with appropriate carvings of game or fish; for though we agree with "Marion Harland" and others, in thinking that this class of ornamentation "savors too much of the poulterers," still if applied judiciously they appear well, and on this piece of furniture are peculiarly handsome. The stag's head surmounting the back, is also of the same material and corresponds with the style of embellishments. This back is separate from the upper part of the sideboard, and is made of a piece of inch thick plank, sawed out on the top in scroll form, in the center of which is the ornaments named above, with oak-leaves below. The door in the center is made of a solid panel, the surface of which is polished and repolished until a uniform porcelain-like solidity is obtained, upon which a picture is painted or transferred, and for which we would recommend a fine engraving.

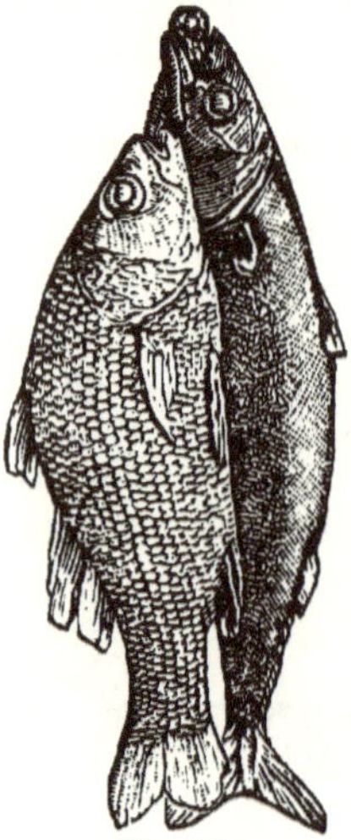

Should carving of fruit be preferred, such a top-piece as Fig. 120, with panel and side-pieces like Figs. 121 will be found equally elegant; the shell ornaments applying to either, and handles, escutcheons, etc., may be procured that are adapted to each;

Fig. 117.

Fig. 118.

oak-leaves and acorns, where game is used; shells, where fish; and grapes with vine-leaves or other fruit, where the various fruit ornaments are preferred; where all are so beautiful, it is difficult to make a selection.

Another elegant sideboard is shown in Fig. 119, which is given more to show a fine form and arrangement than with any idea of recommending the rich ornamentation. Still some of our readers may even desire to imitate this; and with the exception of the top, it may not, after all, be so difficult a matter as would be supposed at the first glance. Let us examine it in detail, and ascertain whether we could not make one at least approaching it in beauty of form and embellishment. For the lower part, we have two cupboards, made in the model with round corners, (but this is not important). Above these two cupboards are drawers of same width, (both about the size of the one previously described). These are separated by wide ornamental mouldings, ornamented with carvings,—such as the floral ornaments described in chapter on bedsteads. This lower part is three feet, four inches high, two feet deep, and five feet long. The embellishment consists in ebonized panels, with a few carved ornaments around both the oblong and diamond-shaped panels.

Next the back part is made: a case fourteen inches deep, three feet, six inches wide, and five feet high, is securely nailed on the bottom part; within this, three shelves are fastened on ornamented iron or carved wooden brackets (the iron ones, of tasteful form and neatly bronzed, are very pretty and possess great strength); above this and across the front, one of the handsome ornamental head-pieces like Figs. 120 and 121, which could be appropriately substituted for the arch. At a point in Fig. 120, (which would be fastened against the top of the frame) an ornamental vase or urn could be placed; or, if the top is desired still higher, a small box about fourteen inches long, ten inches deep, and two feet high, must be fastened securely to the top of the frame-work, the open part out; the edges must be ornamented with leaves, scrolls and mouldings, corresponding strictly in character with the remainder of the work. Within this may be stood an urn or statuette, and on the top, a similar ornament, or one large and a smaller one on each side; by fastening ornaments on the corners of this upper box, an arched form may be given to it similar to the illustration.

Fig. 119.

On each side of the case, containing the shelves, and just at one side of it, a piece of plank two or three inches thick, one foot high, and six inches wide, is nailed in the position shown in the illustration, and behind these pieces, (a few inches at one side) are similar ones supporting brackets, on which stand miniature columns or posts, extending to the top of the case; while upon those in front are figures of "Pomona" and "Flora"; in the original these are of costly bronze, but of which, really charming copies in plaster may be obtained, which may be beautifully bronzed, as also the fluted columns behind. This may appear like a formidable piece of work to undertake, but it is not an impossible thing to accomplish by any means, and where a handsome suite of furniture is desired, the result, if satisfactorily obtained, is well worth the effort, and will amply repay all expenditure of money, labor, care or time.

The various embellishments and adornments on this piece of work can be clearly understood by examining the illustration, and to make a perfect and satisfactory " job " (as the workmen term it), each part must be carefully done. The great beauty of such imitations as this, where every part is rich and elegant,

Fig. 120.

is perfect neatness ; and the carefully finishing up each minute detail, however delicate or complicated it may be.

It is to be regretted that so many imperfect imitations of home-made furniture and home-made elegancies are exhibited, as they are calculated to bring this class of household arrangement into disrepute ; whereas, it being so valuable to many not possessed with abundant means, it should, in every instance, bear witness not only of the beauty, but the durability and perfection to which such work may be brought.

In making such a piece of valuable furniture as this sideboard, which is a noticeable example of first-class furniture, the following rules must be observed if neat and durable work are to be the result : The frame-work must be solid and substantial; if it is of pine, the surface must be neatly painted or stained; rubbed smooth and oiled or varnished, (oiling appears in the best taste) or, better still, ebonized, and polished in the most perfect manner; the wood carvings must be carefully selected, each piece corresponding in style; and not using several kinds; for instance, if fruit and scroll designs—do not use several varieties of the fruit ornaments, (but either grapes and vine-leaves, nuts, or tropical fruit entirely); if the surface is ebonized, these appear best in their natural soft, brown color, without oil or varnish. To have them adhere well, make the surface of the wood (on which they are to be placed) slightly rough, and sprinkled with coarsely powdered charcoal, black pepper or cinders crushed

Fig. 121.

to a powder, allow this to dry, then coat the surface of the carving with rather thick glue (about the consistency of syrup) and after placing the ornament in its place, lay a weight upon it until dry. It is best where possible, to screw these carvings from the back, and they may be obtained with screw-holes made in them.

Where pictures are to be transferred to any smooth surface, it should be made scrupulously clean, and great care should be used to apply it·directly in the position desired—as such an embellishment placed to one side, or in any manner crooked, presents a most careless appearance, and is at once noticed by the critical eye. Attention to these little preliminaries, and neatness as regards the minute details, are the " littles " which insure perfect results.

COTTAGE SIDEBOARDS.

A dwelling to be in perfectly good taste, must be furnished according to its proportions and style. In a small cottage house, the surroundings, as well as the interior decorations and embellishments, should be of a simple, unobtrusive character; the colors quiet, and the light bright, (but not garish) in the Winter; shaded during the hot Summer weather; the furniture unostentatious; while it bears an elegant simplicity in all its features. Here the sideboards just described, could be incongruous, though in another dwelling, no larger perhaps, but of different character, they would appear perfectly appropriate. Many persons of moderate, even humble circumstances, are called sometimes from necessity to reside in large and even elegant dwellings; the rooms are spacious, with high ceilings and imposing windows; the anxious housewife looks with actual dismay upon the task imposed upon her, of furnishing such an abode—understanding fully that the few yards of carpeting, the neat suites of furniture, and diminutive lambrequins which fitted and appeared quite elegant in her old cottage home, would not appear more than " the drop in the bucket " here; this is one of the cases where the various articles we have described will be of infinite value, and even the handsome and massive pieces of furniture prove the " fitting thing." We know of three such cases as the above, that have come under our notice recently, and which have encouraged us to tell others what some women have done.

As a majority of our readers will probably be of the class which reside in less spacious dwellings, we proceed to give some directions for making sideboards, that will correspond with the chairs, bookcases, etc., described in previous chapters, and these " square Gothic " styles will be found unexceptionable as regards beauty of form and general appearance. The dining-room always requires its sideboard, and no matter how simple it may be, if constructed upon good principles, it will be found a convenience of which no housekeeper will be willing to be deprived.

A beautiful cottage sideboard may be made as follows: the height of which, exclusive of the ornamental back, is three feet two inches; its breadth six feet five inches; its depth two feet. The sides of the two closet-like portions which form the ends are of half-inch plank placed vertically, and screwed together by means of ledgers at top and bottom; the back portions of these upright pieces, two inches wide, are carried through the top, as shown, and serving to support the ornamental backboard. Three-quarter inch strips pass diagonally between these end cupboards (as shown in the engraving,) and are let into the backs of the inner upright pieces; and in front strips run at top and bottom from end to end. The panels in the doors are ornamented or embellished in any one of various ways—either by polishing the panel highly and using imitation of marquetry, ivory-inlaying, or transfer pictures—(Decalcomania or engravings, covering with glass or merely varnishing) or with some simple pieces of carvings. Imitation embossed leather looks well in such panels; it is made of French wall-paper, with deep crimson moreen ground and gold embossed figures in raised gold, which is tacked on a panel of half-inch wood; the spaces within the ends may be fitted entirely with shelves, or the upper part may have drawers, though these are always difficult for the amateur to make; a cabinet maker might better be called on for this part of the labor. The whole case must be securely held together by half-inch matched boards, screwed with flat-headed screws from behind, and running horizontally from end to end at the back. That portion of this match-boarding which appears above the top should be decorated with fretwork opening, cut out with the bow-saws, and neatly finished with the carving-tools. A unique and appropriate manner of finishing this work is by using a set of devices such as the Grecian key, etc., and to heat them until scorching hot, then apply them to the surface of the wood—burning the form on in different shades of brown. Unless seen, no one can understand the beauty of this simple embellishment. Our own keys, taken of various sizes, may be made to form a beautiful border for doors, drawers, picture-frames, etc.

The top should consist of one half-inch plank, and be sawed long enough to extend over the ends and top two or three inches. The top may be polished and ornamented, or merely covered with white marbled oil-cloth, of the enameled kind.

SIDE TABLES.

Besides the large dining-table which should always occupy the center of a dining-room, a small table, or even two or more of them, not only appear well but are very convenient for various purposes; as a receptacle for dishes that have been removed or are awaiting the arrangement of the table; to place the dessert upon, and many other like uses. These tables should be long and narrow in form, according to the dimensions of the room, and where this is small, the folding tables which can be put together and set aside after the meal is finished, will be found the best form. These little tables are so simple in construction that they may be easily made at home, and can be ornamented to correspond with the remaining furniture.

A simple side table which upon occasion may be folded and set aside, is made as follows: the frame consists merely of four rods or posts, forming legs and support for the top. These are two inches in diameter, and three feet, six inches long, fastened together, two and two, by long round-headed screws, which allow them to be turned together; across these are two flat strips of one-inch wood, three inches wide and three feet long, which are screwed to the ends of the crossed legs, sawed off flat in order to allow them to be placed flat on the top, after they are opened out; round rods of the same kind are inserted into holes at the lower part, as shown by the illustration. On this frame the top is laid, and in order to make it secure, yet to allow its being removed at any time, four wooden pins about an inch long should be inserted in the four corners of the frame, to enter holes bored in this top, when it is laid in its place on the frame. This frame-work may be made quite ornamental by painting and twining scarlet braid around the crossed-bars, and when covered with a tasteful linen or muslin cover, such as is shown in the model, will form a beautiful addition to a dining-room.

TRAY-COVER.

Materials, fine linen or damask in white or colors,—such as gray or buff. Embroidery cotton, No. 40, drilled thread, No. 20. Tray covers are not only

Fig. 122.

indispensable as a table adornment, but are useful as a protection to elegant and costly trays and to hide the deficiencies in those defaced and worn.

Fig. 123.

Illustration, Fig. 122, shows a beautiful pattern for these covers, and may be adapted to trays of any size. This work is easily done and is extremely elegant as well as durable. This same design may be used as application work, fastening fine linen on strong lace, and button-holing the figures, then working the cross threads in chain-stitch with a fine crotchet needle; afterward cutting away parts of the linen, leaving only the lace and cross-bars.

WINDOW-SCREEN.

Especially useful and appropriate to the dining-room are the elegant screens now so much used to place in windows, and of various styles and varieties, one of which, and a charming specimen of them, is shown in Fig. 124. The mate-

Fig. 124.

rials required are coarse curtain-net, crochet thread No. 40, and black sewing-cotton. The flowers are of the richest character, crocheted and fastened on the net in a graceful group as a center piece, and arranged in the corners and singly around the edge as a border.

These patterns shown in Figs. 125 and 126, offer the opportunity of using the flowers in the effective Irish crochet for other purposes than the screen shown.

On account of the lacing of the net when finished over a frame of polished rods fitted to the size of the window, the net must be cut somewhat smaller than the frame. The shape of one of the middle sized crocheted flowers shown in the screen, is seen in the illustration in its full size, and it is easy to arrange the remainder from this in any desired size and shape, beginning in the middle with a small piece of "Loose chain," this is crocheted round with 1 S C, inserting the hook through both chain links, 1 S C, being always added for the upper and lower leaf-point. The single petals are afterward united by a circle of S C, in order to make the flowers stand out still more ; in sewing on these with stalk-stitch in black silk, the back is turned to the outside. The flower calyxes to be made alone, are sewn on the inner flower edge, partly with visible, partly with invisible single stitches, but have single knots as center. For the small calyx, a small ring of S C, is laid under thick only surrounded by one row of S C, while the larger flower calyx, must have a thick Picot edge as

Fig. 125.

Fig. 126

shown on the full sized leaf in Fig. 126. The flower added to this leaf has a loose chain-ring to join on the leaves, this is crocheted over five times with 1 D C, in treble crochet.

So also is the middle part of the leaf, (illustration) with the right side turned to the outside ; so the middle rib of 18 L Ch join next for one leaf— (half) the following St. 1 S C., 1 D C., 2 T C., 8 D C , 2 H D C., and 4 S C., the other half is then made in an opposite direction. Now follow 2 rows of S C., worked backwards and forwards. The S C. of the first row catch only in the hind link (the front one makes an effective edge for the leaf) but for the second row the crochet is turned and the hook put through *both* links. The points of the finishing edge marked by single stitches in sewing on the leaves, are of common P. which are added always on the second edge St. with 1 S C. rounds of different sizes crocheted in S S. beginning in the middle, give the berries ; the stalks and tendrils are of L Ch. these according to the thickness required are to be crocheted with S. Ch or SC. on one or both sides. Round the leaf border the net ground is to be fastened down very firmly, and this before cutting away the material; the loops to lace on the blind of **L Ch.**, are either put on single or in small bunches and lastly; underneath the leaf edge. They may be crocheted or sewn on as appears most convenient.

Another beautiful window screen is made by basting Swiss muslin upon the net, and after tracing corner pieces like Fig. 127, and a center piece made of four of them in a cluster (the points placed together in the center) then working the outlines with fine embroidery cotton No. 18 in chain-stitch, the grapes in satin-stitch, and after all are completed, cutting away the Swiss from the foundation, leaving only the design. Such screens are

Fig. 127.

exceeding elegant, and give a beautiful finish to a window, besides frequently shutting out unpleasant views.

CHAPTER XIII.

TABLES, STANDS, ETC.

In speaking of the various pieces of furniture required, or perhaps we should say, *desired* for the different apartments, it is our wish to describe certain simple forms of each kind, that may be made by a lady herself, or at least by some member of her family; or, these neither being practicable or necessary, perhaps the nearest carpenter may be called upon. Such varieties of furniture are simple in design and easy of construction, requiring but few tools, and only plain pine wood, with some round-headed screws, brad nails, and some two or three sizes of common nails, hinges and locks, paint, varnish and the usual materials for upholstering, with glass perhaps for some of the doors. These articles, being what is called "home-made," will be honest in construction, and this may be adduced as an argument in favor of their being in good taste, for, according to the highest authority upon this point, "though fitness is not beauty, it is an essential part of beauty, and an article cannot be in good form unless that form explains its *construction* and is adapted to the uses for which it is intended. The form becomes "elegant" when due proportions and appropriate ornamentation or embellishment is added."

Our desire is to give some specimens of plain, simple, but substantial furniture, which, by proper and tasteful enrichment of painting, staining or carving, or the addition of hangings, trimmings and embroidery, may be made so rich and elegant in appearance as to stand the test of critical observation and not offend the eye of correct taste. A certain Gothic air will be preserved in each article, because it appears to us that in this style can most readily be carried out the great principles of making *construction itself decorative.* The articles of "home-made furniture" we explain, have each been made in our own family, and we can recommend them as being strong and durable.

Parlor tables, thirty years back, consisted in the inevitable "center-table," and what was termed a "pier-table," Fig. 128; the latter being a sort of ornamental stand with three sides and a plain back, placed flat against the wall beneath the "pier-glass," which the long, narrow mirror was termed. This table was some four feet in height, with marble slab, and generally richly ornamented with carving and gilding, but was an exceedingly stiff and ungraceful looking piece of furniture. A few years later, the "pier-table" was superseded by the gilded and marble-topped mirror-bracket, introduced for the accommodation of the now extended mirror which reached from the ceiling to the floor, but the popular center-table still held its place, and we may say is still admired by many persons, though the tasteful little *tete-a-tetes* that now dot the spaces of modern parlors, are so very much prettier and give such a dainty appearance to even the small room that they are becoming more and more popular, and bid fair to discard the ancient center-table to the auction room, where perhaps the frame will be purchased to serve in some ice-cream saloon of modest pretensions, and the marble, cut into sections, ornament smaller pieces of furniture, such as brackets or pedestals. Still, for a large room, the library or common sitting-room, nothing can take the place of a firm, neatly made center-table, if by this term is meant a table for the middle or central part of the room; for what can appear so altogether social, so cosy, and withal so convenient?

In a small parlor, however, and it is with this apartment, g r e a t e r or smaller, that we are now dealing, we should advocate the use of several small tables rather than

Fig. 128.

one large one; these to stand on the sides and in the corners, and not to obstruct the limited space in the center. The tiny table which our young ladies doubtless would call " *a love of a thing*," or if a particularly beautiful specimen, a " *perfect love*," is called in England (where it is used for that national institution, the " five o'clock tea,") " Belgravian tables " or " tea-stands." They are Liliputian affairs of only from twenty inches to two and a half feet in height, made with four slender legs, supporting a slab of wood about one-quarter of an inch thick (more or less according to size), which may be from twelve inches to two feet in length and of proportionate width. The methods of embellishing these elegant little affairs are *ad infinitum*.

They may be black, white or colored, inlaid or painted in French style, or the Japanese, Chinese, or plain English. That is, supposing we desire to have one of the light, gay little French stands; first we make a simple frame, like Fig. 129, (which being of pine, and of the very simplest construction can be gotten up for about twenty-five cents). This is rubbed down with " emery," or fine sand-paper, and is then ebonized or painted with the enameled (zinc) paint, made any desired color, or shade of color, a delicate pearl-tint, or one of light sage-gray is pretty for light grounds, though pure white presents equal charms perhaps; this ground should when finished appear like glass with a solid polished surface, and should the zinc-lead fail to secure this, recourse must be had to the varnishing and polishing previously described. Upon this is sketched

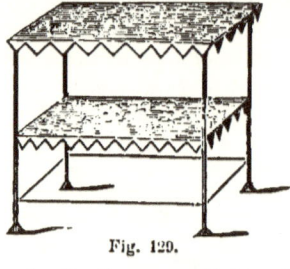

any design desired, such as flowers, birds, or even a pretty scene, or group of figures. This sketching will be best accomplished by using the pounce-bag; thus the outlines of the design and principal parts are drawn upon thin paper, and pricked with a sharp pointed instrument, then placed upon the table, and dusted with charcoal, lamp-black or other powder. Upon carefully raising the paper, the design will appear in small dots on the surface, and is then easily drawn off, using care to

Fig. 129.

make the lines very light. The painting is then done with tube-colors.

As many persons have not the time or ability to thus paint their furniture, we would earnestly recommend them to resort to the Decalcomania pictures for this and *all* work which calls for painted designs. Whatever may be urged in opposition to this imitation, it certainly has born the test of time and experience, and become more and more popular as it has become better known. The writer has had more than the average opportunities for testing the merits of this work, and can testify to its value, and perfect adaptation to household adornment. Wherever Decalcomania is not successful, it is either because the materials are not of good quality or the operator is careless and unskillful. Only procure the very best of materials from those establishments known to be reliable, and follow closely the directions given for the transferring the pictures, and you cannot fail to procure an effect as perfect as a finished water-color, or illuminated design.

By the best materials are meant, imported German and French plates, which are of three kinds; those upon white ground, showing the colors, (though not so vividly as they will appear after having been transferred,) those covered with gold foil, (in order to show the colors upon a black or dark ground,) and the brilliant silver-lined designs, which appear to possess a planished metallic luster that is peculiarly fine, and well adapted to certain kinds of work, as *imitation* of painting on metal, etc. For the other materials, the "fastening varnish" must be of the most reliable kind, warranted to be pure, or the designs will not only curl and peel off soon after the operation, but if it remains then, will not "wear well," but in a short time appear worn and defaced.

The finishing varnish is simply Antique or Demar varnish, and should also be of the finest quality—clear and of the consistency of syrup—not "gumming," nor clouded. With such perfect materials, you will effect results that will give entire satisfaction, and at this time when painted furniture is demanding and receiving fabulous or "fancy" prices, this means of obtaining elegances is not to be lightly esteemed.

Many persons have a fear of attempting to transfer large designs ; there is no necessity for this, for the writer has seen entire suites of furniture thus embellished, where a table, the foot-board of a bed, doors of wardrobe and other large spaces, contained designs eighteen inches in diameter ; and whether these were the oval centers containing a set of scenes in Switzerland, surrounded by a gold scroll-work border, or the charming groups of flowers, mosses and ferns, they are alike lovely, and were done without unusual trouble by a lady. Supposing then that our little French table has been painted with a ground of pearl-gray, or dove-color, on the center we will arrange a group of moss, roses and buds of a delicate pink, with the lovely green and brown leaves ; a graceful border of the same, in smaller buds, and half-blown roses in the corners, (which may be obtained with scroll-designs, etc., arranged with corner pieces and continuous vine for sides and ends).

Around the slender legs, minute roses and buds, (which comes in sheets arranged for edgings) can be put to run spirally from top to bottom. If the table has a shelf, a smaller group of roses, or a simple spray may ornament it, to correspond with the top. The moss roses are mentioned here because the writer has seen and used them with such charming results, and the design in these are so peculiarly beautiful. But morning glories of rich purple, crimson and white, are equally lovely, while upon a white ground the clear turquoise blue of the forget-me-not, or ever beautiful purple of the pansy is not to be surpassed.

Here, we have as choice a little treasure in the way of a table as could possibly be purchased in the store, and costing but a mere trifle, compared to the prices asked for these very articles.

For an Oriental pattern, obtain a quantity of the colored and dyed veneerings, and proceed to ornament your little stand in marquetry, which is now so popular and so altogether elegant. Mr. Eastlake and other of the late writers upon Household Art and Decoration, recommend very highly this mode of enriching furniture, inasmuch as it is again bringing to view one of the ancient arts, now so popular. The *tarsia*, or old Italian marquetry, was used in forming geometrical patterns, or arranged so as to represent natural objects, and so this work may now be applied. This work will doubtless be found a most satisfactory method of enriching tables, cabinets, brackets and such articles of furniture, as it is not only a most fascinating employment, but neither costly nor unusually difficult.

For the groundwork of this ancient style, if of pine, should be stained or ebonized—or better still, make the stand of walnut wood, and inlay upon it.

In this connection we should mention the use of the Autumn-leaves, which produces charming results if well done—and one of the very prettiest of tables the writer has seen, was made from these natural materials as described in "Household Elegancies," page 41.

Chinese and Japanese ornamentation for these little tables is of several kinds, all exceedingly elegant, as this class of work always is.

We will suppose you desire to imitate a set of the tables which are imported. These we find usually come "nested," and slipping one in another, so that when all are "pushed in" the entire four, five or six appear like one table with a deep moulded edge. The edges of the successive tables give the sides and ends the appearance of a moulded panel. The largest of these little tables is two feet long, eighteen inches wide, and two feet six inches high, the smallest only one foot long, eight inches wide and two feet high, the intermediate ones graduated in size to fit each one within the other. These are sometimes arranged in a group, each one drawn out so that it barely rests beneath the edge of the one above it, or they may be scattered in "graceful confusion" about the apartment. We have imitated two styles of these tables, either equally beautiful. In both, the ground was black, then for the one was obtained the dull gold and black designs sold for Potichomania work, consisting of Chinese pagodas, figures, vessels, etc., large scenes for the centers with corner pieces and border, and for the legs and little curved bar across the front, using gold paper cut into narrow strips. The designs were carefully cut out and pasted directly on the tables, and the ground raised by means of repeated coats of paint and varnish. These were when finished quite as elegant as the imported ones from which they were copied. The other set was made of nice pine wood, the outer surface of which was rubbed with emery-paper, and powdered pumice-stone until quite smooth, upon this was placed a design of very simple character, (for inasmuch as this is to imitate difficult inlaying with ivory, it should never be unusually complicated in design, as this would lead to the supposition that it was an imitation, whereas it might better appear as the *genuine* article). The designs therefore, should consist of geometrical figures or conventional forms of animal or vegetable life, such as we see on Chinese work. The border may be composed of a succession of triangles, circles, or other such figures with a few straight bands, these cut from letter-paper, and fastened on the white board of the wood, by means of small needles or pins placed perpendicularly. The ground is stained or ebonized, and upon raising the paper patterns the designs will appear like inlaid-ivory upon the black groundwork. The whole must then receive a coat of fine Demar varnish.

But with all these beautiful methods of making perfect imitations of costly tables, not one of them can exceed in beauty that of the transferred engravings, (given in chapter on modes of embellishing). Select some exquisite engraving, and transfer it as explained, make a border in the same manner from designs taken from papers or books, and the shelf and legs in similar manner, and you have a table that will call forth exclamations of delight from all who behold it.

Such are some of the methods of ornamenting the small tables which impart such an air of graceful ease and negligence, (if we dare to put it,) at once a sign of taste and prosperity, inasmuch as it gives the idea of real hospitality.

Where apartments are spacious and a center-table is desired in addition, it should be either handsomely ornamented or covered. The latter is a most elegant mode of adornment, giving a sort of grace to what would otherwise appear stiff and awkward. It is so easy at the present time to make a rich table-cover, that one would suppose every one would use this tasteful article. A square of cloth of any material, from the stone-colored or white drilling muslin, to the costly damask may with a little skill and taste, be made into a most graceful and elegant cover.

Muslin? you exclaim! Yes, verily muslin! Purchase a square of unbleached sheeting; take this square, and cutting off the selvage, fringe out several inches, and if you desire an extra rich fringe, tie it in knots. Spread this out upon a table or floor, and having cut out some scroll work from paper, arrange first a design in the center with large fern-fronds, leaves of pretty shape and large size, and a few flowers. Make a round or oval frame-work (according to form of table) of your scrolls, placing a spray of fern, etc., here and there through them. Then make corner pieces and border in the same manner. Make a quart of black or colored dye, and with a large brush and a piece of wire-net, or an old sieve, (as shown previously) proceed to cover with spray, according to general rules—which all know. Color fringe also, and from time to time remove certain parts of the fronds and leaves. After all are removed, go over with a small camel's-hair brush, and the dye; veining leaves, putting lines on flowers, and interlining the scrolls. When entirely finished, you will have a durable, and we can safely add, the most elegant cover you could desire.

Scroll work for this purpose is made by using saucers of different sizes, turning them to form a serpentine line. As regards the yellow tinge of the unbleached cloth, it is owing to this very point that Oriental stuffs have that peculiarly rich, soft shade or tone of color. Manufacturers in America, are in the habit of bleaching their cottons and woolens to a dazzling whiteness, whereas the Eastern people leave their cloth with the creamy, delicate tint natural to it, and the consequence is, all *our* goods possess a ghastly white, wherever white is apparent, while Oriental goods have the peculiar softness and richness of shade in the white parts which give tone to the whole.

This subject is occupying the attention of decorative artists at present, and it is to be hoped will result in an improvement in this respect, in which housekeepers will rejoice, as it is the excessive bleaching which renders our cotton and woolen goods so much less durable than Oriental fabrics.

SITTING-ROOM TABLES.

As we have remarked, in library and sitting (or living) room, a table should, if possible, occupy the center of the floor. In small rooms, of course, this is not practicable, but even here, such a table should be used as can be drawn out in the evening, for the family circle to gather around the lamp. Where (as in many small houses is necessary) the dining and sitting-room are one, the modern extension table is well adapted for ordinary use, for not only can it be used as dining table, but pushed together forms a neat center-table. This table requires a rather complicated frame-work, must necessarily be made by a cabinet-maker; but as a neat, plain extension table can be procured for from eight to sixteen dollars, it would appear possible for most families to enjoy this comfort, for this it certainly is, to the housekeeper, who is liable to require an extension of her table at any time, and find it a most inconvenient, perhaps impossible thing to elongate her small family table by means of several small ones, and we believe never was an invention (excepting the sewing-machine), so blessed to woman as this one of an extension table. For the living-room, the table should be strong, neat and solid, without any elaborate ornamentation of carving, and of such height as to form a comfortable desk upon which to write, if occasion requires, and whereupon garments may be cut out, or the various occupations of the family performed by both adults and children.

After making the frame for this table it may be ornamented to correspond with the remaining pieces of furniture, and no more tasteful or suitable embellishment can be applied, we believe, than that of imitating inlaid work (or marquetry), which is easily accomplished and readily kept clean and in order; no knobs of carving to injure or collect the dust, and no projections to catch the dress and be in the way of feet or hands. We should ornament the top of this table in the most beautiful manner possible and leave it without cover. In the center should always stand the evening lamp, but excepting this it should be unfurnished, leaving room for the various accessions of books, work or amusements when they are used.

In recommending an ornamented top we would say emphatically, never allow a marble slab to cover the top of any table in daily domestic use; the cold, hard surface presents such an unfriendly, almost uncomfortable appearance, and is unpleasant to work or write on in the Winter at least. For parlors, halls or chambers, marble slabs appear well, but never in sitting-room or library.

Besides the large central table in the sitting-room, there should be a small table, if room will permit, two or even three of them; a work-stand and a ladies' *escritoire*. A work-stand was some years ago an object of vast importance to the housewife, but since the introduction of the standing work-basket it has changed its character somewhat and is now merely a small table with drawer or drawers for locking up when necessary, for neither the standing basket nor the sewing-machine can quite take the place of the stand. Many persons have one or more, perhaps of the old-fashioned stands still standing in some part of the house, which, if they would bring forward and renovate by ebonizing and putting a line of gilding around the legs and on the drawers; purchase pretty escutcheons for the key-holes in artificial wood-carving and gild these; then embroider a tasteful cover, by cutting out figures from black velveteen and chain-stitching them with gold-colored silk on a piece of cigar or other colored cloth, and lo! she has the tasteful stand shown in Fig. 130, which is now the "height of the fashion," and could not be pur-

chased for less than fourteen dollars as it stands.

Or, take one of the little tables now sold at the stores for three dollars; (if of walnut wood), ornament the legs with gilding, (after ebonizing them,) then have made for the top a box exactly fitting it with lid to raise, and furnished with lock; stain and embellish the front and sides very tastefully, and embroider a tasteful cloth cover for the top, as also for the low shelf (made of a narrow strip of board laid on the bar between the feet) which is very convenient for holding a basket or other article used about sewing. Trim the lower part of this case and the cover of the shelf with fringe, and you have a tasteful work-stand, which costs very little; for truth

Fig. 130.

to tell, any ingenious lady might make the case entirely herself, for the lid need be only a quarter-inch piece of wood with small hinges, and for a trifle a carpenter or cabinet-maker would put a neat cover to fit down into the box, according to the most approved style of box-making; but why not, like another woman we know, learn to do even this piece of cabinet-making your own self? It is not difficult, and merely requires neatness, and it is so pleasant to be independent of the gentlemen. Fig. 131 will testify to this little table being capable of being changed into a most convenient work-stand. The little drawer should be finished with a neat escutcheon, which can be ornamented with gilding or paint.

A pair of the tasteful little hour glass stands, shown in Fig. 132, should adorn every sitting-room, for they not only form one of the most beautiful of embellishments, but are withal capable of being made so useful. No doubt many of our readers understand full well the making of these little articles, but lest *one* should not, we feel loth to omit the description of a pair which are one of the principal features in a room we wot of, and are so exceedingly elegant in their dainty covers that every one who sees them for first time, "turns to look again."

The coverings of furniture and hangings of the one window in this pretty boudoir are in accordance with both rug and paper, and these little stands form a lovely finish to two corners, in which they appear to peculiarly belong. But that our

Fig. 131.

Fig. 132.

readers may have an idea what a perfect little boudoir or morning-room may be made out of exceedingly *common* materials, (?) merely by bringing taste, industry and skill to the rescue; we will digress a little and give a brief sketch of this *multum in parvo*,—a bijou boudoir.

A PRETTY BOUDOIR.

This little apartment, you must know, was a porch built in the angle of the main building, an L, as it is termed; therefore, though the ceiling is high, the room is long for its width; the one window occupying the center of the end opposite the entrance, which is from the back parlor. A good effect was here secured by removing the door (or rather having none made), and introducing curtains of a quiet, but warm reddish brown shade, with gayer stripes, (the material nothing more expensive than the striped woolen and cotton goods, sold for one dollar per yard (double-fold). These in Summer find a substitute in white muslin, with a delicate border of spray-work in blue; the cornice is a strip of pine *door* mouldings ebonized and gilded on the side next the parlor, while the other is a strip of the same enameled with white, and ornamented with clusters of blue convolvuli. The one window has curtains and cornice to correspond, of course; while the six large panes of glass admit a soft glow of light through exquisite designs of Vitromania, consisting of six views in Switzerland of the loveliest character, and a grounding of softest effect in Sepia, with vivid blue Rosaces in each corner. This window, could we but bring it before our readers, would set them "wild" upon the subject of Diaphanie and Vitromania. On the two sides, run long low divans, covered with white *muslin*, so clouded and figured with blue "spray" that it appears like some beautiful material, a decided *novelty*, inasmuch as no one has seen any like it. The effect is charming, however, of that you may rest assured.

The floor has a border of a geometrical pattern, stained to imitate *parquetry*, and though it took both time and patience to accomplish it, has repaid fiftyfold all that was spent upon it, if only in the daily satisfaction it is to look upon a floor so beautiful, saying nothing of the gratification it is to "*weakminded* woman" to hear the oft repeated and enthusiastic praise lavished upon it by all who see it. On this beautiful floor is laid a large and heavy rug. The center was a remnant of exceedingly handsome Brussels carpet, two breadths in width and three yards long; around this heavy braids were sewn, until a long oval rug six feet wide, and twelve long was obtained, which was exceedingly satisfactory. The *rugs* of which the braids were made were old garments, washed and bleached in the sun as far as was possible, then dyed; all the white ones, of a vivid blue, the remainder, various bright colors. This rug was carefully made and has been "*a success.*" It lays on the center of the glossy floor, and is not stretched up to the wall as if it were bound to hide something, or was so flimsy it must needs be held with nails. From this gay, yet not tawdry rug and the pretty divans, the eye rises to the walls, covered with a paper of pearl-gray ground, with a lozenge-shaped vivid blue figure above the dado, which, in this case is what is called by the carpenters, a "chairboard" (the old time wainscot—the architect's and decorator's dado); this is painted in zinc paint of a pearl-gray, two or three shades deeper than the ground of the paper, and headed by a simple two-inch gilt moulding, bought for a moderate price at a picture-frame manufactory. Instead of the usual paper border at the ceiling, a similar gilt moulding finishes the edge of the paper and the ceiling of pearl-gray, calcimining a shade or so lighter than the paper, has a circle of pale blue and white morning-glories in the center, where an iron (or rather heavy wire) rod covered with ivy, descends and supports a pretty lantern of Gothic form. The ivy sprays covering the wire are in this case of wax, colored in several shades of green and a few brown ones, also purple berries here and there.

The corners on each side of the entrance are occupied respectively with a little table and a sewing-machine. The light table is entirely home-made, and consists of a board two feet wide and three long, to each end of which is firmly nailed two other pieces of same width and height, on which are screwed four small casters; this forms a substantial frame, firm, not heavy, and easily rolled from place to place; it is covered with embroidery; three pieces of dark navy-blue pressed flannel; it has upon each side a floral design in Berlin work; on the top is a scene called "The First Ride,"—a little Scotch boy in Tartan plaid and plumed cap, is held on his Shetland pony by his old servant; while in the background is a group leaning on the gate and a cottage door, while far away is a glimpse of the castle-home of the little heir (apparently), with mountains, trees, etc. (Not a difficult pattern to make by any means, and costing but little in time or money, when one thinks of the real value of such work. The entire three designs only occupied the spare minutes of one Autumn and Winter of a woman with four little ones and a full share of this life's busy care.) These designs were tacked on the wood-work with gilt-headed nails, and a deep woolen fringe hung below, with cords and tassels at each corner. We neglected to say that the side-pieces were sawed out (a la Eastlake) at the bottom; that is, a

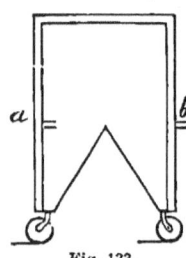

Fig. 133.

triangular section was taken out of the center, thus,— and narrower strips (laths will answer) extend across them from one to the other, at the points *a* and *b*; these are covered with the same cloth and a very narrow (embroidered) floral design. This embroidery is done in *petite-point*, with the canvas drawn out and the design left upon the cloth. This table holds a stereoscope, tray of cards, photographs, parlor kaleidoscope and a few papers or magazines to while away the stray minutes of the "passing occupant" of the easy chair in the corner behind it. This chair is made from the pattern of the corner-chair previously described, and covered with material like the divans.

On each side of the window, the corners are occupied by a pair of "hour-glass stands," covered with blue paper cambric over which are plaited covers of Tarlatan trimmed with puffs and fluted ruffles; a row of pockets around the top hold buttons, trimmings, etc.; and an opening down the center of the lower part forms a bag or case for scraps, patterns or other work-materials necessary in sewing. Dainty bows of Tarlatan edged with the paper cambric pinked out on the edges, and a puff and ruffles of the same with a large bow and ends fastens the dress around the pole.

Above these pretty stands are suspended a pair of Chinese shelves, made of two triangular pieces of board, eighteen inches on the sides, rounded in front, and hung by three blue cords and tassels; the front is ornamented with a strip of card-board cut out in points covered with gold paper, with a Chinese design on the center of each large point, and a gilt bell (a bell-button) suspended on a slender cord. The top of the shelves may be either painted or covered. The effect of these corner shelves and the dainty little stands beneath them is exceedingly lovely. Upon one stand is placed the writing-desk, with a tasteful gold and blue wall-pocket hanging on one side for paper and other writing-materials; on the shelf a few choice books; in front a chair that had once done service in some other house, in a more lofty position doubtless; as it is one of the beautiful colored bamboo chairs, so highly esteemed, and was bought at auction (in a most dilapidated condition,) for fifty cents; but cleaned, varnished and repaired, and covered with a blue tufted cushion over the broken seat, and trimmed with delicate puffings of white Swiss with edgings of fluted ruffles, and it has changed into a most attractive object.

On the other stand is a handsome work-box, once a long cigar-box, which, pierced with holes, and embroidered with zephyr, silk and beads, in imitation of *Indienne* work; pretty feet, made of four English walnuts, painted and gilded, a border, and knob on the lid of clusters of pecans and acorns, treated in the same manner, and the interior lined with blue silk, and fitted up with great care and neatness—all this, and behold an elegant box. The little work-stand is furnished with every article and implement that can possibly be required about sewing, while the footstool in front of the low sewing chair, in connection with the case—made by buttoning down the *dress* of the lower half of the stand, contains all necessary rolls of materials, scraps, etc.

The chair and footstool were both made according to directions given in chapters on these subjects. On the shelf above this stand are three books—not new, but well worn. A Bible and prayer-book, and a Thomas A Kempis, (good helpers for the day's-work commenced in this pretty morning-room).

The walls are furnished with lovely water-color pictures, consisting of bright flowers, soft, green mosses, and wavy looking ferns, Autumn leaves and two landscapes. Two pretty whitewood easels, on brackets of the same, hold photographs, and one large engraving of " *Christ Stilling the Tempest*," on the wide space on one side of the room, balances the two water-color landscapes on the other. In front of the window stands are an aquarium and fern case, both home-made, and resting on an iron stand that once served its time as a sewing-machine table. On each side of the window, three pot-brackets contain a half-dozen flourishing vines and creepers, which clamber up light wire trellises on the sides of the window and thence turn around the walls.

Now every part of this beautiful room is in perfect keeping, nothing garish or "loud," no one thing offending another; but each in harmony with the other, and showing its intention, which is, to make this room, intended for woman's *work*, as pleasant a place as may be, yet testifying in every particular for what it is used ; in which opinion we are sustained by Mr. Conway, who says, " the life of an apartment consists in the degree to which it subserves its end ; the decoration of a *salon* or parlor may well sympathize with the gayety of festive occasions, for they do not exist for the family alone, but in the more private apartments the tired limbs will require rest on chair or couch, and equally the eye will need rest upon soft and subdued shades."

The beautiful table in the illustration, Fig. 134, is connected with another section of our work, wherein the cover richly embroidered with convolvuli is shown, and we would suggest, that a charming effect is produced by using that entire series of embroidered articles on the various pieces of furniture to which

they are adapted. This center-table also shows the beautiful effect of the lace mats, and also of some tasteful ornament in shape of a handsome *Jardiniere*, aquarium, or perhaps a lamp of some fine form. Many persons still cling to the center-table, and consider no room well furnished that does not have its circular table in the center of the floor; and certainly where a group of persons desire to gather about one common center, perhaps to enjoy a Winter's evening game, or examine a set of beautiful or rare pictures, curiosities or books, what presents so perfect and appropriate a scene as the good old fashioned center-table; so though we are fully aware that fashionable people cry out "away with center-

Fig. 134.

tables," we say to those who enjoy their comfortable form and proportions, use your center-table and welcome—only, make for it a tasteful cover. The one here shown is beautiful beyond measure, but among the numerous patterns we offer in the following chapter, many other varieties will afford a large number from which to choose; some extremely simple, others as rich and expensive as may be desired.

The greater the variety among the small stands, the more "stylish" is the arrangement of the room considered. In Fig. 135, is shown a tasteful little round stand, which is rendered peculiarly beautiful by the graceful cover with which it is draped.

This stand is intended to occupy the corner of a sitting-room, and the accommodation of the feathered pet, the beautiful canary, and on this account the lovely table-cover is of material that will not become marred by the splashing of the gay fellow as he takes his morning bath, and dashes the water in a shower over the sides of his fountain.

A square of light-gray linen damask is procured, and the edges frayed out to the depth of four inches for the fringe, next a pretty fancy braid, scarlet, black and white, or a stripe of percale with suitable design, is stitched on each edge with a machine, two rows three inches apart, and (eight inches within the inner one) a third row crossed as the illustration shows.

Between these, a running pattern is done in scarlet and black braid, one row within the other. This is an exceedingly fine piece of work when neatly accomplished, and this cover is very beautiful, moreover it may be washed frequently without any fear of its fading, as the scarlet woolen braid as well as the black will bear frequent washing.

CHESS-TABLES.

It is now so usual for guests to be entertained with the popular games, of chess, checkers, etc., that tables or stands specially adapted to the purpose, are always considered necessary as a part of the furniture of a parlor or library. There are many beautiful methods of making these stands, one of which is, to obtain a plate of heavy glass, of size to fit the top of

Fig. 135.

table, and having drawn out a design of checkers in the center with ornamental figures around. (as shown in the pretty stand Fig. 136,) on paper, pricking the outlines, and transferring the design by rubbing, then drawing it out with a small camel's hair pencil dipped in varnish, afterward painting all the figures with transparent colors (as in Oriental painting) which will appear exquisitely beautiful when thrown out by the black background made with lacquer varnish.

Another way of ornamenting the top of such a stand, is by obtaining a set of

Decalcomania designs for the four borders around the checkers, and painting the squares in black and scarlet or other colors, which is easily done, then covering the whole surface with paint of some contrasting color, upon turning the glass over the designs, checks will appear in their own brilliant tints thrown out by the background. We sometimes are able to purchase engravings, with designs and checks already prepared for a chess-board, when it makes an elegant

piece of work transferred. The glass plate is fastened on the top by a strip of wood moulding, painted to correspond with the rest of the stand, which is handsomely ebonized and gilded on prominent places. The form of such a stand need not of course be circular; a square being more easily made.

Another pretty top for such a stand is shown in Fig. 136. This is made by first polishing the top of the table until a hard, smooth surface like glass is obtained, which may be black or any other shade. On this is traced a border and corner-pieces, and in the center an oval with cards, as shown. Various colors of sealing-wax are dissolved in alcohol, and a brush being appropriated to each, the figures are painted on the colored surface of the table. This work is not difficult and produces the most charming embellishment not only for this stand just described, but for other furniture, cabinets, backs of chairs, and especially for small articles such as wall-pockets, easels, etc.

Fig. 136.

Another handsome table is made by making a pine top very smooth, then drawing the border and central oval figure of cards, to paint them in with white paint slightly tinged with yellow until an ivory tint is obtained. On this to paint, with vivid scarlet and black sealing-wax, the hearts, diamonds, spades and clubs; then cover the ground with stain, or, in other words, to "ebonize" it. This will appear like ivory inlaid work, and is capable of being made surprisingly beautiful. The border and corners should be exceedingly simple in order to appear more characteristic of real inlaid ivory, which seldom presents elaborate designs. The present design is well adapted to this purpose, the conventional trefoils on the border and in the corners merely requiring to be made in three entire leaves and greatly enlarged.

The small walnut tables sold in the stores for three dollars, and frequently procured at the auction-rooms for fifty cents, may be made into elegant little tables for playing various little games upon, by working a cover in Berlin pat-

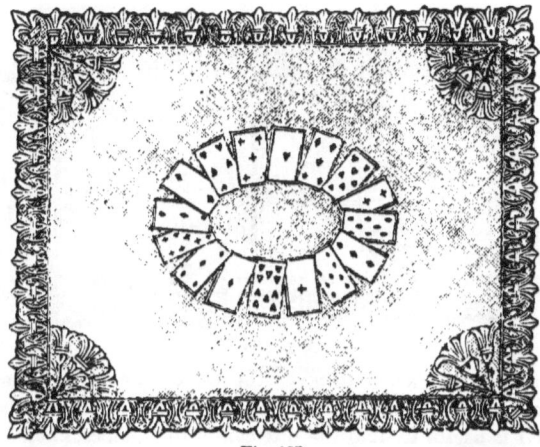

Fig. 137.

tern with zephyr alone, or with zephyr, silk and beads combined, the latter making a remarkably pretty top. The design given in Fig. 138 is appropriate.

Fig. 138.

for such a cover, and may be made to fit the table exactly by applying rows of work outside the border given until the proper size is attained; such designs as

Fig. 139 will make a rich border for this purpose, but by using coarse canvas and working four stitches for each one, the design will be so greatly enlarged

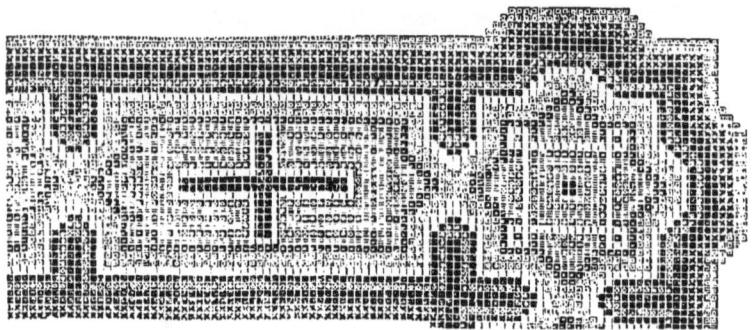

Fig. 139.

that it will be found sufficient to cover the top of the table. A second cover on the shelf sometimes found beneath the top makes a still handsomer stand, and such a shelf is useful to hold the box containing games, chess, cards, etc.

Fig. 140.

After the embroidery is finished, it is stretched tightly over the top of the table and shelf, and tacked closely along the edges with the little gimp or upholsterer's tacks (which are the only kind that will enter the hard wood). On this is placed a narrow moulding of wood, either gilded or carved; and if desired, exceedingly ornamental; the legs and frame-work of the stand may be ebonized and gilded, or painted with enamel in fancy colors.

Fig. 141.

Any table is made handsomer and unusual grace given to it, by the use of a cover, a pretty one of which is shown in Fig. 140. The top is covered with a circle of plain cloth, quilted in diamonds on the sewing-machine with silk of a darker shade, or some contrasting one; around this is sewed (with covered cord inserted between,) a straight strip of embroidery, the full-sized pattern for which is shown in Fig. 141.

The leaves are first thickly formed with working cotton, over which "stuffing" (as it is called,) is worked the satin-stitch embroidery, in coarse silk of contrasting color; the stems are of silk one shade darker.

This lambrequin may be made of material corresponding with the upholstering of the room, or of contrasting colors, if preferred; the only care necessary to be observed being to have the whole harmonize.

The little tables with shelves beneath them are made very much more elegant by simply covering the tops with cloths finished with narrow lambrequins like Fig. 142, tacked on with gilt-headed nails on gimp or strips of cloth pinked out on the edges. The narrow lambrequin is of cloth pinked out and ornamented with satin-stitch embroidery.

Fig. 142.

DESIGN FOR TABLE-COVER.

An elegant table-cover may be made by taking a square or circular piece of flannel of color to correspond with the upholstery or hangings, and transferring to it a border such as shown in Fig. 144. As the full size of this pattern is distinctly shown in Fig. 143, no diffi-culty will be found in doing the work, for which the following variety of mate-rials is required: Silk of many colors, alpaca braid of contrasting color to the ground, and sufficient white braid of the same kind to carry out the orna-mental scallops around the entire bor-der. The figures are done with the various colors, and the design shows the different stitches, satin, chain and half-polka, with a little point Russe, and application with braid. This bor-der will be found one of exceeding beauty, and is worthy the attention of

Fig. 143.   Fig. 144.

any lover of the beautiful. Such a table-cover would cost, in the stores, from twenty-five dollars to a hundred, according to the quality of the cloth and the beauty of the embroidery; yet, worked upon a square of thin cloth or pressed flannel, it may be made up for five dollars or even less.

After basting the braid in place, the knotting is done both on the white scallop-work and also on the ribbon-knots and ends; the graceful, conventional-looking flowers may be made with great rapidity, as also the chain-stitching and loose stitches of the remaining parts. In making covers of this and similar patterns, it will be found more economical to purchase the silk braid etc., by the ounce and from a wholesale establishment.

TABLE-COVER, BORDER AND CORNER.

Another beautiful means of ornamenting table-covers and the edges of curtains, etc., is by the use of the *applique* work. This work is of two kinds, in

Fig. 145.

the one the figures are cut from *Cretonne* or other cloth, and fastened to a ground, by means of chain-stitches, the figures, etc , being arranged just as they

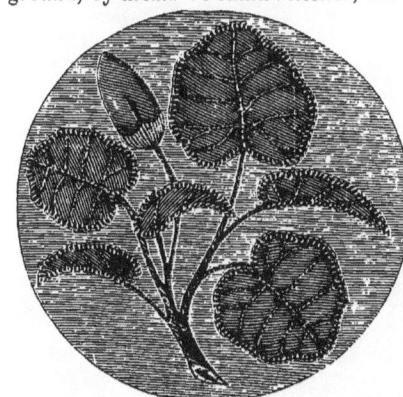

Fig. 146.

appear upon the cloth in all the beauty of a shaded picture, whether it be a pastoral scene, flowers, or other such design; while with the other kind the various parts are cut from cloth, velvet, silk, etc., in proper colors, and the edges covered with chain-stitching, while the various parts of the flowers or other design, are brought out and formed by stitches of different kinds, and other applications that will produce the desired effect.

In Figs. 145 and 146, we have examples of this style, which will be found well adapted to the handsome adornment of a table-cover or curtains. The design is an extremely simple one, consisting only of a waved line of scarlet braid edged on each side with sewing-machine stitching, and held down by a line of herring-bone in black silk. The leaves with three points are cut from scarlet cloth a shade or two darker or lighter, and fastened down on the edge with narrow gold-colored braid, held with black silk stitches taken across at equal distance, about one-eighth of an inch apart. The remaining part of the work is done in silks of all colors used at the discretion, and according to the taste of the operator. In each corner a cluster of leaves like Fig. 146, cut from brown and green merino, silk or velvet is fastened in a simi-

Fig. 147.

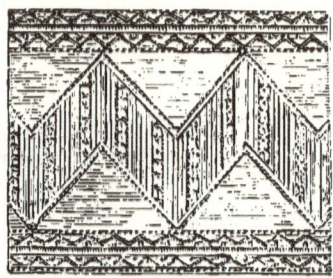

Fig. 148.

lar manner, and a gay star as shown in Fig. 147. Or the various colors of braid may be of the narrower variety, and held by embroidery like Fig. 148, with stitches of various colors on each side. Again, a piece of material of contrasting color from the cloth may have a scallop embroidered with three different colors and a gay dot of large size in satin-stitch above it, while along the edge the braids (named before) may be held in place by stitches.

Fig. 150 is a simple yet elegant border made by stitching ribbon or alpaca

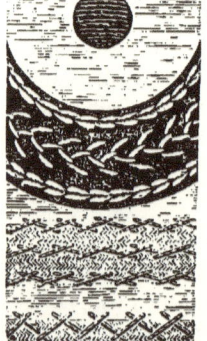

braid with loose stitches of bright colored silk or zephyr, and embroidering across in the center of each figure thus

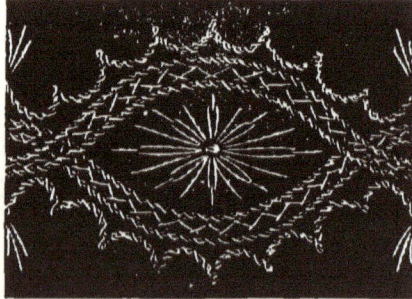

Fig. 149.   Fig. 150.

formed. This with black braid, scarlet, yellow and green stitching, will be found a most beautiful border. Fig. 151 is different from any other given, and is to be applied to pique or damask. The pique may be white or colored, and has a figured percale basted on the center; it is marked off in points, and either cut, turned under on the edges and has a stitching in machine or chain-stitching.

Fig. 153 is also a beautiful design in application embroidery, consisting merely of a border of gray and green velvet leaves upon a light ground. The

Fig. 151.

Fig. 152.

effect is lovely, and with a scalloped edge, this alone makes a simple yet elegant cover, easily accomplished.

The design in Fig. 150 is more easily made than any that have been given, and consists only of a design formed of cord held in place by stitches of silk or wool of any bright shades.

A beautiful and economical cover is made by cutting out a quantity of squares of flannel or cloth, embroidered as shown, and pinked out or notched around the edges and fastened on the cover in rows with dots and stitches as shown in the illustrations, Figs. 151 and 152. As several kinds of materials can be used in these covers and any scraps will answer for the small squares, it will be seen that they may be made quite economical, as they use up, not only the odds and ends of various materials, but the ends of embroidery-silk, remnants of spools of sewing-silk and braid.

Fig. 153.

The last and most elegant border we shall describe, is a superb design in true Oriental style. It is made of two colors of cloth united by means of chain-stitching, and the center design is worked in chain-stitch, point, Russe and half-polka stitches, in all varieties of color. The effect of this *Indienne* design, wrought in all the brilliant tints that can be pro-cured, is surprisingly beautiful. The pattern can be readily understood from the illustration, and the colors may be arranged to suit the taste. It will be perceived that the entire design is given, and the light block unites with the dark continuously. This is the richest cover of this kind we have ever seen.

Other beautiful covers are made by cutting paper patterns of scroll work, and applying these to materials of contrasting colors or shades, cutting them out carefully, and after basting them on in proper position, to stitch a line (along the inner margin,) on the sewing-machine; then cover the raw edge with braid a shade or so darker or lighter than the scroll; next, to work lines and figures, with silks of various bright colors, in chain, point Russe, half-polka and side stitching, in imitation of the Turkish embroideries. A still more simple method is, to use the fine alpaca braids, with stitching on the sewing-machine, using several shades or colors of silk (or cotton even), in plain " lock " or shuttle stitch. Mere straight bands of various colors done in this way, will afford an

Fig. 154.

elegant border, and where sofa and chair-covers, lambrequins, curtains, and table drapery are made *en suite* in this way, it will be found not only an inexpensive, but elegant garniture.

Still another pretty border is made by cutting out deep scallops on one or both edges of the cloth, covering the edges with braid or stitching, and putting a scallop or a row of them above.

Again, the application of flowers and figures from chintz, by means of *applique* embroidery, is another tasteful and economical ornamentation.

Two or three yards of some design that has figures frequently repeated, will be amply sufficient for several covers, (table, lambrequins, etc). The safest method is to fasten the cut figures on the material with a touch of mucilage;

then chain-stitching, a little satin-stitch, perhaps, braid, and side-stitching will hold the edges secure, and make a neat finish. Most Oriental looking hangings can be produced by means of this style of work, and it should be adopted by all those who desire to make their homes tasteful at small expense of time and money.

On the central medallion, copy some of the curious figures and Chinese characters such as you find on tea chests, etc. On the next, diamonds and circles made like Fig. 155, and join the scalloped edges with a colored braid fastened

 with herring-bone stitching; below, add a second row with stitches of coarse silk between. The scallops below are covered with points and braid, and which is clearly shown in the miniature illustration of the section of the cover.

The different Figs. given, though straight, can be readily adapted to the curves in the scallops, when required in this form. On each corner, is a medallion of scarlet and white on the black cloth, the

Fig. 155.   Fig. 156.

palm-leaf figures of which are shown in Fig. 156. The medallion is an oval six inches long, cut out in scallops and united to a scarlet figure two inches deeper, which is embroidered with button-hole stitching on the small scallops around the edge, and further adorned with circular ornaments, but of the smallest size; also a line of dots within the button-hole work on the edge, as is shown in the illustration.

The same medallion just explained, may be continued (reduced in size) around the entire border, or it may be merely worked on the scallops. At the extreme end of each corner below the oval, is a figure composed of three double leaves of yellow silk, with a central single one, each worked around with button-hole stitching, and each alternate one worked with dots and herring-bone, from which the graduated circular figures extend and join the border. If the small illustration and the full-sized figures are closely examined, there can be no difficulty in arranging this handsome cover.

COVER FOR SMALL TABLE.

Another stylish little cover is made thus: Take a piece of cloth two feet in diameter, whether round, oval or square, and of a cigar-color; cut the outer edges in inverted scallops; place this on another piece of cloth of a deep-green shade, and six inches deep, and fasten the scalloped edges with herring-bone stitching in black, on a braid a shade or two darker than the green cloth, beyond which work a Grecian key design in yellow silk. Next cut a strip of

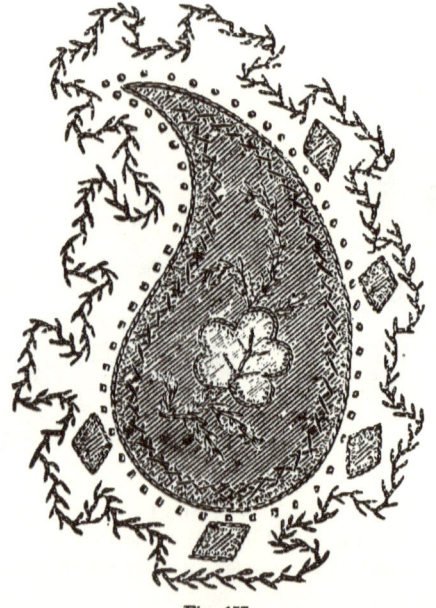

Fig. 157.

black cloth five inches wide, and make the edges slightly scalloped, fitting the one on the green margin with herring-bone stitches and scarlet braid; the other on another band of the cigar-colored cloth eight inches deep, on which arrange a border of palm-leaves adorned with *applique*. Make these palms in all colors, as also the leaf and diamonds surrounding them, and the herring-bone, buttonhole and other fancy stitches used in the embroidery. Thus, in a scarlet palm the leaf may be buff or maize color, with embroidery of browns, reds, etc., in a blue palm. Use a white leaf and black, yellow and crimson embroidery, and thus make as great a variety as possible. The greater the variety and the more brilliantly imposing the colors in these covers, the greater the beauty. In the central medallion a Chinese figure-piece like Fig. 158, may be fastened in application work. Such designs can be found on many kinds of Japanese or Chinese fabrics, and must be cut out and fastened on with button-hole stitching or a braid. Where surroundings are not exactly what is desired, resort may be had to embroidery, as shown in our illustration where the shrubbery and vege-

Fig. 158.

table growth is entirely made of silk stitches, in shades of green and brown, with crimson and yellow flowers. In application work, anything is allowable which will enhance the beauty of the work or make it plainer.

Another handsome little cover is made by using the different colored cloths, as has been described, and putting in the center an embroidered flower in satin-stitch. This, upon a scarlet ground, perhaps, is placed beneath a larger circle, from which a section is cut out, and the edges pinked, as shown in Fig. 159, which is only one-fourth the size. The edges of each piece of cloth are scalloped and embroidered with silks of all colors in one of the designs shown in the design, which exhibits three beautiful patterns, each easy of execution, and which may be rapidly accomplished.

Fig. 159.

TABLE FOR THE BIBLE.

The parlor lectern for the accommodation of the family Bible is spoken of in its proper place, but inasmuch as many persons use a small table for this purpose, we will offer a design for a cushion and cover for such, which will be found extremely elegant and appropriate. The cushion for this purpose should be made to fit the table, and made in what is called "box" form, that is with a narrow strip extending around it between the top and bottom. This piece should be two inches in width, and below it depends the lambrequin. The top of the cushion is first embroidered with the design traced out so as to fit the central part, in a space twelve inches square or less. Around the cushion is fastened a shaped lambrequin ten inches deep, on the front of which is embroidered the monogram I. H. S., with the appropriate leaves and figures, which in our illustration are made in application embroidery with gold thread and cord. The foundation is of purple velvet, the design cut from amber-colored satin, with narrow cord of gold fastened down with yellow silk; the leaves are veined with gold, and the medallion and monogram are made entirely of gold thread. A handsome design is made by using crimson velvet for the foundation, with the

Fig. 160.

designs cut from satin a shade or two lighter or darker, and the dotted raised knots covering the leaves, stems and medallion done with gold thread. The

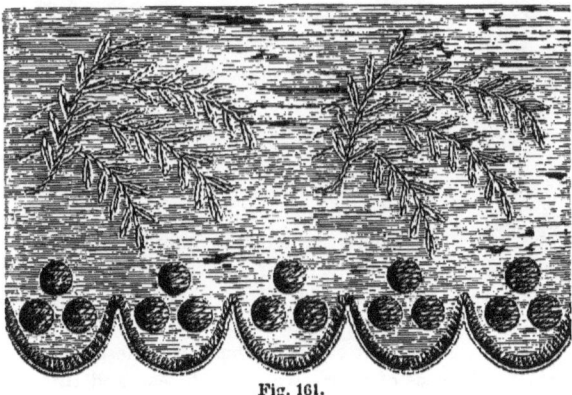

Fig. 161.

monogram is made of gold cord fastened down in the usual manner with gold-colored silk or fine gold thread. The lambrequin must be lined with stiff muslin, or interlined in order to give firmness. The edges are finished with cord, and tassels are fastened to each corner, and also to the corners of the cushion.

BORDER FOR TABLE-COVERS, BED-SPREADS, ETC.

Another beautiful border is shown in Fig 161, and this will be found of easiest accomplishment, as it only consists of a simple scallop, well stuffed with

embroidery cotton under the button-hole stitching of silk, as also the three dots in satin-stitch. The spray of leaves above may be made in various colors, each single spray forming the compound cluster, being different on each leaf of the single sprays in various colors or shades of the same color, as taste dictates; or if preferred, the whole cluster may be of one color, as black, the next scarlet, and so on. When worked with zephyr, this style of cover costs but a trifle, and may be rapidly accomplished.

Fig. 162 shows a lovely border of oak-leaves and acorns in application work, the leaves having been cut from green and brown cloth fastened to the foundation with button-hole stitching of the same color, and veined with a very light shade; the acorns are formed by raising with cotton, and covering with two or three shades of brown, with black and gold-colored silk knotted over the cups. The veins also are made of light shades of brown.

This border is unusually handsome, and a set of curtains and covers of cigar-colored reps, with these oak-leaves in four shades of green cloth, and the acorns of dark brown silks, make one of the richest sets of home made hangings we have ever seen. The leaves may be cut three and four inches long if desired, and a table-cover thus made will repay all the time spent upon it.

Fig. 162.

There are a great number of persons who prefer white covers for sofa and chair-cushions, tidies, and other articles of white muslin, lace or net. These will no doubt hail with delight an opportunity for making, in their spare moments, various beautiful designs for this kind of work. Materials.—A piece of coarse white net fifteen and three-fourths inches wide, and eighteen inches long, coarse embroidery cotton, coarse drilled thread, one yard ribbon one and one-half inches wide.

There is no cover for cushion, or table, as dainty as the ones made of white

Fig. 163.

material; and the style shown in Fig. 163, with the various squares used in making it, are of great beauty and well worthy of imitation. In this pattern, the division of diamond squares, which make, at the corners, triangles, are worked on a straight net foundation, and these have in our model, the size given by the material itself. Each diamond is of forty-four net holes on each side, these being first run round plain with the thread; the plain spaces for

Fig. 164.

colored ribbon to be run in between the net divisions, when counted out, are after the full-sized illustrations below, each darned with a lace pattern, and

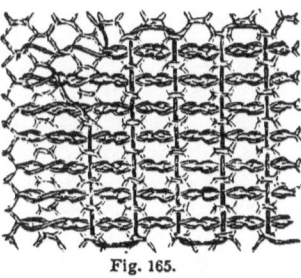

Fig. 165.

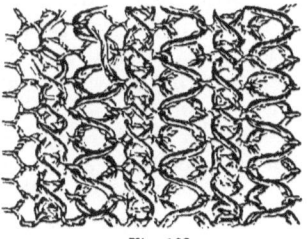

Fig. 166.

with coarse thread; the outer edges of the cover are to be button-holed firm, with which the outer tatted edge is to be caught and worked in. Any tatted edge may be substituted for this one. Colored ribbon is placed under the bound-

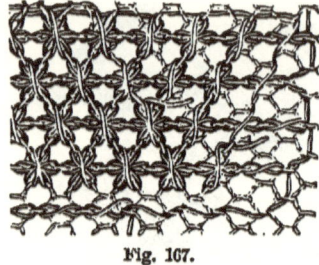

Fig. 167.

Fig. 168.

aries of each net division. Fig. 164 shows a pretty medallion-shaped trimming for inserting between squares of embroidered linen for these white covers.

There can be no excuse for a housekeeper's not having a tasteful cover for

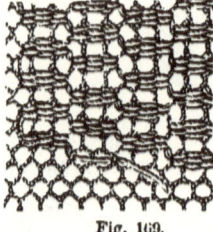

Fig. 169.

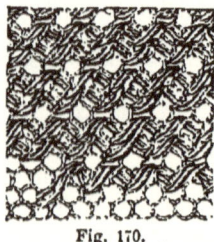

Fig. 170.

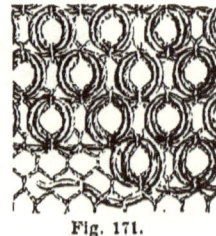

Fig. 171.

her table, surely, in this day of "wonderful bargains" and astonishing imitations, for with a square of double-width reps, or some one of the other pretty stuffs now to be had at such reasonable prices, and a band of five inch velvet ribbon, sewed a few inches from the edge, a unique cover is made at once; or, supposing your table is round or oval, cut a piece to fit the top, then a band six inches wide sewed around it, finished with cord on the seam and a scalloped edge bound with braid on the sewing-machine, or embroidered; otherwise substituting heavy fringe. Covers in imitation of the Indian or Oriental work, are made in many ways. A striking design is shown in Fig. 172, which we will describe so plainly that we believe any one will be able to imitate it. For this, three colors of cloth are required—supposing we name black, scarlet and steel-gray. Cut a piece for the center from the gray cloth, sufficiently large to cover the center of the table, for a distance of two or three feet from the middle point (more or less according to the size of the table); cut the edge out in scallops four inches wide, and rather shallow. Around this place the black, cutting the edge to fit the scallop, and overlapping about one-fourth of an inch, and scalloped on the other edge to correspond in like manner. This piece must be eight inches deep for a large table, six for a small one; next place the scarlet, cutting

Fig. 172.

one edge to fit the scallops, the other left straight; on this join the black again, making both of width to suit the table. Run the different parts together, lay-

Fig. 173.

ing one edge over the other, and stitch together on the sewing-machine; if a chain-stitch, making it come on the outside and using silks of all colors. This done, mark out the figures; long stitches dotting the spaces between the herring-bone, are of black zephyrs. The edges are finished with small points in button-hole stitching, and on each end is a border of plain linen or cotton goods, of color harmonizing with the material used for the center, embroidered with the same colors; a large scallop on the edge is worked closely with scarlet thread in button-hole stitching, while the figure in the center of each scallop is made with scarlet zephyr corresponding with the previous work; the star of the

Fig. 174.

darker, and the coiled circle of the lighter shade. The dot of satin-stitch in the center, of scarlet cotton. This cover is particularly beautiful when made of one of the gray or buff striped table linens, though some extremely handsome ones have been made of the wide striped bed-ticking, and where a fine quality of this article can be procured, it will be found most desirable for covers of various kinds. The colors used in the embroidery may be varied to suit circumstances, of course, and the scarlet is only recommended on account of its being durable and not changing color in washing.

An elegant appearance can be given to a very shabby table by painting and embellishing the legs or pedestal and covering the top with cloth embroidered in the Turkish style, using silks or wools of all bright shades and colors conceivable; putting them in according to convenience or fancy. Such a design as Fig. 174 will make a most gorgeous cover, and be found very easy to enlarge and draw off; for it is not material about its being accurately transcribed, merely giving sufficient resemblance to retain the characteristic points, which are entirely Oriental in appearance. The central circle is chain-stitched, (say in black, with a circle of white beyond) and may be of any size from a tea-cup to a dinner-plate, according to the size of the cover. The star in the center is of shades of gold color, scarlet and from filling made of rows of knots or stitches. Outside of this circle, on the sides, are ten points outlined with green, in arches extending from one to the other; in each point a white

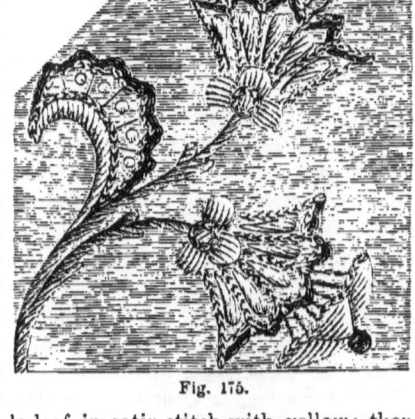

Fig. 175.

and violet figure, while between, a triple leaf in satin-stitch with yellow; then the scallops with dots of straw-color or white. On the top and bottom of circle the graceful arabesque figures are made in silks of various shades of scarlet, yellow, lilac, green, brown and blue, with sufficient white to give the brightness which *white alone* can impart. The second figures upon each side of this corner one, are only one-half as large, but of similar character, and extending from them is a branch of conventional-looking flowers, for which the full patterns, Figs. 175 and 176 will give an accurate guide; and these will aid immensely in forming the preceding parts, as each stitch is clearly defined.

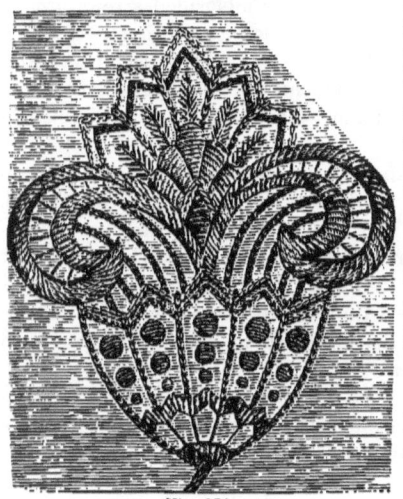

Fig. 176.

The colors may be of any shade preferred, as we have said; but the finest effects are produced in these large flowers by using several shades of one color; and a few strongly contrasting tints, throw these out with full power; black and white in the parts designated (in chain-stitching) add materially to the beauty of the design, and if narrow silk braid is preferred to chain-stitching, it may be used with equally satisfactory results; indeed braid and satin-stitch combined make an elegant cover.

These imposing looking covers, often approximating in richness and beauty of color to the fruits of Eastern looms, or "cunning work" of those wonderfully skillful people who dwell in the lands of the Orient, are well worth the cost of the materials (which purchased at wholesale houses is not extravagant), and the work is fascinating beyond description.

An easy and tasteful cover of the kind is made by using strips of two or three colors, braided with chain-work of narrow worsted braid or zephyr; or to take a square of cloth and sew on lines of alpaca braid with sewing-machine, scarlet with gold-color or yellow; green with black, and black with lilac; above this line, a strip of some flat braid held with point Russe embroidery are placed below (as shown in the diagram, to which they are also screwed).

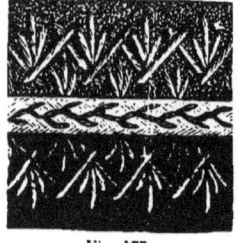

Fig. 177.

Two small triangular blocks are screwed in to prevent any looseness, and also to give strength laterally. The corners of the top are sawed off to give more tasteful form, and green or other colored oil-cloth or other material, such as velveteen or cloth tacked tightly over, the tacks running along on the underside.

Strips of half-inch moulding an inch wide, or a neat beading is fastened with round-headed screws around the edge and over the oil-cloth, and directly above it runs a line of gilt-headed nails, which give a neat finish to this portion of the top. The whole wood-work is finally rubbed smooth with fine emery-paper, and powdered pumice-stone, and either well oiled or varnished.

The large round-headed screws are painted with black lacquer or Japan varnish, or if an extremely elegant finish is intended may be gilded or bronzed. The legs and frame around the lower part, may be ornamented in various ways, either by painting in imitation of inlaying or by fret-work, sawing out ornamental figures. Either of these methods will be characteristic of this kind of work, and in perfect keeping with the workmanship. The appearance of this style of furniture cannot be imagined by merely looking at an illustration, and this table though apparently so simple is exceedingly handsome, but as so very much depends upon the nicety of workmanship and tastefulness in embellishing in articles so simple in form, it is only by examining the object itself that its merits can be fully appreciated or justice done to the style.

COVER FOR TABLE-CUSHIONS OR CURTAINS.

The cover, Fig. 178, is shown in miniature size, and consists of gray and white striped drill or diaper. The pattern is worked on the wide gray stripes

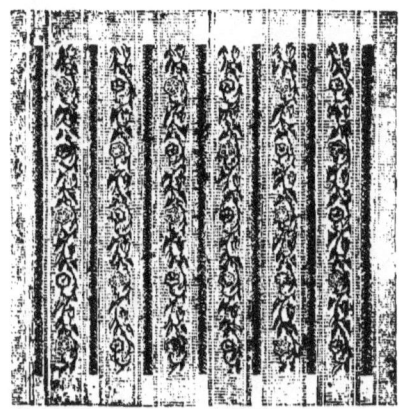

Fig. 178.

Fig. 179.

with colored purse-silk, (or zephyr if striped woolen material is used) in pretty colors in point Russe and herring-bone stitches. The narrow white stripes are marked by black alpaca braid, stitched on with any bright color on the sewing-machine. As a finish to the edge, scallops, bound with braid or colored fringe, will be most appropriate.

The style of cover here shown in Figs. 178 and 179, are now so much used, that ladies are constantly desir-

Fig. 180.

ing new designs, and these are among the most elegant we have yet seen, still so easily made that any one may accomplish them without difficulty. Fig. 181, is shown in the pattern No. 180, and consists of a square of damask or plain linen, white or gray, embroidered with *applique* in scarlet and white braid. The design is marked upon fine white linen lawn, and basted on the colored ground, outlined with the braid, and then cut out as shown; the stems are made of braid or chain-stitching of the cotton. Or as in the pattern No. 180, the design may be fastened on with button-hole stitches of scarlet working cotton. The material may be ecru, and if preferred the white leaves held with black or white.

14

Fig. 182, shows a cover of colored linen braided with black, white, and scarlet braid, and stitches of herring-bone in scarlet and black cotton, the full-sized pattern for which is shown in next Fig., and may be extended to any size.   The

Fig. 181.

Fig. 182.

edges are fringed out and may be tied or not as preferred. For oval trays these may be adapted to the form, and a complete set with coffee and tea-pot cozies to match; egg-covers, mats and dish napkins, give a bright and elegant appearance to the table.

CHAPTER XIV

CHAIRS.

It is a rather popular idea in this "our day and generation," to incline to the *ultra* fashionable; or, to the Eastlake style, because in the old garret lurks some quaint remnant of the olden time in shape of a heavy oak or walnut chair.

Mr. Charles Eastlake, in his "Hints on Household Taste," has immortalized several chairs, celebrated articles of furniture, as samples of perfect style, and obtained permission from the late Earl de la Warr (Knole, Eng.), to make copies of them. Mr. Eastlake found a slip of paper "tucked beneath the web-bing of a settee, which fixed the date of some of the furniture of this ancient mansion indubitably at 1620"; "it hav-ing remained intact since the reign of James 1st." These examples of ancient furniture are eminently adapted to the majority of homes in this country, com-bining, as they do, elegance, simplicity and comfort, and being so easily imita-ted, either by rejuvenating some old and perhaps valued relics, or by getting a house carpenter to make the simple frame-work, which any lady may afterwards cover as elegantly or plainly as desired.

A set of chairs Mr. Eastlake has had made for his own dwelling, after designs of his own. These, also, can be readily imitated, and certainly do possess the ad-vantages he applies to them—simplicity in design, durability and comfortable upholstering. Such chairs could be ob-tained at a small cost, directly from the

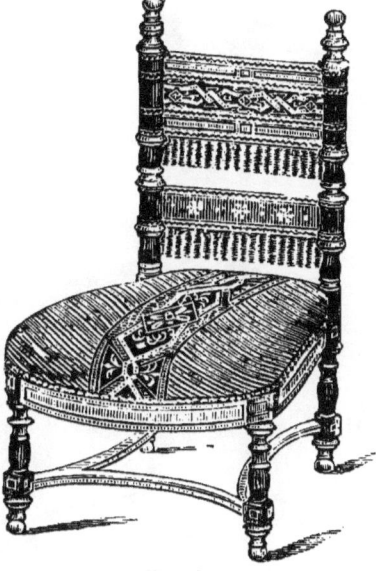

Fig. 183.

manufactory, and "finished up" to suit the taste of the housekeeper; and, in-deed, so many of just such form of chair are to be found in old dwellings, or may be procured at a merely nominal sum from the auction rooms, that we can not but recommend our readers to obtain a few, at least, of these quaint looking articles. With embroidered covers they would be exceedingly elegant, and the wood-work either ebonized or painted with some delicate light tint, in the fine enameled zinc-paint, would make a handsome chair out of a very plain and rough one.

As will be seen, it is not a difficult form to imitate, and the carving may be altered to suit the taste or circumstances of the case; such a chair would look well with a plain panel for the back, embellished with imitation of marquetry, ivory-inlaying or painting, or, in lieu of the last, to apply "transfer" designs,

in some one of the many elegant varieties of this beautiful work. This is a hall chair, but its comfortable proportions and form would appear to recommend it highly as a sitting-room or library seat, in which case upholstering would be necessary on seat and back, the material used in covering to correspond with the furniture of the room, or harmonizing with hangings, carpet and wall embellishment.

Figs. 183 and 184 are illustrations of chairs that have been made elegant simply by the aid of rich and tasteful work, and a little painting and gilding. Such chairs are to be found in many houses, and, perhaps, have been put away out of sight as "old rubbish," but if so, let them be brought forth to the light, well scrubbed, and "scraped," and repainted, as we have directed previously. Across the back and extending round the posts, fasten strips of embroidery in such a manner that they cover the hard wooden strips extending across the back; if desired, these embroidered bands may be lined and slightly padded, to insure comfort to the back. The seat is then covered with a loose cushion, which is tightly stuffed with hair, moss, or even newspapers finely shred. Over this is tacked the cloth or other covering. A double cover with a very thin layer of cotton between, neatly quilted on the sewing-machine like Fig. 184 looks well, as also a diamond pattern in chain-stitching. The bands of embroidery fastened across the seat may be of any kind preferred, either Turkish, Berlin, or *applique*. The lower part of the seat may be still further ornamented by a narrow strip of embroidery, a scalloped lambrequin or a fluted ruffle. The stripe given in Fig. 184, of Berlin work, is fine for this purpose. Many old chairs have a vast deal of carving about them, and though, while shabby and covered with dirt this may

Fig. 184.

not appear sightly; when refreshed with the painting and gilding we have described, they will be more admired, perhaps, than many new pieces of furniture.

In Fig. 186 the upper band on the back is an application design of black velvet fastened with a chain-stitching of gold-colored silk in a variety of colors, which will give the appearance of Oriental embroidery. For common furniture, such as sitting-room footstools, chairs in constant use and other such articles, a good strong bed-ticking (with clear blue and white stripe) if nicely worked with gay-colored zephyrs in "side-stitch," makes beautiful stripes, or, indeed, entire covers, which could never be supposed to have for a *basis* so ordinary a material as bed-ticking.

Fig. 185.

In Fig. 185, we have a plain but beautiful chair, covered with white cotton drilling (or muslin of good quality will answer,) and adorned with monogram and floral design in spray-work, which, as we have said, is a charming means of embellishing.

The monogram is cut from paper and fastened in position on the muslin, the leaves and sprays arranged on back and seat, and the spray cast in the usual manner. The colored spray, violet, crimson, blue and all the varied colors of the aniline dyes, produce a lovely effect upon white or stone-colored drilling, and will be found admirably adapted to the adornment of chamber or sitting-room, where the lambrequins, curtains, furniture-covers, and other appointments require a more *cheery* aspect than other apartments.

The simplicity of the chair of which Figs. 186 and 187 give the back and

Fig. 186.

front view, will render it very appropriate for a hall or chamber, yet when tastefully adorned with embroidered cover, as in our illustration, it is sufficiently tasteful for any apartment. The frame is plain, and could be made with but little trouble or expense. The seat and back are covered with webbing only, as it is proposed to cover both with embroidered cushions.

Figs. 188 and 189 will serve as samples of chairs which may be made exceedingly elegant by gilding the wood-work, and upholstering with stone or lavender-colored velveteen, ornamented with spray-work finished up with India ink and Sepia, thus producing the black figures. Birds, flowers, etc., cut from newspapers, answer well for patterns. White velveteen, when evenly covered with black spray, makes a soft grounding that has a beautiful effect. This

Fig. 187.

is a style of ornamentation that we can heartily recommend as being not only as beautiful as more costly materials, but inexpensive withal. As many do not understand the manner in which the spray is thrown, we give an illustration in Fig. 190.

Figs. 191 and 192 are illustrations showing how two varieties of old and partially worn-out chairs may be renovated and made both comfortable and ornamental.

In this Fig. we have one of the ordinary cane-seated chairs, such as are found in many houses in a shabby, half-worn condition. There are numerous ways of changing these into most delightful sewing and "cozy" chairs, or as the two here shown testify, into really elegant parlor furniture; an entire set thus finished, making a beautiful suite.

For this Fig. obtain four casters, one for each foot, and screw them securely into the wood, adding a solid plate if necessary, in order to give a wider and deeper hold for the screws. Next rub off all the old varnish with a piece of glass, and afterward either polish and re-varnish, or stain and ornament as described in appropriate chapter.

This done, tack a piece of strong webbing over the back, from the top to the seat; on this place sufficient hair, moss, or other filling to produce a thick pad,

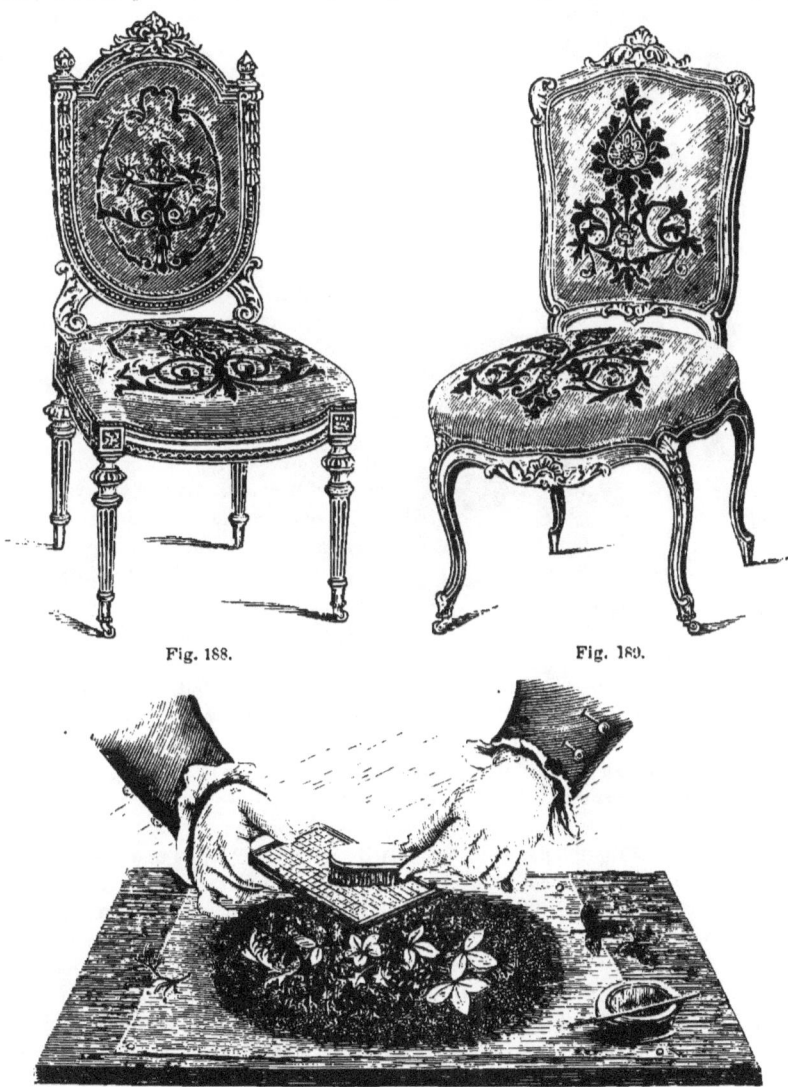

Fig. 188.   Fig. 189.

Fig. 190.—Mode of throwing spray with brush and wire-gauze.

laying several inches on the top, tack a second strip of webbing or coarse crash across the back of the upper panel, and turn the webbing over, thus forming the raised head-piece shown in the illustration; tack the strip closely

Fig. 191.

down the sides, stretching it tightly over the stuffing. Finish the seat in the same manner, and finally cover with any material desired; our figure has a cover of Tycoon rep in striped pattern, costing only 25 cents per yard. Along the front, the cover forms a little lambrequin, and around it, extending up the sides, is a thick woolen cord. As a further finish to our old chair, a strip of coarse Swiss muslin with tatting on each side, covers the gay central stripe, and is fastened on top and bottom with full bows of ribbon, or a piece of the reps pinked out on each edge. Across the lower bar of the back is tacked a strip of heavy fringe which covers the open space between back and seat; but if preferred this may be upholstered by extending the padding continuously from top of back to front of this seat. The legs may be made more ornamental by adding carved wooden rings, or ornaments of any kind desired, but the neat appearance given to the frame-work in the illustration, is done by painting in two colors (with mere lines of buff or white).

Fig. 192, shows a similar article made into a lounging or reading chair, and exceedingly comfortable it is, as we can testify from experience. The first step is to saw off two or three inches from each leg, in order to make the seat lower, as the casters and upholstering, necessarily raise the height and besides, this kind of chair is intended to be *unusually* low. Next, fasten the caster firmly on each leg, and to insure the strength of the casters, those with brass sockets for the admission of the leg will perhaps be best, and are certainly more ornamental, though any neat strong kind will answer.

The next step is to upholster the back and seat, and this is done by first cutting the interlining of some coarse material, two pieces extending entirely across the chair, and allowing at least eight inches on each side, and nine on top and bottom, on account of filling, (which in this chair requires unusual depth,) also cut two side-pieces shaped to the sides of the back and seat as at

A, sew these side-pieces to the under part of the lining, and lay on the filling until six inches deep, then sew the upper part to the sides, and finally make the outside cover of any material desired, slipping it over the padding, and catching the two together at top and bottom. Then with a long sail-needle and strong twine, proceed to catch the back and front together, fastening a button, or tuft of worsted in each place, and using care to make the "buttoning" regular, placing the rows so that the buttons in one row alternate with those in the next. When this is finished, tack the pad to the wooden frame of the chair, and line the back with glazed muslin, and trim around the lower part with deep fringe, a plaited ruffle or ornamental lambrequin as preferred. Finish the

Fig. 192.

edges with heavy cord, and make rosettes for each side of the top, in the center of which let tassels and cord depend. A strip of rich embroidery adds vastly to the elegance of this comfortable chair.

A handsome chair is made, by painting the frame with enameled zinc-white, tinted some delicate shade of pearl-gray, sage-gray, or green, or the lovely tints of lavender, blue-green, or peach-bloom. After varnishing and polishing until a high polish is obtained, the embellishing is commenced by drawing lines lightly on the surface, and painting in with black and white, and adding gold-bronze or color if desired, the forms of these figures will be seen in the illustration, though in a diminutive form. We have seen some of these fancy chairs painted in various bright colors, with tube or sealing-wax paint, and the effect was extremely fine. In the model from which Fig. 193, was taken, the ground is pearl-gray, the lines on the legs are black with edges of gold, narrow bands of scarlet, blue, yellow, and green, with gold and white dividing them, encircle them above and below, and extend along the front, also on the back and supports. The effect of this style of painting these chairs, is more beautiful than can be imagined from this meager description. The cover of our model consists of crimson satin, with a painted design in transparent colors.

Fig. 193.

An equally elegant cover is made by using white velveteen, cutting flowers from paper and arranging ferns, leaves and fine sprays on the outside; cover the ground with spray-work as before shown. In purple, crimson, blue or green aniline dye, the effect is very fine, and the white velveteen so well covered that it is not sufficiently delicate to be easily soiled.

There are many beautiful methods of rejuvenating old chairs, one of which is shown in Fig. 194. This is only a plain walnut chair, and an old and dilapidated one besides, the seat gone, the back badly broken. We shall attack it first, by rubbing it down smoothly with fine emery-paper. This done, we give it a coat of smooth white paint, and this dry, another coat of zinc-white in which sufficient color is added to give a delicate tint of buff, or other color corresponding with the surroundings. Lines of white and some bright color, such as scarlet, black and blue, in style of the old fashioned painted furniture. When dry, give a coat of varnish. Against the back, fasten a cushion either oval or round, covered with an embroidered, or *Cretonne* piece fastened with cord on the edges, and tied in place with bows of ribbon. On the back, tack a piece of colored alpaca or muslin, which will make a neat finish over the panel. The seat is stuffed and covered in the same manner with a cord like that on the back, tacked around the edge.

An exceedingly shabby chair thus renovated, will present a most ornamental appearance. The bright lines of paint on such chairs, gives them a peculiarly tasteful appearance, and very happy effects are produced by using the narrow bands of figures in Decalcomania designs. Scarlet and gold, green and gold, and other combinations variously arranged, may be obtained in these sheets of designs, and the simple narrow bands of color and gold, may be transferred to the smallest spaces.

The Gothic form of chair shown in Fig. 195, will show the beauty of this form of furniture, which, though simple in the extreme, is at once comfortable and elegant. The seat is set low and the wood-work handsomely turned and painted. Such chairs may be readily obtained, or can be made to order for a moderate price, if left entirely unfinished; and this is the very condition in which the amateur decorator desires them, in order to enjoy the pleasure of self-creativeness. Therefore obtaining the rough skeleton fresh from the manufactory, it is rubbed down, stained or painted, varnished and polished

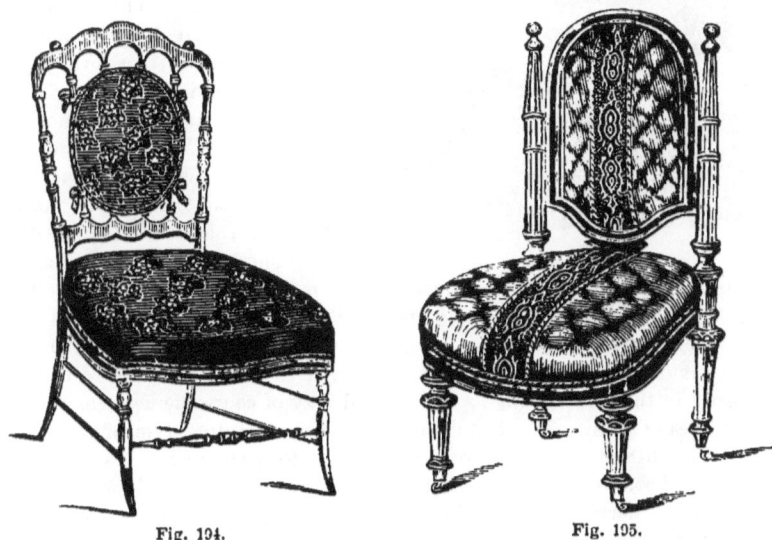

Fig. 194.   Fig. 195.

highly, and finally enriched with gilding and paint of handsome transfers; for parlors, an ebonized frame with lines of gold, or merely narrow bands of delicate color, as white or yellow; or, better still, perhaps, to paint the wood first a yellowish-white, then, arranging narrow lines and some simple borderings cut from paper, fasten them on, painting, or rather staining the surface around in imitation of ebony; then, upon removing the paper, the designs will appear like inlaid wood or ivory. This style of embellishment is capable of wonderfully beautiful effects, and yet is most easily done. The model from which we copied this illustration had a cover of gray damask, upholstered as shown, and finished with embroidered bands, according to one of the patterns we give. A set of such chairs would form a beautiful addition to a parlor, and could be easily got up at a comparatively small cost.

In the chapter on sofas and lounges, we described the manner of changing the old-fashioned "settee" into a comfortable sofa. In our present illustration is the old-fashioned chair found in the wide chimney-corner of the same old kitchen, the two making appropriate companions.

In the olden time, chairs were made much higher than we now consider comfortable for ordinary use; therefore, the first step is to shorten the legs some four inches, and fasten casters on them. This renders the chair of comfortable height, and also makes it less difficult to move, the upholstering, etc., making it quite heavy. The covering is put on in precisely the same manner as the sofa, and where embroidered bands are used for adornment, they may correspond with the sofa. We admire bands of bright colored cloth pinked out on each edge, and embroidered in the middle with chain-stitching in every variety of color. The wooden bottoms to these old chairs and settees are so strong and solid that if desired the spiral springs may be screwed into the wood, and covered with a thick cushion, thus making a most luxurious seat. The manner in which the arms are covered is shown distinctly in the illustration. Any material may of course be used for covering these pieces of furniture, but it should correspond with the style of other articles and the use to which it is to be devoted; if for a sitting-room, a substantial fabric will be most suitable, and it is probable that such a chair would occupy this position, therefore we would recommend strong reps, *Cretonne*, cloth or embroidered bed-ticking.

Fig. 196.

HALL CHAIRS.

The most appropriate chair for the hall is a plain walnut or oak frame, with seat of leather, or the "leather cloth" which Europeans call "American leather cloth." In many cases, the entire chair is of wood, and is so simple in form that almost any one could form the frame, which can afterwards be ornamented with wood-carvings of the "artificial" kind, to correspond with the remaining wood-work. The common "Windsor chair," rubbed down with fine emery-paper and ebonized, makes a handsome hall chair, and when simply ornamented with gilding is really elegant.

For a large hall, and where means will allow the expense, the "church chairs" with high Gothic backs and wooden seats, will be found to furnish handsomely. These may be purchased for five dollars and upward, and really elegant ones are sold at second hand for two and three dollars, which require only cleaning and varnishing or oiling, to make equal to new.

Another beautiful method of enriching such chairs is by painting them in imitation of inlaid wood, the method of doing which we have previously explained. The illustrations, Figs. 197, 198, show good styles for hall chairs, and any one of them may be easily imitated.

A hall should not be crowded with furniture of any kind, and one or two chairs in a small one is all sufficient; while even where this apartment is large, it is better to use a "settee" and other furniture, rather than over-abundance of chairs.

This Gothic style of furniture, the seed of which was planted and flourished in England after the Renaissance, exhibits so many valuable features when applied to furniture, that we feel glad to be able to furnish our readers with a few types of this class, which is so well adapt-ed to the solid, simple furniture appropriate

Fig. 197.

to the majority of American homes. Many persons do not admire the quaint forms of the Gothic; but if not the most perfect in point of beauty it presents a picturesqueness that must be satisfying to the artistic eye.

We take pleasure in giving clear explanations for making various pieces of furniture in this style in our chapter on the library, for which apartment such furniture is peculiarly well adapted. But in the hall it is also appropriate, though at the present time, imposing suites of furniture of this class are exhibited for every apartment in the house. In some of the elegant furniture ware-rooms of this city, not only complete sets of mediæval furniture are made and exhibited, but their arrangement charmingly portrayed in niches specially adapted to this

Fig. 198.

purpose, where the Gothic window, fire-place and various apartments are arranged in true Gothic style.

The hall chair shown in Fig. 198, is one of these models from a firm which makes a specialty of this class of furniture. This chair can be readily made of pine wood, and when ebonized and embellished with painting in imitation of inlaying, will prove as elegant as the specimen given.

A simple yet most picturesque chair for a hall will be seen in Fig. 199. The frame, as will be noticed, is of the rustic order and extremely plain and unpretentious, therefore well adapted to small houses, especially in the country. Having obtained proper branches and put them together in a substantial manner, the seat and upper part of the back are to be covered with canvas and well stuffed; then covered with plain crocheted tidies, edged with a lace of the same character, and tied in place with bows of ribbon. These covers are very tasteful and may be removed and washed when they become soiled. Chairs of this kind are exceedingly appropriate for the veranda, porch or Summer house, if covered with oil-cloth neatly fastened on with gilt-headed tacks. Rustic chairs are usually rather heavy in appearance, but this sample clearly shows that this is not nec-

Fig. 199.

essarily the case, as the one here made is unusually light and graceful, yet perfectly strong and substantial.

THE OCCASIONAL OR RECEPTION CHAIRS.

In the old old time of the Renaissance period, we see from pictures that the fashion was to arrange the regular suite of chairs stiffly around the sides of an apartment, between cabinets, mirrors, tables, and other heavy furniture, while in the center (of large apartments) was a group of four chairs placed back to back, the form appearing much like the round, thickly-stuffed lounging chairs (or "Sleepy Hollows") of this day, which are probably copies of them. This style of arrangement has a most cozy and yet imposing appearance, and would offer many recommendations for a large apartment; but the present style of scattering the light fancy chairs about the room gives an air of graceful careless-ness to the apartment which cannot but please the artistic eye, though care must be taken not to carry the apparent negligence to such a degree that unti-diness is approached.

Allow the regular suite of four or five chairs to occupy the corners and spaces between furniture around the room, keeping them drawn out from the wall; then arrange a few of the lighter and more fanciful varieties about the tables, around the stove or grate, and, if space permit, in the center of the room.

For these occasional chairs, as they are now called, no form is more pleasing and appropriate than the many varieties of the old "camp-stool," of which we

Fig. 200.

Fig. 201.

have such an infinite number of patterns and styles, many of which we give. These are light, graceful, and admirably adapted to the use here named, as they can be so easily folded and transported from place to place The prettiest cover for the backs and seats of these chairs, is embroidered or braided cloth or canvas; and here is opened a wide field for the genius and taste of the ladies of the family. The wooden frames may be highly ornamented by gilding and painting; above and below this a line of the wood is painted in gold and black; then below again a strip of embroidery with a fringe. The lower band of embroidery is simply three scalloped circles of white cloth in application, held by six rows of embroidery, and a heavy chain-stitching around the edge; this also is finished with fringe.

The embellishment on the seat is in application embroidery, and consists of a wide band of cloth (fourteen inches) of a dark crimson color, on which the squares of black velvet, embroidered with shades of gold-color, are fastened with a flat braid sewed on with a sewing-machine.

In Fig. 202, the upper band across the back is a strip of cloth edged on each side, with strips one-half as wide as the band, edged with ornamental braid, a floral design in a satin-stitch embroidery, or with Berlin-work on canvas; below this

Fig. 202.

is a second strip of cloth, embroidered with six separate clusters of flowers and ornamented with tassels. The seat has a crossed band of embroidery corresponding with that across the top, and across the front another matching the lower part of back.

This method of adorning chairs with bands of embroidery is a most beautiful one, and affords wide scope

Fig. 203.

for the inventive and artistic genius of ladies, for they may be made of various materials and in all variety of styles, and as they can be made to cover worn

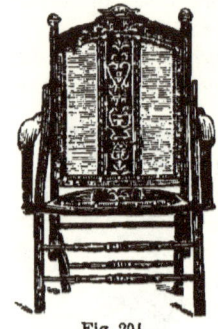

places and soiled spots, they prove "blessings" to the perplexed housekeeper, who has anxiously watched the gradual wearing away of certain spots in the handsome cover of chair or sofa, and felt unable to re-cover during the "hard times," for lo! here is a ready and easy method of renewing the beauty of the furniture, and covering the worn places at the same time, really rendering it handsomer than when in its pristine glory it first came from the store.

Pretty bands are made, by pinking out the edges of two or three colors of cloth or flannel, each narrower than the other, placing them one on the other, and stitching on the machine. Another is made of any striped woolen material of two colors; pink the edges and work each stripe with side-stitch.

Fig. 204.

SITTING-ROOM CHAIRS.

In the sitting or "living"-room, as it is now called, the chairs should all be of the class termed "easy." Be the number few or many, let no one of them be stiff, hard, or high. In this room, devoted to the wants and daily occupation and entertainment of the family, some object should speak of the peculiar taste or requirement or occupation of each member of the loved circle, from the oldest to the youngest. Whether it be the soft-cushioned chair of the aged grandparent in the most comfortable corner, the tufted foot-rest, and newspaper stand of the father, the low rocker and work-basket of the ever-busy house-mother, or the various objects related to each dear child, down to the cradle of the baby-pet, here in this room it is to testify to the world, that this family is one of united love; that at some period during the twenty-four hours, the disbanded group are gathered together again, and here hold sweet communion. Says a late writer, "The life of an apartment consists in the degree to which it subserves its end," and in the living-room the tired limbs require rest on chair or couch, and equally does the eye need rest upon soft and subdued shades.

There is one comfort for those who desire to furnish this, the "dearest room" in all the house, with various kinds of comfortable chairs, and yet have not the well-filled purse wherewith to purchase them, which is, that with a few old "Windsor," or cane-bottomed chairs, or even the homely but very comfortable "splint-bottoms" of the Western States, various cozy and tasteful seats may be made. The very first thing will be to lower the seat, by sawing off two, three or even four inches from each leg, according to the height desired, for what is more uncomfortable than a high chair, or more barren-looking and ungraceful than four long stiff chair-legs?

Having made the chair low, the next point is to make it soft and to cover up all deficiencies as regards broken and disfigured parts; to do this, take any old quilt or "comfort," or, in lieu of these, parts of old worn garments, cotton batting, soft pieces of carpet, or indeed, any material that will serve to make a soft foundation. Tack this covering over the entire chair, from top of back down to the seat, putting on layer after layer until a soft foundation is secured. Next measure the length from the top of back down to the floor in front, (seat and all,) and cutting a lining and outside cover to fit this, make it sufficiently thick with raw cotton or wool to form a comfortable pad, either quilting or buttoning it, and trimming the edges with fringe, gimp or embroidery. Secure this cover on the sides of back with bows of colored flannel, or cloth pinked out on the edges, or button with loops of gay cord and fancy buttons.

By changing the outside material, or using embroidered, braided or ornamented cloth, or in some cases covering only the back and seat, and making a lambrequin for the lower part, or again ornamenting the legs with paint and allowing them to show; as also by varying the trimmings, a set of chairs may readily be made—no two of which are alike—and yet each one not only comfortable, but beautiful little affairs that will prove an ornament to any apartment, and for sewing-chairs they are not to be excelled, even by the handsomely upholstered article of the stores.

For children nothing can be more cunning and really comfortable than kegs or small barrels made and upholstered as described previously. When covered with gay cloth, with the name or monogram wrought on the back, these little chairs always afford infinite satisfaction to the little folks. It is our own plan to embroider some little design suitable for children, or in case this is not practicable to obtain a set of Decalcomania designs, such as the history of " Puss in Boots," "Cinderella" or "Jack the Giant-Killer," or larger pictures of some childish scene or group; these are transferred to ovals, circles or squares of light silk or even glazed colored muslin, which are then fastened as *applique* embroidery, with chain-stitching around the edges.

The little "basket-chairs" used for infants should always have a comfortable, padded cover fastened over them, and the little seat-lid softly cushioned; this cold, hard-looking chair is then changed into a pretty and comfortable piece of furniture, in which "baby" may sit and play by the hour; but to see the poor little head bumping about against the hard basket work, and the tender flesh frequently torn by the projecting points of willow, as is too often the case, is a cruel sight, inasmuch as there is no necessity for it. Besides, a chair thus covered will serve for a whole generation of children; indeed, we know of one used by a family of five successively, then handed to the next

15

generation, and which still appears to be a sound chair; (but its various covers have been legion!)

For the mother's sitting-room chair, what can ever take the place of the old "rocker"? Yet there certainly will be another beatitude added to the list, by the notable housekeepers, when some ingenious person (why not a woman?) invents a rocker that will entirely supersede the forked, horned and spiked affair which has occupied space and ruined walls, furniture and feet for the past centuries. We know full well that there have been several patents taken

out for chairs, the rockers of which are invisible, or, at least, so constructed that they do not rest upon the floor nor project into interminable space before and behind the seat; but this is not the article required, unless indeed such chairs can be made at so low a price that they may be procured quite as cheaply as the rocker now in common use.

These patent rocking-chairs are far too expensive to be purchased by the "million" who most require them, consequently they are never seen save in the houses of the wealthy; and those who procure their pieces of furniture "by the hardest," go on from day to day, having veneering broken out, holes ground into polished panels and the walls worn into

Fig. 205.

chasms, with the incessant vibrations of those great horns in the rear, for *rock*, women will, especially if there is a baby in the question. We would say, though, to every woman who can possibly raise the amount of money required for it, to purchase one of the patent rocking-chairs (for her sitting-room at least), for she will find it money *well spent*.

As we are writing for that class of housekeepers who are desirous of making beautiful homes with the least possible cost, we endeavor, in taking up the furniture adapted to each department and its furniture, to describe the very best ways and means of securing comfortable, and even luxurious furniture, at the least expense. Now as regards the subject of rocking-chairs, those with longest rockers are not either the most comfortable nor the easiest rocked; the rockers should only be sufficiently long to preclude the possibility of tipping over backward or forward; not an inch longer. Very much also depends upon the form of the rocker, which should not be curved too deeply, and which can only be ascertained by trying the motion of the chair. We really know of no more comfortable chair than the homely "splint-bottom rocker" that accompanies the farm-house chair of the western prairies. These quaint-looking but substantial affairs would suit Mr. Eastlake exactly, but as we cannot admire them in their rude state, it has become a subject of importance to make them as tasteful as possible by means of padding and covering Now these chairs cost but two dollars as they come from the store, yet, after upholstering, they will readily sell for ten. It would be wise, therefore, for every one who desires economy and luxury combined in a rocking-chair, to purchase such at once, or several of them, and by means of padding and covering, to make

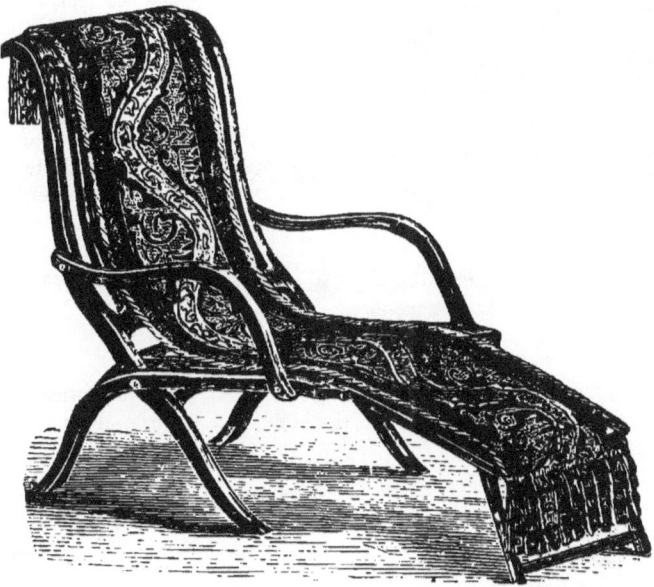

Fig. 206.

them into handsome pieces of furniture. The rockers should be polished and painted, or, better still, ebonized and touched up carefully with lines of gilding.

For the *pater-familias*, the comfortable arm-chair should be always ready. This should be in contrast with the office or store chair he has occupied through the day; or, in default of this, a delightful luxury after a day of toil; therefore it is to be deep and thickly cushioned, with a springy seat and padded arms, and, above all, with the head-rest, in shape of round bolster hung over the back at the upper part of the back.

A good form of chair is shown in Fig. 206, which has extension seat that may be turned down and afford a pleasant rest for the feet, if desired. We give this chair in merely its skeleton frame-work, with embroidered pad, which is thrown over it, after the upholstering is done. This chair is so simple, that any ordin-

Fig. 207.

ary workman may readily make the frame-work; the extension is simply fastened with hinges, as also the legs, both easily folded in and turned on the seat; or, it may have a division in the center also hinged, and the two parts folded together and hooked, may form a front to the bottom of the chair; the latter arrange-ment is preferable, as it does not necessitate the raising of the seat cush-ion. When thickly padded like Fig. 207, this is the best gentleman's reading or lounging chair that can be made.

AN EASY CHAIR.

The term " easy "-chair is frequently a misnomer, and the poetical quotation, so frequently given, " stretched on the rack of a too easy-chair," means very much more than the writer intended, for verily many of the so-called "easy "-chairs of the day are veri-table inquisitorial racks. As many families enjoy the privilege of possessing among their number that blessing, an "ingenious mind," we give the plan of a celebrated chair, called by the imposing name of the "Royal Vic-toria Chair," which pos-sesses so many advantages, and is withal so simple and easily constructed, that we believe many per-

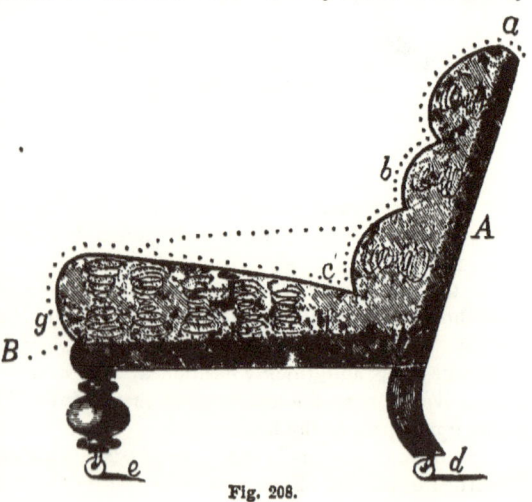

Fig. 208.

sons may follow our example and have one made for themselves, they will never regret it certainly, for to own this chair is to possess a "perfect luxury."

The arms are not shown in the illustration, but they are as simple as the rest of the work; they extend from the back to the end of the seat, and are thickly padded the entire length, and finished with a broad soft cushion on the top, which affords a comfortable rest for the arm. These arms are placed low, not necessitating the uplifting of the arm to an unnatural position, but simply supporting it. Starting from the point A, they extend two-thirds the length of the seat, and gradually slope to the frame at B. The frame-work is of plain solid wood, and as will be seen is perfectly simple, consisting of a back and seat put

Fig. 209.

together at the angle denoted, which is the whole secret of this patent chair, it being planned upon scientific principles, to give perfect support to the back, the seat inclining slightly downward toward the back, instead of tilting forward as chairs generally do; the arms, of plain boards, screwed to back and seat, slope almost imperceptibly toward the edge of the seat, merely sufficient to afford an easy rest for the arms from the elbow to the hand.

This frame is furnished with the spiral-springs, sold by the dozen at any hardware or upholstering establishment, which is fastened into gimlet holes bored in the seat and back; on these a thickly stuffed pad, cut to fit the back, seat and arms, is placed and tacked closely around the frame-work with gilt-headed nails.

The form of the cover is first cut from soft paper—thus:—cut two edge-pieces, shaped like the dotted lines, a, b, c, also for seat f, g, measuring from the top or head to the bottom of the seat h, and the side-pieces of seat from h to i; to these sew the long straight piece fitting between these and across the back and seat of the chair. For the arms, cover the board thickly with the filling and tack over the cover, then make a cushion four or five inches wide and as long as the board, which nail firmly and securely on the top. This chair, which would cost forty dollars in the store, may be nicely got up for five dollars, more or less, according to the material used for upholstering, and will be found in every respect what its name promises, an "Easy Chair."

A Lady's sewing or nursing chair of same construction, but without arms, is shown in Fig. 209, to which rockers may be affixed if desired. This figure will also show the manner of upholstering the back and seat.

SITTING-ROOM ROCKER.

The comfortable looking "rocker" shown in Fig. 210, possesses the advantages of short rockers, and broad, low seat. The form of this chair is rather peculiar, but if examined it will be found that the workmanship is extremely simple, and of the plain Gothic order, thus affording another piece to add to the suite described in chapter on library. Any ingenious person or ordinary mechanic could make such a chair by examining the illustration here given, taken from a home-made article, for the piece of ornamental carving on the top of the back may be easily procured from the artificial wood carvings;

Fig. 210.

and the frame-work or turned posts on the sides of back, may be made merely square, plain round, or be turned at a manufactory, as preferred. The back and seat may be very plain, as it will be covered with the embroidered rug, extending from the top of back, over the seat. This rug in the model is exceedingly ornamental, consisting of a deer cut from brown or gray cloth, and embroidered in shades of brown, as in all application work. The branch and leaves (shown more distinctly in the larger pattern) are of greens and browns in wool or silk,

and the white tracery of silk braid. This design is beautiful in *petite-point*, the colors looking lovely after the canvas is drawn out. The cloth should correspond with other furniture. A reading chair of same kind is shown in the next illustration.

The chair illustrated by Fig. 212, is of such easy construction that it can be made *at home*, without difficulty; or, if this is impracticable, the nearest cabinet-maker or carpenter should make the frame-work without trouble,

Fig. 211.

so plain is the manner of constructing, shown in the engraving, which is left uncushioned on this account. If the carved head-piece is preferred plain, it may be merely a smooth panel of wood, and the entire straight back can have an upholstered cushion, which may continue down and cover the seat, also. The breadth of embroidery may be of any pattern or variety preferred. A good kind for such a chair is simply one width of any striped material such as is shown in Fig. 215, which is worked on the stripes, or between certain of them. If the material is woolen and rich in quality, let the embroidery be of silk, or silk and beads; but if it is linen or cotton, or even low-priced woolen material, the embroidery may be done with zephyr. The point-Russe, chain-stitch, half-polka, and other varieties of those stitches are used in "Turkish embroidery."

We have been delighted by seeing an entire room upholstered with an extremely pretty striped bed-ticking worked with several shaded colors of single zephyr worsted, in the stitches shown in Fig. 215. The effect was beautiful, and the whole appearance of the furniture was as rich and elegant as if the foundation had been costly damask. The style of work used on the stripes here shown are fully described, and the designs, Figs. 213, 214, 215 and 216, will show the various kinds of stitches and materials used on it. Figs. 218 and 219 are designs for the pretty footstool belonging to the chair, which will be readily understood from the various plain patterns both for sides and top.

The beauty and general luxurious appearance of this graceful and comfortable chair are greatly enhanced by its final finishing; the upholstering of back, arms and seat, and the cushion or bolster for the head. The embroidered rug is fastened on with cords and tassel finished with fringe on each end.

CHAIR AND FOOTSTOOL.

Fig. 213 shows the fuschia spray between the stripes on rug of chair, and is done with embroidery silk in satin-stitch. The colors may be varied to suit

Fig. 212.

the taste. Fig. 214 is the stripe upon the sides of the flower embroidery, and is done with narrow silk braid of three colors stitched down with the sewing-

Fig. 213.

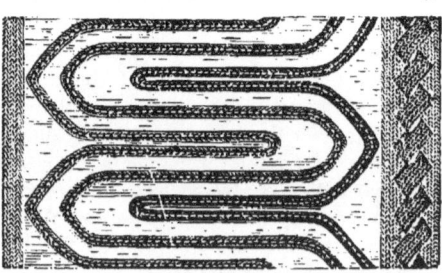

Fig. 214.

machine, both the outer edge and central figure; on the inner side is a strip of braid one inch wide, on which is stitched a row of pointed braid through which is worked a line of some contrasting color as shown in the figure. Figs. 218 and 219 belong to the footstool and are done in satin-chain and point-Russe

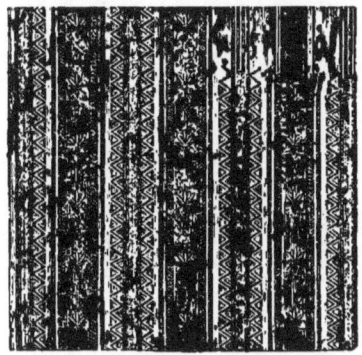

Fig. 215.

Fig. 216.

stitching, with braiding in fancy braid. Fig. 217 shows sample of embroidery upon a striped material; this being done in satin-stitch and braiding, with a little application work in the pointed pieces on each side of the light stripe. "Side" stitch, or the old herring-bone stitch is equally pretty for such stripes. Alpaca braid stitched on a sewing machine, (either in the Grover &

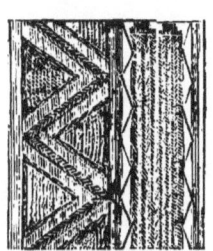

Fig. 217.

Fig. 218.

Baker or Wheeler & Wilson stitch,) will be found a beautiful method of ornamenting trimming for chair and other covers, using contrasting colored thread or silk for the stitching.

THE CORNER EASY CHAIR.

We presume there never has been a home-made chair that has become as popular as the one shown in Fig. 221. The first appearance of this little household star on the domestic stage was several years since, in the columns of

"Hearth and Home," and again in the "American Agriculturist" some years later, in both of which diagrams similar to A and B, with dimensions and directions for making were given. We at once saw the comfort and utility of the arti-

Fig. 219.

cle, and forthwith commenced *building* a similar structure; for indeed so large and heavy was it that it appeared more like a small room than a chair; but it was all it professed to be and ten times more, for so invaluable is it now considered in our family, that we could not be without one, and would not take one hun-

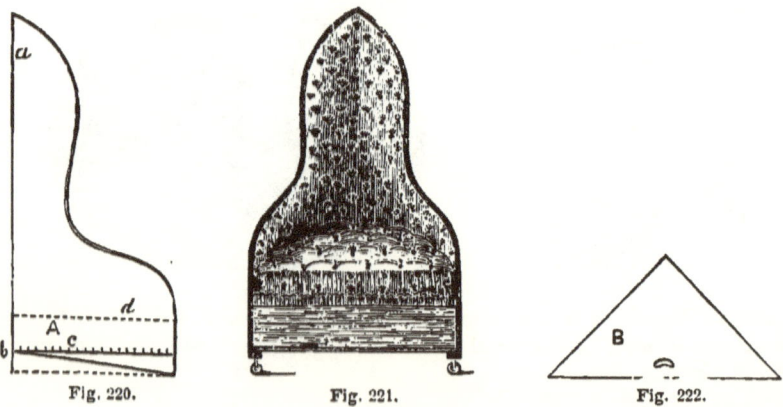

Fig. 220.   Fig. 221.   Fig. 222.

dred dollars for ours could we not obtain another. We do not imagine, however, that ours can be as ponderous an affair as "Faith Rochester's," who tells of it in the "American Agriculturist," and says it served as a cradle for baby, and was of such proportions that she left it when moving to another home.

We think that we have improved somewhat on the original plan, for though ours is a large and deeply cushioned chair, it is by no means a clumsy, cumbrous article of furniture; too unwieldy to move from room to room. It is made thus: Have two boards sawed of "half-inch stuff," four feet by two feet six inches, shaped out from the arms up to the top, as shown in diagram *A*; at the narrowest part, one foot; above (at the widest), three feet; the edges *on the back* must be beveled off in order to let them fit closely together. Two triangular pieces, two feet six inches on the sides, and a board fitting across the front are all the parts required excepting four cleats, two feet six inches long, for the seat to rest upon (for which a lath answers very well). Three strong casters, material for stuffing and covering, and a few yards of gimp or cord, are all that is required for furnishing the chair.

The outside covering may be of any kind desired, whether of common calico or rich damask; and we would here remark that when honored with a handsome cover, our old friend is worthy of a place in the corner of the parlor, (for it is eminently a *corner* ornament). Having screwed the two pieces of board together at *a* and *b*, in diagram *A*, nail on the two lower cleats, just above the bottom (at *c*), place the board *B* on this; and above, at the point *d*, fasten the other cleats as a support for the second triangular board, which thus forms a lid to the box, making a good receptacle for rolls of work, papers or books. (If a lady puts this frame together, she may find it easier to fasten on the cleats preparatory to screwing the back together.) After fastening on the casters, the chair is ready for upholstering, which is done as previously described. In nailing on the upper cleats let them incline gradually downward towards the back, as this makes the seat more comfortable; and in upholstering make a narrow pad, about a half yard wide and six inches thick, for the corner of the back, nailing it along the top and bottom, and covering afterwards with the padding used for the entire chair; this gives the back a soft, rounded appearance.

The cushion and pad for these chairs are made of cloth, embroidered in any style most appropriate for the room they are to furnish. With handsome material and rich embroidery they may be made sufficiently elegant for the parlor, but on the other hand they may be neat and simple, and embellished to suit the rest of the furniture.

The pattern Fig. 223, will be found well adapted to such a chair, and the design is so very simple that even a child may undertake it. It is in *petite-point* embroidery, and we give it for several reasons; first because it may be worked upon any material, as the canvas in this kind of work is drawn out, and leaves the design upon the material beneath, which forms the groundwork. Again, the design is adapted to both back and seat, the square serving for the seat, and frequent repetitions of it for the back. The colors may be selected to suit the worker, and if wrought in various gay tints it will be found a good imitation of Turkish embroidery, though in two colors it is exceedingly beautiful.

The illustration shows plainly the manner of working at A, A, A, A, the

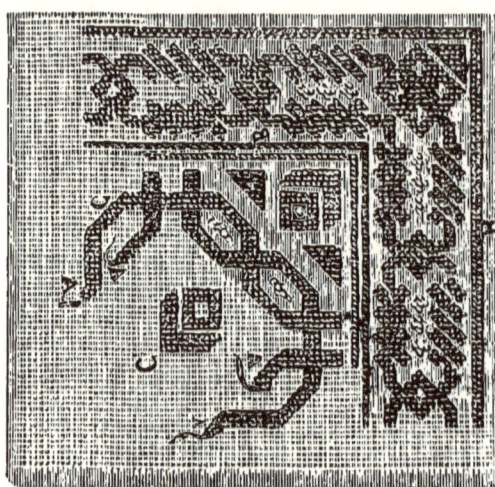

material with a part of the canvas drawn out, and the worked pattern left, B, B, and the pattern worked on the canvas prior to its withdrawal, C, C. Any Berlin pattern will answer for *petite* embroidery, and if strong canvas is used and the stitches not drawn tightly, there is no difficulty in withdrawing the strands. Either "side" or "cross-stitch" answers for this kind of work, but care must be used to work all the stitches to run in the same direction, or an uneven appearance will be the result.

Fig. 223.

A beautiful little sewing-chair is shown in Fig. 224, which may be made from one of the old fashioned cane-bottomed walnut chairs, found in almost every house. First the legs are to be sawed off about four inches, and trimmed neatly down to a graduated point at the bottom as shown in the illustration : Next, procure a dozen turned pieces, which fasten between the rounds and frame, thus giving a more ornamental character to the frame ; the same is done above, using long turned rods, and while purchasing these procure also a few fretwork and carved ornaments, or we would suggest the substituting some pretty artificial carvings of any kind preferred, and by obtaining a catalogue these may be selected to suit the circumstances of the case. This makes the frame-work at once tasteful and appropriate to the after embellishment, which consists in fancy painting. The varnish must be entirely removed from the wood with glass, scrap-

Fig. 224.

ing carefully with the grain of the wood; then rub smooth with emery-paper, and proceed to paint the central part of all the faces with any dark enamel paint (which is mixed with varnish instead of oil); great care should be used to draw the line very carefully, and to paint the lines with a very small brush in order to keep the lines exactly parallel. A charming frame is made by painting the centers dark-gray one-half inch wide, on each side a line of black separating the gray from a scarlet, white and blue border, the black a mere thread of color; the scarlet one-fourth of an inch broad; blue, one-sixteenth of an inch; white between scarlet and blue a narrow line. On the circular rounds use gold, scarlet, blue and black, and gold on the ornaments with lines of color. Embroider a square of navy-blue cloth with gold color and black in clusters, letting one come on each diamond in upholstering the seat.

DINING-ROOM CHAIRS.

The regular set of chairs for the table of a dining-room should all be of one kind, and these should be rather high from the floor, and may be of the simplest, plainest manufacture, yet appear perfectly "genteel."

We have seen a country dining-room which was the perfection of tasteful beauty, yet the table chairs of which were the plain "splint-bottoms" of the prairie. These were repainted until the surface was of one solid, uniform character; then a coat of buff zinc-paint, on which simple lines of black and scarlet made sufficient and beautiful finish. The seats were upholstered with buff linen embellished with spray-work, in black and white, the effect of which was charming, and accorded well with a green and oak carpet and cream-colored paper with a dado of green and gold, made by simply applying a roll of paper the width-wise; a frieze of another pattern arranged in a similar manner, made a beautiful wall covering, and testified to this housewife's knowledge of true artistic arrangement as regards mural decoration.

Fig. 225.

The common cane-seated, or even "Windsor" chairs are wonderfully improved by using a little gold and color on the wood-work, and covering the hard, bare seats with some pretty material corresponding or contrasting harmoniously with the carpet, and fastening these on with brass-headed tacks or cord. An old set of second-hand chairs bought at auction for a trifle, may thus be made into really elegant sets.

Inasmuch as the dining-room is frequently used as a sort of *dolce far niente* place in which to lounge away the leisure moments which should (if possible) succeed the meal time, a few "easy" chairs should grace the corners or be rolled in front of the fire or stove. These chairs may not assume the dainty lightness

of the chamber-set, nor the regular easy "Sleepy Hollow" of the sitting-room, yet they are to be in every way comfortable; therefore we offer an illustration of the best model we have examined for this purpose, and in Fig. 226 will be found a chair at once elegant and yet well adapted to a lounge after dinner. The foundation of this chair may, if desired, be one cf the ever-ready barrel arrangements at once so comfortable and economical. In order to make the frame more tasteful, side pieces of carved walnut may be added to the back and arms, and short legs fastened on the bottom, though casters fastened to the wood of the barrel an-

Fig. 226.

swers every purpose, and are hidden by the fringe of ruffle arranged around the lower part of the frame, as will be seen in the illustration. We have so fully described the covering and stuffing of such a chair that it is useless to repeat these directions. A pretty lace tidy adds greatly to the beauty of such a chair, as also cord, or gilt nails on the edges. The carved pieces on the sides of back and arms are securely screwed or nailed on the solid frame of the barrel.

VERANDA CHAIRS.

The veranda or porch, be it ever so humble, should always be furnished with seats, for, during the pleasant weather, these out-door haunts generally afford the most pleasant place for the family gatherings. In-door chairs and stools should never be carried to the outside of the house for many reasons; they become soiled and disfigured by effects of glaring light, sunshine and dust, and are apt to be forgotten at night, when, perhaps, a storm arises, and the result is "total destruction" to the chair exposed to the drenching rain.

There are many varieties of chairs suitable for this purpose—iron, terra-cotta and handsome wooden kinds, but as these are all more or less expensive, we shall recommend the rustic seats as being not only appropriate but of easiest construction, and costing only the price of a pound or two of nails, and the labor of collecting or ordering a quantity of gnarled roots and branches of trees. In the country, a quantity of what are called "tree-tops," are easily obtained in places where wood-chopping has been going on, and nothing can be better for the purpose than these, covered, as they frequently are, with beautiful bark. Where it is desired to remove the bark, the pieces should first be soaked, when the bark can be easily peeled off. Various patterns may be used for such chairs, several of which we give as a guide to some of our readers, and we would encourage any faint-hearted ladies by telling them that we see daily many perfect specimens of such chairs made by a lady noted for the beauty and delicacy of her hands. Furthermore, let us add, not only chairs and small articles have been thus made, but during last Winter she formed, in sections, an entire rustic bridge, which was put together last Spring, and she is now engaged in con-

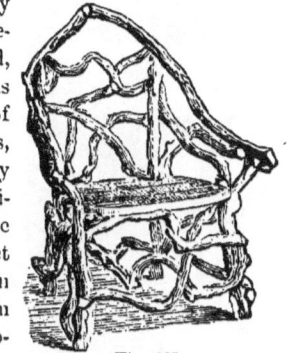

Fig. 227.

structing a lovely little Summer-house. This is done only at odd moments, for she has a large family and is one of those unfortunate (?) persons who, losing the efficient help on which she had been accustomed to rely from her birth, during the late war, has found it doubly hard to learn late in life how to help herself, and perform her own household labor. "What a woman has done a woman can do," is her motto, and could our readers see the charming home she has adorned by means of her own handiwork, we believe they would at once make up their minds to do likewise. We have digressed thus far, with the earnest desire to inspire our readers with an interest in this same rustic work, which shall result in an effort to make some, at least, of the numerous beautiful objects for which Nature so bountifully supplies materials.

We would say here, that this rustic furniture is not suitable for furnishing any apartment in the house, not even the hall, inasmuch as it is a prolific source of dust and dirt, and a safe harbor for insects and "all manner of creeping things." If,

Fig 228.

however, any have a "warm love" for this style of furniture, let each piece be thoroughly cleaned and dried, then varnished with Copal; thus finished, it presents a beautiful appearance, but on account of the complicated workmanship and the numerous nooks and crannies, it requires daily care to keep in good order, and should, once each week, be painted over with kerosene oil,

Fig. 229.

which not only gives it a fresh appearance, but prevents vermin from collecting.

Grape-vines, roots of hazel and laurel, branches of red cedar and spruce pine, with the gnarled tree-laps just mentioned, all afford fine material for this work, which will be found a fascinating employment, and prove far less arduous labor than would be imagined by most persons, who form their ideas of it from the pictures of the various articles which necessarily appear cumbrous and rough, but the more so the pieces are, the greater the ease of constructing.

BED-ROOM CHAIRS.

In purchasing entire suites of bed-room furniture, we generally find that three or four chairs are included, but though these may be ever so richly carved or embellished, or possess all the delicate beauty characteristic of the " Cottage suites," they may be vastly improved by a little upholstering; a pretty embroidered cushion on this one, and a gossamer-like tidy on another. It is these trifles which give a certain air of comfort and elegance to the houses of some persons, while others, with ten times the opportunity, will never make their homes anything more than simply "houses filled with furniture." It is the innumerable little additions which give that air of artistic beauty to certain pieces of furniture; a picture on one, a piece of exquisite embroidery covering parts of another, a little graceful drapery here, and some lovely arrangement of ferns and grasses there, make bald places rich in covering, and lighten up what was otherwise only gloomy.

As Mr. Conway says in mentioning a picture of " St. Cecilia playing on her keys," which ornamented an organ in a house he was visiting: "It is scarcely enough to bring into the house, furniture of a color which is vaguely harmonious with the paper; by a little ornamentation, even the piano, the cabinet, the book-case, may be made to repeat the theme to which the walls have risen."

Many chairs are ugly in the extreme, but if we have (by any means) become the owners of such "eye-sores," there is no reason why we should allow them to annoy us day after day, there is no absolute and irrevocable law by which we are compelled to gaze upon ugly objects, when pretty ones are within our power. Prettiness is not intrenched against the Decalogue, nor "thou shalt make for thyself ugly things," carved upon the tables of the moral law; so let us take our old bed-room chairs and see what we can do to rejuvenate them. First, we have here some old parlor-chairs of that wretched style which never allowed any solid, broad-shouldered man to lean back against them without the embarrassing result of "down goes chair-back, man, and all." Now the two

slender uprights which hold back and seat together, can never be put firmly together again, without the aid of strong *iron* bands, and of course, these would present an extremely rude appearance in the parlor, but as bed-room chairs, we have repaired five of this class, and they prove not only durable, but are much admired.

The first step we take must be to the blacksmith shop, for each one of these chairs require two long iron plates screwed securely to the seat and wood-work of the back, and a brace on the front to hold them firm. This makes the chair stronger than it was when merely supported by the wooden uprights. We next recover the seat and back with material harmonizing with the curtains, and in tasteful contrast with carpet and wall covering. Bands of embroidery on seat and back, aid materially in imparting elegance to these chairs; and for a chamber, a full ruffle from the

Fig. 230.

seat to the floor adds a graceful and dainty appearance, especially in Summer, when light chintz covers may be used to impart that cool delicacy which light materials only can. The iron bands are to be covered with puffs of whatever material covers the chair, and will entirely dispel any idea of this having been an old chair repaired and renovated; presenting only the appearance of tasteful additions, not covered blemishes.

Figs. 232 and 233 show two pieces of furniture which should stand in the bed-room of every house.

We say *the* bed-room, as referring to that particular room known we suppose

16

to every family, the "family-room," where the sick or merely indisposed member of the household always resorts in time of need. Where there is a family

Fig. 231.

of children especially, be they mere babies or quite "grown up," there is generally a desire to be near "mother" when indisposed, and "mother's-room," is therefore the "haven of rest" to each member of the home-circle, as we have observed before. As mother's bed cannot always be at the disposal of the little community, or it may appear desirable to keep it in a state of unruffled neatness, it is always wise to have ready some comfortable, indeed inviting "Sleepy Hollow" for the afflicted; we know of nothing so entirely perfect, and so well adapted to all the requirements of this case, as the arrangement shown in the illustrations, Figs. 232 and 233, which give the chair an ottoman, singly and combined. For the chair, procure one of the large wooden arm-chairs of the cheapest and most comfortable kind, (for spaciousness and proper curve to the back, etc.) are the essential points to recommend such a chair, the finish or style being of no consequence, as the entire wood-work will be covered.

Having secured the chair, first saw off the legs in order to make the seat only one foot from the floor, then screw large casters to each one; this done, proceed to pad the bottom, back and arms as previously directed, the only difference being that in this chair, the arms are to be stuffed as shown in the illustration. A piece of lining and material are cut to fit back and arms, and sufficiently long to turn over the arms in a roll which are carefully stuffed. A

Fig. 232.

piece is cut to fit down the front of each arm, meeting the cover of the seat in front, and finished in the center with a rosette of the material, and a tassel or bunch of woolen balls. The lower part of the front of the chair, and the sides of arms are covered plainly with the material, but for the back, any colored muslin will answer.

A soft cushion should always be placed against the back of such a chair, with a round bolster hung over the back, and an "Afghan" or soft woolen rug, in case the invalid should feel "chilly." A deep heavy woolen fringe, or a ruffle of the material finishes the bottom.

The ottoman is made of a box the same width and height of the chair-seat. The one in our illustration is of a half circular form, but a square will answer the same purpose; casters are screwed to the four corners, and the sides covered in the same manner as the front of the chair, while the lid is padded and then covered. The inside of the box is lined neatly with muslin or paper, and is convenient for holding books, and various trifles an invalid may require, and desire to have near by. The lid of this ottoman is fastened with two hinges and a loop on the front whereby to raise it. In case the person occupying the chair desires to rest, this ottoman drawn to the front of the chair, and the cushion fixed beneath the shoulders, they can recline upon it very comfortably. When not thus used, such a piece of furniture forms a tasteful and useful appendage to any bed-room. If desired, this stool can be made with hinged legs, which turned under, allows it to rest on the floor as a footstool for the chair, it only needs to have them opened out beneath the cushion. We believe most persons (like ourselves) will prefer this way of making it, as the chair requires some support for the feet when used merely to sit in as a lounging chair.

Fig. 233.

The "Sleepy Hollow" barrel chairs have become so well-known that a description of them appears almost useless, yet, as we have never seen any that were made or looked as well as the one shown in Fig. 234, we feel inclined to give our own method of making this useful and economical piece of furniture.

First, the barrel should not be one of the loose, badly-hooped flour barrels which will come apart almost as soon as finished, but a substantial article, not heavy, yet well put together with wooden hoops. Remove the head, and to the bottom fasten four casters; then have the exact form marked out upon the staves, using care to make the sides precisely alike, and giving a graceful curve at that point where the arm turns into the back. At the top, too, instead of simply rounding it, cut out a point and curve down to each arm, as shown in diagram. This will make a more graceful back, and yet be quite as readily

upholstered. Very much depends upon the shape of the barrel, and we prefer a rather short, wide form, to a narrow, high, or long one. About one foot from the bottom nail or screw (around the inside), a number of little blocks for sustaining the "slats," which are to form the bottom; this mode is much better than a solid bottom, on account of lightness and a certain amount of "springiness," the latter being specially the case when flexible wood is used, having thin but tough strips, such as green hickory; but an excellent plan is, where an extremely nice chair is made, to obtain four of the movable coil springs such as are used for "spring bottoms" to beds, and making the bottom of strips crossed over each other, fasten a spring in each

Fig. 234.

intersection. This makes a delightful chair seat. After arranging the seat, proceed to cover the sides and back, and nothing is better for stuffing these chairs than clean, fresh corn-husks, well split and cut, using care to remove all hard parts and washing them perfectly clean, in order to remove all dust; this

makes a very elastic and durable filling. After covering with webbing or other coarse material, and stuffing tightly, cut a paper pattern to fit the entire back and arms, and from it cut two of coarse cheap calico or muslin, and one of the material to be used for outside cover; lay several thicknesses of cotton-batting hair, moss, or other filling, between the two pieces of lining, and stitch them together; then quilt or "tie and button," and tack this when finished on the chair, filling around the edge with a quantity of the stuffing material, and making a round, puffed appearance across the head and on the arms, as shown in the illustration. Next, make and fill a cushion for the seat in the same manner, making it at least

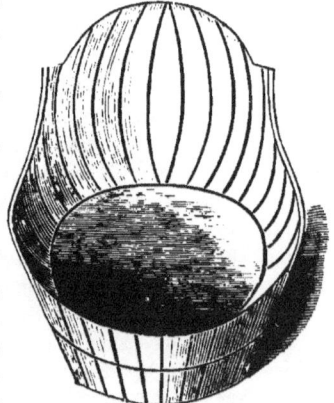

Fig. 235.

eight inches deep, as it must sink into the circular cavity above the slats, and still be seen above, as shown in the finished illustration; around the edge a deep quilted or buttoned side piece is fastened, which gives a most comfortable and handsome appearance to the chair. Our illustration is finished with a fringe and tassels one foot in depth, which covers the piece of wood-work below the cushion, and extends round the sides; rosettes of the material and tassels, are placed on each arm, and a strip of braided cloth ornaments the middle of back and cushion.

A barrel chair thus made will be found a most luxurious seat and well deserving of the name given this comfortable seat, "Sleepy Hollow," for verily it is intended to induce repose, so soft and cozy is the deep cushioned depths of this old barrel. Many of these chairs are clumsy and unjustly condemned on this account, but this is certainly because they are not properly made.

CHAIR-BOLSTERS.

There is no longer the painful necessity of dislocating one's neck in endeavoring to rest the head against the chair-back, for the beautiful bolster now to be found hung against all high-backed chairs not only remedies this evil, but proves a tasteful addition as well. These bolsters are made in every variety of embroidery and in various styles of arrangement, though the form is invariably the same, and the most sensible one that could be devised; a long, round, narrow pillow, neither broad nor deep, but exactly adapted for the purpose designed, a head-rest. We give a number of beautiful designs for these bolsters, any of which will be found easy to make, and not costly as regards material.

Fig. 236 is made of soft merino on the usual round foundation, which being always made in the same manner, we will give here, as it will answer for all

Fig. 236.

the different cushions. Take a piece of bed-ticking, crash, strong muslin, or indeed any material sufficiently substantial to hold the filling without allowing it to work through to the outside cover; in length, let it be eighteen inches, and in width, eighteen. Sew together and turn; then gather one end and sew it around a circular piece four inches in diameter; fill with feathers, curled hair or other material, until it is of good form but not firm and devoid of elasticity; when sufficiently full, gather the other end left open for filling, and sew

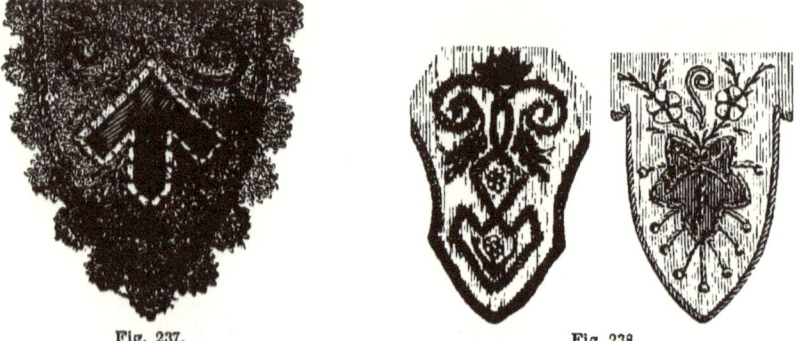

Fig. 237.   Fig. 238.

to a circular piece as at the opposite end; these pieces give a better form to the bolster than if the ends were merely gathered into a knot; it also makes the outside cover set more neatly than if the whole were gathered into one close knot at each end.   Over this pillow the cases are fitted and should always

Fig. 239.

receive the embroidery or other ornamentation before being sewed together. The outer cover should always be sewed together on the sides, and slipped over the stuffed bolster, then gathered at the ends.

In Fig. 241 the merino is ornamented with embroidered leaves, laid one over the other. These leaves may be made in various ways, and are a beautiful method of ornamenting other articles besides these cushions. Fig. 237 shows one of cloth or flannel pinked out on the edges, and embroidered with a figure in application cut from black velvet, and fastened on with white cord, held with stitches of black silk; chain-stitching, point Russe and other stitches of that kind. Figs. 238 in point Russe embroidery, are both pretty for the purpose.

Besides the points the cushion has a protector or tidy made of fine Swiss muslin, with an application design of Nainsook embroidered with chain-

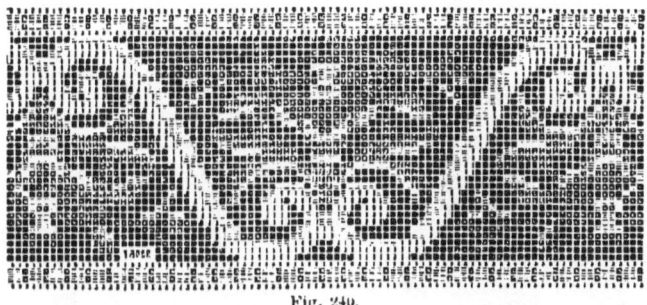

Fig. 240.

stitching of black. This is edged on each side with narrow Swiss edging, and tied with three dainty bows of ribbon. A large button and bunch of tassels finishes each end where the gathers are collected, and from these the cord extends which holds the bolster over the chair. When the muslin cover becomes soiled, it is easily removed and washed. A tasteful mode of embellishing the muslin tidies for these bolsters is by means of spray-work, which if done with indelible ink can be easily washed.

EMBROIDERED CHAIR-PILLOW.

To make the round pillow (or bolster) in Fig. 239, take a piece of brown damask silk, or merino twenty inches long and sixteen inches wide, and lay

Fig. 241.

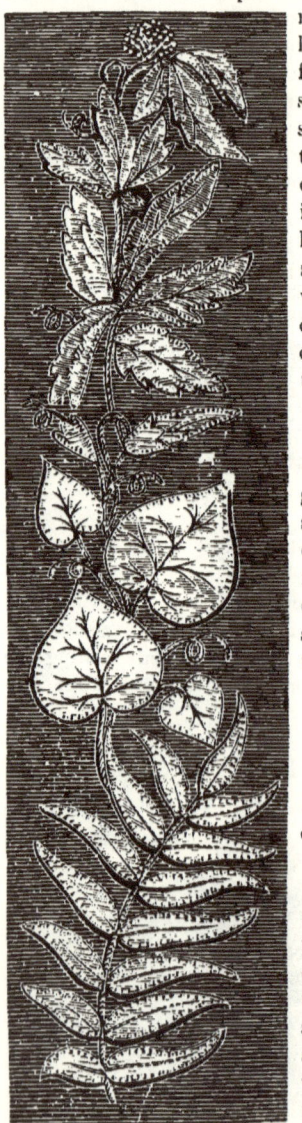

under it a half-inch depth of cotton or wool, making it quite uniform in thickness throughout, then quilt in diamonds one inch long on a sewing-machine, using maize-colored silk for the upper stitches, if done on a Wheeler & Wilson, (or any lock-stitch machine,) if on a chain-stitch reverse the order. Sew the edges neatly together, and gather the one end drawing it up closely. Into this case, the bolster made of ticking or cotton-cloth of some kind, and filled with hair, is slipped and the other end gathered and stefaned in the same manner. These are finished with circular pieces of the material covered over card-board, two inches in diameter, on which a cord and tassel is sewed, and the suspension-cord to pass over the back of the chair, with a bunch of tassels in the center. Next, two strips of canvas three inches wide, and eighteen inches long, are embroidered with zephyr and silk in red, green, black, and white zephyr, with maize-colored silk, which gives a peculiarly rich and brilliant effect. Any strip of work will of course answer for this purpose, provided the colors are well chosen, but the pattern belonging to our model, shown in Fig. 240, will be found specially adapted to this purpose, and cannot be excelled in beauty.

SET IN APPLIQUE EMBROIDERY.

The illustrations here given, show a complete suite of cushions, mats and borders in application embroidery.

The chair-bolster, Fig. 241, has a vine of convolulus leaves and flowers, which may be cut from *Cretonne*, or made by using scraps of colored flannel, velvet and cloth, button-hole stitching the edges, and after touching the backs lightly with thin glue, (or paste with a little glue added,) the separate pieces are held by the veins, and stitches along the edge. The bolster is made in the usual way, and covered with glossy black alpaca, or richer goods, such as satin if preferred. Fig. 242 in small size, forms the lamp-mat; larger a foot-

Fig. 242.

rug for chair or sofa. In the former, it is made of a circular piece of black velvet, ten inches in diameter, the edge pinked-out and ornamented with bands of scarlet silk braid or velvet ribbon, put on (as illustrated by the figure) with a machine stitching, and crimson or pink roses cut from brocade ribbon or silk sewn on, with pink and green silks of several shades in button-hole stitching.

Fig. 243.

For the foot-rug, take a circular piece of heavy flannel or blanket, color black, and pink out around the edges. Obtain a number of scraps from a carpet-store with roses or other flowers in Brussels or velvet carpeting, and cutting them out carefully, fasten on the rug with a large needle and German wool or yarn in over-hand stitches, until the edges are completely covered. Line the rug with coarse canvas or old carpeting. Make a border connecting the clusters of

Fig. 244.

roses with woolen braid, stitching several rows around, and uniting them with cross-pieces woven in and out. This makes a durable and exceedingly handsome rug.

Fig. 243, gives a small and greatly reduced pattern for the border of curtains and bands on furniture. It is a design easily procured on *Cretonne*, and we would advise the use of this material in all these articles excepting the two mats, for which more delicate fabric in the one, heavier, and more durable

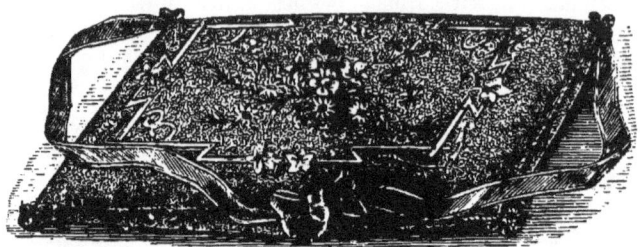

Fig. 245.

in the other, will be found better substitutes. A fancy braid edges the sides of the border, and is arranged in ornamental cross-work at intervals of six

Fig. 246.

inches. The lambrequin, Fig. 244, still continues the same scheme of decoration, and consists as the illustration shows of convolulus blossoms and leaves, with an outside work of fine tracery done in point Russe and chain-stitching in silk of various colors. This lambrequin will be found very beautiful for the mantel, brackets and a hanging *etagere*.

The sofa cushion, Fig. 245, may be made in the usual way, and the upper cover adorned with the design shown in Fig. 246, which beautifully combines both the convolulus and rose patterns, and is finished with a border of the braid, and a suspension ribbon and bow.

CHAPTER XV.

SOFAS, LOUNGES AND DIVANS.

A room is scarcely considered completely furnished in this day without its sofa, lounge or divan. The old-fashioned "settle" or "settee" of years past, is scarcely to be found in any dwelling of the present time, though now and then in some farm house kitchen, the "old arm-chair" and quaint "settee" may still be found opposite the now closed fire-place. If there should happen to be any of the old-time pieces of furniture in any of your houses, bring them forth, and, according to the "heavy Gothic," change them into most artistic shape copied from the prescribed patterns described by Mr. Eastlake, of "The Ancient Sofa in long gallery at Knole;" or "The Settee in Billiard-room at Knole;" for these heir-looms are at least two hundred and sixty years old, and the former so celebrated as to have been introduced into a painting by Mr. Marcus Stone, exhibited in the Royal Academy, England, a few years since. The sofa here spoken of is stuffed with feathers, and two cushions filled with the same, cover the seat. The old-time settee could easily be made to appear precisely like this sofa, by covering the straight sides and back with coarse sacking of some kind, and filling between with feathers if you will, or any substitute at hand. Then make square box-cushions for each end, and cover the sides with a straight piece of the covering material; make two large feather cushions for the seat (dividing the seat with them); finally, resurrect some ancient damask or other faded material from the trunks in the garret, with a quantity of heavy fringe, and with these cover and ornament the structure, and your old settee is changed into "the most luxurious form of couch that could be desired."

In England, in the most elegant mansions, the divan has become one of the principal features in house furnishing, and as the custom of adopting Oriental luxury is becoming popular among the higher classes, the introduction of the Persian divan, with rugs of leopard skins and hangings of rich Eastern looms, is esteemed the perfection of comfort and elegance combined.

When there are recesses on the sides of a chimney, as is the case in many houses, nothing furnishes better than a pair of divans, filling the spaces entirely; or, in the case of a bay window, a narrow divan running entirely around the projection beneath the sash, has a remarkably cozy, pretty effect.

The divan proper is simply a wooden frame as long and wide as desired, and about eighteen inches from the floor, furnished with casters. This simple box is covered first with some heavy material, such as a worn quilt, carpeting or blanket, tacked on smoothly over the entire back, seat and arms. On the seat, an elastic mattress of considerable depth is placed, which should be covered with the material intended for upholstering the front, sides, back, and a set of cushions (from five to seven), which must be made large and square, and be firmly stuffed with hair, feathers or moss. These are piled two and two upon the ends, and three are stood up against the back. A row of brass-headed nails or a heavy cord or braid, may finish the edges of the front, back and arms, and tassels the corners of the end-cushions. After covering, the upholstering should be finished by sewing the cushion of back and seat through with buttons or tufts of wool in diamond, similar to a mattress.

Where the sides of a room or a window are furnished with this Oriental luxury, they should be made extremely narrow—not more than one foot in depth, and finished without large cushions, or merely long narrow ones placed across the ends. Such a finish to a large apartment will be found exceedingly elegant, and for a living-room nothing can be more convenient or impart a greater air of cozy comfort.

Where windows extend to the floor, with merely a panel beneath the seat, the shallow cushioned divans are a charming finish, as they give the appearance of the old-fashioned cushioned window-seat, connected so delightfully with the tales of our childhood. Where (as is the case in many houses) the window-seat is too high to be cushioned, a small divan should always be placed beneath, and these may be only boxes neatly covered and cushioned, which can be utilized as receptacles for work, rolls of pieces, scraps and papers, or, perhaps, for dusters, brushes, in the nursery for the toys, in a chamber for shoes, bed or toilet linen.

The low wall-divans are pretty, simply covered with colored drilling, or brown linen bound with colored braid, and an elegant effect is produced by covering with coarse Turkish toweling and crash, worked with scarlet zephyr, and bound with alpaca braid of the same color. The shades of brown contrasted with the red are extremely tasteful, and impart a most cheery aspect to an otherwise rather dull room. Low divans extending along a wall are of great value as a protection against chairs being pressed against and breaking the plaster.

The plain turned lounges with straight back and arms (made entirely of beaded rails and bars) are exceedingly quaint looking, and neatly cushioned and embellished with fancy painting, make really elegant looking pieces of furniture, eminently adapted for hall and the more simple kind of library furniture. These may be purchased for from three to six dollars; the lower priced ones having no back, require cushions. These simple lounges, made almost exclusively for country use, are generally made with the legs entirely too high to appear graceful. They should, therefore, prior to embellishing them, have two or three inches sawed from each leg, and casters fastened on. The embellishment may consist in ebonizing and painting on the upper part of the pointed (Gothic) back, with a band of color around each bead, which gives a beautiful appearance to the wood-work. The higher priced of these lounges is generally arranged with a double seat which may be turned over, and thus an *impromptu* bed is improvised at short notice, which makes this simple piece of furniture of great value, in a small dwelling especially. This double seat is merely a light frame (fitting the bottom of the lounge) with slats running horizontally; hinges connect it to the front of the seat, and three strong pieces of wood the length of the height from the floor, fastened each with a hinge to the opposite side, are thus made to fold over against the bottom when not in use, and in case of using, are arranged so that they fall to the floor when the half is turned over; and thus a full sized bed may be formed with but little trouble. A lounge that can

Fig. 247.

be used for its legitimate purpose during the day, and at night turned into a bed, is of great value in a sitting-room, as in case of sickness or a crowded house it can be used as we have described, and in a family-room this is no small consideration.

We give the design of Fig. 247 to show how an old and worn sofa may be repaired and renewed. Supposing the seat, arms and back have become worn, procure sufficient material of whatever kind desired, and, measuring the size of each part accurately, fit the cover over and tack firmly to the wooden frame. The arms will require the greatest care, and as the form varies so greatly it is impossible to give a particular pattern, but it is not a difficult matter to cut the shape of back and arms with front piece, as shown in the illustration; in our own family it is such a usual thing for us to re cover our furniture, that it has come to be considered as simple a job as the making of a dress or shirt.

Nothing helps the appearance of a sofa so much or imparts such an air of comfort as cushions. Where the depth will not admit of back-cushions, divide the covering of the back and tack it, so that when filled it will simulate cushions as in the illustration. The old-fashioned bolsters are again much esteemed, and give a quaint and cozy appearance to the seat. After covering the sofa as described, finish off with cord or flat furniture gimp and fresh tassels; fringe around the bottom is very elegant if deep and heavy.

An Afghan rug, either crocheted or of silk or soft woolen goods, should be hung across the arm and back of every sofa; not only because it imparts a certain air of graceful and luxurious taste, but also for the sensible reason that it is really necessary and the preventive of many a cold when the sofa is used,

Fig. 248.

as it frequently is, for a brief siesta. For this purpose, nothing can be better than parts of old discarded silk dresses, made into some tasteful design of patchwork.

The illustration, Fig. 248, is given to show our readers how an old sofa may be renovated and made to appear really tasteful as well as comfortable. This was an old hair-cloth covered "abomination," which was always a slippery and severely ugly piece of furniture. At last, "Father Time" punished its numerous faults by repeated hard knocks, until it was no longer presentable, and we concluded to attack it with vigor and make a change in its appearance, as well as its power of giving comfort; for the springs having become broken and displaced, and the stuffing matted, it was no longer the sleek, hard, smoothly rounded piece of furniture which was considered so exceedingly elegant, and the discomfort of which we so meekly endured because it was the fashion. By turning the entire sofa upside down and removing the webbing beneath, we could gain access to the springs; which were then re-arranged, and in some cases replaced with the spiral ones (purchased by the dozen at the hardware stores); the canvas was then put back and closely tacked, and the under part of the work was accomplished. Next, the entire cover of hair-cloth was removed, and the stuffing taken out, picked loose, washed and dried; then replaced and covered with a piece of old bed-quilt, which is very much softer than mere ticking or canvas. We then cut a pattern of the back, seat and arms, and from it cut the outside of a brown twilled cloth, two yards wide, costing one dollar and seventy-five cents per yard; two yards covered the entire sofa, excepting the back, for which we used muslin. On this was laid three thicknesses of cotton-batting (requiring six rolls); we found this an easier method of quilting than to do it after tacking on the cover. With neat black woolen buttons we then caught the out side cotton and a lining of old material together in regular dia-monds, and fastened them on the wrong side.

The back, seat and arms thus quilted were finished with a row of ornamental tacks, and furniture gimp or cord. On the front the woodwork was covered with a piece of the goods, with cord on each edge and a fall of long and heavy fringe below, but this may have a substitute in form of a

Fig. 249.

lambrequin or scantily gathered ruffle. The pretty cushion finishing our now neat and comfortable sofa, is shown in Fig. 249, though any pretty design will answer equally well.

We hope our illustration, Fig. 250, will aid some of our readers to utilize the old-fashioned "settee" that are still to be found in many an old farm-house kitchen, or, perhaps, has been stowed out of sight in the ancient garret, consid-ered only an "eye-sore" to the tasteful. Bring it forth, and at once saw off at least three inches from the feet; have casters fitted to the corner ones, using the kind with brass sockets, into which the legs may be securely screwed. The next step is to cover those hard, uncomfortable rails and upright rods which used to so lacerate our feelings and injure our spines; this is done by tacking a piece of canvas or ticking along the upper edge of the back, and along the back of the seat, and proceed in the same way with the arms; tack a similar cover on the other side and fill between tightly with moss, feathers, corn-husks or any other suitable material. Next, make a similar cushion for the seat, but do not tack it on until covered and fastened through, which is the next step, both with back and arms. The back is fastened through with a long sail-maker's needle, strong cord, a button or tuft of zephyr being fastened between each stitch, and the cord tied on the back. Care must be used to tie in the center between each

Fig. 250.

two bars, thus making the diamonds of uniform size. In making the cushion for the seat, allow sufficient to cover the edge, and extend down to the round running along the front and ends, to which it must be tacked, the ends being covered from the arms. In order to make the appearance still more attractive, bands of embroidery, fringe, and gilt-headed tacks may be used, as shown in the copy of our own model.

BED-LOUNGE.

It is frequently a great accommodation to have in sitting-room or library some opportunity of arranging an *impromptu* bed; indeed, either in living-room, *boudoir*, or library, a tasteful lounge so constructed as to admit of being changed into a bed, is a real comfort. In Fig. 251 such a lounge is shown, the construction of which is so simple that any one may undertake it.

It consists of a long, narrow box seven feet in length and four in width. To the bottom, turned feet with casters are screwed, and in the box is fitted a "spring bottom," on which a comfortable mattress is placed. To the one end of the box a piece of board two feet high is firmly screwed, as a support for the pillow. This forms the frame-work of the lounge, which is next to be neatly covered with any material preferred ; first, however, the head-board should be padded by tacking a portion of an old quilt, or several folds of blanket over it beneath the cover. The material is then covered over and fastened with gilt-

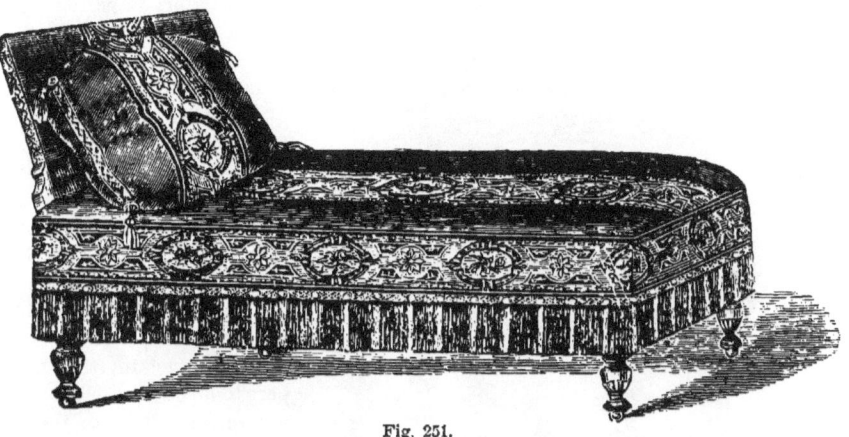

Fig. 251.

headed tacks, the same being applied to the cushion of the seat, with a fall of heavy woolen fringe below it.

In our model from which the illustration is copied, the cover is dark green reps embellished with strips of embroidery, which we have applied to this purpose with fine effect. If preferred, however, a braided pattern may be used, and we have found a cover of wide striped bed-ticking worked on the white stripes with the various colors of zephyrs in herring-bone or point Russe stitches, not only beautiful, but durable as well.

17

CHAPTER XVI.

OTTOMANS.

Besides the sofas and chairs required in a tasteful room, there is much elegance, and that indescribable air of "easy and sociable" comfort imparted by the addition of what might be called the promiscuous seats, the stool and little *tete-a-tete* sofas; the quaint little chair and corner "cozy," but perhaps above all the beautiful ottoman with its low soft cushion and easy-rolling casters, that

allow it to be propelled from one spot to another, with the mere touch of hand or foot. Every room may have one or more of these tasteful seats, which rolled out in the center of the floor near the fire, or in front of some pleasant window, gives an inviting aspect to an otherwise simple apartment. It is to these little adjuncts indeed, rather than to the regular "*suite*" of furniture that an apartment receives its principal and most pleasant aspect. Whether in parlor, bed-room, living or dining-room, the ottoman should

Fig. 252.

always have a place among the first, simply as a seat perhaps, though even here if *made in box form*, it might better be devoted to holding dusters, or perhaps the boxes of cards, chess, and other games frequently scattered about in inconvenient places. In the chamber and living-room these receptacles for shoes, rolls of work or papers are invaluable, and in the dining-room, when lined with oil-cloth, they afford a ready place wherein to deposit the dishes that have been removed. This class of ottoman is always made like a deep box or case, and such should always be the kind used in any room excepting the parlor, where it may be in more ornamental form if desired, several pretty plans of which we offer as samples, which any one may readily carry out herself, as the embroidery, lambrequins and general outside ornamentation forms the principal features in these articles of furniture.

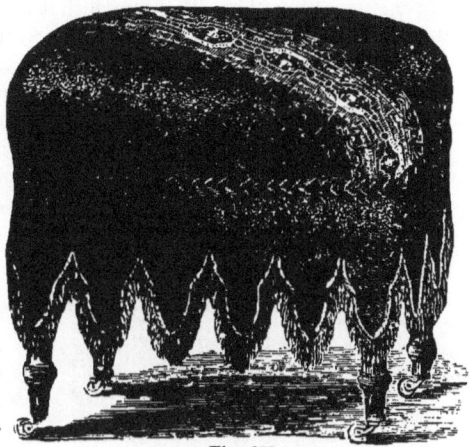

Fig. 253.

Fig. 252, illustrates an elegant ottoman with carved frame, which we give in order to show how an old but handsome article of this kind, may be upholstered and made more beautiful than in the beginning, and we frequently find exceedingly elegant frames of the kind sold at second-hand for a trifling sum, it is well to know various ways by which they may be repaired and beautified. The carved framework is ornamented with black lacquer and gilding. The covering of material like the upholstering of the chairs, etc. On the top, a tufted cushion is fastened and edged with a cord, over which is tied a square of black velveteen, trimmed with a border of lace, fastened on as shown in four bands; heavy cords and tassels trim the edges and tie the corners. The lace for such a cover is pretty made of tatting a wide insertion and edging on each side. This ottoman is unusually chaste and artistic in appearance.

Fig. 254.

The next figure, 253, shows a more simple frame, which is easily constructed, if instead of making the tasteful open frame-work curved, it is straight as also the legs. By this change it will be clearly seen how easily such a frame may be made, and it is at once so light and tasteful that it will be found one of the best forms for this article. Four or five strips of wood run longitudinally from the seat, which is thus rendered "*springy*"; on this, a long stuffed cushion covered with reps or other material is stretched smoothly over, and finished with a band in contrasting color, richly embroidered in Turkish embroidery with silks of all colors.

Fig. 254 is a copy of an old ottoman that had had many new covers but none that had been admired as much as the present one, consisting of a piece of brown woolen stuff, the color of the chairs, sofa, etc., with a lambrequin of scarlet velveteen, trimmed with fringe and gimp. Across the top, diagonally, is a band of the velveteen embroidered in various colors in a running design, using *petite* point, drawing out the threads of the canvas. As will be seen, this made a useful and handsome cover.

A beautiful design for the band will be found in the running pattern, Fig.

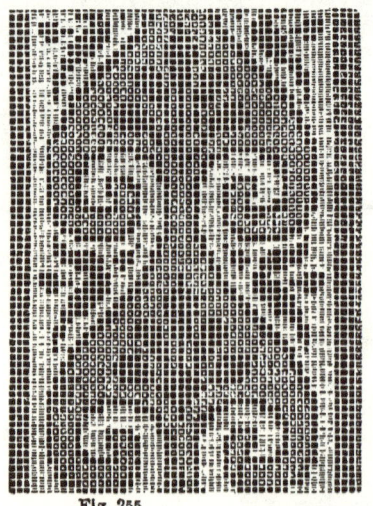

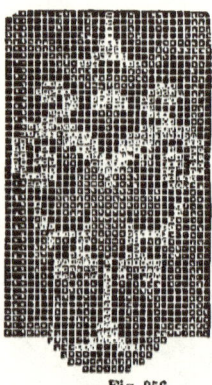

Fig. 255.   Fig. 256.

255, which though simple, is rich and striking worked either in four shades of one color, or of four different colors, as preferred.

The ottoman, Fig. 254, is very handsome, though its foundation may be nothing more than a common square box obtained from the nearest grocery, unless the beveled corners is preferred, in which case a box can be made of the form shown in the figure. This is covered with any dark material, and instead of the fringe, a deep, scant ruffle or lambrequin may be substituted with equal effect. The top is covered with velveteen, and is put on in four separate cushions, or rather these are simulated by the embroidered bands which cross the top. A beautiful Tapestry design for these bands is shown in Fig. 256, which worked on coarse canvas will appear several inches in width. Beads may be substituted, if preferred, using four for each stitch.

The *tete-a-tete* form of ottoman is always elegant, and has withal such a cozy appearance that it makes a corner, otherwise empty and inhospitable of aspect, put on a most sociable appearance, conducive of agreeable intercourse. The ottoman here displayed will explain itself in point of form, and is upholstered with any material that may correspond with the remaining furniture; and to add to the beauty of the appearance, circular pieces of embroidery cover each seat.

With regard to such furniture as this, it is not the mere frame that is costly, but the after work of stuffing and covering; and it is with the object of inducing ladies to furnish their houses tastefully, by performing this part of the labor themselves, that we append such specimens of furniture as the foregoing. By visiting a turning establishment, or, as we have before said, securing the services of a neat carpenter during the leisure season, such frames, or the various parts of them, may be purchased at a very low figure, and made up by the housekeeper herself into the most elegant suites. It is by examining such models as these that a correct taste is formed; and frequently persons are prevented from surrounding themselves with elegancies for the simple reason that they know of no such forms and do not possess models from which to copy. For this reason, we give throughout this volume many perfect models of beautiful furniture, in order that our tasteful readers may have a guide from which they, or perhaps some ingenious mechanic of their neighborhood may be able to make articles quite as elegant.

EMBROIDERED OTTOMAN.

The foundation of this ottoman is a square, pine-wood box, fourteen inches high and two feet four inches square. The sides are covered with any plain material convenient, and casters fastened under the corners. A wide fringe covers the sides, and should be thick and heavy, though a deep puff slightly full may be substituted, if more convenient. A cushion thickly tufted covers the top, and is finished on the sides with a wide puff and lengthwise plaited strips, with tassels at each corner. A pretty combination of colors for such an ottoman is to make the top and plaited sides of the cushion of maroon, and the puff below black, with maroon and black fringe and

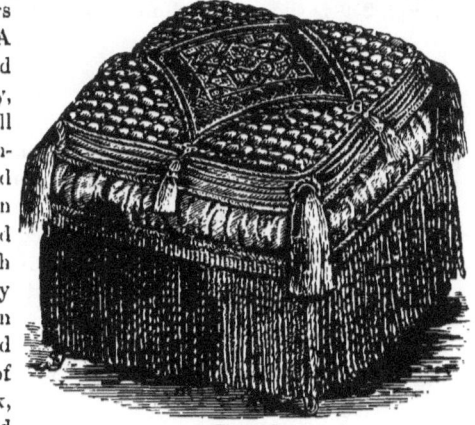

Fig. 257.

tassels. A cover of embroidery also ornaments the top and adds greatly to the elegance of the appearance. Fig. 258 shows one-fourth the size of the embroidery which is done in the new Gobelin embroidery. We have spoken of the

Fig 258.

peculiar elegance of this style of embroidery, and would only remark here that it is specially adapted for this class of work.

In Fig. 259 is shown a quaint ottoman which has a richly carved frame, but

Fig. 259.

it is shown here more on account of the cover than to explain the framework, and for the reason that it exhibits a method of covering a worn seat by means of application work of a different style from any we have shown. Here a piece of light gray (or other colored) cloth, or even fine flannel is covered with black silk or velveteen; a design with center piece, border and corners marked out on it, and worked in button-hole stitching. The intermediate cloth is then cut away, leaving the design in the black upon the light ground. The effect in this combination is exceedingly beautiful, and this will be found a durable cover for chairs, cushions, and upholstering in general.

Fig. 260.

In Fig 260 a plain frame easily made is covered with a strong piece of rug-work embroidered with coarse double zephyr in star stitch, which consists of a

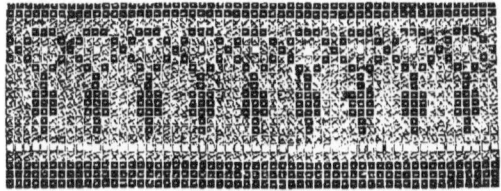

Fig. 261.

common cross stitch recross-ed. Designs like Figs. 261 and 262, with a border, will be found the best type for such work; the canvas being coarse will of course greatly enlarge the size.

A few such ottomans will be found of inestimable ser-vice in the various apart-ments, especially if there are children to be accommodated, for these tasteful little seats are always highly apprecia-

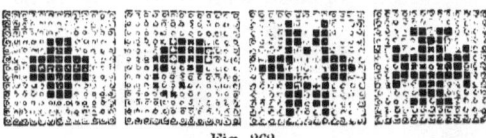

Fig. 262.

ted by the "pigmies," besides adding a graceful appearance to an apartment.

ROUND HASSOCK IN PATCHWORK, (MOSAIC DESIGN).

MATERIALS.—A round box, cloth, silk or merino of three colors, (black, light and dark,) strong lining, woolen braid, (one inch wide,) woolen fringe, and material for filling. The design for the patchwork of this hassock is a mosaic design, commenced with a star made of the light and dark color, the diamonds of which it is made, being two and one-half inches on each side, with a row around it of two diamonds sewed together (one light, the other dark) and a diamond of the darker, and one of the lighter alternately, as large again as those composing the star, between the space thus formed are five sided figures or blocks of black, and beyond these are blocks of the three colors, (triangles of

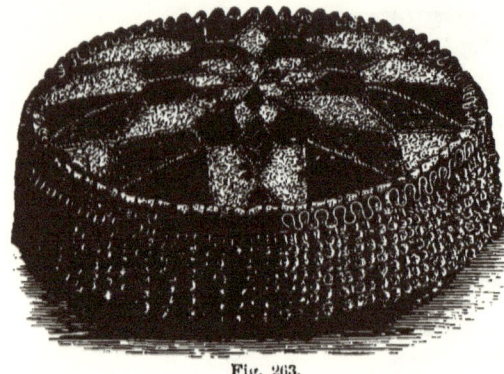

black, and irregular blocks of light and dark) cut to fit the spaces and completing the mosaic circle. The sides of the box are covered with dark colored or black alpaca or other material covered with fringe, or this may have as a substitute a plaiting of the material. After stretching the covering and patchwork over the stuffing in the box, cover the edge with plaited

Fig. 263.

braid, and fasten casters on the bottom of the box.

Those accustomed to making fancy patchwork, understand that each block must be tacked or basted over stiff paper or card-board, and the blocks overstitched closely, then carefully pressed with a warm iron on the wrong side, after which the lining must be removed.

FOOTSTOOL AND BRIOCHES.

The footstool and brioche are the usual accompaniments to the sofa and "easy" or "lounging chair," and give such an air of comfort to the room, that all tasteful people have them scattered through their apartments, the parlor especially. Many footstools are by their elegance made costly affairs, yet no piece of furniture is capable of being made extremely elegant at so small a cost, for not only will any small sized wooden box, a foot square, admit of being changed into an exceedingly beautiful one, but many

Fig. 264.

scraps of carpet and pieces of cloth, can be used with equal effect for the purpose, as also remnants of trimming, tassels, etc. Take for instance the model,

Fig. 264, which appears (as it readily is) an elegant stool, it cost nothing for *new* material, and is one that can be specially recommended, inasmuch as it will be found a means of using the jet and bugle trimmings that were so fashionable on ladies' garments a few years ago, and of which many have mourned the loss, as they were expensive and did not grow shabby by use, so that laid away for so long a time they appear equal to new.

But concerning this stool: the foundation was a large-sized cheese box fourteen inches in diameter. This was tightly stuffed with moss and covered with ticking, allowing it to rise above the edge of the box, as shown in the illustration. As regards the cover, the original was made entirely from fragments of a discarded walking dress, parts of the overskirt, a brown poplin, forming the puff around the sides, allowing the strip sufficiently long to pass once around (and one-third over for fulness); also measuring rather over the length, which gives a pretty appearance to the puff. Four triangular pieces, rather more than the width of one-eighth of the circumference, cut from the lower skirt, (which was of poplin a shade or two darker than that around the bottom), were allowed long enough to make slightly full, and were caught to the ticking cover of the top, as shown in the illustration. The edges covered with the trimming put on the ornamental square made of the velveteen jacket belonging to the suit, which, being black, made a beautiful yet quiet contrast. This cross was cut so that the sections, four in number, covered the spaces between the puffs of the top. The whole was trimmed with rich jet gimp and edging, with silk cord forming a looped cross on the top, and tastefully coiled around the edge. Other materials may be substituted for these, of course, which were only given to show how certain old and available fragments may be made to serve a good end, and yet an elegant object be the result. A similar box may be covered and orna-
mented in a variety of ways. Fig. 265
shows one covered with cloth matching
the sofa, and with an embroidered strip
fastened across the center. The embroidery should match the sofa and
chairs, if possible, and a suite thus finished will be found exceedingly beautiful. If preferred, application embroidery may be substituted, and will

Fig. 265.

be found extremely effective, besides using the small scraps of cloth always to be found in the scrap-bag.

A beautiful form of footstool will be seen in Fig. 266, which is made with a frame of wood on four short carved legs. The frame is exceedingly rich, being embellished with carved designs; but an equally handsome one may be made by having recourse to the wood carvings, and on such a stool to paint these with black lacquer and use a little gilding on certain parts, would make an elegant finish. The top is then covered with a hard cushion over which is arranged the beautiful star-shaped center of the cover. This, in the one illustrated, is com-

posed of blue soutache embroidered in satin-stitch, with a beautiful design of roses and forget-me-nots. This star is cut with eight points, trimmed around with narrow fringe and gimp above the pinked-out edge. Puffings of satin fill each of the points; these are cut in large triangles and gathered on the three sides, thus forming full triangular puffs, the edges of which are cov-

Fig. 266.

ered with the overlapping of the points of the star.

This embroidery is extremely beautiful in application embroidery; in this case cut the rose in the center from three shades of rose-colored velvet, button-hole stitching the edges with silk of like shade, and fastening each petal with long stitches in the center, folding one over the other in a natural manner. The forget-me-nots are cut from blue satin worked with fine blue silk on the outer edges; the leaves are of various shades of green and brown cloth, silk or

Fig. 267.

satin, held by stitches of the same shade. The fine tracery is done in chain and half-polka stitching with light shades of green.

A more beautiful brioche than Fig. 267 cannot be conceived. It consists of the usual foundation stuffed sufficiently to be firm yet elastic, over which the elegant cover is sewn. To make this, take a strip of black velveteen, sufficiently long to extend around the cushion, and eight inches deep; line with paper cambric and cut one edge into points, which bind over and cover with cord. Cut a circular piece of the same material of size to cover the top of cushion and reach the ends of the points described; cut the outer edge into regular points as many in number as will correspond with those in the edge, and trim in the same manner. On the center, transfer a design in application, in rich, bright colors; or other varieties of embroidery may be substituted, if preferred. Next, make full diamond-shaped puffs of crimson satin, which sew

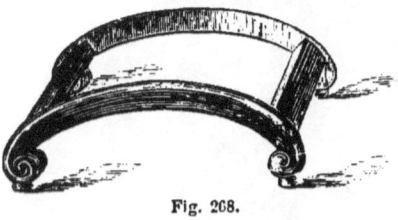

Fig. 268.

into the openings made by fastening the lower points and top together. Trim each corner with a crimson button, and make a ring and loop of cord on one side.

An elegant little footstool is shown in Fig. 269, the frame of which is so easily made that, even though a person may not be able to construct it themselves, they will get any ordinary carpenter to make it for a trifling sum. Over this frame is stretched a piece of strong canvas, tacked closely around the edge of the frame. If made of pine, the sides and feet should be stained or ebonized, but the upholstering, it will be observed, covers the ends. On this tightly stretched foundation is tacked a cushion stuffed until perfectly firm and smooth, over which is fixed the beautifully embroidered cover of Turkish work, in all shades and colors, which will be found a capital means of using the

Fig. 269.

many "odds and ends" of sewing and embroidery silk found in the work-box of every family.

Fig. 270 will be found another method of using old material. Two colors presenting strong contrasts are woven, basket fashion, to form the octagonal cover; or it may be round or square, if desired. We have found black alpaca and strips of bright color (scarlet, blue, or other vivid color), worked up well in this cover; but of course any materials may be substituted, and even several used, only using care to have them contrasted, half light and half dark. Strong crash, or even carpeting, will form the foundation, cutting eight side pieces, ten inches long, and four wide, with a bottom fitting the octagonal

Fig. 270.

figure thus formed, and the top held in loosely in order to form a high, rounding upper surface. This case is tightly packed with bran, moss or other material. For the cover, take pieces of the lighter material, with which cover the sides;

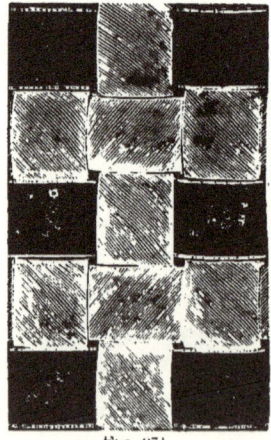

Fig. 271.

Fig. 272.

then cutting pieces of each four inches wide, fold them together lengthwise, and baste or press them; when a quantity of these have been made, proceed to braid them, as shown in Fig. 271. Where the material is not heavy, a strip of muslin laid in between the folds of the cloth will make a stronger cover. Rows of white porcelain buttons (of the ball kind) finish the edges; and rosettes made according to Fig. 272, of the material plaited, ornament each section of the octagon sides. This will be found a beautiful hassock.

FOOTSTOOL OF VELVET AND APPLICATION WORK

A beautiful footstool is made by cutting out a square of floor oil-cloth, rounding the corners and hollowing out the center of each side as shown in the illustration. Cut also a strip of the same six inches high, and with a strong needle and coarse "patent linen-thread," sew t h i s along the bottom uniting the ends at one of the sides; cover this on the top with coarse muslin held on very loose, (in order to fill in the puffing of the cover 'of velvet) s t u ff this tightly with corn-husks, hair or moss, and t h e case or foundation is r e a d y for

Fig. 273.

the after embellishment. Make a case of crimson velveteen by cutting a square one-third larger than the oil-cloth bottom, also a piece to fit the sides, sew the ends of the latter together and measuring it into four equal parts, sew, fit the square also measured into four parts to this, and gathering the edges sew these two firmly together, and fit it over the stool, sewing the bottom securely around the oil-cloth, and finish with a thick woolen cord. Next, take two smaller squares of gray and yellow silk or fine cashmere, baste them to-

Fig. 274.

gether slightly and mark out a design, such as is seen in the illustration, embroider the outlines with button-hole stitching, and when finished cut away

the yellow silk (or satin) from the surrounding parts, and figures will remain upon the gray grounding. Cut the outside in leaves and four bands, and fasten the square upon the hassock with yellow cord of finer size than is used on the edges of the stool. A wooden handle with the cord passed through, and tassels and fringe

Fig. 275.

around the sides and on the corners finish this beautiful stool, which is sufficiently elegant for parlors handsomely furnished.

An exceedingly handsome brioche of square form is seen in Fig. 274. It has for its foundation a strong case of canvas or carpeting stuffed very tightly, and tied down on the top in the way that mattresses are upholstered. The cover is *Cretonne* in the original model, but any other may be used. Around the sides is a plaited ruffle, edged with gimp and tacked in every under-plait; against the canvas side piece a heavy cord is sewed around the bottom edge, and a quilling two and a half inches deep, pinked out or edged with gimp, covers the raw edges around the upper part, with full bows of the same at each corner.

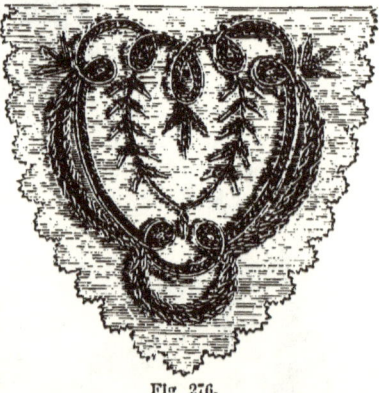

Fig 276.

The beautiful brioche, Fig. 275, is made by covering a circular bottom (of floor oil-cloth or other strong material) with muslin, and sewing around an edge of strong material, held sufficiently full to form a round puffed edge; a circular top one-third less in size than the bottom is then sewed to the other edge, and the stuffing put in until a solid cushion is formed. The cover of this brioche is extremely beautiful.

The sides are covered with a puffing of black cloth, with eight points of scarlet pinked out on the edges, and embroidered with chain-stitching and point Russe embroidery (No. 1 shows the design) in shades of gold and brown silk. A quilted circle of the black cloth covers the top with an ornamental square, fastened over, of the scarlet cloth embroidered according to No. 2, which shows one corner and a figure of the side, which is merely to be extended, as shown in the full illustration. This square has a section cut out from the center and displays an embroidered design on white cloth like pattern No. 3, which gives

Fig. 277.

Fig. 278.

one-third of the cluster, and will show clearly the style of embroidery, which is satin-stitch in shades of scarlet and brown, with a little yellow in the small flowers. This brioche is sufficiently rich and elegant to correspond with hand-

Fig. 279.

some surroundings, yet may be made quite simple, if desired, and still preserve the beauty of the design.

In the chapter on rugs has been given the method of tanning and preparing small skins and sheep or lambskins; in Fig. 279 one of these will be seen applied most appropriately to the covering of a brioche. For persons who suffer (as many

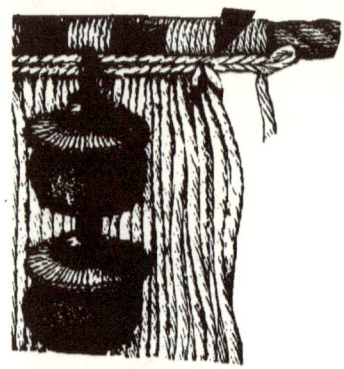

Fig. 280.

do) with cold feet, this footstool will exhibit the advantage not only of resting the feet, but keeping them comfortable. A case is stuffed, as has been described, and over it the lambskin is sewn; or, if a box has been used, it can be tacked around the edges. The sides are covered with cloth or carpeting, and a heavy woolen fringe made of covered buttons with a woolen ball beneath and a bead above, strung on cord as shown in the section A, which are hung over the heavy fringe; or a plaited ruffle of cloth may be substituted. The wool may be dyed in color, or white skins in imitation of ermine. Squirrel skins look well for such a stool.

CHAPTER XVII

SOFA CUSHIONS.

The comfort and luxuriance of a sofa, lounge or divan, is greatly enhanced by having cushions—one or more—placed at the ends and against the back, if the depth will admit of it. These cushions are generally one of the principal features in a tasteful parlor, as they are capable of being made exceedingly rich and elegant by the embroidery of various kinds with which ladies have it in their power to lavishly adorn them.

The cushion itself should be firm, yet elastic, but never so soft that it will not admit of being placed on end and hold its upright position. Hair is the very best material for filling, on account of its elasticity, but various substitutes are used, such as moss, fine shavings, wool, corn-husks, straw, and a new patent material highly esteemed by many. Paper torn into very small pieces and used generously until the case is tightly stuffed, makes an excellent filling, which retains its elasticity for a long time. As we have already noticed, feathers were used in the olden times for filling both bed and cushions of sofas, and, when well stuffed with a good article, this stuffing is perhaps better than any we have named, excepting hair. For sofa pillows, the form should be either oblong or square, the old-fashioned round bolster being no longer used, and justly condemned on account of its uncomfortable form.

For chairs, however, a round long bolster or cushion has come into use, which is to be highly recommended as a most comfortable, even luxurious finish; for the head and back often require a support which a high backed chair fails to afford. We offer some beautiful patterns for both sofa and chair cushions, to our readers, and have endeavored to give those which they can easily imitate.

SOFA CUSHION WITH TATTING AND CRAPE.

Materials: White satin, lilac crape, purse silk in lilac the same color as the crape, yellow, brown, and shaded green silk, fine bonnet wire, muslin, and wool or hair.

Definition of abbreviations: Dk., double knot; that is, one front and one end knot; P, Picot; Jsph-kn, Josephine knot, consisting of six to ten end knots.

The cushion seen in illustration, Fig. 281, is made first of the usual muslin case stuffed with wool or hair, and is twelve inches in diameter cut out in twelve

18

large scallops three-fourths of an inch deep. The eight in the center should be about six inches, sloping gradually to the edges. This cushion is covered

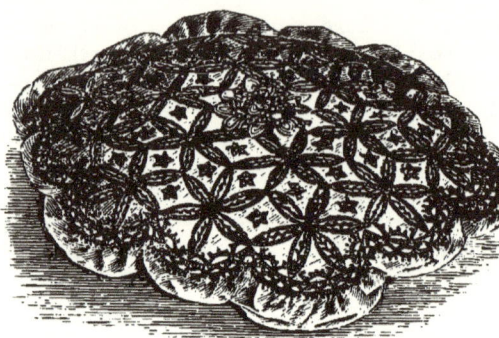

underneath with white alpaca or satin, and on top with a white satin embroidered with crape and a tatted decoration.

The curve trimming going around the scallops is of single white satin stripes, each seven and one-half inches long and two and one-half inches wide, cut on the crosswise, which, laid double, are folded between the two stuff layers of the

Fig. 281.

upper and lower coverings of the cushion, and fastened with the ends coming over each other. The violet group making the middle of the cushion, to be tatted in separate parts, which are fastened on a card-board, round, two and one-fourth inches large, covered with lilac crape, Fig. 282, and are to be

tatted in separate parts, which are fastened on a card-board, round, two one-half inches in diameter, covered with lilac crape. Fig. 281 gives the full size and shows the arrangement.

Each violet has two lilac-leaf circles, graduated in size and put over each other; they are each made of five closed loops, and in the center a large Jsphkn (yellow), forming the calyx. The five loops of the first leaf-circle are each time of 16 Dk., with 1 P. in the center, the five loops lying over on the contrary

Fig. 282.

of the second leaf-circle of 12 Dk., with 1 middle P., and always 1 small Jsphkn in the middle, working after the completion of every loop; to begin the same the working thread is to be thrown tight in the middle P. of the required loop. The Jsphkn makes the leaf filling up, by being joined at the loop close. The violet buds, fastened on wire stalks twisted over with green silks, are arranged of three loops, united at the middle P. and 1 small Jsphkn in the middle, of the same size as mentioned for the second leaf-circle of the violets. To begin the leaves worked with green shaded silk, the green wire stalks reaching up at the back to the leaf-point, to give more strength, is tatted with 1

Fig. 283.

closed loop of 26 Dk., with middle P., 2 side P., and 1 large Jsphkn in the middle. Then round this middle loop, according to the size of the leaf, taking in the helping thread Q; 5 curves united at the P. are made. The number of knots and Picots in each following curve is to be enlarged as required. For the join of the Jsphkn, which are tatted as an outer finish, besides on the two smallest middle leaves, on all the other ones, the necessary number of P. are also to be made. The stalk tatted by taking in the helping thread with brown silk is of 12—15 Dk.

Illustration, Fig. 283 gives in the full size the embroidery design and edging lace for this cushion, and this is to be put on in such a manner that sufficient room is left in the middle of the foundation for the group of violets just described. The embroidery pattern is traced out on paper, then laid over with three layers of lilac crape, making the outlines of this by running round several times with lilac saddlers' or purse silk, and edging this line on both sides with lilac button-hole stitches, catching one in the other, which gives a thick, corded appearance to the edge. The inner space of these stars are filled in, as shown, with point Russe stitches ; and after all are done, the material outside the outlines is carefully cut away. The outer edge all around is marked by the middle line of the lace tatted with lilac silk, for the beginning of which a row of Jsphkn is first knotted on to this line on the outside. Two rows of curves, each of 10 Dk, taking in the helping thread with 3 P. equally divided, over which, according to illustration Fig. 283, are to be arranged opposite each other, thus complete the lace-work cover. The single flowers simulating violets, which are put on between the lace design as a running pattern, are made as already described, and add vastly to the beauty of this truly elegant cushion. The tatting of the various parts makes pleasant work for spare minutes, and by picking them up in this way now and then, such a cushion has the most tedious part finished before a person is aware of it.

SOFA CUSHION OR COVER.

Materials : Colored satin or merino, white cloth, wood-brown and green shaded purse silk, and floss silk in white, blue, lilac, green, scarlet, yellow, etc., etc.

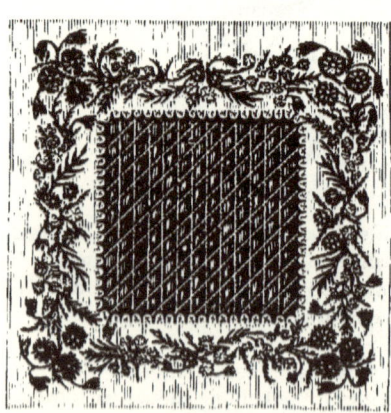

A square of blue satin (seven one-half inches) is laid on thin wadding, and quilted on the sewing-machine with white silk in diamond across the block diagonally. The edge border of white cloth or merino, or some neutral shade, if preferred, as stone, or light ecru ; is decorated with a flower wreath worked in variegated but tastefully arranged colors ; one corner is shown in Fig. 285, of full size for a cushion cover ; is sufficient for one-eighth and can be extended from this, as all the varieties of flowers and leaves are shown. All the flowers are worked with coarse embroidery ; the stems and fine tracery with saddlers'

Fig. 284.

twist silk. The green calyxes of the corn-flowers are stretched over net with brown silk. Asters arranged in groups appear in one place, blue with yellow

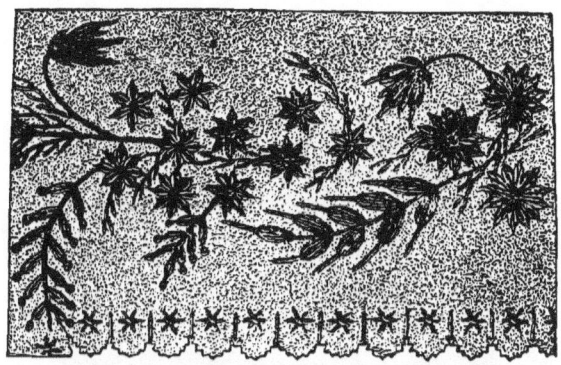

Fig. 285.

calyx; in another cherry or pink and white with green knots. The centers of the large flowers are scarlet, lilac, white, crimson and pink; the fox-gloves in

Fig. 286.

lilac, the bottoms of the bell-shaped flowers green, the top of green dotted with a shade darker, the petals purple, white and lavender; the stars and long stitches holding the pinked-out edge in place, are of black and gold color. A heavy cord and tassels finish the edges and corners of this beautiful cushion.

This same design will be found equally effective as a table or chair cover, a sofa rug, or bed or cradle quilt, and has the recommendation of novelty and unusual richness of effect. The color, of course, may be varied to suit the furniture or hangings of the rooms.

Fig. 288 is made of a square of cashmere or merino of any color that will harmonize with the upholstery of the room, on which is set a circular piece of velvet or cloth of contrasting color, on which has been previously embroidered a pretty design in Berlin work; on this again is set a second circle cut out in ornamental form, as shown in the illustration, a pretty cord or narrow braid holding down and covering the raw edges. A little white braid-work on this circle (which is a lighter shade of cloth than the central circle) will add to the richness of the appearance, and in each scallop of the circle is an application of leaves cut from

Fig. 287.

green or brown cloth, veined and fastened with stitching of silk. In the original from which this was copied, the foundation is brown damask, the cen-

Fig. 288.

tral circle, white velvet, embroidered in rich colors, the scroll circle surrounding this of buff satin, with chain-stitching in black and white silk, edged with three cords in as many shades of crimson. The *applique* leaves in three shades of green velvet and silk, with half-polka stitching in lighter shades. Cord and tassels of silk are looped and fastened to each corner with cord extended around the edges. This cushion is exceedingly beautiful, and if desired a Berlin wool design may be used in the center.

PATTERN FOR SOFA CUSHION—RUG-WORK.

The style of work shown in the sofa cushion, Fig. 289, is something novel, and at the same time extremely beautiful. It is worked on fine canvas, and the design of butterflies, beetles, and various insects, with bright green and brown leaves is quite unique.

The contrast is very fine, with the lovely Oriental bright colors of the insects, giving an extremely artistic effect to the wreath of vine-leaves

Fig. 289.

climbing over a trellis-work of slender rods, the shades of a reddish-brown, stone-gray (in five shades) with pale-yellow floss silk for the lightest color. A pale soft pea-green lace-like ground of fine purse silk for the center, agree best with the bright green and brown of the leaves, and shows out the metallic colors of the silken insects, while the outer corners are filled in with black (or other dark color) in zephyr, with common cross-stitch. The insects are worked with floss silk in fine side-stitch, using four stitches for one, but the filling is in cross-stitch; then the frame-work is in ordinary cross-stitch, which gives a peculiarly prominent appearance to the outside parts, making it appear as if it stood out from the central portion. A person who understands Berlin-work will have no difficulty in tracing the design from the illustration. The canvas should be twenty-three inches square. After the work is finished, the cushion is

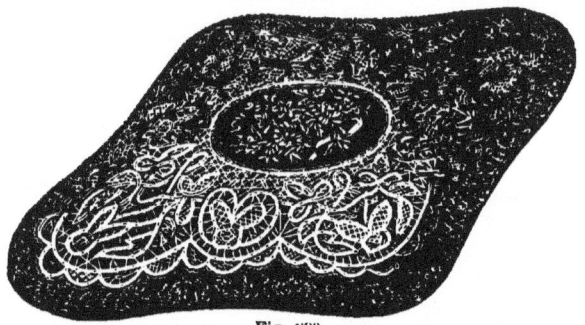

Fig. 290.

lined upon the under side with green or brown material, and finished with a heavy cord and tassels around the edge and corners.

Point-lace work is now so popular with ladies, that the heavier kinds of braid and coarser thread are being applied to household embellishment as well as to the mere personal articles, and exquisite covers for cushions, tidies, and various other knickknacks, are now being made, which add a peculiar delicacy to the apartment they beautify.

The sofa pillow, Fig. 290, is first covered with crimson damask, on which is embroidered a floral design in satin-stitch and white silk, the edge finished with a plaited ruffle of the damask, edged with loose button-hole stitch in the white silk. Over this is fastened the lovely point-lace tidy.

A beautiful and easy kind of fancy work, is shown in the sofa-cushion, Fig. 291, which will answer equally well for table-covers, curtain-borders and chair-bolsters; indeed a complete set, made in this

Fig. 291.

way, will be found exceedingly handsome, and at the same time inexpensive. This work consists of a foundation of printed flannel, such as the imitation of ermine with black spots, bordered with a point Russe embroidery, This border is cut in four strips two and one-half inches wide, and embroidered

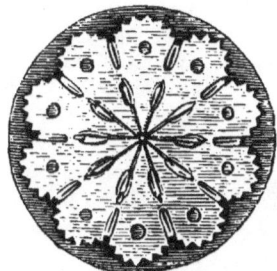

Fig. 292.

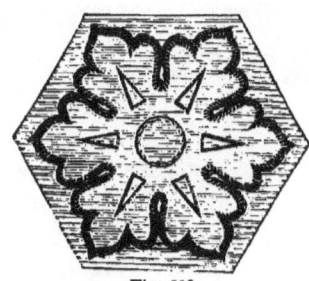

Fig. 293.

on the edges like the patterns, Figs. 292 and 293, in point Russe, chain and half-polka stitches.

The foundation of ermine, or flame dotted flannel, has each figure edged with

Fig. 294.

button-hole stitching of green, scarlet, yellow, orange, violet and blue; a stitch of the same kind in contrasting color, and somewhat long, is taken across the dark place enclosed in each flame or spot; this center should be about twelve inches square. The border of scarlet flannel is pinked out on each edge and worked with white. The transparent white flannel rosettes are pinked or embroidered in button-hole stitch, and are fastened on the scarlet stripe with colors, as black, orange, blue and scarlet silk. This pattern also makes an ele-

Fig. 295.

Fig. 296.

gant bed or cradle-spread, or is very ornamental thrown over the back of sofa or lounge as an Afghan or rug.

FOOTSTOOL (HASSOCK).

The materials required for the beautiful hassock shown in Fig. 297, are a strip of scarlet merino or fine flannel four and one-half inches wide, and twenty and one-fourth inches long; two strips of black cloth the same length, and each eight and one-half inches wide; small pieces of satin in Turkish blue and myrtle green; some scarlet cloth forty and one-fourth inches, scarlet silk braid, yellow

braid one-half inch broad, and a like quantity of the same braid three-fourths of an inch broad (a scarlet braid edged with yellow would be best, perhaps, if obtainable; otherwise, stitch the two together), twenty-seven and one-fourth inches of twisted black woolen fringe two

Fig. 297.

and three-fourths inches deep, embroidery silks in black, white, light-chestnut, brown, blue and green (like the satin); purse silk in two dark shades of chestnut brown, light-brown silk, and sewing silk of different colors.

The under cushion is thirteen and one-half inches square, and stuffed with hair, moss, or finely split corn-husks. The middle strip (made according to the pattern), is of scarlet merino, and we will make the mode of embroidering it plain by description and application to the figures. It will be noticed that the embroidery is of flowers in the center; the round flower is of blue satin, the leaf

Fig. 298.

green, fastened down with deep button-hole stitching of black silk edged with half-polka stitches of black and white silk; these extend *alternately* the entire length of the strip. The remainder of the embroidery between these flowers and leaves are done in the three shades of brown silk in half-polka or dovetailed satin-stitch. Next, the edge of the scarlet merino (5) and the black strips (1) on each side of it, are to be united by the narrow scarlet and yellow braid (2) which is to be stitched on the two edges, using the darkest brown silk and a close chain-stitch. Next the widest fancy braid (4), and between it and the narrow braid (2) are the rows of vandykes—upon each side—(3), which are of brown, green and blue embroidering silk in satin and half-polka stitching, with chain-stitching on each side. The pillow is finished with tassels on the corners made of the black woolen fringe wound together and headed with rosettes of scarlet cloth pinked out on the edge and laid in plaits; the widest and outer strip for these is one and one-half inches wide and twelve inches long; the smaller one in the center one inch wide and ten inches long. The central scarlet embroidered strip of the hassock with a black strip on each side, is sewed on the one side of the cushion, and a cover of scarlet or black material sewed over the opposite side, the edges pinked-

Fig. 299.

out and folded over the edges of the outer side, thus covering the rough unfinished ends of the pieced strips, and making a neat finish to both sides.

This hassock is one of special beauty, and, if desired, a sofa cushion and a chair bolster may be made in the same manner, thus making a complete and handsome set.

The beautiful sofa cushion, Fig. 300, is one of the most elegant specimens of *applique* embroidery, and is composed of the richest colors and combination of beautiful materials, being a group of wild flowers with gorgeous butterflies, etc.

The model from which the little sketch was taken is upon dark-brown cloth ground, the group shaded in every rich and resplendent colors, but with skillful fingers, taste and good ideas of combining colors, it will not be difficult for our

Fig. 300.

readers to invent shades and arrangements that will be quite satisfactory. The large leaves are all cut from various shades of green velvet, silk and merino, the edges buttonholed, and the veins made of yellow, white and green silk, as the case may be; when laid on the cloth these are in some cases raised with a little edge turned over. The strawberries and some flowers have a little cotton laid beneath them, to give a rounded appearance. The grass and stems are made with silk, some in half-polka, others in satin and chain-stitches. With the blue, green leaves and sprigs are mixed, some of very light colors, and others of brown in various shades. Close to the clusters of foxgloves, which is the most projecting flower, a stately bough of lilac campanulas is placed, at the side a cluster of unripe nuts of pale greens shaded over into brown, and white strawberry blossoms peep forth from between the dark green leaves, and have an extremely pretty effect as contrasted with the vivid scarlet berries, dotted with pale yellow. The small golden dandelions enliven the whole, as they stand out in all their bright saucy prettiness from the long pointed leaves, and the red blossoms of the beautiful heath are scattered over the whole with fine effect, giving a light airy look to the group. Work all these fine leaves with various shades of bright green silk in herring-bone and chain-stitches, and add the beautiful tints of wood-browns, putting several shades of pink at the points of the small feathery sprays. The curving border of contrasting colored cloth is to be applied with herring-bone stitches of yellow silk.

CHAPTER XVIII.

SOFA RUGS OR AFGHANS.

Every sofa and lounge should be furnished with its soft, warm rug or Afghan, for not only are these articles of great comfort and convenience to a person resting, when suffering from fatigue or indisposition, but they add a peculiar aspect of luxuriance to the apartment, especially if made of bright, Oriental-looking woolen stuffs, whether of richly crocheted stripes, or some woolen strip or figure, covered with curious Turkish designs.

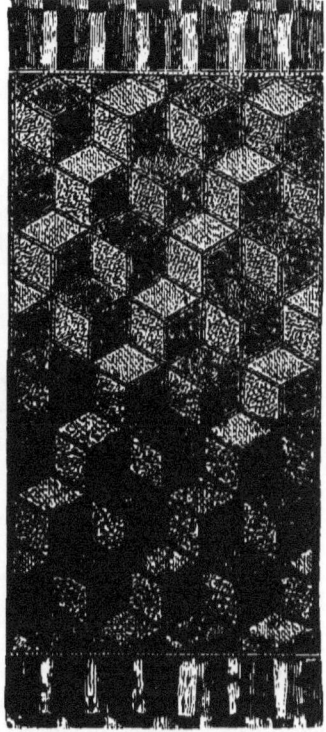

Many of the crochet stitches suitable for such rugs are so exceedingly simple, and yet so beautiful when nicely wrought, that we feel inclined to urge all our readers to procure sufficient zephyr for such a one and commence it forthwith; or, if this is not possible, take all the bright scraps of silk or woolen goods, and make them into a piece of patchwork, of some tasteful pattern, either block or star design; when sufficient to make a cover has been pieced, (about two and a half yards long, and two yards wide) lay a layer of sheet wool or cotton on a lining made perhaps of parts of discarded silk or soft woolen dresses, and the patchwork on it; then with pretty buttons, or tufts of bright zephyr—sew the two parts together in diamonds.

Fig. 301 shows a section of the box-pattern patchwork; made of black, light and white diamonds, in this model of six colors of silk goods, with chain-stitching (on each seam) of embroidery silk. Silk fringe finishes each edge, and a cord the side edges. These blocks may

Fig. 301.

be made of any size, from one to several inches, and thus prove valuable as a means of utilizing scraps. A beautiful effect may be produced by a tasteful arrangement of colors, either silk or woolen, in the accompanying illustration, of circular blocks of patchwork. The central pieces are hexagonal in form of block, and on their equal sides are arranged six perfect squares, one of which unites each two of the blocks, lengthwise, and as the five blocks— this central one and two on each side in the hexagonal blocks are of one kind of material, either plaid or plain, tney form a running pattern, which is continued on through the entire work. The triangular pieces uniting the squares, must also be divided into sets of light and dark, as shown in the two blocks given as a

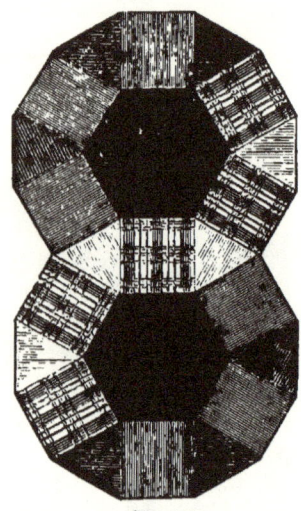

Fig. 302.

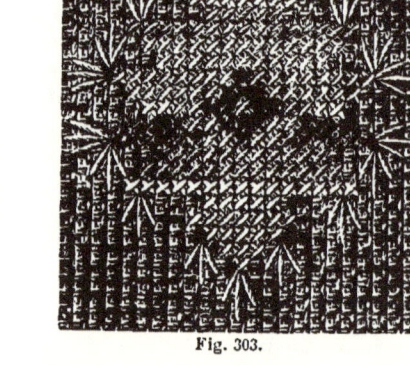

Fig. 303.

guide; the running pattern of light and dark, as well as the hexagonal figures, form a mosaic pattern, when the various colors are arranged tastefully together.

All the care required in making these blocks, is to use five square dark blocks, and five square light ones; to each four blocks; uniting them with light and dark shades of some different color in triangular blocks. All the pieces must be first sewed on letter paper before overseaming them together.

This pattern also appears well arranged in stripes, a row of two blocks in width of the patchwork united by velvet ribbon, or silk if preferred. In this case, the blocks must be set on a strip of material slightly wider than their width.

A HANDSOME RUG.

MATERIALS :—Double zephyr, green, scarlet and white, with the same colors in single zephyr for the fringe. Embroidery silk. black, violet, silver-gray, brown, blue and maize color. All the stripes of which this rug is composed are in common Tunic stitch, worked over with cross and other ornamental stitches laid loosely.

The length of the rug is sixty-one and one-half and sixty-three and three-fourths inches; the width, fifty-one and one-fourth inches; each stripe two and three-fourths and six and one-fourth inches wide, begins with one stitch; in the next following rows at each side edge is increased by one stitch until sixteen and thirty-two stitches, making the points of the wide and narrow stripes. The stripes are then continued without interruption, and finished with a point as begun. A row of green crossbars, yellow embroidery

Fig. 304.

and stars with green knot calyxof floss silk, make the border for the six narrow black stripes. The shapes in bright colors, worked in cross-stitch for the five wide stripes, will be understood from the illustration, and may be arranged according to the taste of the worker. The variegated colors are chosen in the best possible harmony with the ground-colors, white in the center, scarlet; then green on the sides. On the corners of the two side stripes and middle one at the opposite end, use yellow bordered black diamond squares and black embroidery stitches, but on the latter these are also yellow like the diamond edge. The stripes are

Fig. 305.

joined by a row of single crochet of maize-colored zephyr. This is a most elegant rug and not difficult to make. If desired, the colors may be altered to suit the taste.

A rich and beautiful cover is made, by cutting large squares of different colors in flannel, or merino, and braiding each one with some tasteful design, then putting these various blocks together with long strips edged also with braid. Where a mass of many colors are thus put together a most elegant cover of Oriental character is formed, and will richly repay the labor and material spent upon it, as such a one could not be purchased under a high price.

INFANT'S RUG.

This rug, intended for the baby's perambulator, is given to show a beautiful method for applying those exquisite tatted rosettes which some ladies make so

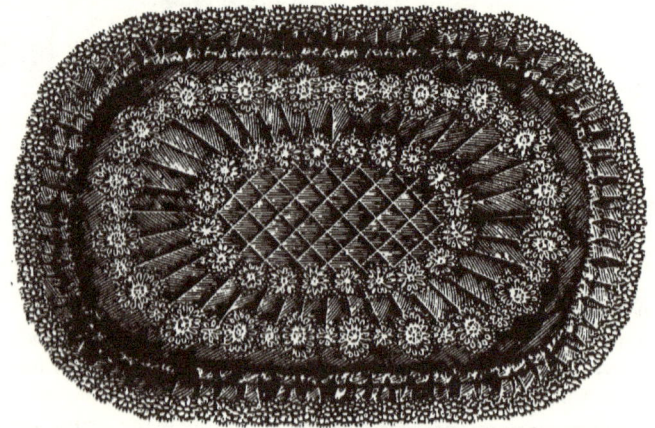

Fig. 306.

rapidly and perfectly. The shape of the rug is oval, or rather an *oblong-square*, with the corners rounded (though the description may appear rather paradox-

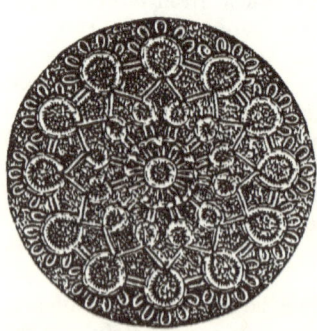

Fig. 307.

ical). The material is silk of any pretty color, lined with soft flannel.

On the foundation, tatted rosettes are sewed in rows alternating with quilted circles. Around the outer edge is a plaited frill finished with fine tatted edging, and pinked on the inner edge. The tatted rosette is shown full size in the illustration annexed, but if preferred an equally pretty effect is given by using circular pieces of lace, with edging or tatting around the outside.

An entirely different specimen of a sofa rug is shown in Fig. 308, which consists of strips of vari-colored merinoes, embroidered with the Turkish designs shown in Figs. *a, b, c, d,* and put together with damask or reps. The colors of the merinoes are scarlet, green, yellow and blue, put together with brown or gray.

The scarlet ground is worked with black and

Fig. 308.

gold-colored silks in the oval figures as in Fig. *a,* and with green and violet in the central forms, bordered with orange and brown. Fig. *b,* the green ground has a conventional shaped flower composed of two sets of colors, yellow - brown, scarlet and black in the one, maize-color, dark brown and yellow in the other, with edge of scarlet and black. In Fig. *c,* the corn-colored stripe has palms of three shades of scarlet and brown, with edge of white.

Fig *d* is composed of arabesque figures in all shades that may be convenient, using pieces of any length, so that a curious mingled design, such as is seen in some of the Turkish embroideries, is produced; this stripe might better be

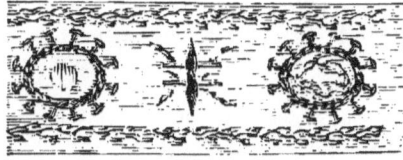

Fig. 309 *a.*

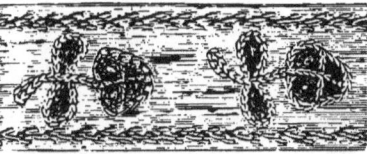

Fig. 310 *b.*

worked last, and will be a happy method of using up all odds and ends of silk left from the other strips. Line with silk or merino, quilting a layer of sheet wool or cotton between, by tying a knot or tiny rosette of ribbon or silk, in diamonds, at intervals of four or five inches.

A rug of entirely different character is made with *application* embroidery upon a foundation of merino, which may be either in stripes of different colors or of one entire piece. The *Cretonne* cloth affords beautiful designs for this work, but a different style of embroidery is shown in Fig. 313,

Fig. 311 *c.*

19

where the *silhouette* designs afford a humorous ornamentation upon a piece of damask o merino. The silhouette figures for *applique* work are cut from black

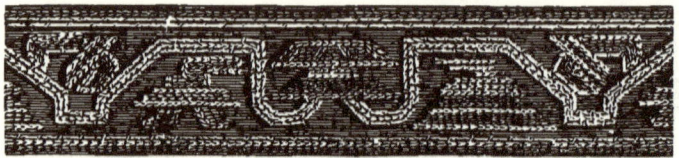

Fig. 312 d.

Fig. 313.

and white cloth, embroidered with white and dark gray, sufficiently to form the prominent parts of the figure.

Designs for such groups may be obtained in paper at the Art stores for a few cents, and from these copies can be taken by pricking around the edges and outlines of the entire group—then placing it in position on the cloth and pouncing with white powder, which will leave the design upon the cloth in tiny dots. With a light pencil these marks are then traced out carefully, and the cloth cut in proper form. Next baste the various parts made of black upon the cloth, and in the same manner prepare the white figures (if there be any), basting them against the black, as shown in the illustration, and with black and white silk buttonhole stitch the edges to the foundation, and finally trace out the various parts with white and gray silk, wherever lines appear in the paper silhouette.

This will be found very fascinating employment, especially for the young people, and for a lounge in a living-room, or gentleman's lounging-chair, such rugs will be found exceedingly satisfactory, and affords great amusement. A border and edge on the sides of chain-stitching (in black and white) with scroll patterns at the ends, will finish such a rug appropriately.

RUG IN SPOTTED CROCHET.

Use double zephyr and a large Afghan needle. First row, make a long chain of stitches; very loosely form a loop on each of the first three, which will give you then four loops on the needle; reduce these to one by passing the wool through all four at a time, which forms the first spot. The second is formed in the same manner. The first loop is drawn through the same stitch as the third of the first spot, and the two others through the two next stitches of the foundation chain. All the row is worked in the same way.

In the following rows, the first and third loops are made in the openings on each side of the spot, and the second in the top of the spot itself. In the illustration, a dot shows the place of the first loop, and a cross that of the third. The whole of this easy pattern is worked in the same way. It may be made in stripes of various colors, or in shades of one color. These crocheted rugs, as we have intimated, are eminently adapted to the purpose here named, forming a soft warm cover, the gay colors of which give a most luxurious appearance to an apartment, and when the sofa and curtains, or general tint of the room

Fig. 314.

is of quiet, subdued shades, will present a charming contrast, like a gleam of sunlight across a sky covered with soft clouds.

This spotted pattern has a very curious, and at the same time beautiful appearance, and is so easily accomplished that even a child may undertake it.

CHAPTER XIX.

MISCELLANEOUS ELEGANCIES FOR THE VARIOUS APARTMENTS OF THE DWELLING.

BESIDES the various articles we have described as necessary furniture for the different rooms of the house, there are innumerable knickknacks and articles, both useful and ornamental, which add greatly to the elegant appearance and comfort of the house in general. A few of these, at least, we will endeavor to describe, but many more can be made from the directions given for such work, in the two previous works of the "Household Series," Household Elegancies and Ladies' Fancy Work.

Every bed in the house should be furnished with one or two *negligee* pockets,

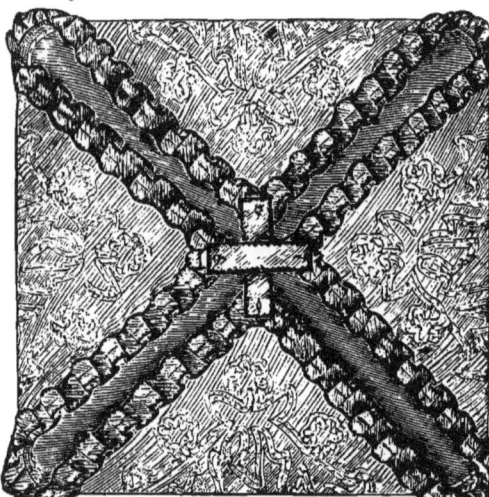

Fig. 315.

in which the night dresses may be placed, instead of resorting to the careless habit of placing them beneath the pillow. These envelopes or pockets may be made as simply or elaborately as desired. A very neat style is shown in Fig. 315, which consists of a square of pique one yard in size, richly braided, with a center and four corner pieces, the latter of which show, when folded over on the side, as explained by the illustration. A quilling of edged cambric sewed around the four corners, and straps of the same buttoned across, finish this neat case, and is shown in pretty contrast on a lining of pink, blue, or other colored cambric.

Another pretty pocket is made by quilting two pieces of material, with a slight layer of cotton between, and finishing with embroidery on the edges; also by using spray-work on Swiss muslin, with colored lining and fluted ruffles on the edges. Such tasteful pockets placed below the pillows add a neat and beautiful finish to the bed.

Cut the petals of the poppies of red cloth or velvet, and fasten them partly with single half-polka and button-hole stitches, and partly dove tailed satin stitch, with several shades of scarlet silk. Work the spikes with yellow filling and saddlers' silk in chain-stitch, and the corn flowers with blue silk in satin stitch. The stamens are worked in knotted stitch with yellow silk, and the forget-me-nots with turquoise blue silk. Cut the large leaves from dark green cloth, and apply them with half-polka stitches of green silk. The veins, stems and leaflets are worked partly in satin and partly in half-polka stitches, with green, brown, and yellow saddlers' silk. On the outer edge of the lambrequin apply gray silk, satin or velvet, and edge it partly with button-hole stitches and partly with gold-colored cord.

HAIR PINCUSHION.

For this pretty cushion, take a common collar box about six inches in diameter and two inches or more in height, and fill it with hair or wool so that

it is raised well in the middle, and slopes gradually to the sides. Cover this with a piece of loose knitting, in any scraps of yarn or worsted on hand. Then knit an over-cover of a bright color suiting the trimmings of the remaining toilet articles, such as the " hair receiver," " catch-all," " comb and brush case," and pincushion. For each of these covers,

Fig. 316.

make a foundation of thirty sts. (stitches) with fine wooden knitting needles, and going back and forth on these work thirty rounds, all knit plain, and then

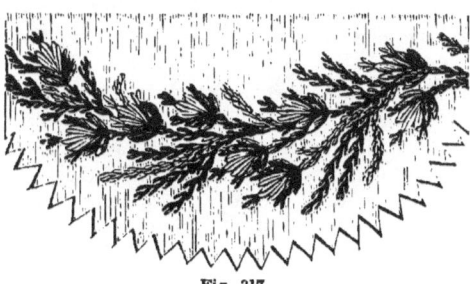

Fig. 317.

cast off. Or a circular piece may be crocheted in the usual short and long stitches. Having sewed both under and over-cover closely to the edge of the box, cut off the corners of the piece (if knitted, square), and trim the side of the box with a box-plaited ruche of ribbon, suiting the cover in color, and two inches wide. Above this fasten an embroidered border, worked on white flannel or merino, the design of which is given in Fig. 317, in chain, herring-bone and point Russe stitches, with green silk of various shades, and flowers corresponding in color with the trimmings, using three or four shades. The edge is cut out in points, or pinked, as most convenient; above this, around the edge, is a ruching of ribbon one and a quarter inches wide.

BABY'S CRIB.

In houses where the apartments are small, it is frequently a matter of great importance to have certain articles of furniture in a portable shape, so that they may be put out of the way occasionally. The cradle or cot, especially, is frequently a subject of great annoyance, and the neat mother when expect-

Fig. 318.   Fig. 319.

ing company, and baby is not occupying its crib, would gladly put it out of sight; for such situations as these, the elegant folding cot shown in Fig. 318, would prove a boon indeed.

This simple little affair is made only of four rods, slender but strong, fastened together with screws that allow of its being turned up in the compact form shown in Fig. 319. The bed itself is made like a hammock, of merino, reps, damask, etc., with a strong interlining of canvas with quilting to hold the parts together. Our small elegant model of blue quilted silk, is trimmed with a Swiss muslin frill trimmed with lace and a puffing lined with blue, and medallions of lace edged with fine Valenciennes or tatting; this is caught up around the sides with bows of the silk or ribbon.

Around the entire edge of the hammock a strong piece of rope is fastened, which not only strengthens this part, but gives the long boat shape to the cot when opened out. A mattress, pillow, etc., will fold inside the hammock. At the head of the cot a strong rod is screwed, which bends over the top and sustains a drapery of light muslin matching the other hangings. This slips in a socket prepared for it, and is easily removed and hung away.

MATS FOR WASH-STAND.

A wash-stand should always be provided with a set of mats, upon which the various articles may be placed, in order to avoid soiling or scratching the sur-

Fig. 320.

Fig. 321.

face, whether it be marble or wood, or covered with material of any kind. In Fig. 324, is shown a beautiful pitcher, embellished with a transfer in Decalco-

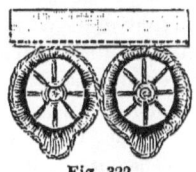

Fig. 322.

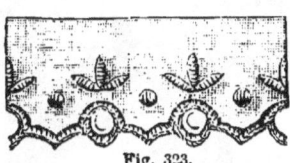

Fig. 323.

mania, and standing upon a mat of two colors of linen. An open border is traced out, of which the patterns, 320, 321, 322 and 323, and the one around the illustration are good examples, and after finishing the embroidery, the open parts are cut away, showing the colored linen beneath. A pretty combination is white and gray linen with scarlet embroidery, or white and buff with black. Embroidery cotton No. 20, is best for this work, and the mats should be lined with baize reaching as far as the embroidered edge, hemming it down around the edge, or using a line of sewing-machine stitching. These mats are equally pretty as

Fig. 324.

tray-covers, and where used for a pitcher, etc., an oval circle, or square of fine enameled oil-cloth, embroidered in scallops around the edge may be cut to fit within the embroidered border, as shown in the illustration, and is a preventive of dampness and soiling, or the effects of heat, where hot coffee or tea-pots are placed on them.

WALL-POCKET FOR BRUSHES AND COMBS.

Fig. 325, shows a wall-pocket for brushes and combs, carved from black-walnut, with the bracket-saws and carving tools. Make the back of a piece of wood one-fourth of an inch thick, fourteen inches high, and the front six wide at the top, four at the bottom, and six and three-quarters high, with triangular side-pieces four inches wide and six and three-quarters long, forming a box or

Fig. 325.

pocket. The front is ornamented with application embroidery, worked on a foundation of brown carriage leather or enameled oil-cloth.

To work this embroidery, cut the foundation of the material in shape of the front of the pocket, and the foundation figures of rings and square of oiled lines or light colored enameled oil-cloth, and arrange them in place, cutting through the square, passing it through the rings, and covering the slit with the rings. The square is fastened on the foundation with point Russe, and knotted stitches of brown silk, and edged with button-hole stitches of the same. The rings are ornamented with herring-bone stitches of yellow-brown silk. The remainder of the embroidery is done with point Russe embroidery, and knotted stitches of maize-colored silk. After finishing the embroidery, interlay it with card-board, and line both back and sides with enameled oil-cloth, place it against the fret-work of the front, and fasten securely. This will be found an elegant pocket, and easily made.

BRUSH CASE.

As the nail and tooth brushes used on the wash-stand necessarily become damp, and in order to preserve them it is necessary to dry them as quickly as possible; it becomes a matter worthy of attention to provide some means of doing this effectually, yet neatly, and perhaps tastefully.

The china stands with perforated bottoms are objected to by many persons, and sometimes occupy too much space, whereas the case we show in the illustration, Fig. 326, may be hung against the wall above the stand, and would prove a beautiful addition to the stand and toilet table combined, described in another chapter.

The case here copied, was from a model made of pine-wood, eight inches square, sawed off to form a perfect hexagon. On this was screwed a half-circle, fitting the

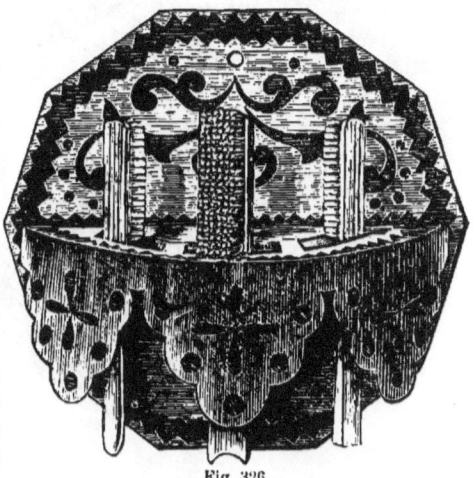

Fig. 326.

center, in which were cut openings to admit the brushes, and adorned with a lambrequin, cut from green oil-cloth, cut out in design figures as shown, and lined beneath with black velveteen, which showing through the openings has a beautiful effect. The pine back (for which heavy pasteboard may be substituted) was covered in like manner, and the back part lined with muslin, glued neatly over. The shelf was covered with the oil-cloth tacked neatly down beneath the lambrequin, and when finished, a beautiful, though simple and easily made case, was the result.

FOOT RUGS.

The efforts made of late years to introduce the luxuriousness of Oriental life into this and other countries has led to the use of many exceedingly attractive and comfortable articles of domestic furniture; among which may be named the soft rugs and beautiful mats, which in Eastern lands cover the costly marble floors in rich profusion.

Whenever a custom prevails, which has good sense to govern its adoption, we should always use it to the best advantage, both for ourselves and others; and the use of rugs is at once so great an advantage to an apartment, both as regards appearance and comfort, that we feel glad to be able to assist our readers in making several varieties, at small cost. We may all admire the elegant imported rugs, rich in Eastern workmanship, or even the Turkish rug, sent us from

Fig. 327.

Germany, and which is an imitation altogether so beautiful and perfect, that none need hesitate to use it; but as even the latter is comparatively costly, many would be obliged to forego the use of this comfortable luxury altogether, were it not, that even elegant specimens of the same may be made at home.

The sheep and lambskin rugs are beautiful, placed before the sofa or chair, but there are many other kinds which can be made of various materials, and form such attractive objects (on an otherwise bare floor, perhaps, or as cover to a shabby carpet) that many ladies will gladly avail themselves of this method of giving an air of comfort to their rooms.

The first illustration is for a circular rug, the foundation of which may be a piece of worn carpeting, crash or other substantial material. The star in the center is cut from any bright woolen material, about eighteen inches in diameter, which is fastened on a circular piece of cloth in some contrasting color; or better still, on a section of woolen drugget-cloth of some inconspicuous design, or plain ground. Coarse and strong wool or thread with chain or button-hole stitching covers the edges, and forms the center; strips of flannel pinked-out on the edges, extend to the edge of the star and confine it; these strips and the points of the star are finished with long stitches of the wool used on the edges, three in a cluster forming rays.

The cloth beyond the star is cut into divisions for the first circle; two inches are cut, then a space left of the same length, then another two-inch slit, and so on around the circle, care being used (by measuring) to have the spaces come out correctly when they meet around the circle. In the second circle, allow the spaces about a half-inch longer, on account of the widening of the circle, and the third circle still larger. The arrangement will be understood from the illustration. Through these slits are woven strips of the cloth forming the star, sewing each strip firmly down at each end on the under side of the rug. Each strand is finished outside with the embroidery. The outer edge is ornamented with a braided plait made of several kinds of cloth sewed into four long strands, and then plaited.

This forms a gay and beautiful rug, especially pretty under a chair or round table; moreover, it is easily kept clean and free from dust, on account of its being so flat, and having no tufted or puffed work. Mats and rugs admit of being made in bright colors; indeed, they rather demand these shades, and thus give

Fig. 328.

a cheery aspect to a room where the remaining furniture is of the quiet and subdued order.

Application embroidery forms a beautiful method of ornamenting rugs, as shown in Fig. 328, in which a circular piece of drugget cloth is pinked out around the edges, and above it is worked a row of simple chain-stitching. In the center is a star formed by cutting out two squares (hollowed out a little on the sides), and placing them on each other, on the light foundation of cloth cut out in form of a cross with broad rounded ends. Besides the central star, eight circular pieces of the same cloth are fastened around it with black worsted braid. (Alpaca braid folded and stitched on the sewing-machine.) Between the four divisions of the cross are circular pieces of cloth of a different color from either the ground or central parts just described, which are held in place by bands of alpaca braid stitched down on the sewing-machine. Beyond these is a circle of leaves cut from heavy cloth, and fastened on with a chain-stitching of coarse thread or wool. These leaves may be of various colored scraps. This mat, in shades of green and brown, with embroidery of golden tints, is one of the most beautiful that can be made.

The next illustration, Fig. 329, is a beautiful rug and most easily made. It consists of a foundation of cloth on which is wrought a border of cloth of any bright color, sewed over rope (about as thick as is used for clothes-lines); about

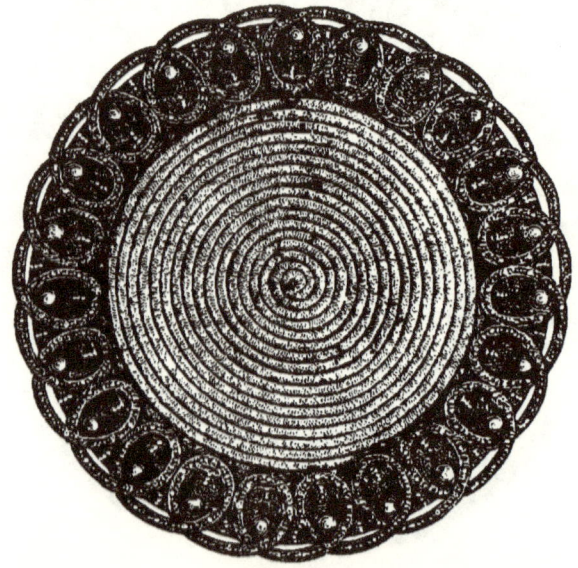

Fig. 329.

two dozen large woolen balls (made over circles of card-board in the usual way) are placed at the intersection of each coil of the rope, as it is wound around the edge of the rug.

Within the border (which is about twelve inches deep) the covered rope is coiled, one row within another, until it ends in the center. We have seen a mat of this kind, the foundation of which was a circle of crimson ingrain carpet of small mixed design; the rope around the border was covered with a corn-colored figured flannel, and the woolen balls of black and shades of corn-color (ranging from brownish-yellow to light gold color) gave a lovely effect. The small buttons of white-porcelain, three in a row, on the edges of the foundation, give a very pretty finish to the edge, and the rope covered with a piece of Scotch plaid, in various bright colors, being cut on the bias, made a bright and curious center that excited much wonder and many praises.

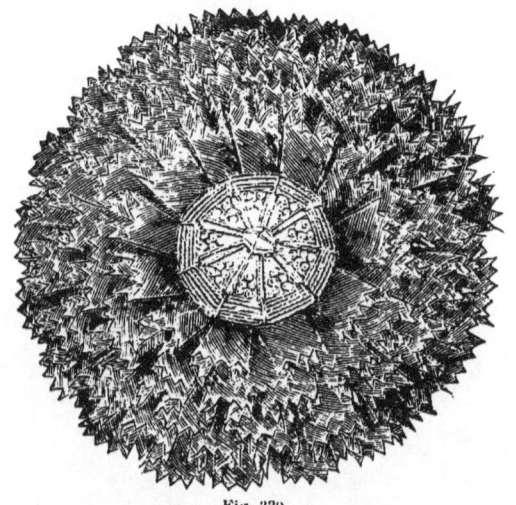

Fig. 330.

Simple as this rug may appear, it is exceedingly pretty, and the one here copied was made entirely of old materials. The most beautiful rugs imaginable are made with plaited rosettes of merino flannel or other such material.

Two forms of such rosettes are given in Figs. 330 and 331. In Fig. 330 the material is pinked-out on one edge, and plaited in close box-plaits; then sewed on a circular foundation of stiff cloth, such as a piece of pilot-cloth, or drugget.

These circles should be about three inches in diameter, and the rosette is finished in the center with a button, either a f a n c y variety or a mould covered with

Fig. 331.

any bright material. These rosettes may be of various materials, or of one or two, and are sewed firmly on a strong foundation of carpet or cloth. Fig. 331 is made in the same manner, but is finished on top with a cluster of leaves of the material worked over the edges.

BRAIDED RUG.

Fig. 332 shows a rug which is not only neat and even tasteful, but economical withal; as it *may be* made of old garments or pieces of carpet. It may consist of any number of colors or of blacks, light and dark pieces mixed, promiscuously.

Strips are cut about two inches wide, until a quantity of each color is accumulated (and this will be found a nice task for children or for " occasional " pastime work to " pick up" at odd moments). As regards material, any pieces will answer, whether woolen or cotton, and carpeting cut into pieces one inch wide, will make an article both strong and durable. The pieces are sewed to-

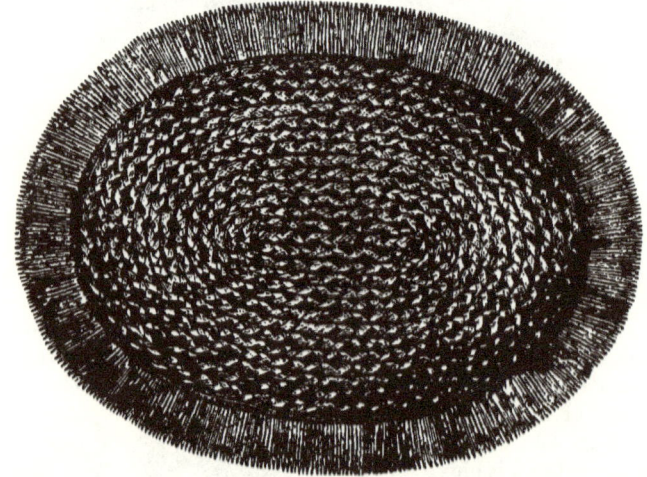

Fig. 332.

gether (as for carpet rags), then folded lengthwise, and three strands, (black, lighter shade, or some bright color, and white) are braided together; then commencing in the center, a piece a few inches in length is taken, and placing it flat, the braid is turned round and sewed down one side of it, coiled round the other end and so on, until the entire mat is sewed, coil after coil, around this center; this gives an oval shape. If the rug is desired round it will require the central coil to be worked round only an inch of braid, instead of a strip of central braid. After sewing the braids together with strong patent thread in over-stitch, it may be sewed on a foundation of crash or carpet, or left unlined, as most convenient; if lined it will require binding around the edge. The fringe is made of raveled carpeting.

In Fig. 333 we have an entirely different rug. This is made either of lambskin, carpeting, or heavy cloth in the center, around which is fastened a border of dark cloth ornamented with application embroidery. Beautiful designs such as are shown on the illustration, may be found in *applique*, and all that remains to be done is to cut the separate part carefully out, and after arranging and basting down the various figures, to fasten them to the foundation and cover the edges with chain-stitching, using a shade of the color found in the designs; for instance, in the leaves several shades of green or brown; in the deers' heads, various shades of dun; and so through all the parts. In some cases, the design

Fig. 333.

is cut out of self-colored cloth and applied to the foundation by means of embroidery, introducing various stitches, such as half-polka, point Russe, chain and coral stitches. This requires not only skill in embroidery but considerable knowledge of colors, as the whole formation of birds and other prominent objects, depends altogether upon the arrangement of colors. In certain kinds of woolen goods very appropriate designs are found, as also in silks, the only objection being the tendency in this class of goods to fray on the cut edge, and we have found it an excellent plan where we have used such, to touch the edges with a little nice, clear gum arabic, and work over closely (after it dries) in button hole stitch.

BRAIDED RUG.

Those acquainted with the manner of making the "quilled braid," as it was called in the old days, can apply it to the manufacture of beautiful and ser-

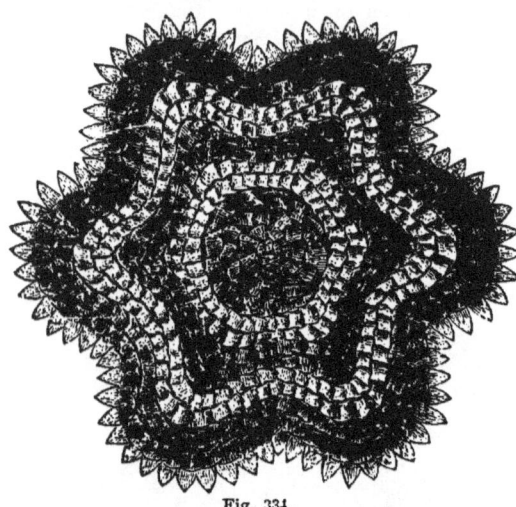

viceable rugs, for parlor or sitting-room floor. The materials required are wide, woolen braid or strips of cloth of two or more colors, a piece of canvas or carpeting for the foundation, and strong thread.

The accompanying figures clearly show the *modus operandi* of plaiting the braids, if any are unacquainted with the simple performance.

Scarlet and black, green and brown, or a row each of various colors, will all be found beautiful for these braids, which, when finished

Fig. 334.

are sewn on the foundation which has been cut to proper form; a tasteful one of which is shown in Fig. 334. The form of arranging the braids, which are

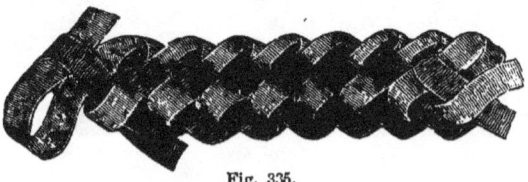

Fig. 335.

shown in one-half size in the diagrams 335 and 336, is plainly marked in the illustration of the rug.

Where such rugs are made of old cloth, (which, by-the-way, will be found a

Fig. 336.

most useful manner of utilizing old fragments or pieces of discarded garments) they must be cut into strips and run together along the edge, thus making long inch-wide pieces, of which the braids are plaited. The edge is finished with cloth pinked-out on the edge, or perhaps merely cut into points and sewed around the foundation beneath the first and outer row of braids.

SHEEPSKIN RUGS.

Mats should be placed in front of each door, and here instead of being the rough sort required upon the outer step or in the vestibule, they should be made of some soft, bright-colored material. In the country where sheepskins are abundant, nothing can be more appropriate than a rug of soft, woolly sheepskin. After the skins are removed from the animal and cleaned, any woman may tan and "card them," and finish by making thoroughly white or coloring with aniline dyes. The process for preparing such skins is as follows:—

Take two nice long-wooled skins and well wash in strong suds, made of one gallon soft water, one table-spoonful of sal soda and one-fourth pound of good soap. Make the water boiling hot, and work the skins, one at a time, thoroughly in it, then pass through another weaker suds, placing the skins in it while boiling hot, and allowing to remain until sufficiently cool to handle; squeeze them well between the hands, and pass once or twice through a clothes-wringer made moderately tight. Rinse in clean, cold water, and dry off by wiping and shaking. Next dissolve one-half pound alum and one-half pound of salt in hot water, and put into sufficient water to cover the skins; soak in this for twelve or fifteen hours, or overnight, and hang across a fence or frame to drain; when well drained, spread on a board or against a building, nailing at the corners and frequently stretching; while still a little damp, sprinkle over the flesh side one ounce saltpetre and one ounce alum, powdered and well mixed; rub in thoroughly. Lay the two skins together (wool out) and hang in the shade for three days, turning them over each day; then separating them, take a dull knife and scrape carefully to remove any remnants of flesh or skin that may remain, trim into proper shape, and with powdered pumice-stone and a hard pad well rub the whole surface, and finally finish by wiping briskly with a woolen cloth. They will be extremely soft, white and pliable, and, either white or colored, will make durable and beautiful rugs. Lambskins thus prepared are well adapted for small rugs.

FUR RUG WITH EMBROIDERY.

There are many persons who have the opportunity of obtaining fur or skins of various kinds, especially in the Western States, where the gentlemen of the family spend a portion of each year in long hunting excursions and return laden with their spoils; sometimes, perhaps, consisting of a fine buffalo or otter

20

skin. Of these, all understand the value and mode of making into something valuable, but in this connection, we desire to bring before our readers the manner of utilizing even small and (dare we term them so?) common skins, such as rabbit, squirrel, opossum, raccoon, and even the domestic cat. Many perhaps will smile to see that pussy may be made into a thing of use and beauty, but if the furriers will use her skin for muffs and tippets, surely we may for rugs etc.

In the chapter on modes of embellishing will be found many recipes and explanations of useful methods of applying certain things, and among

Fig. 337.

them the manner of tanning such skins, which even a lady may undertake if she is not over-fastidious, in which case, doubtless some of the gentlemen would undertake the operation. Once tanned, and these small skins may be cut and pieced together very readily; thus forming beautiful rugs, such as the one shown in the illustration, which is made of rabbit skins fastened upon a strong foundation (in the present case a piece of worn-out carpeting), and around it a border of scarlet flannel, braided and embroidered with shades of yellow and brown zephyr. A thick cord and woolen fringe finishes as elegant a floor-rug as can be wanted by even the most fastidious taste.

CHAPTER XX.

CLOTHES-HAMPERS AND BAGS.

ONE very necessary article in a bedroom is a basket or box, hamper or bag for soiled linen, and inasmuch as these articles are not in themselves elegant pieces of furniture, it behooves the tasteful and tidy housewife to render them so by the pretty designs she is enabled to put upon them, in form of covers, lambrequins, etc., or in the case of the useful bag by making it elegant with embroidery or crochet-work.

Fig. 338 shows a plain wicker-work hamper, which becoming defaced by long usage, has been covered with a lambrequin, made of old materials entirely, and consisting of black cloth, taken from gentlemen's wear, white, scarlet and green woolen materials (old

Fig. 338.   Fig. 339.

dresses). These are cut into four sets of points, placed one above the other on four sides of the basket, and between them points of black velveteen Fig. 340

embroidered with long stitches of zephyr in yellow and scarlet, and pinked-out on the edge. Each of the colored points are pinked and dotted with contrasting colors. The lid is covered with four sets of points arranged in a similar manner, and the edge of both lid and basket are finished with a plaiting of one of the materials, folded over on each edge and stitched securely down. Tassels finish the points. Should the handles or ring of the lid have been torn off, replace with wire, covered with alpaca braid or crochet-work, and a very forlorn-looking hamper may be changed into a most tasteful appendage to the room

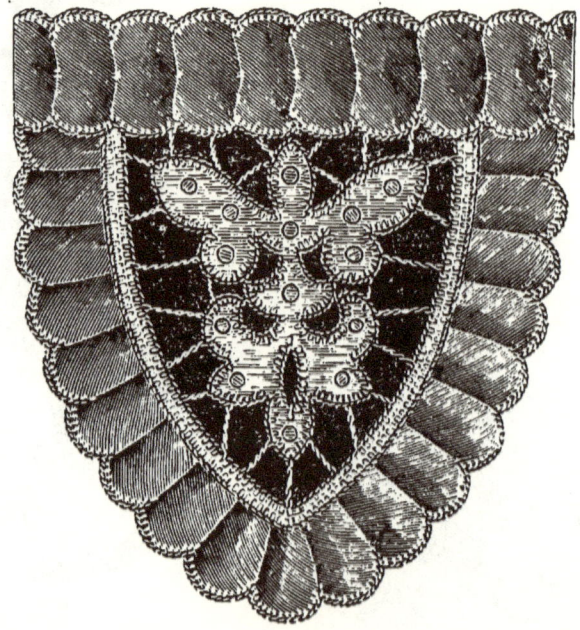

Fig. 340.

which will prove quite an ornament to the corner nearest the bed; the tassels which finish the lambrequins are made of strips of the different colored cloths, those on the points three inches long, those between four inches. Full quilled ruchings of the alpaca are tacked around the edges, top and bottom, also on the edge of lid, which has a ring of covered wire for lifting. This box may, if more convenient, be covered with linen, and be adorned with points of white, pink, buff or other colored cambrics, embroidered with white.

The bag for soiled clothing or bedroom linen is indispensable, and should be found at the head of each bedstead. As pretty and tasteful articles therefore are more grateful to the tasteful, than those devoid of beauty, it is far wiser to make these articles so that they may have some pretensions to the elegant, and for this reason we append a few simple patterns for these articles.

Fig. 339 is made of a straight piece of linen one and a half yards wide, and three-quarters of a yard long, which is laid in plaits at the bottom around a circular piece of card-board four inches in diameter, covered with the material, and at the top finished with a casing, through which two drawing-cords are passed. The whole surface of the bag is adorned with figures in *applique*, cut from colored chintz, and fastened with button-hole stitching. A ruching of bright colored chintz-work in scallops

Fig. 341.   Fig. 342.

on each edge, divides the length of the bag into three parts, the upper two finished with the fringes placed in different directions, the lower parts with drapes, in Guipure embroidery; the full size shown in Fig. 339, and consisting of a scalloped bias strip, button-holed on the edges, with a design figure in the center, held with stitches as shown.

Another handsome bag is made by crocheting an upper part and fitting it around an embroidered bottom made of six vandykes of linen embroidered and finished at the top with a shaped lambrequin to correspond. Three designs for the drapes are shown in Figs. 342, 343 and 345 either of which are beautiful for the purpose.

In Fig. 341, the lower part of the bag is made of striped goods, either bed-ticking, chintz or pique, embroidered in various colors with zephyrs, and stitching on the sewing-machine, with a heading of linen, gray or colored, braided with fancy cord and edged with a narrow braid button-hole stitched on the edges. This forms a gay and inexpensive bag, and may prove pretty work for

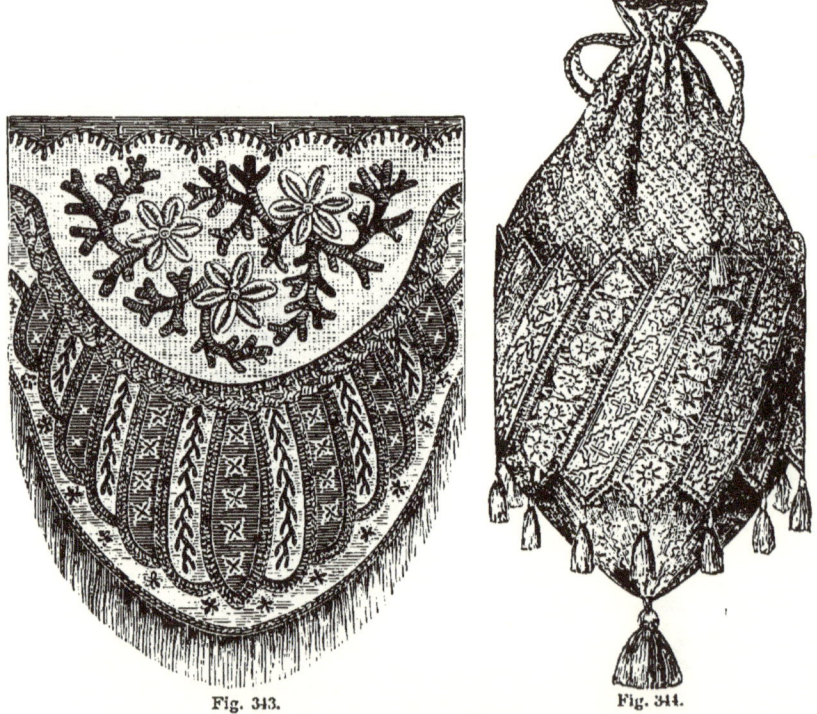

Fig. 343.   Fig. 344.

the little girls of the family, as it is very simple to work in herring-bone be-tween stripes.

In Fig. 343 we find an elegant drape formed of gray pique at the bottom, dotted with star-shaped stitches in coarse silk or zephyr; above this leaves (of which the central one shows the form) diminishing in size as it runs towards the upper part; each leaf made of alternate scarlet and buff linen, embroidered with white and black, (black on the buff and white on the scarlet leaves). The coral work above is in scarlet, first formed with cord and covered closely with the stitches; the circular flowers are buff, made in the same manner. This piece is finished with a scalloped edge fastened with button-hole stitching. At the bottom is a linen or woolen fringe.

Another pretty drape, and one easily made, is shown in Fig. 342, and consists merely of the application of " serpentine " braid, plain twilled tape, and button-hole stitching. The design will explain itself perfectly.

These various drapes may be used for many purposes, and the colors can be varied to suit circumstances. In the last one, for instance, the " serpentine "

Fig. 345.

braid may be scarlet or white, and the stitches on the colored tape of any desired shade.

Fig. 344 is a bright, fanciful-looking bag, the central part of which is covered with stripes, one of heavy, the other of open work, placed in a sloping direction, the lower points of which stand out beyond the firm foundation below of six firm pieces of stuff, each four and three-quarters inches deep, and four inches wide below; at the, top these points are sewn to the bag-part, made of loose chain crochet-work. Scarlet merino stripes with rosettes of tatting, and various intermediate stripes of green, yellow, white, etc., each embroidered with some contrasting color, as buff with scarlet, black with green, blue with white, scarlet with black, and white with pink, would make a beautiful contrast, and be found exceedingly handsome for such a bag, or, indeed, for stripes in lambrequins, etc.

Fig. 346 shows a home-made clothes-hamper, which in appearance is quite as handsome as the purchased baskets, and can be made at a trifling cost. It

consists of one of the circular wooden firkins in which eggs, etc., are sent from a distance, and can be purchased at a grocery for a few cents (two shillings perhaps). This is neatly lined with muslin on the inside, either tacking or pasting it smoothly around the sides, and covering the bottom with a circular piece. Next, some strong wire is procured and, first, a circular piece is made to come within one inch of the edge of the bottom, and to this four pieces, coiled as shown in the illustration, are fastened firmly, as feet, while four others are bent around and up against the

Fig. 346.

sides of the box, turned over square and taken up again; first, however, slipping a wire ring between the opening, and then tying it securely at the top, where a full bow of ribbon hides the join; a hoop of the wire also passes round the box and is joined to these four uprights by small pieces, as shown in the figure. The wire supports and feet are all painted with scarlet lacquer or varnished. The entire outside of the box and lid are covered with black alpaca, and on the lid is arranged a star in *applique* work, with flannel or merino e m b r o i d e r e d and pinked, or notched as shown in the pattern, Fig. 348; and around the center of the box is a similar point, Fig. 347, either embroidered like Fig. 348, or with a center of woolen

Fig. 347.

Fig. 348.

lace (as shown on the center of Fig. 349) on the point. These points may be in one or various colors.

A box about two feet high and the same width and height, makes a convenient receptacle for soiled linen where space must be economized, as it can be used as a seat as well. To line it neatly within is the first step, and next to cover it with any goods convenient; the model is of striped material. On the

Fig. 349.

lid a stuffed pad is tacked, and the whole is finished with a quilling of some contrasting color, an ornamental button or a gilt-headed nail being placed in the center of each plait. Casters may be placed at the four lower corners if desired, and a strong loop nailed on the lid, wherewith to raise it.

CLOTHES BASKET WITH LAMBREQUINS.

A pretty style of hamper for soiled linen is shown in the accompanying illustration, and may be readily made by any lady of taste, possessing a knowledge of embroidery by application, or *applique* work, as it is called. The frame of the basket consists first of a circular piece of wood, or a hoop twelve inches, and a second hoop fifteen inches in diameter, united by four bars of thick wire twenty-nine inches long, bent into the form shown in the illustration, with four shorter pieces, two feet long, bound around the lower part. Four inches of the wire is turned into a coil at the top, and ornamented with rings of wire. In this frame-work sets the basket, made of strong pasteboard twenty inches high, fitting in the frame at top and bottom, and strengthened with wire sewed around each edge. This is lined with table oil-cloth, glazed muslin or even paper, and covered on the outside with striped goods to suit the hangings, etc., of the room, and adorned with a woven braid simulating

Fig. 350.

the hoop around wicker baskets; a lid cut of four pieces of pasteboard, with a small hoop of wire giving the round form, and a circular piece on the top is covered and finished in like manner. This lid is six inches high and has a scalloped strip of pasteboard one inch wide sewed around the top, covered with

Fig. 351.

the stripe and bound with braid; across this a wire handle is fastened. Around the top edge of the basket is fastened a piece of wire coiled with a cord of bright color, as also the feet and frame-work. The wire frame is neatly bronzed or covered with lacquer. The elegant lambrequins are worked upon a foundation of gray cloth in application, satin and half-polka stitches.

INDEX.

HOUSEHOLD ELEGANCIES.

The most beautiful Ladies' Book ever published. Get it for your Work Basket
or Parlor. A Beautiful Gift to Friends.

BY HENRY T. WILLIAMS AND MRS. C. S. JONES.

VOL. 2—WILLIAMS' HOUSEHOLD SERIES.

A splendid new book on Household Art, devoted to a multitude of topics, interesting to ladies everywhere.

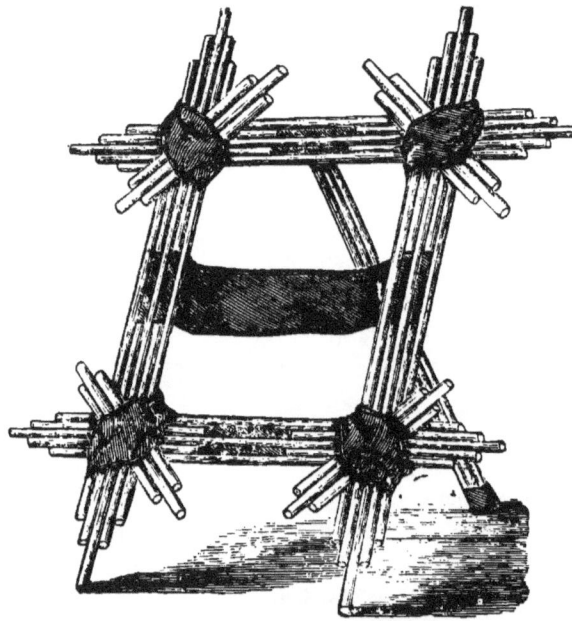

CONTENTS.

Hundreds of exquisite illustrations decorate the pages, which are full to overflowing with hints and devices to every lady, how to ornament her home cheaply, tastefully and delightfully, with fancy articles of her own construction. By far the most popular and elegant gift book of the year—300 pages. Price $1.50. Sent post-paid by mail.

ADDRESS HENRY T. WILLIAMS, PUBLISHER,

P. O. Box 6205. 46 BEEKMAN STREET, NEW YORK.

Ladies' Fancy Work,

OR

HOME RECREATIONS

IN

Art & Household Taste.

Just published, a Charming New Book with above title. A Companion Volume to

Household Elegancies and Window Gardening,

Issued in same size and style, profusely illustrated with engravings of superior execution, and devoted to many topics of Household taste, Fancy Work for the ladies, and containing hundreds of suggestions of Home decorations.

VOLUME THREE

OF

Williams' Household Series.

CONTENTS.

Among the topics which "Ladies' Fancy Work" treats of, are—Feather Work, Paper Flowers, Fire Screens, Shrines, Rustic Pictures, a charming series of designs for Easter Crosses, Straw Ornaments, Shell Flowers and Shell Work, Bead Mosaic, and Fish Scale Embroidery, Hair Work, Card-board Ornaments, Fancy Rubber Work, Cottage Foot Rests, Window Garden Decorations, Crochet Work, designs in Embroidery, and an immense number of designs of other Fancy Work to delight all lovers of Household Art and recreation.

Price sent post-paid by mail, $1.50.

Address, HENRY T. WILLIAMS, Publisher,

P. O. Box 6,205.   46 Beekman Street, New York.

Window Gardening.

By HENRY T. WILLIAMS,

Editor Ladies' Floral Cabinet N. Y.

RICHLY ILLUSTRATED WITH EXQUISITE ENGRAVINGS.

An Elegant Book, with 250 Fine Engravings and 300 Pages,

Containing a Descriptive List of all Plants Suitable for Window Culture.

A ready and invaluable aid to all who wish to adorn their houses in the easiest and most successful manner with plants or vines, or flowers. Instructions are given as to the best selection of plants for Baskets or Ferneries and Wardian Cases. Several chapters are devoted to Hanging Baskets, Climbing Vines, Smilax, and the Ivy, for decorative purposes. Bulbs for House Culture are fully described; also ornamental Plants for Dinner Table Decoration. Other topics are well considered, such as Balcony Gardens, House Top Gardening, Watering Plants, Home Conservatories, Fountains, Vases, Flower Stands, Soil, Air, Temperature, Propagation, Floral Boxes, the Aquarium, Rustic Conveniences for Household Ornament, and directions in detail for the general management of in-door plants for the entire year throughout the Winter, Spring, Summer and Fall. The volume is profusely illustrated with choice engravings, and pains have been taken to make it one of the most attractive books ever issued, from the American Press. For sale or supplied by Bookstores everywhere, or sent post-paid by mail on receipt of price.

Price, $1.50.

Every Woman Her Own Flower Gardener.

By Daisy Eyebright, (Mrs. S. O. Johnson.)

A delightful little volume, written by a lady fond of flowers, as a special help and assistance to others interested in out-door flower gardening. Simple directions are given, how to lay out and plant Flower Borders, Ribbon Beds, and arrange ornamental plants. Among the topics treated are Geraniums, Fuchsias, Bulbs. Ornamental Flowering Shrubs, Everlasting Flowers, Ornamental Grasses, Coleus, Pæonics. Shade Trees, Garden Vegetables, Old Fashioned Flowers, Annual Flowers, Perennials, Ornamental Vines, Lawns, Insects, Manures, Watering Soils, When and How to Plant, Dahlias, Lilies, Gladiolus, Verbenas, Cannas, Balsams, Portulaccas, and nearly all the popular varieties of flowers and shrubs. The book contains 148 pages, is charmingly written by one deeply in love with the subject, who appreciates the tastes of ladies and aims to do good with agreeable, kindly advice on home gardening. For sale or supplied by Bookstores everywhere.

Price, in handsome Pamphlet Covers, 50 cents; bound in Cloth, $1; postpaid by mail.

Address HENRY T. WILLIAMS, Publisher,

46 Beekman Street, N. Y.

ORNAMENTAL DESIGNS

—FOR—

Fret-Work, Scroll Sawing, Fancy Carving,

—AND—

HOME DECORATIONS.

Fret-Sawing has become an art of such wonderful popularity that the interest in it has been shared by both amateurs and professionals to an astonishing extent. Hundreds are earning large sums of pocket-money by cutting these beautiful household ornaments, and selling among friends or acquaintances, or at the art stores.

Ladies and the Young Folks find in it a fascinating recreation, and are making dozens of fancy articles at small cost, to decorate their homes in a charming manner, or to give as Holiday Presents to friends. The following books contain mechanical designs of full size for immediate use, and are invaluable alike to the amateurs, ladies, young folks, mechanics, architects, and all of professional skill.

PART 1 contains full size designs for Picture Frames, Small Brackets, Book Racks, Fancy Letters and Figures, Ornaments, Wall Pockets, etc. (Has patterns worth at usual prices over $8.) Price, 75 cts , post-paid by mail.

PART 2 is devoted exclusively to designs of Brackets of medium to large size, all entirely new, and of the most tasteful detail and execution. (Contains over 50 plans, worth at least $15.) Price $1.00, by mail, post-paid.

PART 3 is devoted to Fancy Work, Ladies' Work Baskets, Easels, Crosses, Match Boxes, Pen Racks, Paper Cutters, Calendar Frames, Thermometer Stands, Watch Pockets, Fruit Baskets, Table Platters, etc. Nearly 100 designs, many of them really exquisite. Price, $1.

The above books contain over 300 patterns, all beautifully printed in blue color. These books are the only ones yet issued in the U. S. The patterns are mostly original, designed expressly for these books, and in execution, choice selection, taste, cheapness, they may be safely esteemed the best collection yet produced! The whole series of three costing but $2.75, contains upwards of 300 patterns, worth at usual values over $30. All sent post-paid by mail, on receipt of price.

Bracket and Fret Saw.

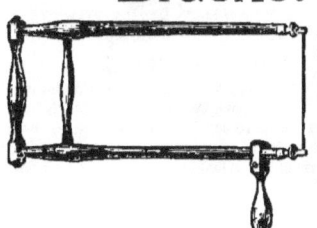

With this Bracket Saw, the designs and directions, very desirable articles can be made for Fairs, etc., which will sell quickly and at a good profit. With it you can *make beautiful articles for presentation gifts.* With it you can *help beautify your homes.* With it you can *make money.* To parents desiring a USEFUL GIFT for their children, we would call attention to this Bracket and Fret Saw, for it not only affords *great pleasure, but it helps to cultivate a mechanical taste.*

Price with 25 bracket and ornamental designs, 6 bracket saw blades, also full directions for use. Sent by mail for $1.25.

Address HENRY T. WILLIAMS, Publisher,

46 Beekman Street, New York.

Part 4, Price 50 Cents.—A new book of Fret Saw designs, containing many tasteful patterns, entirely new and of special elegance, is now in press, and will be issued early in October.